Princess Fredericka Devereaux's Christmas Wish List

1. A special first holiday season for my baby son, Leo.

2. Mistletoe hung with care throughout the palace.

3. A beautiful stocking for Leo, embroidered with his name—and maybe one for my new bodyguard, Treat?

4. The ability to stop gazing at Treat from afar!

5. An evening snuggling under a blanket with my sexy guard to watch old Christmas movies.

6. A feast fit for a princess and my prince(s)— Leo and Treat!

7. A father for Leo...and the husband of my dreams?

* * *

Royal Babies:
A new generation of little princes—and princesses!

A ROYAL CHRISTMAS PROPOSAL

BY
LEANNE BANKS

Published in Great Britain 2014
by Mills & Boon, an imprint of Harlequin (UK) Limited,
Eton House, 18-24 Paradise Road, Richmond, Surrey, TW9 1SR

© 2014 Leanne Banks

ISBN: 978-0-263-91338-5

23-1214

Harlequin (UK) Limited's policy is to use papers that are natural, renewable and recyclable products and made from wood grown in sustainable forests. The logging and manufacturing processes conform to the legal environmental regulations of the country of origin.

Printed and bound in Spain
by CPI, Barcelona

Leanne Banks is a *New York Times* and *USA TODAY* bestselling author who is surprised every time she realizes how many books she has written. Leanne loves chocolate, the beach and new adventures. To name a few, Leanne has ridden an elephant, stood on an ostrich egg (no, it didn't break), gone parasailing and done indoor skydiving. Leanne loves writing romance because she believes in the power and magic of love. She lives in Virginia with her family and a four-and-a-half-pound Pomeranian named Bijou. Visit her website, www.leannebanks.com.

This book is dedicated to all the parents who have gone the extra mile, two miles or one hundred miles for your child's well-being. Thank you for your love and devotion. You've made the world a better place.

Chapter One

Princess Fredericka hoped her brother wasn't going to be impossible.

She knew she had made more than her share of mistakes. She'd been a wild child when she'd been a teenager and terrified her family with her antics. Everyone had breathed a sigh of relief when she'd gotten married, because she'd appeared to calm down. In many ways she had, but she'd learned things didn't always turn out the way one expected. She'd managed to make the best of what life had dealt her. Ericka knew her brother Stefan, the ruling prince of Chantaine, however, would have a hard time seeing her as a competent single mother to her adorable son, Leo.

She resisted the urge to fidget as she waited to be invited into her brother's office. She nodded at staff members as they hung holiday greenery and put candles in the window. Ericka suspected the Christmas decorations had been ordered by Eve, her brother's wife. Ericka barely remembered seeing Christmas decorations when she had been growing up in the palace. With the exception of the huge Christmas tree in one of the formal rooms, one might not have known the holiday existed. Of course, the deep chill between her mother and father hadn't helped matters.

Her father, Prince Edward, had been a philanderer and an absentee father and husband. Her mother had felt trapped and bitter. Ericka remembered wishing only that she could run away. She'd done exactly that in more than one way, which was why she suspected this was going to be a messy discussion. Stefan was extremely protective.

The door to Stefan's office finally opened. "Your Highness, Princess Fredericka, please come in," Stefan's assistant said.

She nodded. "Thank you very much," she said, then entered her brother's office while the assistant left the room. "Stefan," she greeted, walking toward her brother. She noticed a wisp of a couple gray streaks on the sides of his dark hair. The burden of his position was obviously weighing on him.

She kissed his cheek and he kissed hers. "How are you?" she asked.

"I'm well," he said. "I'm more concerned about you and Leonardo."

Ericka smiled. "Leo and I are great. I'm happy to be back in Chantaine after spending the last year with Tina in Texas."

"You could have spent the last year here in Chantaine," he said, and rounded his desk to sit in his chair.

Ericka sat in the chair across from her brother, watching him as he tented his fingers and studied her. "I think it was good to be with Tina in Texas during my pregnancy and delivery. She and her husband were supportive, and it was fun having their daughter, Katarina, around. She's quite the spitfire. Little ones put everything in perspective."

"True," Stefan said, giving a serious nod. "I think it would be best for you and Leo to live at the palace."

Ericka's stomach twisted and she bit the inside of her lip. She hated to go up against Stefan but knew it was necessary. "I think not," she said. "I've found a lovely gated cottage and a nanny. I think this will be best for Leo and me."

Stefan frowned. "But what about security? You and Leo need to be protected. That would be much easier within the palace walls."

Ericka shook her head. "The palace isn't the place for me. If you think about it, it's not the place for most of us. None of your siblings live here. I apologize for how this may sound, but the palace feels claustrophobic. I don't want that for Leo."

"He's a baby," Stefan said. "How will he know?"

"Babies sense more than you think. He would sense my tension. Leo and I need our own place. As I said, I have found a wonderful nanny and I've arranged for therapy for his hearing disability."

Stefan pressed his lips together. "Is there any chance you're wrong about his hearing? He's so young."

"No," she said, remembering the grief she'd suffered when she'd learned her perfect Leo couldn't hear. The doctors had tested Leo before she'd left the hospital with him, and many more tests had followed. "He has a hearing disability and I'm determined to make sure he gets the best treatment available."

"I can't believe you don't think living in the palace would make your life easier," Stefan said. "And your son's life safer."

Ericka shook her head. "Don't try to guilt me into doing things your way, Stefan. I have to follow my best inner guidance. I have to be my own expert. I'm counting on you to be supportive."

Stefan sighed. "This situation is going to put a lot of pressure on you. I hesitate to bring up the past, but—"

"You're talking about the time I spent in rehab in my teens," she said. Ericka couldn't blame any of her family for being concerned, but if she'd successfully survived her most recent humiliation, she could handle anything. "I'm lucky I learned to avoid chemicals early on. I haven't had a drink in nearly a decade. I learned to wake up every morning and make the decision that I'm not going to drink or use drugs that day."

Stefan nodded. "It's obvious you've come a long way, but I still don't want you to be overwhelmed."

"I'm going to be overwhelmed at times," she assured him. "I have a baby. Being a mother is new. But I'm a Devereaux and I'm not the weak link you may have once thought I was."

"I never said you were the weak link," he said with a dark frown.

"Well, maybe you just thought it," she said gently with a smile and lifted her hand when she could see he was going to protest. "It doesn't matter. You'll soon see there's more to me than you thought. I'll be very happy in my cozy cottage."

"Okay," he said reluctantly. "As you wish. However, I insist on providing you with security. You'll have a guard within the next couple of days."

Ericka made a face. "If you insist," she said. "Just make sure whoever you choose is low-profile or they'll get on my nerves. No one too pushy."

"I do insist, and I'll make sure you have the best security possible. You're working for the palace, so protection is more than appropriate. The new rules specify that if any of the Devereaux family is working for Chantaine, they shall be given security. You're taking over the coordination for the conference for The Royal Society for A Better World, although I don't know how you expect to do it with a baby and no husband," he said.

"Single mothers have been accomplishing great things for ages," she said. "I'll have a nanny and two sisters willing to help."

"Along with Eve," Stefan said of his wife. "She would kill me if I didn't offer her assistance."

Ericka smiled still amazed at the change Eve had wrought in her brother. The two were soul mates. Her happiness faded a little when she thought of her own future romantic prognosis. She wasn't sure her soul mate existed. Brushing the thought aside, she knew it was silly for her to waste one moment on any ideas about romance. She had no time or energy for a man in her life right now.

"You're always welcome at the palace if you should change your mind."

"Thank you, but I won't," she said. "Now shall we cover a few issues about the upcoming conference?"

Stefan shot her a smile that held a hint of approval. "Down to business already?"

"I've been ready," she said, and powered up her tablet.

Two days later, Stefan sent Ericka a text message informing her that one of his assistants would be bringing her security detail to her for introduction. Ericka frowned at her phone in response. This wasn't the best time. She was tired and hadn't even taken a shower yet. Leo hadn't slept well and had been fussy throughout the night. Even though Nanny Marley was more than able to care for Leo, Ericka had wanted to soothe him. Ericka was finding it more difficult than she'd planned to turn Leo's care over to someone else.

Silly. Ericka had never considered herself overly nurturing, but Leo had provoked powerful changes within her. Of course now that sunlight streamed through the windows of the cottage, Leo slept peacefully.

Yawning, she pulled her hair into a topknot and quickly changed clothes. She dashed to the bathroom to splash water on her face and brush her teeth. The introduction with her security detail shouldn't take any longer than five minutes. After that, she planned to sneak in a little nap before working. Before Leo, Ericka would never have considered meeting someone without being turned out to as close to perfection as possible. Having a baby had changed her priorities.

A knock sounded at the door and she rushed to answer it. Leo was already being treated for his hearing disability with infant hearing aids, and Ericka never knew what sounds might awaken him.

Spotting her brother's assistant through the glass

window beside the door, she opened it. She immediately caught sight of a man standing just behind
her brother's assistant. He stood at least as tall as her
brother-in-law from Texas. Over six feet tall. How
was this subtle? she wondered. He would stick out
like a sore thumb in Chantaine. What had her brother
been thinking?

"Hello, Your Highness. Rolf here," her brother's
assistant said as he made a quick bow. "I'm here to
introduce you to your primary security detail. Mr.
Montreat Walker."

Ericka nodded toward Rolf then turned to Mr.
Walker out of politeness. "Mr. Walker."

He gave a half-hearted dip of his head. "You can
call me Treat," he said in a Texas twang.

"Oh, really," she said, thinking he was not a treat.
With his stubborn chin and too-broad shoulders, he
looked as if he would be a pain in her derriere. "Mr.
Walker," she said then turned to Rolf, who appeared
to be cowering from both her and Mr. *Treat* Walker.
"Thank you so much for stopping by. I'll be in touch
with Stefan."

"I'd like to check your home security system
first," Mr. Walker said.

"Excuse me," she replied, unable to hide her dis-
approval.

"Yes," the overly tall, overly muscular, overly
American man, said. "I've been hired to protect you.
I need to make sure your home is adequately secure."

"I have a security system," she told him.

"Then you won't mind me checking it," he said.

Actually, she would, but she couldn't say that. She shrugged and opened her door widely. "Don't wake my baby."

He lifted his eyebrows for a half-beat then stepped forward. "I'll do the best I can, but I will need to test your alarm system."

Ericka stared at Rolf. "Please tell my brother I'll be in touch," she said.

"Yes, Your Highness," he said before he dipped his head and walked away.

"I'm a done deal," Mr. Walker said to her. "Your brother has made his decision."

Ericka tried to look down her nose at him, but he was too darn tall. "Nothing is a done deal."

Mr. Walker shrugged. "Good luck. I'll check your system."

Ericka frowned at him as he swaggered through the hallway. "I told you not to wake my baby."

Mr. Walker paused and turned to look at her. "How strong is his hearing disorder?"

Ericka could have cried at his question. If only she knew how extensive his hearing loss was. Even the doctors had told her the measurement for his hearing disorder could change. "Profound. He's been awake most of the night."

Mr. Walker nodded. "I'll check the house. I'll have

to test the alarm system some time. You let me know when I can do that without startling him."

If only he *could* startle Leo, Ericka thought. If only she could make a sound that would startle him. Ericka stared after Mr. Walker, hating him and liking him at the same time. What could he possibly know about having a child with special needs? Nothing, she suspected. His life had probably been perfect. No troubles. No trials.

Leo's future was full of trials. She stiffened her back. She needed to cushion her child in his infancy and make him strong for his future years. Her job was to provide the perfect amount of support and hope. Whatever that was.

A flash of fur passed between them.

Mr. Walker frowned. "Was that a cat?"

"Yes. The doctor said Leo would benefit from a pet."

He frowned in confusion. "A cat? Don't they sleep twenty-three out of twenty-four hours a day?"

"Sam is awake much more than that, plus he watches after Leo."

"You mean, he stalks your baby," Mr. Walker said.

She blinked. "He does no such thing. Sam protects Leo. He's probably studying you right now to make sure you won't hurt the baby."

Mr. Walker lifted a dark eyebrow. "This is one more challenge for implementing a sound security system."

She lifted her head. "Sam stays. We brought him back from Texas. My brother insisted he was neutered before we arrived. Stefan doesn't want any more potent cats on the island. He's afraid Chantaine will end up with too many cats."

"Understandable," Mr. Walker said. "Practical."

"Mr. Walker, you need to understand that you're dealing with a very human element. My son. I know that the people of Chantaine don't hold a grudge against me. They're delighted I have returned."

"But there could be one person who's not delighted," he said. "And I'm here to protect you from that person."

Ericka stared into his dark eyes and knew he would protect her from anything. She held his gaze for a long moment and saw a flash of tenderness. It surprised her. How could a man who appeared so hard be kind?

If he couldn't be kind to her son, she had no use for him. If he couldn't tolerate her cat, he would be dismissed.

Treat Walker looked into Princess Fredericka's disapproving blue eyes. He'd read her file. She'd been known as the teenage wild-child beauty. She'd even made a few trips to rehab before she'd gotten herself straightened out and married a French film director.

Although the princess had returned to Chantaine frequently for public and family events, she'd seemed to prefer life out of the limelight. With the exception of red carpet appearances with her husband, Fredericka had focused more of her time on studies in fine arts.

When her husband fell for a younger actress, Fredericka's life began to fall apart. The combination of the scandal and her pregnancy had been overwhelming, so she'd disappeared to live in Texas with her older sister during her pregnancy.

At first glance, she looked a little too perfect. With her aristocratic bone structure, she could have modeled for a Renaissance sculptor. Although she was trying to hold him in cool contempt, he glimpsed humanity and a little bit of fear in her eyes, a hint of purple shadows that showed she wasn't sleeping well.

Taking care of an infant with serious hearing loss could be hard on anyone, especially since she appeared to be trying to do most of it on her own. "Your son," he said. "He's lucky you have the resources to give him the best help he needs. Not everyone can get their child the right kind of help."

Her eyebrows knitted slightly. "Money can't solve everything. The choices may be difficult," she said before she turned away from him.

Ericka spent the day juggling caring for Leo and planning her work schedule. Since the nanny had gone to market, Ericka carried Leo in a cloth baby carrier against her chest as she talked on the phone.

Leo quickly drifted off to sleep and Ericka answered a few calls. When he began to drool against her collar, she suspected he was ready for genuine nap in his crib. Just as she pulled him from the cloth carrier and set him in his crib, he let out a squeak of protest.

Wincing, Ericka immediately placed her hand over his tummy. Her sister had taught her this trick. Leo didn't like the abruptness of being detached after being held. A little more of a human connection seemed to soothe him and he gave a little snorty baby sigh. Ericka held her hand on him for several more moments, staring at his rosy, plump cheeks and dark eyelashes against his perfect skin. Pride and love welled up inside her. He was the most beautiful thing she'd ever seen in her life.

Carefully backing away, Ericka turned around and pulled the door partway closed behind her. Then she walked straight into a wall. Or, it felt like a wall until it swore under its breath. Her heart hammering in panic, she opened her mouth to scream at the same time she looked up into the hard face of Mr. Walker.

She slumped in relief and he immediately clasped her arms as if he thought she were going to faint. The notion annoyed her, "Remove your hands from me," she said in the icy tone she'd learned from one of her governesses.

He immediately released her and she stumbled backward, glaring at me. "I thought you had left to get an alarm system. What are you doing here now? And why didn't you knock?"

"First, since I'm your security detail, I'm like a member of the family. I don't have to knock," he said.

"Oh, yes, you do," she said. "You're not family. You're staff. All staff knocks before entering."

"Plus I didn't want to wake your baby if he was sleeping," he continued.

She opened her mouth then closed it, feeling as if someone had let the air out of her balloon. "Well," she said, desperate to establish some boundaries with this man who seemed to take up entirely too much space. "You shouldn't come up behind me like that and startle me. There's no excuse for that."

"I was examining the hallway for the best alarm system."

He was so implacable, she thought, her irritation growing. "I'm not sure this is going to work," she said, and walked past him. "My nanny and I are working perfectly well together. Your presence is disruptive."

"Give me a couple days," he said. "You'll barely notice I'm around."

That did it, she thought. Mr. Walker was going back to the States. She would talk with Stefan that afternoon.

Except Stefan wasn't picking up his private cell phone, and his assistant said he was indisposed. Stalling tactics. Ericka recognized them because he'd used them before on rare occasions when he wanted things his way. She considered calling Stefan's wife, Eve, but with two young children and another on the way, Eve had her hands full. Besides, this was between her and Stefan.

Ericka made another call. "Bernard, this is Ericka again. How are you?"

"Quite well, Your Highness."

"I realize Stefan is quite busy today," she said.

"Yes, yes, he is," Bernard said.

"Lots of activity in his palace office," she said.

"It's often busy in the Prince's office. As you know, he works hard for the people of Chantaine."

"Of course he does. Since he is at the Palace office today, I'll just scoot over for a quick visit. I promise it won't take more than a moment or two. Ciao," she said.

"But, but, but—"

Ericka disconnected the call and smiled grimly to herself. Two could play this little game. Stefan would be hard-pressed to avoid her if she was standing outside his office.

Ericka found Nanny Marley taking a well-earned break reading in the sunroom. "Marley, I need to make a quick trip to the palace. I won't be gone long."

"Yes, Your Highness. I'll keep an ear out for him."

Ericka shook her finger at the sweet middle-aged woman. "We've already discussed this. You're not supposed to address me as 'Your Highness.' Please call me Ericka."

"I keep forgetting," the woman said. "It just doesn't feel respectful."

"It's my wish," Ericka said. "So that makes it respectful. Please?"

"Yes, Miss Ericka," Nanny Marley said.

Ericka smiled. "That's a little closer. I'll be back soon."

"No hurries on my account, ma'am," the nanny said.

Ericka drove her tiny smart car through the winding streets of Chantaine. Her route to the palace took her past the view of the azure ocean trickling against a white sandy beach. She'd never realized how much she'd missed her homeland until she'd returned. In fact, she'd fought the idea of ever returning. She'd had too many memories of feeling confined and suffocated in Chantaine. Leaving had felt so freeing.

Even now, she felt twinges from her memories, but she was determined to keep her feelings and future in perspective. One of her most important decisions had been not to live at the palace. Another important decision had been to hire Nanny Marley. The next decision would be to get rid of her assigned security man, Mr. Walker.

As she pulled up to the palace, the gates were opened and she was waved through. Parking her car at the side of the main building, she touched her finger to the sensor that would allow her inside the door. Her shoes echoed on the marble floor of the hallways as she made her way to her brother's office. The same office had once belonged to her father, although her father had spent far less time performing royal duties and much more time on his yacht with his mistress du jour. She'd always found it amazing that her father had managed to sire six legitimate children despite his numerous affairs. Now that Ericka was grown, she could look back and see that her mother had continued to have children in hopes of truly winning her father's heart. Unfortunately, her mother's wish had never come true.

Ericka's stomach knotted as she remembered feeling that same sense of desperation at losing her husband. She'd been all too aware of the deterioration of his feelings for her. In fact, she'd made love with him in a final effort to win him back. When she thought of how weak she'd been, she could hardly bear it. It had taken her over a year to find herself again and get centered. She never wanted to be that weak woman, dependent on a man again. Never.

Reaching her brother's office, she knocked on the door and waited. Impatience nicked at her and she knocked again.

The door swung open and one of her brother's assistants dipped his head. "Your Highness," he said.

"I need to see my brother," she said.

"But he's—"

"It won't take long. I promise. Stefan," she called. "I know you're in there. Do you really want me yelling outside your office?"

Her brother's assistant groaned and seconds later, he backed away, allowing her entrance. Stefan frowned at her. "I just got off a conference call with two dukes from Spain and Italy."

"Great timing," she said, and shot him a broad smile. "I thought you might be signing off around this time."

"I actually had some other items on my list," he said, his irritation clear.

"I imagine they could wait until tomorrow. Eve and your little ones would probably love to see you tonight."

His hard gaze softened. "You're probably right. Eve is worn out by the end of the day with this pregnancy, although she would deny it."

"You married a strong woman," she said.

"So I did," Stefan said. "I suspect you're here to complain about your new security man."

"Your suspicion is correct. I specifically requested someone low key, who won't interrupt my routine or bring undue attention."

"Mr. Jackson will work out with no problem. He comes highly recommended. I wanted the best for you and Leo."

"You gave me the Texas version of the Jolly Green

Giant. He's been an interruption since he walked through the door. He doesn't like the cat—"

"Can't blame him there," Stefan muttered.

"Leo likes the cat," she said.

"Leo doesn't know any better," Stefan retorted. "Listen, you haven't even given Mr. Walker a chance. He hasn't been there a whole day. The least you can do is give him a trial period."

"One more day," she said.

Stefan shook his head. "At least a week. He left an assignment in the States at my request."

"I don't need this kind of invasion into my privacy. I can't believe you think Leo or I are at risk here in Chantaine."

"You forget Eve's encounter with that crowd before we were married," he said.

"That's different. I won't be doing nearly as many appearances since I'm focusing on the conference. Any time I'm making an appearance, you can assign someone from your security detail for me."

Stefan sighed. "I don't like to frighten you, but I don't trust your ex-husband. How do you know he won't try to use Leo to get some sort of settlement?"

Ericka's blood ran cold at the thought. She swallowed over a lump of fear and shook it off. "My ex-husband couldn't be less interested in Leo. He knew I was pregnant when I left."

"He could change his mind. If he does, I want to be ready for him."

Chapter Two

Treat heard two voices coming from the den of the house as he walked down the hall. He stopped outside the den and watched as the princess used sign language while she gazed at her computer tablet. The baby sat next to her with his eyes closed, apparently asleep.

"So, how did you like that, Leo?" she asked and turned to look at her child. She gave a soft laugh. "Bored you to sleep, right?"

She sighed. "Well, maybe we can get you to extend your little nap in your crib," she said as she gently picked up the baby and stood. She turned and met his gaze.

Treat saw the way her body stiffened slightly.

"Anything I can do for you? I've decided to focus security around the perimeter of the property and give you and your nanny a panic button."

"Fine," she said with a total lack of interest. "I'm going to try to put Leo down now. He has a hard time sleeping unless he can see me or I'm holding him."

"Maybe it has something to do with his other senses being heightened. Do you leave a light on in the bedroom?" he asked.

"No. I hadn't thought of that," she said. "I use room darkening shades for him during the day."

Treat shrugged. "Just something to think about. He's probably a very visual guy."

She studied him for a moment. "I'll do some research."

He nodded. "Looked like you were doing well with the sign language," he said.

"You know sign language?" she asked.

"A little. Not enough to get any—" he said, and wiggled his hands for the sign for applause.

Her lips twitched in an almost smile. "I've got a long way to go. Right now, though, I'm putting my big guy to bed. I'm glad you won't be concentrating as much on alarming the house. Leo may not be able to hear the alarms, but it would be startling for Nanny and me."

"I hear you," he said. "Listen, do you mind if I take a swim in the pool at night? It's one of the ways I like to stay in shape."

He felt her gaze dip to his shoulders then she blinked and cleared her throat. "Of course not," she said. "Excuse me while I put Leo to bed."

Treat felt something wrap around his ankles and watched Sam wind around him. He frowned.

"Looks like Sam likes you," Princess Fredericka said.

Treat watched her as she retreated down the hallway. He shifted from one foot to the other and narrowed his eyes. Sam looked up at him and gave a meow. He glared down at the cat, but the cat continued to mark him. Glancing toward the hallway, he thought about the woman who'd just left the room. He'd expected a snooty princess. At first glance, maybe she was. But in less than twenty-four hours, he'd glimpsed something else. A princess trying to teach herself and her baby son sign language? She wasn't what he'd expected.

Treat felt a strange gnawing sensation in his gut. He hadn't felt anything like it in a long time. In fact, he hadn't felt much of anything for a long time. He'd made sure not to invest in anything too emotional. His life hadn't allowed for it once he'd suffered that last professional football injury. Treat hadn't gotten truly involved with a woman in several years. He'd been too busy trying to make a living. Once he'd switched to security, he'd decided to make his fortune with it. The past few years he'd worked nonstop with his partner to build their security business.

Now, he was making the step to take the business international.

He needed cooperation from Princess Fredericka and he also needed not to get emotionally involved. No problem, he told himself.

Another near-sleepless night, Ericka thought as she rubbed her face when the sun shone through the crack of her window coverings. She wasn't sure when Leo had fallen asleep for more than an hour, but she planned to check out night lights and anything else that might help him. She'd finally turned on a lamp in the hallway. She wondered if that had helped.

Nanny was more than ready to step up, but Ericka had a hard time handing over Leo's care when he seemed so distressed. Now, however, she had calls and plans to make and she wouldn't feel quite so guilty handing Leo over to his nanny. Ericka was so exhausted that she knew she needed help.

Lying on her back in her bed, she took several deep breaths and stared up at the ceiling. She needed to open the blinds, she told herself. She'd recently read that exposure to light during the first thirty minutes of her day would make her feel more awake.

"Wake up, Ericka," she urged herself and dragged herself from her bed. She thrust herself under a shower, brushed her teeth then stumbled toward the kitchen where Nanny sat at the table.

"You should have woken me. That's why I'm here," she said, offering Ericka a cup of coffee.

"He was just on the edge," Ericka said, accepting the coffee and taking a long draw. "He kept going to sleep and waking up. Then going to sleep and waking up."

"You should have awakened me after the first time," Nanny said.

"I think it became a challenge," Ericka said.

"Oh," Nanny said in a dark voice. "That's bad. No one should ever challenge a Devereaux."

Ericka laughed and took another long drink from her coffee. "You're so right." She paused a half beat. "The security man suggested I do something with light to help Leo. Something about his sight being a strong sense. So I'm going to do some research."

"This from the American?"

Ericka nodded. "Who knew?"

Nanny shook her head. "I would not have expected that."

"Neither would I have," Ericka said.

Nanny lifted her hands in the sign language for applause. "Good for you. Good for Leo."

Ericka smiled and echoed the sign language. "We're working on it," she said. "In the meantime, it's time for me to go to work."

"Drink another cup of coffee," Nanny said.

Ericka extended her mug up toward the woman, who refilled her cup. "I'm so glad I don't have to meet face-to-face with anyone today. Thank goodness this is a phone day."

"Take a nap midday then have juice and a cookie," Nanny said. "It will be good for you."

Ericka chuckled, but she couldn't help thinking Nanny had a good point. Maybe, if everyone took a nap after lunch followed by a snack of juice and a cookie, then the world would be a better place. She would be less cranky. That was for sure.

She made several calls throughout the day. Coffee kept her going. Just before dinner, she signed off and typed some final notes on her laptop. The conference planning was coming along. She was pleased with her progress.

Ericka stood and shook her body to release her stiffness and tension. A short dip in the pool would do her good, she thought, and she went to her bedroom to change into a bathing suit. It was dinner time, but she was more interested in the sensation of sinking into water than eating. Thank goodness the pool was heated.

Ericka stepped down the stairs into the pool, pausing before the last step. The water was cooler than she'd expected. She finally took that last step and let out a little squeal. Sinking down to her neck, she shivered, but quickly adjusted.

She took a deep breath then plunged her face in the water and began to swim. She made it to the far wall and turned then swam back. Out of breath, she paused and chastised herself. "Go," she muttered to herself and swam another lap. She returned and grasped the side of the pool, gasping for air.

A warm hand covered hers on the side of the pool. "Are you okay?"

Surprised, she inhaled water and coughed. And coughed. And coughed. She felt a splash beside her and a thump on her back. She hacked a couple more times then took a low, careful breath through her nostrils.

"Did you have to startle me?" she finally managed, looking up at Mr. Walker who was fully dressed in jeans and a polo shirt. Drenched, he stared down at her, his shirt clinging to his perfectly muscled body.

"I thought you were drowning," he said. "You kept gasping for air but ducking your head under the water."

"I was pushing myself to go a little farther. I realize it may look pathetic in your eyes, but I haven't had a lot of physical exercise during the last few months."

"Oh," he said, watching her as she continued to catch her breath.

"Have you ever had a baby?" she asked.

His mouth twitched in a cockeyed smile. "Not that I can remember."

Ericka took a deep breath and headed toward the

steps. She felt his hands on her waist guiding her. "That's not—"

"No problem," he said, continuing to help her up the steps.

Her heart raced at his touch and she didn't like the sensation. "Let go of me. I'm fine."

He didn't release her until she was steady. She resented the fact that she wasn't steady one minute earlier. She resented him, too.

"I was just taking a swim," she said.

He stepped up beside her in his wet street cloths and looked down at her. "Maybe you shouldn't do as many laps next time."

"I didn't do that many," she retorted.

"Cut yourself some slack. Isn't your baby still waking up every night?" he asked.

"Yes," she said.

"And you don't let the nanny take over nearly often enough, then," he said.

Ericka took another deep breath, hating that he was speaking the truth. She so wanted him to be wrong. "I can handle it."

"I'm your security detail," he said, and extended his hand. "I can't let you drown yourself."

She ignored his hand and walked away, her limbs heavy from her exertion. "You ruined my swim."

"I saved you from drowning," he corrected.

She turned around and stared at him. "You are a total pain and you will be gone in six days."

He gave a crooked smile again. "Your brother insisted that you give me a trial period."

Ericka scowled. *I hate you*, she wanted to say. "Good night. You'll be gone soon enough," she said, and then turned to walk away.

"You know Beethoven wrote some of his most famous work when he was deaf," he said.

She stopped and her heart stopped, too. Ericka took a deep breath, more moved by his words than she would ever want to admit. "Good night," she repeated, although even she would admit she sounded less hostile.

Although she turned on a light in Leo's room, he still awakened in the middle of the night and screamed bloody murder. Nanny was there to help, but Ericka felt responsible. She was his mother. She was the one who should soothe him back to sleep. As soon as she drew him into her arms, he quieted.

As she rocked him in the middle of the night, she wondered if she would ever be the mother he needed. He was such a precious soul. How could she be all he needed?

She dozed a bit with him in her lap then rose and carefully placed him in the crib, keeping her hand on him for several moments. She felt him drift to sleep and carefully walked away.

An hour later, he awakened again. This time, she let Nanny take him. At the same time, she felt like a failure. Why couldn't she help her son so that he would sleep through the night?

Exhausted, she awakened later than usual and forced herself to climb out of bed. Stumbling toward the bath, she splashed her face with water and brushed her teeth then headed for the kitchen for coffee. She wanted to mainline it through her veins.

Nanny offered her a cup. "Would you like cream and sugar, ma'am?"

"That sounds wonderful," Ericka said. "Have you gotten any sleep since four am?"

"Yes, ma'am, I have," Nanny said. "His royal self gave it up after half a bottle. Men," she said, shaking her head. "It's all about food."

Ericka chuckled and took a sip of her coffee. "So true. And this morning?"

"He's still asleep," Nanny said.

"That can be good," Ericka said. "And bad."

Nanny nodded. "I'll take a nap in just a few moments," she said.

"I'm thinking of hiring back-up assistance for cooking and cleaning," Ericka said.

"It shouldn't be necessary," Nanny said. "I know our arrangement is for me to return to my apartment a few days every month. Is that a problem?" the woman asked with a worried expression.

"Not at all. Trust me, you are irreplaceable. I think a little additional back-up may help. For both of us,"

Ericka said. "Leo has us coming and going. There's too much of cooking and cleaning left to do."

"Well, it's not as if you're a woman of leisure," Nanny said. "You work very hard."

Ericka felt a sliver of relief. "Thank you for saying that. I somehow feel as if I should manage all of this on my own."

Nanny shook her head. "Never. It's not as if you have a husband," she said, and then covered her mouth as if she were shocked by her frank words.

Ericka shook her head. "Don't worry. What you say is true. I'm just trying to figure it all out."

"And you're doing a wonderful job," Nanny said. "Don't be so hard on yourself. It won't help you get any job done, motherhood or your other duties."

Ericka made more phone calls to continue to secure the arrangements for the upcoming conference. Her sister Bridget called in between calls. "Hello, Bridget, how are you?"

"Pregnant and busy with the twins and all the animals my husband insists on having at our so-called ranch. When I agreed to marry a Texan doctor, I didn't realize he was serious about recreating home on the range here in Chantaine," Bridget said in a mock huffy voice.

Ericka smiled at her sister's tone. Although Bridget had been known as the socialite in her family, she'd been tamed when she'd fallen in love with her doctor husband and the two nephews he'd adopted. "More animals? Horses, cattle, goats. You're turning into a zoo,"

"Oh, darling, we became a zoo a long time ago," she said. "Now, I know you're busy, but Pippa, Eve and I want to have a get-together for lunch before I get much closer to my due date. Before you know it, it will be Christmas. Or I'll be in labor. One of the two."

"I'd love to," Ericka said, "but I'm feeling strapped for time. Between caring for Leo and planning the conference…"

"I feel terrible that you've had to take over the conference, but when the doctor put me on limited activity, it squashed my schedule even more. You have a nanny and back-up, don't you?"

"I have a wonderful nanny, but I think I'm going to have to get someone part-time for shopping and errands," Ericka said.

Bridget made a tsk-ing sound. "You should have done that right away. Trying to do too much. You're starting to act like overachiever Valentina before her husband took her away from us."

Ericka smiled at the description. Bridget had nailed Tina's personality perfectly. "I'm not sure I'll ever measure up to those standards," Ericka said.

"Well, you have too much right now, so I think you should ask for a loaner or referral from the palace. Anyone they recommend will have been properly vetted. You can ask for a few choices," Bridget said.

"I've been trying to avoid placing any extra burdens on the palace," she confessed.

"Oh, yes. I know all about it. Stefan is huffing and puffing because you won't stay at the palace where he can make sure you're safe and secure. Can't blame you for wanting to escape, though. Even though I live in a circus with these five-year old twins and all these animals, I much prefer living outside the walls. But I insist you let the palace help you out. I also insist you join us for lunch day after tomorrow. No arguments," Bridget said in her best no-nonsense voice.

"All right," Ericka said. "When did you become so bossy?"

"You get a family of instant twin baby boys and you'll be amazed how bossy you become. Ciao, darling. Go eat some chocolate and have some wine. Drink an extra glass for me."

Although reluctant, Ericka put in a call to palace personnel. Two applicants would apply tomorrow. She fed the baby and carried him around for a while. Suddenly it was eight o'clock and she was tired and cranky. Thank goodness for Nanny. She thought about how Bridget had suggested wine and chocolate, but she was in the mood for something different. Something she'd had when she was pregnant and living in Texas.

A peanut butter and bacon sandwich.

* * *

Treat followed the scent of bacon inside the house. He'd missed that smell. "Bacon?" he said.

Ericka whirled around to look at him. "Technically pancetta."

"Smells like bacon," he said.

"It's not quite the same thing," she said. "But I'll make do. If I burn it enough and put it on top of peanut butter, it won't matter that much."

"Peanut butter?" he echoed, impressed by her determination.

She nodded and turned back to her frying pan. "My brother-in-law from Texas turned me onto this when I was pregnant. It has turned into one of my favorite stress foods."

She flipped the pancetta onto a paper towel while she slathered a slice of bread with a peanut butter.

"Hey," Treat said. "Do you have any extra bacon?"

"Pancetta," she corrected.

"It smells great," he said.

She chuckled. "Here you go."

"I think I want to try it with peanut butter," he said.

She slid him a sideways glance. "I don't have a lot of extra peanut butter," she said. "My sister from Texas sends it to me."

"Okay," Treat said. "I'll just take the bacon."

She gave a heavy sigh and pulled out two more slices of bread. Slapping some peanut butter on a slice, she followed with a helping of crispy pancetta and squished the sandwich together. She handed it to him on a plate. "Eat at your own risk."

"I'll brave it," he said, then took a big bite and savored the flavors. He took another bite to assess. "It's delicious. The pancetta's a little strong, but it's still delicious."

"Agreed," Ericka said. "I'm trying to figure out how to get American bacon, although I know I've just offended every Italian I've ever met."

"The pancetta's not bad," he said, taking another big bite of the sandwich.

"No, but I want cheap bacon," she said, and took a bite of her own sandwich.

"If anyone should be able to get it, you should," he said. "You're a princess."

"We have importation rules," she said, and continued to eat her sandwich. "I wonder if I talked to Stefan. Or if I kept my mouth shut and asked Tina to send me American bacon…"

"What a scandal that could be," he said. "Princess Fredericka imports forbidden bacon."

She slid a quelling glance at him, then chuckled. "I suppose you're right. I could be importing so much worse."

He swallowed the rest of his sandwich and nodded. He brushed off his hands. "So right. Time for bed?"

She met his gaze and choked on her sandwich.

Treat smacked her on her back. He wondered if he should perform the Heimlich.

Ericka coughed then stepped away from him. "I'm fine," she insisted, coughing.

"You sure?" he asked.

"Yes," she said, still coughing.

He poured a glass of water and offered it to her.

Ericka sipped it then took a shallow breath. "I think you're right. It's time to go to bed."

Treat nodded. "Let me know if you need me for anything."

"I'm fine, Mr. Walker," she said.

"Call me Treat," he said.

"Treat?" she echoed and shook her head. "What an interesting name."

"Montreat," he said. "The name was shortened."

"Oh," she said, and then nodded.

"Kinda like Fredericka was shortened to Ericka."

"Interesting," she said. "Mr. Walker. Good night."

"Good night, Princess Fredericka," he said.

"I need to clean up," she said.

"I can do that," he said. "Go on up to bed. You need your sleep."

She paused a moment. "If you insist, Mr. Walker."

"Treat," he corrected.

She paused a long moment. "Treat," she finally said in a soft voice. The sound of his name from her lips did something to him. He would have to figure that out later.

"Night," he said as he watched her leave the room. Treat cleaned the pan and dishes then prowled the kitchen. Fifteen minutes later, he heard the sound of Leo crying. He knew Ericka would get up and cradle her baby. He also knew she needed rest.

Treat climbed the stairs. He nearly bumped into Ericka.

"What are you doing here?" she whispered.

"I'm checking on your baby," he said.

"I can take care of that," she told him.

"But maybe you shouldn't," he said. "Even Saint Ericka needs a rest."

She scowled at him. "I've never said I'm a saint."

"Then stop trying to look like one," he said. "Go back to bed."

"Who will hold Leo?" she asked.

"I will," he said.

"You?" she asked. "You look like you would be better with a football."

"Football, baby, they're close to the same."

"A baby is close to a football?" she said, clearly alarmed.

"I'm joking," he said. "I've rocked a baby before. Trust me."

"Why should I?" she asked.

"Your brother did," he said. "He vetted me six times from Sunday."

Ericka sighed, clearly so weary she could hardly stand. "Just for a few minutes," she said. "Just a few minutes. Then wake me up. I can handle this." She turned toward her room and Treat felt a crazy quiet sense of victory as he entered the nursery and picked up the baby.

Chapter Three

Ericka awakened in the night and listened for sounds from the baby monitor. Nothing. She stared up at the ceiling then closed her eyes and told herself she should go back to sleep. Leo wasn't crying. All was well.

Except the football player was looking after her baby. Rising and pushing her covers aside, she shook her head at herself. She must have been out of her mind to put Leo in his care. Rushing to the nursery, she carefully pushed the door open and saw Treat moving the beam of a flashlight against the ceiling. He saw her and lifted his fingers to his lips to urge her to remain quiet.

Ericka looked at Leo whose sleepy gaze followed

the light. His eyelids drooped then opened then finally closed. She tilted her head and looked at Treat in silence. He placed the flashlight on the small dresser then stood and ushered her out of the room, gently closing the door behind them.

"What was that about?" she asked.

"I told you he might like more light," he said.

"That's why I put a nightlight in there," she said.

"I think he likes something more active. It's a challenge to track a moving light. He's a smart little guy," he said.

Ericka took in Treat's last words and it was all she could do not to burst into tears. Although she believed Leo was smart, she hadn't heard anyone else say those exact words. He'd been called beautiful and alert, but no one had called him smart. Ericka bit her lip, determined to pull her emotions in check. "Yes, he is smart," she said as she crossed her arms over her chest. "Thank you for looking after him. It's not really your job."

"I don't require a lot of sleep," he said.

"I envy you that," she muttered. Suddenly she realized how close he stood to her. She could smell the faint scent of soap and shampoo. He was so tall, she thought, and told herself she found that fact off-putting. She looked into his eyes and her stomach took a strange dip. *What was that?* She took a quick short breath and looked away. "You can go to bed.

Nanny and I should be able to handle it now. Thank you again."

"No problem," he said, and walked past her down the hallway to the front door. He slept in the small guest suite. Attached to the cottage, the suite had its own door. For a moment, she wondered what he did all day in that suite when he wasn't figuring out new ways to protect her and Leo. It occurred to her that all that solitary confinement would make her batty. Sure, she enjoyed quiet moments enjoying art. She especially missed those moments lately, but Ericka needed human connection. She wondered if Treat did.

Suddenly realizing she'd been thinking about him for at least three full moments, she shook her head and reminded herself that she didn't care if Treat needed human connection or not. She just wanted him to stay out of the way so she could do what she needed to do.

Treat returned to the guest suite but felt like a caged animal. He felt he shouldn't leave the property to go for a run, so he decided to take a swim. Maybe that would relax him. He slid into the pool and the water felt warm against his skin, probably because the night air was cool. Automatically swimming several laps, he waited for the exercise and the monotony of motion to ease his mind.

Being around the princess's baby brought back

memories of his disabled brother, Jerry. Jerry had been born with multiple deformities, both mental and physical, but he'd had a good soul. Treat had seen it in his young brother's eyes and smile.

Treat had noticed that Leo didn't smile as frequently. Leo looked as if he were trying to figure everything out. The baby appeared to want every bit of information he could get and he wanted it immediately. A demanding baby, he thought, and not just because of his hearing loss.

His brother, Jerry, had been demanding due to his health issues which had been enormous. After Treat's father died when he was a teenager, Treat had watched his mother struggle to pay medical bills. He had cared for Jerry whenever he could, but his mother had pushed him to take a football scholarship. It had always been Treat's dream to make a lot of money so that he could take care of both his mother and Jerry.

But Jerry had died during Treat's junior year in college and he'd lost his mother just one year later. She hadn't even seen Treat graduate. Treat had felt like a rudderless boat after that.

Even though he knew the princess's situation was far different than his mother's, he caught glimpses of the same emotions he'd seen in his mother's eyes. Fear, worry, weariness. He also saw a helluva lot of determination. Ericka would make sure Leo received every bit of education and attention he needed. She could have taken an easier way out, but he could tell she would be actively involved in every decision in that baby's life. Leo was damn lucky, not just because his mother was a princess, but because she was so devoted.

Treat swam a few more laps. The vision of the princess and Leo stomped through his mind. Swimming hadn't extricated them from his consciousness, but maybe the exercise would help him sleep. Her Highness was making a bigger impact on him than he'd expected.

Ericka rose early and conducted two teleconferences. She much preferred regular phone calls because for those, she didn't need to apply make-up or fix her hair. During another call later in the morning, she received the disturbing news that young royals from Sergenia were in danger and needed to leave their small country due to unrest.

Ericka turned off her phone and did a session with Leo. She showed him several works of art and signed the best she could. "Here is da Vinci's Mona Lisa," she said, lifting her computer tablet. "He was a brilliant artist. As was Raphael." She pulled up a photo of one of Raphael's paintings. "I can't wait to show you Michelangelo's sculpture of David," she told her son. "It's beyond amazing. There's nothing like it," she said, and waved the hand toward her face making the sign for amazing.

"I must have been way behind," Treat said from the doorway. "I didn't know anything about da Vinci until I was in my teens. Unless you count the Teenage Mutant Ninja Turtles."

"Who are they?" she asked, feeling a strange rush of pleasure when she saw him.

"Cartoon turtle characters named after some of the great artists of the Renaissance," he said. "Michelangelo, Raphael, Donatello and Leonardo."

"How clever," she said.

He chuckled. "You learned about the real artists. I learned about the cartoon characters."

Ericka frowned in sympathy. "How unfortunate," she said.

He chuckled again. "No worries. I received a little more education later on and saw pictures of the Renaissance artists. I'm okay. Just not as cultured as you are."

Ericka met his gaze and felt her stomach jump. "You can learn."

"I do my best. Are you ready to go out for your luncheon with your sisters?"

"Yes" she said, standing as she remembered. "Nanny will take care of Leo."

"I'm sure he's exhausted from his morning lecture," he said.

She narrowed her eyes at him. "Are you saying I'm boring him?"

Treat lifted his hands. "Not me."

"I need to freshen up," she said. "I'll be back in a moment. Nanny Marley," she called and walked down the hall.

Treat walked over to look at Leo. "How ya doing big guy? Wanna talk football?"

Leo kicked and stared at him, making grunting sounds.

"Just so you know, Bonnie Sloan was one of the first deaf NFL football players. You can do anything you want," Treat said. "When you get a little older, maybe we can toss the pigskin."

A half-beat later, Nanny Marley entered the room. "How's he doing?"

"He's just received a very cultural tutoring session," Treat said.

Nanny nodded and smiled. "Her Highness is highly motivated to expose Leo to art, culture and science."

"What about sports?" he asked.

"That may be someone else's job," Nanny said.

Princess Fredericka strode into the hallway. "Ready," she said, and quickly ran to Leo to give him a kiss on his chubby cheek.

"Yes, Your Highness," Treat said, and walked with her out of the house.

"You don't have to call me 'Your Highness,'" she said.

"Oh, really," he said. "Then what do I call you?"

"For the remainder of your service, you may call

me Ericka in private," she said as she walked to the car.

"And what do I call you in public?" he asked.

"Miss," she said. "Just call me Miss."

"Done and done, Ericka," he said as he helped her into the car.

Just a few moments later, Treat drove to the café where Ericka planned to meet her sisters and sister-in-law. Although she was more than willing to hop out as he approached the curb, he refused to let her out. "I'll escort you into the café," he said.

"Well, don't expect to stay," she told him as he parked the car. "There will already be security for the rest of the crowd. You'll be superfluous."

"Superfluous," he echoed as he walked her into the café.

She gave a heavy sigh. "It's not an attack against your masculinity. When it comes to security, my brother Stefan provides overkill."

"I'm glad he's protective. You are all valuable to him and many others," Treat said. "There's your table. I'll be outside. Call me if you need me."

Ericka was still contemplating his statement about how valuable she and her sisters were, but Bridget stood, in her immense pregnancy, and extended her arms.

"Ericka, come here and give me a big hug. I need it. Maybe you can squeeze away some of my swelling," Bridget said.

Ericka smiled and rushed toward her sister and gave Bridget a hug as big as her pregnancy. "So good to see you. You look great."

"I'll look so much better in a few weeks. Look at Eve. She's doing fabulously. Six months pregnant and she looks like she could deliver after a full day of plowing fields."

"I hope not," Eve said, kissing Ericka on the cheek. "How's our little boy Leo?"

"Wonderful when he sleeps," Ericka said. "Which doesn't seem to happen at night."

"Oh, no," Pippa, Ericka's other sister said. "Hopefully, he'll sleep soon."

Ericka felt Pippa search her face and wished she could hide her emotions.

"You should call me for help," Pippa said.

"You're busy with your own baby," Ericka said.

"Not too busy for family. Any news on treatment?" Pippa asked.

"We're still working with hearing aids, but we haven't seen any improvement. Surgery may be in his future, but I want to make sure he's ready for it. Even with surgery, I'll teach him sign language. Of course, I'm learning it, too."

"You know the rest of us will be right there with you," she said. "We're happy to learn sign language. It would be good for the children. It would be good for all of us."

Ericka's heart swelled and she felt her eyes fill

with tears. "You're so sweet," she said, embracing Pippa. "So very sweet."

"Oh, stop," Pippa said. "Let's have a nice holiday lunch."

Ericka sat down with her sisters and sister-in-law and enjoyed a non-alcoholic cranberry spritzer along with a salad then a chicken crepe. Afterward, the women enjoyed chocolate mousse pie.

"Delicious," Bridget said.

"I agree," Ericka said.

"Stefan says you're doing a great job with the royal society conference," Bridget said.

Eve nodded. "He said the same to me."

"And me," Pippa added.

Ericka felt her cheeks heat with self-consciousness. "Thanks. Our colleagues have been very responsive."

"Good to hear," Eve said.

"I did receive an unsettling call this morning. You know that Sergenia is experiencing some unrest and the princesses and prince need a place to go. I think Chantaine would be perfect."

"But we're such a small country. How could they possibly hide here?" Pippa asked.

"Different identities and jobs." Ericka said. "They're amenable to such a plan."

"But would Stefan agree?" Bridget asked. "He has always wanted to remain neutral."

"Perhaps with the proper pressure," Ericka said, then glanced at Eve. "I hate to ask you."

"Give me more details later and I'll see what I can do. He's a stubborn, but wonderful, man," Eve said. "That's why we all love him."

"True," Pippa murmured then lifted her glass of soda. "To good health, happiness and the future of the Devereaux family."

"Here, here," Eve said. Bridget echoed the cheer as did Ericka.

"And next week, we meet publicly for the lighting of the royal Christmas tree," Eve said. "Bridget excused."

"If I can be there, I will," Bridget said, and then took another sip of her cranberry beverage. "In the meantime, we've just added a couple new goats to our zoo. Too many in my opinion. Do any of you want a goat?"

Silence followed. No takers. Ericka nearly choked over her spritzer, but she swallowed hard to quell the urge so that Bridget wouldn't mistake any sound she made as interest in taking on one of her goats.

After hugs all around, the women headed out the door. Ericka waited for her sisters and sister-in-law to leave then strode outside. A crowd awaited her, taking her by surprise.

"Hello," she managed and Treat appeared by her side.

Several people rushed toward her and Treat stepped in front of her. "Go to the car," he instructed her. "It's behind you."

Ericka rushed into the vehicle and Treat followed, driving her away from the crowd. "Next time, you won't leave last," he said sternly. "The crowd caught on after your sisters left."

"I was merely being polite," she protested.

"Next time you'll leave at the same time they leave or before," he said. "Think about it. If I hadn't been there, you could have been crushed."

She wanted to argue, but she knew he was right. She had underestimated how much the people wanted to connect with the royals. Now that she was a mother, she had to think more carefully about her safety. Thank goodness Treat had been there to protect her.

As he drove into her gated cottage, she felt a sense of safety settle over her. He helped her out of the car. "Thank you," she said quietly. "I was so busy fighting for my independence that I didn't realize I was sacrificing security." She looked into his gaze and noticed a scrape and a trickle of blood on his forehead. "You were hurt."

He shook his head. "Someone just got a little pushy."

Horrified, she lifted her hand. "I'm so sorry. We need to bandage it," she said.

"It's no big deal," he said. "Trust me. I've suffered much worse. Are you okay?"

"Me?" she echoed. "I'm fine. You took care of me."

"Good," he said. "Go inside. Take a break or a

nap. I'll be in the guest room unless you want to go anywhere."

"Of course," she said, standing on the porch as he walked away, wanting to put a bandage on his wound.

She felt a bit stupid after fighting her brother and Treat. As much as she wanted to think she could walk around like anyone else, she just couldn't. And she needed to face that fact for both herself and Leo.

The next day, the artificial pre-lit Christmas arrived outside her well-secured gate. Treat brought it inside. "Good news. There are only three pieces."

She looked at the mark on his forehead and pressed her lips together in concern.

"Stop staring at my little mark," he said, waving his hand in her face. "We need to get this tree put up for Leo. Where is the little sleep-stealer, anyway?"

"I hate to wake him," she said.

Treat dropped his chin and shook his head. "Well, he sure doesn't mind waking you. Besides, this will be a great visual experience for him."

"You're right," she said, clapping her hands as she strode toward the nursery and went against every motherly instinct by waking him. His sweet little eyebrows frowned as she lifted him from his crib.

"Trust me," she said. "You're gonna love this." Ericka was determined to continue talking to Leo even though he couldn't hear a word she was saying. In a few months, if he got the surgery, he would be able to hear her, so she needed to keep talking to him. Shifting him slightly, she grabbed his infant seat and walked to the den. "We're ready," she said as she set Leo into his seat.

"All right, all right," Treat said. "Let's rock and roll."

In a stunningly short amount of time, he put the tree up. Leo squirmed and sucked on his pacifier, but didn't cry.

Treat plugged in the lights and Leo stopped squirming and sucking, gaping at the lights.

"He loves it," Ericka said, delighted. "He loves the lights."

Treat smiled and nodded. "Bet he'll love it even more after we put on the ornaments."

"Oh," she said. "In the top of my closet in my bedroom. My sister gave them to me. I'll get them."

"No," he said. "You stay here. I'll get them."

Ericka turned to Leo and cooed. "You like the lights, don't you? Christmas is a wonderful time of love and hope, Leo," she said to her sweet infant son. "Never ever forget that."

Treat returned with the two boxes of ornaments and garland. "I hope you have some ornament hangers."

'I'm sure Valentina included them. We just need to find them," she said, and opened the boxes. It took only a few seconds to locate the hangers. "Here they are."

"Let's get moving, then. Garland first," he said as he began to spread the garland around the tree.

Ericka helped adjust the greenery. A half beat later, he grabbed a handful of hangers. Before she knew it, he hung five ornaments.

"Wait a minute," she muttered and began to hang silver and red balls. "You seem quite experienced at this."

"I was usually assigned the job of setting of the Christmas tree and decorating it," he said.

"Did you set a speed record?" she asked, hanging more ornaments.

"I wanted the tree decorated and then I wanted out of the house," he said, adding five more ornaments in no time at all.

"Why?" she asked, searching his gaze. "Why did you want out of your house?"

He shrugged as he hung the ornaments. "It wasn't all silver bells and gingerbread at my house," he said. "But that tree was good for everyone and I liked seeing it every time I came into the house. It was sad when we took it down on New Year's Day."

Ericka nodded. "I don't remember putting up the tree or taking it down. The rest of the palace felt cold. I remember wishing I could sleep under the tree, but, of course that wasn't possible. Last year, I

spent Christmas with my sister in Texas. It was a totally different experience. I want to give that to Leo."

"You are," Treat said, and hung several more ornaments.

Within five minutes, they had mostly finished
decorating.

Treat stepped away and gazed at the tree in approval. "Looks good."

Leo gave a high-pitched squeal of delight.

Ericka looked at her son then at Treat. "That's a
first," she said.

"Well, it's his first Christmas. I'm gonna take that
as a thumbs up. If he was looking at a Picasso, I
might interpret it differently."

Ericka shook her head and laughed. His comment
gave her a wonderful, surprising sense of lightness
that she'd rarely experienced since she'd given birth
to Leo. Everything felt so serious, so important. So
dire.

She looked at Leo and he smiled and laughed.
Joy filled her, starting in her belly and shooting up
to her chest, throat and cheeks. She laughed again,
staring at Leo and savoring his joy.

The moment was delightful and sacred. She
couldn't have explained it in any language, but she
was so glad she'd brought Leo to Chantaine and decided to have Christmas in this cottage. Her heart
was so full that her eyes burned with tears.

"Thank you," she said, then began to repeat it in

every language she knew. *"Grazie, Merci, Gracias, Danke..."*

He put his finger over her mouth. "I get it," he said. "You're welcome." He looked at Leo and grinned. "You're very welcome."

Ericka sucked in a teeny tiny breath into her tight chest and nodded.

"I need to check the perimeter," he said, and met her gaze. "You've done well."

"Me?" she squeaked. "You're the one who put this together in no time."

"Don't underestimate yourself. Or Leo," he said, and walked away.

She watched him leave, then she burst into tears and stroked Leo's face as he stared at the Christmas tree in wonder.

That night, Treat did his job and he made sure the house was secure. He made sure the princess and Leo were secure. He stayed away from his precious charges but watched over them.

Grabbing a sandwich, he ate it then took a swim. He swam several laps and the water felt good over his body. Finally, he stopped and hung over the edge of the pool. He took several deep breaths to clear his head.

Images of Leo swam through his brain. The princess permeated his mind. Treat shook his head and swam several more laps. He was caught between driving himself to the point where he was forced to sleep and the point where he had to stay awake to take care of the princess and Leo.

Chapter Four

The cat greeted Treat as he entered the den the next morning, and he immediately realized that he needed to secure the tree. He raced to his room to retrieve twine then returned to the den.

"What are you doing? Why are you running around?" Princess Fredericka asked, appearing in the doorway, her hair mussed from sleep as she pulled a light robe around her.

"Because I need to secure this tree," he said. "I should have done it yesterday."

"Why?" she asked, clearly bemused.

"Because you have a cat," he said. "And cats love to tear up Christmas trees."

"Oh," she said, her sexy, sweet lips forming a perfect O.

Treat scanned the floor to make sure Sam hadn't already grabbed a few ornaments. Then he wrapped twine around the tree and tied it around a vent plug. He wrapped more twine around the tree and a chair leg. He wasn't all that happy with that choice, but he figured it was better than nothing.

Treat decided to place a nail in the wall and wrap yet another bit of twine around it.

"You think that's enough?" she asked.

"I hope so," he said. "But cats are clever and destructive."

"Sam won't be destructive. He's very sweet."

"How long have you had a cat?" he asked.

"Three months here. Longer in Texas," she said.

"How much longer in Texas?" he asked.

She shrugged. "Four months. Why?"

"Has Sam ever seen a Christmas tree?"

"No," she said then winced. "Problem?"

"Not now," he said, making a final tie from the tree.

The tuxedo cat looked at Treat innocently and began to wrap around his ankles. "Oh, look," she said. "He likes you."

"No, he's trying to rub his scent on me probably because he doesn't like my human smell."

Fredericka sniffed. "I don't smell anything."

Sam gave a meow.

"Time for breakfast," she said

Treat watched as the cat proudly strode to the kitchen with its tail upright. "What are Sam's habits?"

Fredericka shrugged. "He sleeps a lot during the day. He jumps on the shelf above Leo's crib and watches over him at night. He meows if we don't respond quickly enough to Leo's cries."

"Hmm," he said as he walked around the kitchen. He glanced on the top of the refrigerator and saw several plush toys. Pulling them down, he glanced at Fredericka. "Did you put these up here?"

She glanced at the toys and frowned in confusion. "No. Two of those are Leo's toys. One is a Christmas tree ornament."

Treat nodded. "Cats are sneaky," he said.

Fredericka frowned. "Maybe so, but Sam watches over Leo, so it's okay if he takes a few toys. It's not as if Leo will notice. He has tons of toys. Christmas is coming."

"You're defending your cat against your son?"

"Sam watches over Leo. Soon enough, Leo will hold onto his toys and Sam won't get any of them." She shot him a sideways glance. "Why don't you like Sam?"

Discomfort flooded through him. "It's not Sam."

"Then what is it?"

"I brought home a kitten one time. My dad made me give it away," he confessed.

"Oh," Fredericka said, her voice full of sympathy.

"Don't feel sorry for me," he said.

"Oh, I don't," she said. "I wanted a puppy when I lived at the palace and that was a big no-go." She glanced downward. "Sam is hugging your ankles again."

Treat looked down at the cat as he wound around his feet and shook his head. "I'm telling you he doesn't like my scent, so he's trying to replace the way I smell with the way he smells."

"Is that why he's purring?" she asked, crossing her arms over her chest.

Treat heard the sound and stared at the cat. He felt a softening toward the feline. Then he shook it off. "I have no idea why he's purring."

"I do," she said. "He's purring because he likes you. He's purring because you're a guy and he's glad to have another guy in the house."

You're nuts, he wanted to say, but he didn't. "I need to get some work done. Call me if you need me." He felt the gazes of both Fredericka and Puss in Boots on him as he strode back to the guest suite. This gig was getting weird.

After making a few calls, Ericka diapered and dressed Leo for a trip to the hospital to test his hearing. Before she left, Treat stepped in front of her car and waved his hands.

"Where are you going?" he called.

She pressed down the button to push down her window. "I'm taking Leo to get his hearing checked," she said.

"Why didn't you tell me?" he asked, stepping next to her window. "It's not on the schedule you gave me."

"I didn't put all the appointments on there. The doctor told me I could wait a week or two later for testing, but I don't want to wait," she said, and shook her head. "It may sound crazy, but I need to prepare myself if he's going to have surgery. It's serious surgery," she said. "It won't be performed until after Christmas, but I don't want to wait a long time for it. This surgery could help him speak and perform just like other kids by the time he hits five or six years old. At the same time, we'll continue sign language and other therapy. It's complicated. I don't expect you to understand."

Treat shoved his hands into the pockets of his jeans. "I understand more than you think," he said.

Ericka felt a crazy connection and bit her lip. "I need to go," she said.

"Well, get into the passenger seat because I'm going with you," he said as he opened her car door.

"This is not necessary," she told him. "I can handle this on my own."

"Not this time, Princess," he said with the smile of a shark.

"Don't call me princess," she said while she rounded the car to take the passenger seat.

"Okay," he said, sliding into the driver's seat. "If I don't call you princess, what do I call you?"

"Ericka," she said through her teeth.

He drove to the hospital and she wasn't sure if she was glad for his presence or not. She squirmed in her seat and glanced back at Leo as he dozed in his infant safety seat.

"You okay?" he asked.

"I'm fine, thank you," she said.

"You don't sound fine," he said.

She took a deep breath, but didn't reply.

"What's the worst thing that could happen during this examination?" he asked.

She frowned at his question. "I hadn't thought of that."

"Well, do," he said as he drove toward the hospital. "Are you afraid he has a tumor?"

"Oh, heavens, no," she said. "No tumors. I was just hoping his hearing would improve."

"And if it doesn't?" he prompted.

"Then we'll learn sign language and he'll get surgery. The prospect of surgery terrifies me," she said, her stomach knotting.

"Will he have the surgery tomorrow?" he asked.

"No," she said, staring at him. "It will be months."

"So you'll have time to prepare," he said.

She took a deep breath. "Yes, I will."

"Take more deep breaths," he said. "You're a strong woman. You can handle this. You'll get Leo through this."

Ericka knitted her eyebrows. "How do you know that?"

"I'm an excellent judge of character," he said. "Before I met you, I thought you were a prissy princess. You've already proved you're more than that."

Nonplussed, Ericka didn't know how to respond. She wasn't sure if she should be insulted or complimented. "Why did you think I was prissy?" she asked.

"Press," he said. "Press was all wrong."

She felt a soft warmth infuse her. She sank back into her seat and smiled. "I didn't like you when I first met you."

"I know," he said.

She glanced over at him. "You're too tall, too big."

"Someone may have felt more secure because of that," he muttered.

"I found you intrusive," she said, and slit her eyes at him. "Sam didn't, though."

"Sam wants another man around the house. He likes Leo, even though he steals his toys."

"I had no idea Sam was stealing toys and ornaments," she said.

"Cats are crafty," he said.

"You like Sam," she said. "Admit it."

"I don't trust him," he said. "But he seems like a good cat."

"You don't trust easily," she said.

"I don't," he admitted.

"Neither do I," she told him and looked out the window as he pulled into the hospital parking lot.

"Want me to wait or come in?" he asked as he pulled to the outpatient entrance.

"Wait please," she said as she got out of the passenger seat. She released Leo from his infant seat and held him against her. "We'll be back in about an hour."

Treat guided the car into a parking space and sat for five minutes that felt like forever. He got out of the car and paced the parking lot for thirty minutes. He checked his watch and did a few push-ups followed by planks. Glancing at his watch, he took several breaths and paced five more times around the parking lot.

Standing next to the car, he jogged in place and looked at the door to the hospital. Finally Ericka appeared with Leo in her arms. She didn't look happy as she walked toward the car.

"Hey," he said.

"Don't ask," she said with tears in her eyes. She began to put Leo in his infant safety seat. Treat helped her. She opened the door to the passenger side of the car and stepped inside.

Treat slide inside the vehicle and started the engine. Despite the sound of the engine, the silence between Ericka and him was deafening. She must have been terribly disappointed by the test results.

He backed out of the parking space and began the drive home. After five minutes of complete silence, he spoke. "Do you know who Thomas Edison is?"

"Of course, but I don't know much about him," she said.

"He was an American inventor," he said. "He invented the light bulb and is credited as the father of electricity. He was deaf."

She took a quick sharp breath. "I didn't know that."

"Leo is going to be an amazing man. He has an amazing mother."

Ericka looked away from him, outside the window and squished her eyes together. She didn't want to cry. She really, really didn't want to cry, but tears streams out the sides of her eyes. *Oh, heaven help her.* She sniffed and prayed that Treat wouldn't hear her.

She couldn't manage a word during the rest of the trip home and she breathed a sigh of relief as Treat pulled into the driveway. "Thanks for driving us," she said.

"No problem. I'm supposed to keep you safe," he said. "Another thought. Francisco Goya was a successful deaf artist."

She met his gaze and smiled at him. "Thank you for the encouragement."

"Even bad news isn't bad news," he said. "With any kind of news, you can make a plan."

She felt the click of certainty inside her. "Thank you," she said. "Really."

He shrugged. "Anytime. Let me help you with Leo."

"I can handle it," she said.

"Of course you can," he said. "But you don't always have to."

Treat picked up the baby from his infant seat and carried him inside the front door.

"Oh, brilliant," she said, seeing a package. "It's a rotating solar toy that promises to gently light up the nursery ceiling. I ordered it a few days ago."

"It could work," he said.

"You don't believe in it," she said.

He lifted one of his hands because he was carrying Leo in the other. "It's got to be better than waving a flashlight around in the middle of the night."

She pressed her lips together. "True."

Treat took Leo to the nursery. He set the baby down in his crib. "I'll set it up for you while you change his diaper."

"Are you afraid of dirty diapers?" she asked with a sly smile.

"I wouldn't use the term *afraid*," he said, then

returned to the front door to get the package while Nanny Marley appeared in the doorway.

"Oh, you're back," she said. "I was doing a bit of laundry so I didn't hear you come in at first. Any news on little Leo's hearing?" she asked as she headed for the nursery.

"I don't think the test showed any improvement," Treat said, carrying the package.

"Oh, dear," Nanny said, and sighed. "We have so many reasons to remain positive. He is a beautiful, healthy baby."

"That, he is," Treat agreed as he allowed Nanny to precede him into the nursery.

"Why, thank you," she said. "What a lovely gentleman."

Ericka looked up at him and twitched her lips in humor. "Gentleman?"

"Hey, I know a few things about manners. I wasn't raised in a barn. Let me open this box and see what tools I'll need," he said.

"And I'll take the baby. Perhaps he could use a bit of tummy time after riding in the car," Nanny said.

"Perfect," Ericka said, lifting the baby from the crib and kissing him on both chubby cheeks. "You can do some push-ups and planks and rolling over followed by a bottle. Then you'll have the best nap ever."

Leo smiled his toothless grin in response and Ericka gave him another squeeze. Then she handed him over to Nanny.

"You're a good mother," he said, and then turned back to the project.

"Thank you," she said, then gave a soft deprecating chuckle. "I'm muddling through. Are you sure I can't help you put the solar system together?" she asked.

"I've got it," he replied. "Don't you usually have some calls to return?"

"Always," Ericka said. "I'll check in later."

Treat watched Ericka walking away, enjoying the sway of her hips. Her blond hair skimmed her shoulders and her shapely pale calves peeked beneath the dress she wore. Treat couldn't help imagining what she would look like if that dress fell from her delicate shoulders down her back, over that ripe rear end to the floor.

Then he realized he was imagining the woman he was supposed to protect naked. Treat swore under his breath and gritted his teeth. He needed to keep his distance. He needed to keep a clear head. This job would make a huge difference in his future. Treat could *not* be attracted to the princess. For too many reasons to count.

Ericka frowned as she talked to the man speaking on behalf of the country of Sergenia's royal family. "I'm sorry, but I don't understand what you're asking," she said to a man named William Monroe.

"As you know, Sergenia has two princesses and a prince to represent their kingdom, but there is so much unrest. The royal family is in danger."

"And how can I help you with that?" she asked, drumming her fingers on an end table as she pumped her crossed leg.

"The royal family of Sergenia would like to seek asylum in your country," Mr. Monroe said.

"Asylum," she echoed, automatically stiffening. She knew Stefan would never agree to such an arrangement. "Public asylum? Do you really think that's wise? If there are people who have ill will for the Sergenia family, shouldn't they be secretly sheltered?"

"Possibly, but—"

"Mr. Monroe, I know my brother will not be willing to make a public issue. If you are looking for a place for the royal family to hide, then that may be a different situation," she said.

Silence followed. "The royal family would be grateful for the opportunity to reside in your country until the unrest in Sergenia has subsided," he finally said.

Ericka bit her lip. Heaven help her, this was not her area of expertise. "I'll research the matter and get back to you."

"Please don't wait long," Mr. Monroe said, then disconnected the call.

Ericka rubbed her forehead and stood. She felt as if she'd been given a huge responsibility. If she didn't respond appropriately, then the lives of the Sergenia royal family could be at stake. She said a silent prayer as she paced the den. She knitted her hands together. She would have to convince Stefan that hiding the Sergenia royals in Chantaine was the right thing to do.

Heaven help her.

Taking a deep breath, she headed for the kitchen and fixed herself a cup of tea. Sipping it, she sank into a seat. All was quiet in the house. Surprisingly enough, Leo was still napping after his active morning and early afternoon. She half wondered if she should awaken him. She didn't want him napping so long that he wouldn't sleep tonight.

Wandering down the hall, she spotted Nanny Marley reading in the sitting room.

"He's still asleep?" Ericka asked.

Nanny looked up from her book and nodded. "Yes, ma'am. I can wake him if you like," she said.

"I hesitate to do that," she said. "Sleeping babies and all that."

"True," Nanny said. She nodded toward the video screen. "He must've worn himself out this morning."

"Maybe we should do that more often," Ericka said, then laughed.

"Perhaps," Nanny said. "We must be careful not to coddle him due to his—"

"Hearing issues," Ericka finished for the woman and nodded. "He's a strong, smart baby. He needs exercise and stimulation. Treat mentioned that he especially needs visual stimulation due to his deafness."

"That sounds right to me," Nanny said. "Although heaven knows you've exposed him to sign language. You've been as perfect a mother as could be."

Ericka sighed. "I'm not sure about that, but I'm working on it. We're so lucky to have you."

Nanny smiled. "You're a lovely girl. Leo will turn out fine. Trust my word," she said.

Ericka could only hope Nanny's words would be true. Soon enough, Leo awakened. Ericka fed him and conducted the sign language lesson even though Leo seemed a bit bored. She lifted his hands so that he could physically experience the meaning of the signs. He seemed to enjoy the physical engagement.

Deciding to take him outside for a bit, she put a tiny hat over her ears and put him into his stroller. The second she opened the gate, however, Treat appeared.

"An evening walk?" he asked, meeting her gaze.

"I thought he might enjoy it," she said. "I don't get him out often enough."

"Aside from his busy day today," he said, walking beside her.

She noticed again his height and his wide shoulders. "Do you exercise every day?"

"Five out of seven days," he said. "Why do you ask?"

"I just wondered. You seem very athletic," she said.

"I always have been," he said. "I went to college on a football scholarship. I thought my future was in football."

"But not," she said.

"An injury can change your life in an instant," he said.

"But you don't appear injured," she said.

"I exercise to compensate," he said. "I was told that another football injury could cripple me."

"Yet, you're a security man," she said. "You don't worry."

He laughed. "Security is much more mental than football. If someone tackles me, they probably won't weigh over two hundred pounds. If they do, I'll mess up my knee for a better reason than chasing pigskin."

Her respect for him went up another notch. "I'm starting to understand why Stefan chose you," she said. "Not that I like it any better."

Treat chuckled again. "I told you I would disappear into your household."

"Not yet," she said. "I didn't get a chance to look at the solar system ceiling light. What do you think?"

"Really?" he asked.

"Really," she said as she studied him.

"I want one of my own."

Ericka couldn't contain a laugh. "Why?"

"This thing is slick. Glow-in-the-dark planets with a remote control battery-operated light. I don't sleep that well, but I think this thing might lull me to sleep," he said.

"It sounds even better than I thought it would be," she said.

"If you ever decide to get rid of it…"

She smiled at him, liking his combination of toughness and masculinity. How could she explain that she liked the fact that he coveted her son's new solar system night light? How utterly strange.

Chapter Five

Despite Leo's new toy, he still didn't sleep through the night. Ericka discovered, however, that after a change and some cuddles, she could set him down in the crib and put on the solar system light and he would fall asleep. Although she was weary, her mind was busy with concerns about the Sergenian royals, not to mention the public service announcement she, a British Duke and an Italian royal would make to support clean water for everyone that was scheduled for the next day. Her sister Pippa was in town and had agreed to entertain the visitors with sightseeing and dinner after the commercial was filmed. She tossed and turned until Leo's cries awakened her early the next morning.

After feeding him, she handed him over to Nanny while she showered and got ready for the shooting of the commercial. As she fixed her hair and applied cosmetics, she realized she'd forgotten how long it took to transform herself to the polished state that was de rigueur when she lived in France with her ex-husband. Now that she was a mom, she couldn't imagine investing so much time in a daily routine.

She brushed a kiss on Leo's forehead, leaving a lipstick print. "Oops. I didn't mean to mark you," she said, and dabbed at it with her fingers.

"Oh, don't worry about it," Nanny said. "I'll take care of it. Besides, it just shows how much he's loved."

"If you say so," Ericka said skeptically. "Something tells me he won't like a lipstick print from me once he hits his teen years. Oh, heavens, I can't believe that thought crossed my mind. I'm so focused on getting him to his one-year birthday."

"And that's the way it should be," Nanny said. "I've had two teenaged children. No need to go there before necessary. I hope your photo shoot goes well."

"Thanks, Nanny," she said as she walked out the front door to where Treat stood by the car. Dressed in a jacket, white shirt and dark slacks, he looked dark and powerful. With his sunglasses hiding his eyes, he had an air of mystery.

She felt a twist of awareness at his extreme masculinity. He did nothing to tone it down, although she wasn't sure if that was even possible.

"Good morning," she said. "How are you?"

"Good," he said as he opened the passenger door then rounded the car to get inside. "And you?" He started the car and used the remote to open the gate.

"Well, thank you. You'll be happy to know the new solar system seemed to help Leo with his sleep. He woke up in the middle of the night, but then fell right back to sleep after I turned on the timed light. I wish I could say the same about my own sleep. Too much on my mind," she said. "Did you sleep well?"

"I got about four hours," he said.

She cringed. "That's not enough for me."

"I don't require much. You know how it goes. Everything gets quiet and your mind wakes up. I took a swim and that helped."

"In the middle of the night? I didn't hear you," she said, wondering what thoughts kept him awake at night.

"I hope not," he said with a chuckle.

"Maybe I should try that next time I have a hard time sleeping," she said. "Go for a swim."

"Let me know if you decide to do that," he said as he continued to drive toward the beach selected for the shooting of the public service announcement. "I don't want you drowning."

"I'll have you know I'm an excellent swimmer. I was raised on an island and my father made sure all of could swim. He didn't pay much attention to us other than that, but he was adamant that we all learn to swim well."

"He didn't pay much attention to you?" he echoed. "Don't you have several siblings? Why have children if you don't want to pay any attention to them?"

"Yes, there are six of us. He had children for the sake of progeny. Plus, if there were more of us, he could send us off to make appearances and he could go yachting. He loved his yacht. More than anything," she murmured, remembering how often he'd been absent due to his love of the sea and perhaps several women.

"Interesting," Treat said. "That wasn't in the report Stefan gave me."

"Oh, it wouldn't be. Stefan rarely says anything disparaging privately about my father and he would never put such a thing in writing. What was in that report, anyway?"

"Just every fact about you since your birth," he said.

"Oh, Lord," she said, feeling a rush of embarrassment. "I'm sure he made sure to note the face that I was the bad princess during my teenage years."

"It wasn't worded exactly that way, but…"

"I've changed," she said firmly.

"I can tell," he said. "He also gave a few details about your ex-husband."

"Stefan doesn't trust my ex-husband," she said.

"Should he?"

"I suppose not," Ericka said as she looked out the window. "I prefer not to think about him. I don't see him or have to deal with him, so to me, he doesn't exist."

"What about the fact that he is Leo's father?" he asked.

"He knew I was pregnant when I left him and he's made no effort to contact me since. Leo's birth made the news, but I've stayed out of the spotlight and I won't discuss him during interviews except to say that Leo is beautiful and growing by leaps and bounds."

"Works for me," he said, and pulled alongside the beach where several others were already setting up the commercial.

Fighting a sudden attack of nerves, she took a deep breath. "I hope this goes quickly," she muttered as he helped her out of the car.

"Why? Many women would envy your beauty," he said.

"I've never enjoyed being in front of the camera," she told him.

"But you married a filmmaker," he said.

"I wasn't in the films," she told him. "The reason I married my husband was because he took me away from Chantaine. My life wasn't studied under a microscope in France. At that time, I just wanted to escape scrutiny. The only time I had to put on a show was for a premiere or awards show."

"If you hate it so much, why did you agree to do it?"

"It's for an excellent cause. It's a very small sacrifice on my part to raise awareness. If my tiny contribution can wield influence, than I should use it." She gave a silly half smile, half moue. "Time to be a grown-up."

Treat walked behind her as she headed for the small group on the beach. She wore a simple blue dress that skimmed her curves without being too tight. Classy, feminine and, in his mind, sexy. Walking in the sand exaggerated the sway of her hips. She probably cursed the way her hair fluttered in the wind. To others, she may have appeared a smiling, friendly, blue-eyed blonde, but he knew there was a lot going on under that pale, creamy skin and "Her Highness" label.

Ericka was complicated with a heart like a mama bear for her baby and devotion to her country and sisters and brothers. She was so busy with the demands of her life that Treat wondered if she had any idea how beautiful she was. He was finding himself thinking about her far more than he should. She was a job, a means to an end. He'd protected other beautiful women. Why was she different?

He watched as she patiently did her part during

each take, and there were several. Finally, two hours later, the director appeared satisfied and Ericka took several moments to speak to each person at the shoot. She also gave Pippa a hug and thanked the Duke and Italian royal for their participation.

Treat escorted her to the car and she sank into her seat. "Thank goodness that's over," she said. "Everyone was wonderful, but we all seemed to mess up on different takes."

"Where to now?" he asked, sensing she'd felt a little trapped by the experience. It wasn't quite midday.

She glanced at him in surprise. "Home, I guess."

Treat nodded. "Home, it is."

She let out a sigh. "Well, maybe we could make one stop along the way."

Treat nodded again. "Where?"

"Gelato. There's a place in town that makes fabulous gelato, almost as good as Italian. I already know I want dark chocolate," she said. "You'll have to get some, too, but you're not allowed to choose vanilla."

Treat smiled, but mentally planned the visit in his head in order to protect Ericka from unpleasant surprises. "What if I like vanilla?"

"Then you'll have to choose that a different time," she said.

"As you wish, Your Highness," he said.

"Don't start with that now," she warned him, but laughed.

Treat hadn't seen her this playful even when she

was playing with her son. It was as if every exchange with Leo had a serious undertone. Following her directions to the gelato shop, he secured a parking spot down the block and escorted her to the shop.

"You're going to love this," she told him as he constantly watched their surroundings both inside and outside.

Two servers, one male and one female, dressed in uniforms stared at Ericka in surprise.

"Your Highness?" the young woman finally managed.

"You weren't supposed to notice," Ericka whispered and smiled. "You have the best gelato in Chantaine and I want a scoop of dark chocolate."

"Yes, of course, ma'am," the woman said as she prepared Ericka's gelato.

"What kind do you want?" Ericka asked Treat with a curious expression on her face.

"You choose," he said, his attention focused on their surroundings.

"That's no fun," she said, her face falling. "Do you prefer fruit or chocolate?"

"Fruit," he said. "I'll take the berry gelato."

Treat took a bite of his and was surprised by the vivid flavor.

"Excellent, isn't it?" she asked, savoring a bite of her own.

He watched her lick her lips and felt his gut tighten in awareness.

Suddenly the waitress came up to their table again. "Your Highness, would you possibly allow us to take a photo with you?"

Ericka wrinkled her nose. "Then everyone will think I'm playing hooky," she said.

"Oh, no," the female server said. "We can say your visit was official business."

Ericka laughed. "Okay, but I'm not sure how you can sell that. Treat, would you mind taking a photo with this lovely woman's smart phone?"

Treat nodded and took the photos. "Just give us ten minutes before you post it for the world to see," he told her. "Finish in the car?" he asked Ericka. At her nod, he escorted her to the car. He inhaled his small portion of the dessert and started the car.

"Already finished?" she asked, still taking slow bites of her own.

"I wanted to get on the road before there's a crowd," he said.

"Oh, I was so busy enjoying the outing that I forgot you're working," she said.

"Your brother wouldn't forgive me if I forgot to protect you," he said. "That's always number one."

She sighed and took her last bite of gelato. "Well, it was nice while it lasted. Hope it wasn't too much of a trial," she said, and shot him a glance from beneath her eyelashes that almost looked flirtatious.

Treat felt that pull in his gut again. He would have to put a stop to it. He'd figure out how soon enough, he promised himself. In the meantime, he shook his head. "I can't think of any man who would consider that a trial," he told her in a dry tone. At the same time, she seemed to be playing havoc with a place inside him he'd considered sewn up tight and under wraps.

"Thanks for the field trip." She sighed and leaned her head back against the headrest in the car. "Maybe my sister Bridget is right. She keeps saying I need to get out more, but I don't like leaving Leo."

"You could take him out every now and then. Has he been to the beach?"

"Not since he was an infant. I'm afraid the paparazzi will catch a photo of him wearing his hearing aids. I want to protect him as long as I can," she said.

Treat shrugged. "You could always go early in the morning and put a hat on him," he said. "For that matter, you could put him in the pool, too."

"I'll see," she said. "Like you said, my number one job is to protect him."

"Are you afraid of the questions?" he asked.

She looked away for a moment as if she didn't appreciate his query. "Perhaps. I don't have all the answers. I may never. I don't want anyone to make fun of him. That would break my heart."

"Oh, I don't know about that. You've got a strong mama-bear thing going on. If anyone caused harm to your baby in any way, I wouldn't be surprised if you broke some bones."

"That may be a slight exaggeration. I'm not normally a violent person."

"But if someone threatened Leo?"

"I like to think it would never get that far," she said.

Treat gave a short, emphatic nod and pulled the car past the gate to the front door. Cutting the engine, he rounded the car and helped her out of the vehicle.

"Thank you," she said. "My new part-time genie planned to prepare an afternoon meal today. Would you like to join us?"

"Thanks," he said, knowing such a move would be dangerous. "But I have computer work."

Her eyes darkened with a twinge of disappointment. "Of course. Ciao, then," she said as she walked into the cottage.

Treat stood there, looking after her, for a full moment after she closed the door behind her. His attraction to her was ridiculous. She was the princess of a Mediterranean island for Pete's sake. He was a wrong-side-of-the tracks kid from Texas. He knew he wasn't the kind of man who would normally catch her eye. He had to be careful. He knew enough about security to know that these situations could be emotionally intense for some people although he'd never had a problem before. He sure as shooting didn't need a problem now, especially since this job could help him expand his company internationally. He'd worked hard the past several years. He didn't want to lose all his hard-won progress just because he was developing a stupid crush on a princess.

Raking his hand through his hair, he returned to the guest suite and turned on his laptop then grabbed one of the jars of peanut butter he'd brought with him from the States and slapped a peanut butter sandwich together before he returned to his desk. The welcome screen rose to greet him. There was always work to do, he told himself. Work that would help him forget everything he had lost so quickly in his college year. Work was a panacea. Always.

Treat checked the perimeter several times then knocked on the door to the house that evening. Nanny answered. "How are you tonight, Mr. Walker?"

"I'm fine. How are you, the princess and the baby?" he asked.

"All well. The baby appears quite charmed with his new ceiling mobile of the solar system. Her Highness has either been working all afternoon or playing sign language games with Leo. I swear that woman hardly ever stops. I would just like to see her get a full night's rest."

Treat smiled and nodded. He could always count on Nanny giving him a mouthful of information. "I'm glad to hear everything is going well. I hope everyone has a good evening. I'm only a few steps away. Call me if you need me."

"Yes, sir," she said.

Treat returned to his suite and made a few calls.

His agreement with Stefan allowed him to continue to make future business plans and contacts. So far, it was quiet job, but he never let down his guard. Not even when he slept. He'd set multiple alarms and had a backup with the palace.

Hours later, he looked at the clock and realized he needed to hit the sack. He did a weight workout in the suite, but still felt restless, so he put on a swimsuit and went to the pool. Lap after lap, he took then felt a slight disturbance in the water. Rising, he looked around and saw Ericka hanging on to the side of the wall.

He took several breaths. "What are you doing here?" he asked.

"You said you swim when you can't sleep. Why can't I do the same?" she asked.

He studied her for a long, hard moment and saw that she wasn't being coquettish. She, like him, just wanted a decent night of sleep. "Have you tried meditation?" he asked.

She sighed. "The trouble with meditation is that I keep interrupting the oms with what I worry about."

He chuckled, easily identifying with her quandary, although he struggled with more regrets than worries. "Okay, start your laps. I'll sit on the side to make sure you're okay."

"I'll do fine," she told him with a prim frown and began swimming.

He couldn't fault her form and he liked that she

didn't move too quickly. A nice, steady pace. She did a flip turn against the wall and he was impressed yet again. On her back, she kicked like a pro. After the next turn, she did a great breaststroke, tagged the wall and did another length of breaststroke.

She smiled as she approached him, taking several heaving breaths. "I was never good at butterfly."

"Looks like you're good at everything else," he said.

She gulped in several more breaths. "Again, my father encouraged competitive swimming."

"That can be good and bad," he said.

"It was probably one of the few good things he did," she said. "I need a few more laps."

She did a few more and he couldn't help admiring her body. He liked her combination of athleticism and feminine softness. She relied on the breaststroke for a couple more laps then turned on her back and did the backstroke for two more laps.

She grabbed the side of the pool and gasped for breath. "I think that's enough for now," she said.

"Should you have stopped sooner?" he asked.

"No. You always have to push yourself when you're swimming," she said, still taking deep breaths. "Even if you feel like you're dying."

"And this is why I want you to let me know if you decide to do night swimming," he said.

"Spoilsport," she said as she rested her head on

the side of the pool. "The water feels nice at night, doesn't it?"

He nodded. "Do you worry about Leo at night?"

"Yes," she said. "I worry about what I may have done during my pregnancy that caused his deafness."

"Isn't this a genetic issue?"

"Most likely," she said. "But I still wonder. I wonder if I could have prevented it."

"You couldn't have," he said.

"How can you be so confident? How can you know that I did everything possible to protect Leo during my pregnancy?"

"Because I know you did. I know you couldn't prevent his deafness," he said. "And you can't make his world perfect now. It's okay that you can't. You just need to be his mom and love him no matter what. You can't fix everything. You don't have to."

Ericka sighed. "I wish I had superpowers and could fix everything."

"Stop wishing," he said. "Just do what you can every day. You get to the end of the day, say a prayer and enjoy a full night of rest every night."

She chuckled. "A full night of rest every night?" she echoed. "That's a fantasy world for me."

"Do another four laps," he said.

"I'm tired," she protested.

"Not tired enough," he told her. "You're still arguing."

She groaned, but did the laps, albeit slowly. After

the fourth, she dragged herself out of the pool. "You're not as bad as my father, but you're close. I'm way tired."

"Good. Maybe you'll sleep now," he said. "Let Nanny do her job if Leo awakens during the night."

"It makes me feel like a slacker when I don't get up with him at night," she said.

"Take a break. It's not as if you have a husband to take a turn," he said.

Ericka bit her lip. "And that's another subject. No father figure for him."

"He's got plenty of father figures. More than most," Treat said. "Your brothers. Your brothers-in-law. I hear there's more one road to Mecca. You're taking it."

"If you say so," she said, wrapping a towel around her.

"I do. Now you're growing very sleepy. Very sleepy. Your eyes are closing," he said.

"You're a good guy, Treat, but you're no hypnotist."

"Bet you fall asleep within five minutes," he said.

"But will I stay asleep?" she asked.

"Yes," he said, then waited until she left to swim ten more laps. He wanted Ericka more than ever.

Chapter Six

The next night, Ericka sent Treat a text informing him that she planned to take Leo for an early morning trip to the ocean. Ericka had strange feelings about Treat. He showed her a lot of heart then totally backed away as if he wanted to remain as professional as possible.

That's what he should do, she told herself as she crawled into bed and pulled the sheets up to her chin. That's what she and Stefan wanted. A true professional. It was his good heart that was wearing her down. It was his good heart that made her feel both weak and strong. And she totally needed to get over those feelings.

She took a deep breath and tried the meditation

exercise she'd learned earlier in the day, and surprisingly enough, she drifted off to sleep.

Reality smudged with dreams. *Treat took her into his arms and his body felt so strong and muscular. His heartbeat drummed against her chest.*

"I want you," he confessed. "I want you, but I shouldn't."

She felt herself melt in his arms. "I want you, too. I was afraid I was the only one."

"No," he said, and lowered his mouth to hers. He slid his tongue between her lips and she drank in the taste of him. She couldn't prevent herself from rubbing her chest against his.

He groaned in response. "You feel so good," he said. "I want more of you," he told her. "I want you naked."

Her heart beat so quickly she wondered if she would faint. She slid her fingers through his short hair and opened her mouth for a soulful kiss.

Moments later, as if through magic, her clothes floated away, as did his. Her nipples meshed against his hard chest. She felt him naked against her from head to toe. He took her mouth and the kiss seemed to go on forever and ever.

"I can't get enough of you," he muttered against her lips as he slid his hand between them and rubbed her where she was swollen and needy. "Can't get enough."

"I want you," she said. "I need you..."

Groaning, he pushed her legs apart and...

Ericka reached for him, arching her body. "*Treat...*"

A sound permeated her dream. A baby crying. Ericka sat up in bed, fully aroused and full of want and need. She gasped for breath and shook her head, chasing consciousness. "Oh, my—"

She shook her head again and realized she was hearing Leo's cry. Rubbing her forehead, she climbed from her bed and went to the nursery. She clicked on the light for the solar system and waited a few seconds. She could hear Leo squirming in his crib then he quieted. She felt him slurp his thumb into his mouth as he studied the lights on the ceiling.

He was comforting himself, she realized. He needed a little extra help, but he was working at it, sucking his thumb and staring at the solar system. Her chest tightened and she felt a tear run down her cheek at the realization. Her baby boy was doing the best he could. She would do the best she could for him even if the best she could do frightened her nearly to death.

Ericka returned to bed and waited for sounds from Leo, but he remained quiet, hopefully sleeping. She tried meditation, but she fell asleep during the middle of it. Proof she was exhausted, but also felt safe. She would have to think about that safe feeling to-morrow. Or the next day.

* * *

The next morning, Ericka arose to the sound of her alarm and dragged herself out of bed. Despite her drowsiness, excitement raced through her. She was taking Leo to the beach!

She stripped then pulled on her bathing suit followed by a pair of shorts and a t-shirt. She went to her bathroom, splashed her face with water and brushed her teeth.

"Your Highness?" Nanny said, wearing her night robe, as Ericka entered the hallway. "I believe the baby is asleep."

"For how long?" Ericka asked.

"Most of the night," the older woman said. "I only heard him once and he quickly went back to sleep or I would have gotten up with him."

"It's the solar system," Ericka whispered. "I pray it continues to work. In the meantime, I'm taking him to the beach."

Nanny's eyes widened. "The beach? Are you sure that's wise? Won't the water be too cool for him?"

"If it is, he can enjoy the sand. This baby lives on an island and he's only been to the beach once. I want him to experience the ocean, if only for a few minutes."

Nanny gave a thoughtful nod. "I think it's a good idea. The boy loves new experiences."

Ericka smiled, glad Nanny approved of her idea. Even though Ericka knew it was the right thing to do,

Nanny's affirmation added to her confidence. "See you later," she said. "Go back to bed."

"As you wish, ma'am," Nanny said, tightening the belt of her robe and returning to her room.

Ericka rushed to the nursery and broke one of her cardinal rules. She awakened Leo. He blinked his sleepy eyes and rubbed them then met her gaze as she changed his diaper.

"Good morning," she whispered, even though she knew he couldn't hear him. She signed the words and repeated them then smiled.

He smiled his toothless grin in return.

"Aren't you handsome," she said to him and stroked his forehead. She grabbed a few more articles of clothing and a bottle. He was hungry and quickly downed the formula. Ericka lifted him against her shoulder and a burp escaped. "Aren't you the efficient one this morning?" she asked, then grabbed her diaper bag and raced out the door.

Treat was waiting next to the car. Her heart leaped at the sight of him. She told herself to ignore her wayward reaction to him.

"You think he's ready for the ocean?" he asked.

"We'll start with the sand and end with the ocean. I don't want him to get too cold," she said, and placed Leo in the infant safety seat. "I think he's ready for an adventure."

"He's always ready for an adventure," Treat said.

She glanced at him. "And how do you know that?"

Treat shrugged. "He's just that kind of guy."

Ericka stuck a pacifier in Leo's mouth and he suckled it for all he was worth, as if he knew this would be one of his first great adventures.

Sliding into the passenger seat, Ericka gave Treat direction to the privately owned beach of the Devereaux family. Although the beach was private, it was no match for the long lenses of cameras from the paparazzi. Since it was December and early morning, however, they had a great shot at avoiding the photographers.

Treat pulled down a sandy road and stopped when the beach was in sight. "I think we're here."

"I think we are," she said, excitement thrumming through her. Pulling on a baseball cap, she got out of the car before Treat could assist her and started to release Leo from his safety seat. She began to pick him up.

"Hat," Treat reminded her, and she paused.

"Right. Thanks," she said as she put a ball cap on the baby's head.

Leo stared at her, still sucking on his pacifier. His expression seemed to say, *Are you sure you know what you're doing? I don't know if I like this thing on my head.*

"You're gonna love the cap," she told him and pulled him against herself.

The trio walked toward the gentle lap of the waves on the beach. Not too far from the surf, she sank onto the sand and put Leo between her legs. "How do you like this?" she asked, and stroked his head while keeping his cap in face.

Leo continued to suck on his pacifier as he stared at the surf.

Ericka lifted a handful of sand and spilled it over his tiny palm. He glanced down at his hand and she repeated the motion. His sucking slowed as he studied the sand in his hand. A few seconds later, he dipped his hand into the sand and squeezed his fingers through it.

"Good for you," she said, patting his arm. "You're a smart one."

Leo played in the sand for the next several moments and Ericka loved watching him explore.

"Are you sure you want to try the ocean? It may be a bit cold," Treat said.

"I agree," she said. "Maybe we could just dip his feet in it."

Treat grabbed Leo against him and pulled Ericka rise to her feet. They took a few steps into the ocean.

"A little chilly," she said.

"We can let him have his own opinion," Treat said and, still holding Leo against him, he dipped the baby's feet in the ocean.

Leo paused again in suckling his pacifier.

"How was that for you, big guy?" he asked, and then dipped his tiny feet into the surf again.

Leo kicked his feet and legs.

Ericka laughed. "I don't know if that's a yes or no."

"He's not screaming, so let's call it a yes," Treat said as he dipped the baby's feet in a wave once more. Leo opened his mouth and cackled, dropping his pacifier. Treat caught the paci before it fell into the ocean.

Ericka stretched out her hands for Leo, and Treat passed the baby to her. "You may be an ocean baby, after all," she said. "We'll have to bring you again."

"Are you going to take a dip?" Treat asked.

"Not this time," she said. "It's a little cool for me."

He nodded, staring out at the ocean. "I only went to the ocean twice when I was growing up. Loved it both times. Once, we went in winter and I swam even though it was freezing cold," he said, then chuckled.

"You should go now," she urged.

He shook his head. "I can't be protecting you if I'm swimming in the ocean."

She sighed. "Well, darn."

"I'll come back another time on my day off," he said.

"What day off?" she asked as they walked out of the water. "You haven't taken a day off since you started."

"I will sometime," he said.

"But then I won't get to see you swim in the ocean," she said.

"I'm sure I wouldn't win any prizes for form," he told her. "You won't be missing much."

"I bet you dive into the waves," she said.

He looked at her and his lips lifted in a half-grin. "Who are you? The psychic princess?"

She walked on the sand toward the car. "That's what I want to see. You diving into the waves."

"Why?" he asked.

"I'd like to see what you were like as a kid," she said.

He shook his head. "The kid in me doesn't come out very often. The kid had a complicated childhood."

"How complicated?"

"I told you more than enough. You're a client," he reminded her.

His statement felt like a smack in her face. She took a quick breath. "You were just part of an amazing, private experience. How many times have you taken a baby with his mom for a dip in the ocean?"

"Never," he admitted.

"Leo and I are not just clients," she told him tersely, and put Leo into his car seat. "Do you have his pacifier?"

"Here," he said, and pressed the pacifier into her hand.

He opened the passenger door and she slid into her seat without looking at him. She heard and felt Treat get into the car and start the ignition. She kept her gaze trained forward. She was so incredibly insulted and not sure why. Why should she care what staff thought of her?

"Sorry," he said as he pulled past the gate to the front door and stopped. "That was out of line. I've dealt with kids before, but not infants. And not you. I just need to keep my head on straight."

Her heart turned over at the intent expression on his face. His gaze forced her to think more about how she was feeling at this moment. This *was* a job for him, one that would end. He was a human being with feelings. Deeper feelings than she'd expected. He was the first man who'd inspired crazy emotions inside her. Emotions she hadn't felt in a long time. The situation was very complicated, but that didn't change the fact that she wanted him.

"I understand," she said. "I'll get Leo inside for his bottle and a nap."

"And your morning full of work," he said, stepping out of the car. He unhooked Leo from his car seat. "You did good, big guy," he murmured to the baby. "Want me to bring him inside?"

"I can do it," she said, taking Leo into her arms. She inhaled his baby scent and gave him a kiss on his chubby cheek. "Thank you," she said, and walked into the cottage. Feeling Treat's gaze on her as she walked, Ericka felt a tiny sliver of comfort. He was as affected by her as she was by him. She wasn't completely alone. Small comfort, she told herself. Neither could do anything about their feelings.

Ericka looked down at Leo as he stared up at

her. Maybe doing nothing was for the best. She had enough on her hands and in her arms.

That afternoon Ericka decided to pay a visit to the palace. She needed to talk to Stefan personally. Despite the fact that her biggest concern was Leo, thoughts of the Sergenian royals plagued her. She needed to get Stefan on her side.

Treat insisted on driving her and she did all she could not to think about the dream she'd had the other night and how much he affected her and how hard it was to be this close to him. When they arrived at the palace, she nearly leaped out of the car. "I'll be back soon."

She'd called ahead and Stefan had agreed to meet with her provided she wasn't complaining about security. Truth was, her security could complain about her, but that was another story.

His assistant opened his office door at her second knock. "Your Highness," the assistant said.

"Good afternoon," she said as she walked toward Stefan.

He stepped from behind his desk and kissed her on the cheek. "You sounded upset," he said.

She kissed him on the cheek in return. "I'm concerned. I received a call about the royal family of Sergenia."

"The country has experienced a lot of unrest," he said.

She nodded. "The royal family is in danger. They need a place to go."

He gave her a thoughtful look. "You know we don't get involved in the politics of other countries."

"This isn't about politics," she said. "It's about people. What if one of us had needed a place to go because Chantaine had become more violent?"

"We take care of our people," he said. "We put our people first. That's why Chantaine is peaceful."

"But this isn't asking a lot. They just need a place to disappear," she said.

Stefan shook his head. "I appreciate your good heart, but I have to think about the greater good. I don't want violent people from Sergenia taking revenge on our citizens."

"But if we kept it secret—"

"Fredericka," he said. "The answer is no."

She understood her brother's point, but her heart still tugged at the thought of the young Sergenian royals in danger. She'd done research on them. They were good people.

She bit her lip. "You know I could have done this behind your back."

He narrowed his eyes in a way that would have intimidated her five years ago. Not so much today. "I hope your honor as a Devereaux means more to you than that."

"I hope you'll think about the Devereaux honor and how we're trying to make a new name for ourselves. Please reconsider." She lifted her hand when he opened his mouth. "Don't say anything, just please reconsider. Have a good evening in your very safe palace, in your very safe country. Not all are quite so fortunate," she said as she walked out of his office.

Striding out of the palace, she found Treat waiting for her just outside the door. He quickly exited the car and assisted her inside. Ericka jerked her seatbelt into place.

"That was fast," he said, sliding back into his seat and pulling out of the parking area.

"Fast, but not successful. Being honest and honorable can be a total pain," she muttered.

Ericka felt Treat's gaze on her as he stopped at a stop sign. "Honor? Honest? You want to explain?"

"Not really," she said, feeling extremely frustrated. "Everyone thinks I have this superficial job where all I do is plan meetings with other members of royalty, but other things can happen. I can get calls that are more than fluff. What am I supposed to do about those calls?"

"What are you talking about?" he asked.

Ericka took a deep breath and crossed her arms over her chest. "Nothing."

"Doesn't sound like nothing to me, but as long as it doesn't affect your security," he said.

"Of course it doesn't affect my security," she said, and sighed. "It affects the security of the royals in Sergenia, but if you repeat that, I truly will kill you."

He gave a whistle. "Sergenia. Oh, that place is a mess."

"Yes, it is, and the royals need a place to go," she said.

"Here? Chantaine? Why here?" he asked. "Why not a larger country?"

"You must agree we're a bit more isolated. We're not a target," she said.

"True, I guess. I take it Stefan didn't agree."

"He didn't, but I'm not giving up," she said. "I put in the initial guilt screws. I'll try again in a few days."

He glanced at her and chuckled. "You're a little scary when you get determined."

She smiled back at him. "I'll take that as a compliment."

Shortly later, they arrived back at the cottage and Ericka thanked Treat as she entered the house. Nanny greeted her, holding Leo in her arms.

"He's been a bit fussy this afternoon. The hearing doctor called the house phone. I couldn't get to it in time. I think he left a message."

Ericka glanced at her cell phone and spotted a missed call from Leo's doctor. She listened to the message and her stomach fell. The doctor confirmed what she had already sensed. Leo was profoundly deaf. But he could have life changing surgery in January or February.

The news left her in a quandary because the surgery presented a fair amount of risk. The possibility of endangering Leo crippled her. In normal circumstances, she would want to put it off. The flip side was that if Leo's surgery was successful, he would be able to speak normally and hear more than he ever could with hearing aids.

Ericka went to Nanny and extended her arms. "I'd like to hold him for a while," she said.

"Of course," Nanny said. "Simon left groceries and dinner. Would you like some soup?"

"That sounds perfect," Ericka said as she carried Leo to the den. He stared up at her with his wide blue eyes. "How are you doing, little man? I thought you would be all tuckered out from your adventure in the ocean this morning."

Leo squirmed in her arms and Ericka realized her darling baby had gas. "Maybe I can help," she said, sitting down and putting his tummy over her knees. He gave several burps and let air out his backside then seemed to relax.

She pulled him onto her lap. "Better now?"

He made a moue, but didn't cry. "Bet you're hungry now," she said. "Let's get a bottle." She went to the kitchen and pulled a bottle from the refrigerator as Nanny heated soup on the stove.

"Gas," Ericka said.

"That explains the crankiness. I hope he'll sleep well tonight," Nanny said.

"Me, too," Ericka said as she gave Leo his bottle.

He sucked it down in no time. She burped him repeatedly then put him to bed. He was so drowsy he looked as if he were craving rest.

Crossing her fingers, Ericka returned to the kitchen and accepted the bowl of soup Nanny had heated for her. "Thank you so much," she said. "It's been quite a day."

"I'll say," Nanny said. "You've been up since nearly the crack of dawn. I bet you're ready for some sleep yourself."

"I am, but I hate for you to take the tortured night shift," Ericka said as she sipped her soup.

"Remember, I can sleep when he does. You have work to do. Don't you worry about me," Nanny replied, and patted Ericka's back.

But Ericka couldn't help feeling *she* should be the one getting up with Leo.

Chapter Seven

Despite her qualms, Ericka gave into her longing for a full night's rest and allowed Nanny to take the night shift. She heard a couple of peeps from the baby monitor, but no prolonged crying. When she rose, she felt rested and refreshed, a condition she rarely experienced these days.

Making her way into the kitchen, she found Nanny sneezing into a tissue. "Bless you and good morning," Ericka said. "I hope Leo didn't keep you up too much last night."

"Not at all, ma'am, but I fear I'm getting a cold. I've been washing my hands, but I feel as if I need to spray myself with anti-germ cleaner so I won't pass this on to you or the baby," Nanny said then sneezed again.

"You look miserable," Ericka said. "Perhaps you should take a day or two to recuperate."

"I hate to leave you without help," Nanny said.

"I have Simon for food and errands. You've just given me the gift of a full night of sleep. I think I can manage for a couple days."

"Are you sure?"

Ericka nodded. "You'll get better sooner if you rest. And take some of Simon's soup with you. He made quite a bit of it," she said, going to the refrigerator and pulling out the crock of soup. She poured some into a storage container and gave it to Nanny.

"You're too good to me," Nanny said.

"Not at all," Ericka said. "I hope you feel better soon."

Nanny left for her small apartment in town and Ericka quickly took a shower then started working on a spreadsheet of workshops for the upcoming conference. In the middle of a telephone call with one of the prospective speakers, she heard Leo cry out. Quickly ending the call, she went to the nursery, changed his diaper and brought him into the den with her. She gave him his bottle, made the sign for milk and moved his hand to make the same sign.

Leo clapped his hand against hers and cackled.

Ericka couldn't resist smiling. "We'll keep working on it," she said, while he sucked down his formula. As soon as he finished, she burped him several times. A gassy baby was not a happy baby.

"Time for sign language class," she said, then clicked on the pre-recorded video on her laptop. Sitting on the floor, she propped Leo on her lap and repeated the words from the tutor and performed the signs then helped move his hands into the signs.

A knock sounded at the front door and she glanced toward it. Who—

Treat poked his head inside and she felt an unwelcome surge of pleasure at just the sight of him. *Oh, please. Get a grip*, she told herself.

"Just checking on you. I noticed Nanny left earlier."

"We're fine. Nanny was fighting a cold and losing, so I thought it would be best for everyone for her to take a couple days off."

"Good call," he said. "How's he doing with sign language?"

She chuckled and shook her head. "I think he's more interested in giving me a high five and having fun, but I've been told most babies don't start signing until six months."

"Nothing wrong with both of you having fun," he said. "He's a fun kid."

She felt a slight easing inside her and let out a breath. "I'm trying so hard to do everything correctly that I sometimes forget about having fun."

"Think about when you were a kid. Didn't you learn better when you were having fun?" he asked.

She thought back to her childhood and remembered strict nannies and teachers. There had been one or two that had relaxed the rules at times. "I guess you're right."

Sam strolled into the room and began to rub his face on Treat's jeans. He looked down at the cat in confusion. "He does this nearly every time I come into the house. Doesn't he know that I'm not really a cat person?"

Amused, she tried to keep a serious face. "It's obvious that he's determined to make you love him," she said.

Treat rolled his eyes, but bent down to rub the cat behind his ears. Sam closed his eyes in contentment.

Leo squirmed and let out a little shriek, waving his hands toward Sam. Hearing the baby, Sam obligingly strolled next to Ericka and Leo. Leo patted the cat. He hadn't quite learned the technique of stroking. Sam tolerated the petting then slinked toward the kitchen.

"Does the cat always let Leo pet him?" Treat asked.

"More times than not," she said, rising from the floor. "I think Sam believes his job is to watch Leo."

"A watch cat instead of a watch dog," he said. "Looks like it's working. I'll let you get back to whatever you're doing."

"I'm getting ready to eat lunch. Simon brought soup and a pasta meal that could feed a dozen. Would you like to join us?" she asked.

She saw a flicker of hesitation, as if he wanted to stay. He shook his head and she hated the knot of disappointment she felt in the pit of her stomach.

"Thanks, but I'll have to pass," he said.

Why? she wanted to ask, but swallowed the question. She wasn't asking for a lifetime commitment. She just wanted a little company, and the more time she spent with him, the more curious she became about him. But he was clearly determined to keep his distance. She should accept that and be done with her thoughts about him.

Deliberately forcing herself to stop thinking about Treat, she made sure Leo got in some tummy time, watching him grunt and groan as he did baby push-ups. She placed one of his favorite toys in his peripheral vision to see if she could tempt him to roll over. He worked hard but wasn't quite ready. When he started to cry, she scooped him and gave him the toy, praising him even though she knew he couldn't hear him. She wanted to stay in the habit of praising him for the day when he could hear her, possibly after his surgery in January.

He was drooling like a fountain and rubbing his eyes, so she put him down for his afternoon nap and returned to her work. Less than an hour later, she heard him crying. Surprised, she turned on his solar system toy. That only worked for a few more minutes. She brought him with her into the den and put him in his infant seat with toys hanging in front of him, but he continued to fuss.

She spent most of the rest of the afternoon walking the floor with him in his arms. Fearing he might be catching Nanny's cold, she touched his face and body, but he didn't appear to have a fever. He did, however, seem to be chewing on his pacifier more than sucking on it.

"You're teething," she said, feeling like a dumb bunny. "Maybe some ice?"

The night turned into an endless search of relief for Leo's sore gums. She felt as if she tried everything, but nothing worked for more than fifteen minutes.

Changing into her pajamas, Ericka rocked Leo in the rocking chair beside his bed. He calmed and she put him in his crib then headed for her own bed. Not long later, he cried again and Ericka tried the solar system, but it was clear that Leo was hurting. She rocked him again, put him down and headed again for her bed. Just as she fell asleep, Leo cried out again.

For the five hundredth time during the past four months, Ericka encountered the truth again: *this is single motherhood*. Sometimes it was one day at a time. Other times it was five minutes at a time. Tonight was the latter. She rocked then turned on the solar system light until it all became a blur. Sometime after midnight, she wondered if this night would ever end.

Treat took a swim and looked at the lights in the cottage. He noticed that some form of light kept illuminating the nursery. The room went dark and he swam a few more laps then paused. The light from the nursery flickered on again.

Deciding to give it a few more minutes, he returned to the guest suite, took a shower and pulled on sweat pants and a tank. Restless, he walked outside and looked at the nursery window. The light was on. Well, darn. He was going to have to do something.

Treat waited a few more moments and the room went dark. Edgy, he decided to check on the princess and her baby. He unlocked the door, approving of the fact that Ericka had indeed locked it, and walked down the hall to the nursery. The door was ajar, so he walked inside to silence. Ericka was crumpled into a rocking chair, clearly asleep. Treat walked closer to the crib and saw that Leo was sprawled on his back, also asleep.

Putting his hands on his hips, Treat assessed the situation. He definitely didn't want to wake the baby, but Ericka needed to be in bed. As soon as possible. Taking a silent deep breath, he approached her and touched her arm. She didn't awaken. It must have been a rough evening, he thought. Sliding his hands underneath her, he picked her up and carried her to her room.

He gently put her on her bed and her eyelids flickered. She looked up at him and batted her eyes again, as if to clear them. "Treat?"

"Yeah," he said, his face inches from her.

Her eyebrow wrinkled. "What—"

"You fell asleep in the nursery and looked uncomfortable, so I brought you back to your bed," he said.

"Leo?" she asked and his heart softened because she automatically asked about her son even though she wasn't totally conscious.

"He's sleeping. Looks like a deep sleep," he said.

"Oh, thank goodness. Poor thing. He's teething," she said.

"Ah," he said, unable to pull away from her.

For a fraction of a second, she lowered her eyelids then looked him straight in the eye. "Thank you," she whispered and wrapped her hand around his neck and kissed him.

Her mouth was so soft and sweet he immediately wanted more. He wanted to taste her. And heaven forbid, take her. He slid his tongue past her lips and tasted a delicious combination of citrus and mint. He felt her lift her fingers through his hair and a rush of arousal raced through him.

Her combination of sweet and spicy undid him. Treat couldn't stop himself from devouring her mouth. She opened easily to him, making him want more and more. She pulled him down against her. He gave into her urging and relished the sensation of her warm, feminine body beneath his. It would be all too easy to kiss away her nightclothes then kiss her all over her body. All too easy to touch her in all her secret places and make her ready and wanting for him. All too easy to thrust inside…

Treat was suddenly so hard with need he trembled from it. She kissed him again, thrusting her sweet tongue in his mouth. He swallowed a thousand curses at how she made him feel. Strong, tender, fierce. Out of control.

He couldn't get out of control. He could not.

Even as she wriggled beneath him and took him with her mouth, he knew he needed to draw back. For her sake and his.

It was tough, but he did it. He pulled back, gasping for air. "Whoa," he muttered.

"Wow," she said, her eyelids half-shuttering her eyes in a sexy glance. She slid her hands down his shoulders to his arms.

She made him feel strong, sexy and all too aware of the fact that he hadn't been with a woman in a long time. But she was different. She wasn't just any woman.

"I didn't mean for that to happen," he said.

"But it was a good thing to happen," she said. The expression in her eyes was so inviting he had to look away.

"Can't deny that," he admitted, and kissed her on her cheek. Her lips were far too dangerous. "You need sleep," he said. "Get it while you can."

"I won't forget that kiss," she whispered.

"Neither will I," he said, and forced himself to rise from the bed. Then he forced himself to walk out of her bedroom and out of the cottage. His body was hot, his heart was hammering in his chest and he was hard with want and need. Returning to the guest suite, he headed straight for the bathroom. He stripped off his clothes and stepped into a cold shower. Standing under the cold spray, he waited for relief from his need for Ericka. He waited for fifteen minutes, but relief never arrived.

Leaving the shower, he dried himself off and pulled on a pair of underwear. He went to his self-made gym and began to work out. An hour later, his muscles were tired, but his brain still drifted toward the sensation of Ericka's body and mouth beneath his. He wondered if he would ever be able to rid himself of the memory.

Ericka slept like the dead until Leo's cry awakened her from the baby monitor. Stumbling from her bed, she walked to the bedroom and spotted Sam mewing on the shelf above Leo. "Okay, okay," she said. "I'm here."

She looked down at Leo and put her hand on his tummy. "How are you feeling today, sweetie?"

Leo squirmed and wiggled then smiled at her. Ericka's heart squeezed tight. "Good for you, sweetheart," she cooed as she changed his diaper. "How are your gums? Are they a little better?" she asked.

Leo giggled and her heart caught again.

"You are clearly a morning guy," she said while she lifted him into her arms. Carrying him to the kitchen, she pulled a bottle from the fridge and sat in the den and fed him. Burping was compulsory and she squeezed several gas bubbles from him.

"So let's do little sign language while you're fresh," she said, turning on a video lesson.

She lifted his hands to follow the signs during the lessons, but again, Leo seemed to prefer playing patty-cake. She laughed. "Come on. Give me a try for cat. You can do that," she said, pointing at Sam who stared at them as if they crazy. She gave the sign of stroking a cat's whiskers and helped Leo do the same. "Cat," she repeated.

Sensing he was being discussed, Sam came closer and allowed Leo to pet him. He gave a meow then walked away. Leo grunted and waved toward Sam.

"Leo loves Sam, doesn't he?" she said then gave her baby a squeeze.

Leo wasn't drooling quite as much today, so she hoped he would rest more comfortably during his naps. She put him down for his morning nap and was surprised that he slept soundly, but Ericka was no fool. She used the time to make several phone calls and get work done. When he awakened over an hour later, Ericka fed him and kept him awake until he grew cranky. Then she put him to bed.

After that, Ericka couldn't stop thinking about Treat and how his body had felt against hers, how his mouth had felt against hers. She couldn't remember when she had felt more like a woman, more wanted in a man's arms. She could still taste him on her lips.

Her heart hammered in her chest at the thought of him. She wanted to be with him, to feel his mouth on hers, to feel him on her…inside her.

Ericka bit her lip, thinking and plotting and planning. The last time she'd attempted to seduce a man, it had been her ex-husband. This, her second time, she planned to seduce her bodyguard and the thought of it made her so nervous she could hardly stand it.

Leo was cooperative. He awakened early evening and she fed and played with him. Apparently his gums weren't hurting tonight. Great for her and him.

She rocked him to sleep and he easily settled into sleep. It seemed like a miracle to her. Or, perhaps, destiny, she thought, and dressed in a skimpy black tank dress. She fluffed her hair and said a crazy prayer then pressed the intercom button for Treat. "Do you mind coming over to the cottage?"

"No problem. I'll be right over," Treat said.

Ericka sat on the sofa. Then she stood. Then she sat down again.

Treat walked through the front door. "Problem?" he asked.

"Yes," she said, her heart thumping in her chest. "My problem is that I want you very, very much."

Treat took a deep breath. "Ericka," he said.

"I've put my feelings on a plate. Can you do the same?" she asked.

Treat closed his eyes and looked away. "You know this is wrong," he finally said.

"Wrong?" she echoed, rising from the sofa. "But we're adults. We can determine what's best for us."

Treat shook his head. "I can't do this," he said. "If I'm with you, I don't know how I can be rational and protect you the way I need to," he said. "It's not that I don't want you," he said.

Ericka struggled with his rejection. "Right," she said, trying to figure out her next step since her first step had clearly failed.

"No, really—"

"Oh, stop," she said. "You clearly have no problem resisting my attempt at seduction. Enough humiliation. Let's just go to our separate beds."

"You're wrong," he said, moving toward her. "I do want—"

"Stop," she said, lifting her hand. "I made a mistake and now we're both uncomfortable. Let's just try to forget it all."

"I can't do that," he said.

"You may have an easier time than I will," she

said. "Good night, or as my sister-in-law Eve would say, sweet dreams."

Ericka walked to her bedroom and stripped off her dress. She suddenly felt a century old and as sexy as a stone. Humiliated, she put on her comfy jammies and climbed into her bed. Treat was not in her future and she needed to forget that mind-blowing kiss they'd shared. It had been an illusion. He might say that he wanted her, but he clearly didn't want her as much as she wanted him.

She needed to shut those desires and needs down. Now and forever.

The following afternoon, Nanny returned appearing less congested and more rested.

Ericka decided she needed a little outing, so she told Treat she wanted to visit her sister but also told him she wanted to drive herself. He could follow in his own vehicle. After her failed attempt at seduction last night, she couldn't bear the prospect of him in such close quarters with her.

Driving her small car onto Bridget's ranch, she pulled to a stop and skipped to the front door. She knocked.

Seconds later, Bridget, immensely pregnant, opened the door and squealed. "You're here. Where's the baby?"

"Resting," Ericka said. "I just needed a sister visit."

"Well, you've got one. Come on inside," Bridget said, and led her inside to a comfortable sunroom. "You picked a good day. The twins are in a quiet mood. Playing Lego. Under all that quietness, I'm convinced they're trying to take over the world. My husband says swelling from my pregnancy is making me crazy, but I know better."

Ericka gave a circular nod. "If you say so."

"I'm just kidding," Bridget said. "How's sweetie-pie Leo?"

"Perfect," she said, sinking into a comfortable couch. "But I think I may need to get out a little more often."

"Getting a little crazy?" Bridget asked.

"I wouldn't have put it that way," Ericka said, but knew Bridget had nailed it.

"Well, why not kill two birds with one stone?" Bridget asked, clapping her hands together. "As you know, the royal family is hosting a holiday art event. I know a hot, young Italian guy who could cheer you up," she said.

"Italians flatter too much," Ericka said.

"There are times when we could all use a little flattery. I'm not asking you to marry him. Just enjoy him for the evening. You don't even have to take him to bed," Bridget said.

Ericka stared at her sister in shock. "Bridget, shame on you. I'm not that desperate."

"Of course you aren't," she said. "But you could

use a little fun. I'm looking out for your mental health," she said.

Ericka couldn't help chuckling. "I'm not sure this is a good idea. I was thinking a luncheon or a visit to our museum."

"This is similar to a visit to a museum. You'll just dress up a little more and enjoy the company of an attractive man. Like I said, it's not forever. You could use a little fun. You're looking a little unnecessarily serious and cranky," Bridget said.

Ericka blinked. "That's sounds a bit insulting."

"Just tell me you'll go on the date," Bridget said.

Ericka took a deep breath. She clearly needed to get out. She was getting way too hung up over a bodyguard who didn't want to be with her. "I'll do it."

Bridget clapped her hands together. "Great. I can't wait to talk to Antonio."

Ericka visited with the twin boys and a few of the animals. She promised to bring Leo soon. As she got into her small car, she spotted Treat waiting. She waved at him because it seemed like the right thing to do. Then she drove home. Along the way, she wondered if she should have agreed to the blind date via Bridget, but she hoped it would be a very welcome distraction.

She needed to stop thinking about Treat. Maybe Antonio would help. Arriving at the cottage, she stepped out of the car and waved toward Treat as he pulled in behind her. "I'm going to a formal event tomorrow night. Representing the Devereaux family. The palace will provide a car."

He met her gaze. "This is new."

She shrugged. "Good to know we're keeping the job interesting. Ciao," she said as she walked into the cottage.

Chapter Eight

The next day, Ericka awakened early to the sound of Leo's lusty cry. She waved Nanny back to her bed as she made her way to her son's room. Today, she was determined to brighten her outlook. Perhaps Bridget was right. She'd become too serious for anyone's good. She had plenty going for her. She had a healthy, happy baby. Her child's nanny adored him. She had a supportive family and she lived in a lovely cottage on a beautiful neighborhood.

Ericka looked down at Leo as he whined. "Good morning, beautiful boy," she said, putting her hand on his chest to comfort him then stroking his face. She smiled and he quit crying. After changing his diaper, she put in his hearing aids even though she now knew they helped his hearing very little, if at all.

"I bet you would like a bottle," she said, and carried him to the kitchen where she grabbed a bottle from the refrigerator. He slurped down his nourishment and she helped him burp. If she were following her normal schedule, she would share a little sign language session with him then move on to tummy time, but the sun was shining brightly and she'd heard the weather should be reasonably warm.

She decided to take Leo for a stroll. With a cap over his head covering his hearing aids, even if the paparazzi took a picture, they wouldn't spot anything unusual. She changed into jeans and a light jacket and put a jacket on Leo, grabbed the stroller and headed out the door. The sun was so bright Leo squinted his eyes.

"Sorry about that, sweetie," she said as she pulled the top of the stroller forward to offer him a little shade. She walked to the gate and pushed the button for it to open. Just as she walked through it, she heard footsteps behind her. Glancing behind her, she saw Treat and felt a strange combination of excitement and annoyance.

"What are you doing?" he asked, catching up to her.

"I'm taking Leo for a stroll," she said.

"You're supposed to tell me," he said.

"Nothing personal, but I didn't want to invite

you." She shrugged. "Well, maybe it is personal," she said. "I'm not going far."

"It doesn't matter. I need to have eyes on you if you leave the gate. Anything could happen," he said.

"But it probably won't at seven a.m.," she pointed out. "Most of the citizens of Chantaine don't rise much before nine." She frowned. "This is Leo's first stroll in a week. Don't ruin it."

He blinked and lifted his hand. "Okay. Just pretend I'm not here."

"Not likely," she muttered under her breath but gave it a good effort. She looked at the trees and her neighbor's well-tended garden. She tried to take a deep breath and fill her mind with so many good thoughts that they would crowd out her awareness of Treat. After a few moments of walking, she stopped to check on Leo. The little sneak appeared to be sleeping.

"You little rascal," she said, adjusting his jacket.

She felt Treat look over her shoulder. "Sleeping on the job?"

"I was hoping this would be stimulating for him, offering him a new experience." She chuckled.

"You really can't blame him. He's nicely bundled and shaded. The temperature is perfect with a little breeze. The movement of the stroller probably lulled him to sleep. Perfect nap situation," he said.

She looked up at him and began pushing the stroller again. "Are you a nap person?"

"I can be, but I'll only go fifteen minutes tops."

"When I sleep, I like it to last for hours and hours without interruption," she said.

"Says the single mother of a baby," he said with a nod of understanding. "There's a reason sleep deprivation is used as a form of torture."

"It's really much better than those first couple of months. It helps if I look back at how things were when I first came home from the hospital with him. I have Nanny and she's an enormous help."

"And the solar system on the ceiling," he added with a half grin.

That half grin made her stomach take a dip. She looked away. "Yes, the solar system." She turned silent and fretted over her feelings.

"You don't need to be uncomfortable with me because of what happened the other night," he said.

Upset by his ridiculous comment, she rounded on him. "Of course I'm uncomfortable with you. I tried to seduce you and you didn't want me in return. The situation is beyond awkward and—"

"I didn't say I didn't want you," he said. "I just know I can't have you. It's for the best."

Her heart skipped a beat when he confessed in a double negative sort of way that some part of him perhaps did want her. Her heart seemed to want to ignore the latter part of what he'd just said. Her heart was being very foolish, she told herself and she closed her eyes, shaking her head. "I'm not sure talking about this is going to help," she said, and opened her eyes. "But I'm doing some things to help alleviate my…" She took another breath. "Complete humiliation."

"Ericka…" he said.

She lifted her hand to cut him off. "Please. If we must talk, choose another subject." She turned the stroller around and headed for the cottage at a brisk pace.

Treat stayed right by her side. "How do you like those Broncos?"

She glanced at him in confusion. "Broncos? What on earth—"

"You said change the subject. I said the first thing that came to mind. Denver Broncos," he said. "Football."

"Oh, American football," she said. "I remember that Valentina's husband is a big fan, but he favors another team. Rangers?" she guessed.

"That's baseball. Sounds like he could be a Texas fan," he said.

"Texans. That's what it is," she said. "And Ackies?"

"Aggies. That's college football. They're from Texas, too," he said.

"Where are these Broncos from?" she asked. "Didn't you grow up in Texas?"

"Yes, but I had to expand my loyalties when I played pro for Kansas City," he said.

"I didn't realize you played professionally. Was Kansas City a good team?" she asked.

"They were pretty good when I was with them, but I was on the injured list way too often," he said.

"Does it ever hurt?" she asked. "Wherever you were injured," she said.

He chuckled. "I got injured all over my body at one time or another, so I'd be in bad shape if I hurt all over. But my left knee took the worst of it. I work out every day, but I can tell you when it's going to rain because my knee lets me know."

"How upset were you when you had to quit playing?" she asked.

"I was pretty disappointed, but I didn't have time to mope. With no family left, I didn't have a place to land. I had to switch gears as quickly as possible. Luckily I had a buddy who wanted a partner for a security business. I lived on SpaghettiOs for a while, but I'm eating better now."

"SpaghettiOs?" she echoed.

"Spaghetti and meatballs in a can," he said.

"Oh, that sounds disgusting," she said. "Your palate must be destroyed from that. No wonder you turn down Simon's food."

"I'm sure Simon's food is delicious. I just don't want you to think you've got to feed me. I can handle that."

She nodded. "I'm curious. How do you handle that? What do you eat?"

He rubbed his jaw as if her question made him uncomfortable. "Nothing you would want," he said.

"Okay," she said. "But answer my question."

He sighed. "I didn't want you to know that I eat a lot of peanut butter and canned soup."

She wrinkled her nose. "That's ridiculous. You're so determined to stay away from me in the cottage that you give up gourmet food for peanut butter. Unless you're eating peanut butter and bacon. Otherwise you deserve your bad food," she told him.

He stared at her in surprise.

"I feel better now. And look, we're at the gate so you can go back to your man cave and eat some peanut butter. Ciao," she said as she pushed the stroller to the front door. Pulling Leo up into her arms, she hugged him close. "When you grow up to be a man, try not to drive women crazy," she told him.

Leo looked up at her with wide, innocent eyes and smiled. Her heart swelled with love. "Oh, darn. You're already too gorgeous. The female race is doomed," she said, then kissed his chubby cheek.

Ericka divided the rest of her day between caring for Leo and doing work for the palace. She would likely be out late tonight due to the Christmas Art Show, and she tried to balance the demands of childcare with Nanny so that Nanny wouldn't become overwhelmed. Ericka treasured Nanny's presence and was actually a bit terrified of losing her. She couldn't imagine replacing the sweet woman.

As she showered and fixed her hair and make-up, she felt a mixture of emotions. Part of her regretted her decision. What had she been thinking? She wasn't ready to start dating and she truly didn't have time for it. At the same time, a shot of excitement raced through her when she picked out an emerald-green dress she'd worn pre-pregnancy from her closet, *and it fit.*

It hit her that she had totally lost confidence in herself. Before her marriage, she'd had plenty of male admirers. Since her divorce and pregnancy, when she looked in the mirror she saw a tired woman, dumped by her husband, with zero sex appeal. Because she'd been so busy trying to take care of Leo and make a life for her baby and herself, she hadn't realized how much her husband's betrayal had affected her self-esteem as a woman.

Ericka closed her eyes for a moment then looked in the mirror. Maybe it was time to push the reset button. She was no longer the young naive woman who'd married her husband and agreed to follow wherever he led. True, she was often tired and felt more vulnerable than she liked. But she was stronger now.

Treat wasn't all that comfortable with the event tonight. He was accustomed to Ericka staying in the cottage with the baby. Although he knew he shouldn't care, he did. He worked out, took care of online reports, showered and shaved, but he still didn't feel great about tonight. He needed to keep his feelings hidden, however. He dressed in slacks, dress shirt, tie and sport jacket. That should do the trick. At least for tonight.

He went outside and waited for the car from the palace. He understood that he would be riding in the front with the driver while some Italian businessman rode in the back with Ericka. The thought of it made him lose his taste for everything, but he needed to conceal his feelings.

The expansive limousine arrived and Treat waved them into a spot in front. He held up the universal sign for stop then went into the cottage. Nanny was holding Leo. "Is she ready?" he asked.

"I think so," Nanny said as she walked down the hallway. "I think your vehicle has arrived, miss," she called to a closed door.

The door flung open and Nanny gasped. "You're so beautiful."

Ericka rounded the corner in the hall and smiled. "You're so sweet," Ericka said, and then walked down the hall in a formal emerald-green dress and a cream-colored stole.

Treat succeeded in staring at her without dropping his jaw, but it was tough. She looked more beautiful than a beauty queen. She looked like a princess.

She glanced at him and nodded. "Good evening," she said. "I may need a little extra help getting in and out of the palace vehicle. I haven't been wearing heels much lately."

"I can do that," he said.

"Thank you," she said, walking toward Nanny and Leo. She pressed a kiss against the baby's cheek, leaving a lipstick stain that many men would welcome, including himself.

Treat escorted her to the vehicle and Mr. Italian stepped outside. He was a not-too-young man with model looks and a muscular frame. Treat had wondered if Antonio was just a pretty face, but apparently the man operated several companies.

Antonio bowed slightly then took Ericka's hand and lifted it to his lips.

At that moment, Treat hated Antonio.

"You look very beautiful, Your Highness. Please allow me to assist you into the limousine."

She met his gaze and smiled. "Thank you so very much, Antonio. I appreciate your help."

And Treat hated the man even more.

The couple neglected to close the window between the driver and backseat, so Treat was able to hear nearly every word Antonio and Ericka exchanged. Antonio flirted. Ericka responded lightly. Antonia flirted more. Ericka smiled and sat closer to him.

He couldn't stand it when she smiled at Antonio. It made him want to break every window in the car, but he held it all in. He had a job to do.

Treat escorted the couple into the event for the

Christmas Art Exhibit. As Ericka allowed Antonio to hold her hand, he clenched his fists together. The two of them wandered through the exhibit, studying and discussing the works of art.

After a time, Antonio grabbed two glasses of champagne and offered one to Ericka. She accepted, smiled and clicked her glass against his.

Antonio pressed a kiss against her wrist and it lasted a few seconds too long for Treat. Frowning, he wondered if Ericka was asking for more than she wanted to deliver.

Should he question her?

At the same time, Treat was concerned that Antonio might be expecting more from the end of the night than he might get. He forced himself to block out his jealous feelings and focused on his job as protector.

Another hour passed and he watched as Antonio kissed her hands and drew her against him. Ericka laughed and appeared to flirt with him. Treat could tell that Antonio was becoming more intent and drawn in by Ericka.

Antonio finally took a break and dismissed himself, most likely to the restroom. Treat approached Ericka. "May I have a word with you?" he asked.

"Of course," she said, and allowed him to guide her to the lobby of the art center. "Is there a problem?"

"There could be," he said. "I'm concerned that

Antonio may want more from you than you want to give."

She lifted her chin. "Maybe I can deliver what he wants. At least he finds me attractive and he's not afraid to admit it."

Treat ground his teeth. "I'm not afraid to admit my attraction for you," he told her. "I'm just trying to draw a line of professionalism."

"Enjoy that line," she told him and turned away.

"Ericka," he said, tugging her arm.

The princess glanced down at his hand on her arm. "Yes?"

He pulled her closer and pressed his mouth against hers, sliding his tongue inside, tasting and taking her. She was deliciously sweet in a forbidden way. She tasted like sin and heaven at the same time.

He forced himself to draw back and looked deep in her eyes.

"You are such a pain in the butt," she said breathlessly, and stalked away from him.

Treat stared after her, completely aroused. This *cake* assignment was turning into his worst nightmare.

Ericka tried her very best to pay attention to Antonio, but he mind was stuck on the kiss she'd shared with Treat. Her lips burned, her heart hammered and all her womanly places swelled and moistened. Staring into Antonio's lustful eyes, she couldn't summon the least bit of interest.

"Antonio," she said. "I'm so sorry, but I think I should leave. I'm not feeling well."

"You are ill?" he asked, his brown eyes tilting in concern.

"The nanny for my son has been sick. I hope I haven't caught her cold." That much was true, although Ericka was suffering from a different kind of illness. Complete lust for her bodyguard.

"I'm so sorry, but I think I should go home," she said.

Disappointment crossed Antonio's handsome face. "Of course," he said. "Let's leave right away."

Antonio escorted Ericka to the palace limo with such a gentlemanly attitude that she felt guilty. At the same time, she knew she shouldn't lead him on. They rode quietly through the streets of Chantaine toward her cottage. Finally, they passed through the gates and the doors of the limo opened.

Antonio attempted a passionate kiss, but Ericka couldn't find it in herself to pretend. She pulled back and smiled. "Thank you. I really should go."

"Call me if you change your mind," he said.

"Good night," she said as she stepped out of the car.

Treat took her hand and helped her stand.

As the limo rode away, Treat turned away. "Regrets? You wish you had stayed with him?"

"You made that plenty difficult when you kissed me," she said.

"Maybe I shouldn't have," he said.

"Don't start with that now," she said. "My American brother-in-law once gave me a great quote. *Go big or go home.* What are you going to do?"

"If I followed my professional guidance, I would walk you to the cottage door and go back to my room," he said.

She crossed her arms over her chest. *If he rejected her again...*

"If I follow every other urge and need, I would take you back to my room and make love to you."

She bit the inside of her lip. "What are you going to do?"

"Are you sure you want this?" he asked her. "Because once I take you into that room, I'm not going to want to stop."

Ericka bit her lip. She couldn't remember a time that she'd wanted a man more than at this moment. "Take me with you," she whispered.

Sweeping her into his arms, he took her to his room and bed, releasing her onto his mattress. "You're so beautiful. You have no idea," he said, pulling off his tie, jacket, shirt and slacks.

Ericka's heart slammed so hard against her chest she couldn't find any words to respond to him. She opened her mouth, but no words came out.

"Just tell me what you want," he told her. "Because I want to give it to you."

How could she say that all she wanted was him? She took several deep breaths and swallowed hard. "You," she finally managed. "All I want is you."

She slid her hands over his muscular chest and arms and lower.

"Oh, Ericka, you're too much, but you make me want more," he said.

He kissed her and caressed her body with his hands and mouth. Every breath, every heartbeat made him want more of her. Her lips tasted like cherries and felt like sex.

"You're just too good," he said.

"I want you," she said, sliding hers hands down between his legs.

Treat nearly burst out of control, but he reined himself in. "I'm trying to pace myself," he told her, covering her hands with his.

"Don't do that," she said, meeting his gaze. "Give me all of you."

Her expression nearly sent him over the edge, but he hung on long enough to put on protection. Then he pushed her sweet white thighs apart and plunged inside.

She gasped.

He stopped. "Okay?"

She closed her eyes, then wriggled against him.

He swallowed a groan. "What are you doing?" he muttered.

"You. I'm doing you," she said. She wriggled again as she lifted her mouth to his.

That's when Treat lost control. He just wanted her way too much. Thrusting inside her, he watched her as her eyes darkened in arousal.

She felt so good and tasted so sweet, he thought as he clutched Ericka's derriere, then flew into the most intimate moment he'd ever experienced. He flew high in the sky and wanted more than anything to take Ericka with him.

"Come with me," he urged, sliding his hands over her sweet body.

When he felt that she hadn't gone over the top, he slid his hand between their bodies. She wiggled against him. Again and again.

"Give me you," he said. "Give me you." He continued to rub her sweet spot and she clung to him.

Finally she clenched and rippled against him, her climax producing a ricochet through her to him. "Oh," she whispered. "Wow."

He couldn't help smiling at her response at he pulled her against him. "Yeah. Oh. Wow."

Chapter Nine

"You know this wasn't the wisest thing for us to do," he said. "I don't want anything to damage your reputation. I'm not concerned about my own situation—"

"Oh, stop being a saint and stop trying to play my big brother when you're my lover," she said.

"I'm not trying to play your big brother," he told her. "But it's my job to protect you."

Sighing, she pushed her hair behind her ear. "It's lovely of you to protect me, but I'd rather you make love to me."

"But you need to make a decision. Do you want to keep this between you and me? Or do you want it public?"

Frowning, she sighed again. "I actually don't want anyone in my business. I don't want anyone studying Leo. I don't want anyone analyzing you and me under a microscope. It's strange, but I feel protective of my relationship of you and me. Do we need a contract for this?" she asked.

He gave a rough chuckle and pulled her against him. "No." He slid his fingers through her hair and rubbed his mouth against hers. "No contract. This is just between you and me," he said, then he made love to her again.

At 2:00 a.m., she awakened to silence and listened for the sound of Leo. It took a few moments for her to realize that she was in Treat's bed and man cave. She sat up. "I need to go," she whispered.

Treat slid his hand over her arms. "What's wrong?"

"I need to check on Leo. I can't hear if he's crying. I can't hear if he's okay," she said. "I'm sorry."

"No. It's okay," he said, rising. "Let me walk you to the cottage."

Both of them dressed. It felt odd to Ericka to put on her now crumpled formal gown. She ran her fingers through her hair. "Hopefully Nanny won't be up for my walk of shame, although I'm actually quite proud. How am I going to hide my feelings from Nanny?" Ericka asked him. "She's so intuitive."

"It'll be okay. Just don't discuss it," he told her

as he escorted her from his suite. "She's too discreet to ask."

"That's true," she said. "Otherwise I would blab on and on about my feelings.

"Brush your teeth," he suggested.

"What?" she asked then covered her mouth. "Is my breath bad?"

"No," he said. "Just tell her you need to brush your teeth because there was too much garlic in the appetizers. She'll run. Who wants to smell too much garlic?"

She narrowed her eyes at him. "Are you sure I don't smell like garlic?"

He lowered his mouth and gave her a soulful, thorough kiss then pulled back. "What do you think?"

"Guess not," she said, and flung her arms around his neck. "Oh, I want to stay with you, but I need to check on Leo."

He returned her embrace. "I'm here. Not going anywhere."

Ericka slumped against him for one luxurious moment, and then pulled back. "Good night," she said as she walked into the cottage.

Closing the door quietly behind her, she stood in the foyer and listened. Was Leo awake?

Silence pervaded the cottage. Who would have thought? she thought and walked on tiptoe to her bedroom, listening for any sound, especially any sound from Leo. But there was nothing. She quickly changed into bedclothes and sat on her bed waiting for sounds from Leo on the baby monitor. Nothing.

Unable to still her concern, she broke her second cardinal rule of the evening and peeked into the nursery. She walked next to the crib and saw that Leo was breathing. No need to put a mirror under his nose and mouth. He was sleeping.

Go, go, she told herself and headed for her bedroom. She brushed her teeth then dashed into bed, wishing Treat were with her. His body had warmed and comforted her. Her feelings for him were far more than sexual, and that was dangerous. But withering from fear and need…wasn't that more dangerous?

Stumbling into bed, she fell into a deep, deep sleep.

What felt like fifteen minutes later, Leo's cry broke into her slumber. She checked her alarm clock. It had been five hours not fifteen minutes, actually.

Dashing out of bed, she raced to the nursery and changed his diaper. "Need a bottle?" she asked, giving the sign language for bottle.

Leo's gaze was fixed on her face.

She slowed down and smiled at him.

After a few seconds he smiled and kicked in return.

"Aren't you the best baby in the world," she cooed as she lifted him in her arms. She carried him to the kitchen and brought his bottle out of the refrigerator. He immediately began sucking it down. She was thankful for his appetite. To her, it was a sign of a healthy baby. In that case, he was extremely healthy.

She burped him several times then carried him into the den and put him on her shoulder. He wiggled and rooted then settled down and took a little nap.

"Thank you," she whispered, and leaned her head against the back of the sofa. She drifted off to sleep.

A half hour later, Leo awakened and gave a cry. Ericka shrugged off her slumber and took a sniff. Definitely time for a diaper change. She encountered a very messy diaper and decided to give him a quick bath. Leo had a love-hate relationship with baths, so Ericka always made sure his water temperature was very warm, but not quite hot.

Talking to him the entire time despite the fact that he couldn't hear a word, she bathed him in the kitchen sink. Quickly washing him, she rinsed him then pulled him out of the sink and wrapped him in a towel.

"How's that?" she asked. "Pretty darn good, don't you think?"

Leo nuzzled against her and for several moments, he remained still, safe and warm in the towel. She pressed a thousand kisses on his sweet forehead.

Leo began to squirm. Ericka gently rubbed him with a towel then diapered and dressed him. Putting him in his crib she rested her hand on his chest.

He kicked and played and fussed a little then fell asleep again

When he fell asleep, she was certain she had the best baby in the world.

Treat paced the man cave. He was clearly an animal. How could he have given into his feelings for Ericka? He was supposed to protect her, not ravish her.

Continuing to pace, he thought about the night they'd shared. He couldn't remember feeling such desire for a woman. He'd barely kept his head on straight until that Italian guy had begun to vie for her affection. It was crazy, but after that he couldn't deny his feelings. He had wanted her so much. He still wanted her.

He realized he may as well kiss his plans for business expansion via Prince Stefan good-bye. But he couldn't quit on Ericka and Leo. He didn't know how he could ever quit on them. They'd wrapped their tentacles around his heart. The only way he could turn away from her now was if she officially told him she didn't want him. Treat knew deep inside that the time would come when she didn't want him in her life. How could a life between a princess and a boy born on the wrong side of the tracks in Texas ever work out?

Still glowing from the night she'd shared with Treat, Ericka had to force herself to concentrate on her work for the palace. Toward the end of her designated work time, she received a sobering call with another urgent request for the Sergenian royal family to stay in Chantaine. She had to figure out how to persuade Stefan to give his permission. Feeling her frustration build, she decided to step outside for some fresh air and bumped into Treat.

Her heart jumped in her chest. "Hi," she said, feeling suddenly shy.

"Hi to you," he said, his gaze seeming to envelope her from head to toe. "Everything okay? I thought I would check in." He paused a half-beat. "Are you okay?" he asked and his second query somehow felt more personal.

"We're fine. I'm mostly fine," she said as she walked to take a seat by the pool. Treat sat across from her. "I just received another more urgent request for the Sergenian royal family to come to Chantaine. Stefan has already said no. I wish I could find a way to change his mind."

Treat nodded thoughtfully and leaned forward. "There are a few things you can try. Start out the conversation with something you've accomplished. Is there something you've done lately that would impress him?"

"I think he'll be impressed with two of the speakers who have given me last-minute acceptances for the conference. They're both internationally renowned in their fields and one is a winner of a Nobel prize in medicine."

"Sounds good. The next step is to talk to him at the right time of day. When is quitting time for him?" he asked.

"Usually between four and five. Why does that matter?"

"It means he won't have anything else he's trying to get off his plate," Treat said. "Finally, give him reasons that this decision is in his best interest."

"That's going to be difficult," she said glumly.

"It doesn't have to benefit him immediately. The potential benefit could come down the road."

She nodded. "I'll ask Stefan's assistant to look at his schedule for tomorrow and plan to go then. In the meantime, Simon has brought over an immense pan of lasagna. There's no way Nanny and I can eat it. And I won't even force you to dine with me in the cottage," she said, unable to keep herself from making the cheeky comment.

Treat leaned forward and lightly touched her knee. "Ah, but dining with you would make it taste so much better."

In a flash, he'd gone from consultant to seducer and she felt the difference throughout her body. "I've been thinking about you and me all day," she said. "I realized it's not going to be all that easy for us to—" She cleared her throat. "Be together." She frowned, feeling both anxious and extremely uncomfortable.

"I want to have time with you without prying eyes, but Nanny is here five days a week or more. I want you, but I want our privacy. Nanny is off two days from now."

"It's okay," he said, squeezing her leg. "It will be okay. I won't sneak into your bedroom unless you invite me."

The sensual expression on his face made her so weak in the knees that she was grateful she was sitting down. "It's not that I don't want to invite you," she whispered.

"We'll work it out," he said, and rose to his feet.

Ericka stiffened her own knees and walked toward the door to the cottage. "Why does it seem so much easier for you than me?" Ericka asked. "You appear to be in perfect control, when I'm not." Unable to resist the urge, she stood on tiptoe and brushed her lips against his. He swept her away from the cottage door and windows and took her mouth in a sensual, all-encompassing kiss.

He drew back and his eyes looked like black fire. "Does that look like complete control?" he asked.

Ericka tried to catch her breath and mind so she could form words. "I don't know if it's perfect control or not," she said, and then took another breath. "But I like it."

Treat chuckled. "I do, too," he said. "I'll check in on you later."

Ericka returned to the cottage and immediately

fixed a glass of ice water for herself. Like many Europeans, she'd never been big on ice, but after that blazing kiss from Treat, she wondered if an ice bath would be appropriate.

Treat popped in for a few moments later that evening and accepted a large helping of lasagna. Ericka was relieved Nanny wasn't in the room because the electricity between Treat and herself was so strong she was surprised her hair didn't stand on end.

Ericka spent the rest of her evening trying not to think about Treat and preparing for her meeting with her brother. While Nanny took care of Leo, Ericka wrote out every word she wanted to say and when she reread it, she could see that Stefan would fall asleep if she talked this long without taking a breath, so she edited it twice.

By that time, she was putting herself to sleep. Crawling into bed, she couldn't help remembering how wonderful it had felt to have Treat's arms around her. A little damning voice inside her reminded her she had no time for his warm arms and lovemaking, but she pushed it aside. For now.

The following afternoon, Treat drove her to the palace. Ericka was too nervous to chat. When he pulled outside the side entrance, she grabbed for the door. He stopped her with his hand. "Take a deep breath," he said. "Or two. Remember, you're very persuasive."

She took a deep breath and winced. "It's just Stefan is so accustomed to saying no. Sometimes I wonder if it's his favorite word."

"You don't have to take no for an answer," he told her. "You didn't take it last time. Your will is just as strong as his, maybe more if it's something you care about passionately."

She gave a quick nod. "Thanks for the support." She went into the palace. She gave a tight smile of welcome to the staff she encountered then paused long enough to take another deep breath before she knocked on Stefan's office door. His assistant immediately allowed her inside and Stefan stood as she entered.

"You're looking well," he said, and stepped from behind his desk and kissed her on the forehead. "Is Leo letting you have a little more sleep?"

"When he's not teething, he is. I bought a new gadget that hangs from the ceiling and lights up. I think it gives him a temporary distraction," she said.

"You'll have to tell Eve about it. She's got several months before her due date, but it never hurts to be well-prepared when you have an infant," he said as he motioned to one of the two chairs beside his desk.

Ericka sat down and he followed. "You had something you wanted to discuss with me,"

"Yes, first I wanted to tell you about the two speakers who've recently accepted invites to the conference. Hector Suavez, a foremost expert in making sanitary water available in developing countries, has agreed to speak. Along with Dr. Albert Shoen, winner of the Nobel Prize in physiology."

Stefan gave a nod of approval. "Well done. I can see that you were the right person to take on the task of this conference. I'm very pleased."

"I am, too. It also appears that several of the attendees want to put together a roundtable so they can discuss how to make trips to various countries in need of assistance."

"Again, well done," Stefan said.

"Now onto a concern that I have," she began.

"This isn't about your bodyguard, is it? I know his probationary time period has passed," he said.

"No. He's fine. Not too intrusive and he's surprisingly good with Leo," she said.

"Good to hear," he said, leaning back in his seat.

"I've heard from a representative for the Sergenian royals again," she began.

"I've already discussed this. I said no and I meant it," he said.

"What if the royals temporarily gave up their identities and took jobs?" she asked. "We don't have to announce that they're living here, and the whole situation is temporary. They're not asking to become citizens and stay here forever."

"But why here?" he asked. "Why not a large city where they could easily get lost?"

"You're forgetting that their country doesn't have

many large cities. Part of the reason they want to stay in Chantaine is because it's not as well-known as other places."

"That's still no reason for us to get embroiled in this kind of controversy," he said.

Ericka ground her teeth in frustration. "You've always said you want to be a better ruler than our father. Here is a chance for you to show it. He avoided controversy like the plague. You are stronger than that," she said. "This is the right thing to do."

When Stefan stared at her in silence, she lifted her chin. "What if these were your children? Wouldn't you want someone to show some compassion toward them?"

His expression changed minutely. His eyes softened and he rubbed his finger between his eyebrows. "I'll think about it," he said.

"No," she said. "The royals need to come to Chantaine now. You must say yes."

"I must?" he echoed.

"Yes, you must," she said without flinching.

Stefan sighed. "You're going to nag me to death until I agree to this, aren't you?"

"Yes, I am," she said.

"Okay, but there will be strict rules. They can't be seen in public with each other. They'll have to temporarily give up their identities and they will have to work," he said.

"Done," she said, then stood. "Thank you. I knew I could count on you."

He rose to his feet. "I'm still not sure this is going to work," he said.

"I'll make it work," she said, and kissed her brother on his cheek.

"You've turned into quite the soldier, Ericka," he said. "I'm proud of you."

Her eyes filled with a surprising burst of moisture. "High praise from you."

Calmly walking from the palace, she stepped toward the car. Treat helped her inside and shot her a look of inquiry.

"He's going to let them come to Chantaine. I'm so happy I could dance on the roof," she said.

"I wish I could take you to one," he said, grinning at her obvious joy.

It was all she could do not to throw herself into his arms in celebration. "On second thought, I'm not sure dancing on a rooftop is a good idea, but I do know a wonderful little bar on the ocean. I could have a martini and you could have a beer," she suggested, delighted with the prospect.

"Are you sure this is a good idea? You, me in public like that?" he said.

"As long as we don't kiss each other, it should be okay. It's just a drink on a Monday night. They can't be busy," she said.

"If you're sure," he said, looking decidedly un-excited.

"If you can't be a little more cheerful then just let me go into the bar by myself so I can enjoy my martini in peace," she said.

"As if I would ever allow that," he said.

"Allow?" she echoed in irritation. "Just because you're my security detail doesn't mean you have to watch me every minute."

"You say that like it's a trial," he said, tossing her a glance full of heat.

His expression took the punch out of her defiance. She closed her eyes and smiled. "I'm just going to enjoy this moment," she said.

Moments later as they arrived at the bar, Treat watched Ericka pulled her hair into a ponytail and perch her sunglasses on her nose. "Ready," she said.

"It's dark outside. Don't you think you'll look a little odd wearing your sunglasses?" he asked.

"It will make me less recognizable," she said, and stumbled on the walkway.

He quickly righted her. "And if you fall because you can't see?"

"Then you'll catch me," she said with a smile full of charm.

Treat wasn't sure what to expect next from her. From the beginning, he'd known she was a strong-willed woman and she could be heartbreakingly fervent about people she was determined to protect. But that wasn't all. He'd held her in his arms and she'd kissed him with a passion that that made his head spin. She'd apparently just taken Stefan to task, yet now she was determined to savor the moment.

As Ericka had predicted, only a few patrons occupied the bar when they entered.

"Let's take a table by the ocean," she urged, leading the way and stumbling again.

Treat grabbed her around her waist and guided her to a table. "If you keep falling, they're not going to want to serve you any more alcohol," he said.

"Oh, posh," she said dismissively and waggled her fingers toward a server who immediately responded.

"Good evening. How can I help you?"

"Years ago, you made this lovely martini during the holidays. I can't remember the name," she said.

He nodded. "We called it Hollytini," he said, and then listed the ingredients. "We renamed it the Holiday Princess because rumor has it that it was one of Princess Fredericka's favorite drinks."

Ericka cleared her throat. "Is that so? Isn't that something?" she said to Treat.

"Isn't it?" he said. "I'll take a glass of beer."

"Yes, sir. And you'd like the Holiday Princess," he confirmed.

"Yes, please, but can you leave out the alcohol?"

He paused then nodded. "Of course," he said as he walked away.

"I thought you wanted to celebrate with a drink," Treat said.

"I don't drink anymore," she said nonchalantly. "What I really wanted was to look at the ocean while I sit in this romantic bar with my lover."

Her words delivered a one-two punch. In another circumstance he would be all over her, but this time he couldn't. He had to show restraint.

The server delivered the drinks and she lifted hers. "Cheers," she said.

He took a drink of beer. "To Chantaine's Holiday Princess."

They lingered a few moments and Ericka told him about one of the many times she'd sneaked away from the palace to hit the clubs with friends.

"You must have been a terror," he said. "No wonder your brother hired me. You should know that you wouldn't have succeeded in any of that if I'd been your security detail."

"I would have detested you for being a fussbudget," she said.

He shook his head. "Wouldn't have changed a thing."

She smiled and took another sip of drink. "I'm way past high school."

"I'll say," he agreed and paid the bill before they left. As soon as they got into the car, she threw herself in his arms.

"I want to be with you. How can I possibly wait

for Nanny's day off?" she whispered and pressed her mouth against his.

Treat kissed her in return then pulled back. "We need to go back to the cottage. Now fasten your seatbelt and stay in your seat," he instructed firmly.

As soon as he pulled into the driveway, she began kissing him again. After just a few minutes, the windows steamed up and Treat felt like a horny teenager. Taking a deep breath, he set her away from him. "We're adults. We can handle this."

She frowned at him. "There you go being all responsible. You make it look so easy."

"I told you it's not easy," he said, his lower body hard with need. "I'll show you at the right time. Unless you want Nanny to know about us, now is the not the right time."

She sighed. "You're right. I apologize. You probably think I'm some desperately needy woman."

He put his hand on hers. "I don't. I think you're an amazing and passionate woman. I need to protect you, and not just because it's my job."

Chapter Ten

The next morning, Treat received a call from the palace. "Mr. Walker, this is Glendall Winningham from the Palace Public Relations Department. We understand a story with photos about Princess Fredericka has hit an online paparazzi site. The palace prefers to be informed ahead of time of any possibilities of these kinds of stories. We will make a statement if necessary, but I had to tell you because interest in the princess may be elevated due to this story. I'm emailing the link to the story right away. Good day."

Treat blinked as the call was disconnected. He hadn't said a word, but he'd sure gotten an earful from the palace. Dread rumbled in his stomach. A story about Ericka? With photographers?

He pulled up his email and immediately read the story. Who Is Princess Fredericka's New Mystery Man? A dark photo of her wearing her sunglasses sitting at bar with Treat supplemented the story.

He swore under his breath. This was what he'd wanted to avoid. If the paparazzi decided Ericka was interesting, she and Leo would be hard-pressed to find a moment of peace outside the gated cottage. He'd glimpsed the few steps she'd taken to enjoy a few outings. Now that would be nixed unless she was willing to risk more invasions of her privacy.

Rubbing his face, he considered doubling the warning system all the way to the curb. It would result in extra false alarms, but if it kept a telescopic lens from capturing little Leo wearing hearing aids, it would be worth it. Ericka was finding her way of dealing with the delights and challenges of meeting Leo's special needs. She didn't need any extra pressure from the press about it.

After he'd examined ways to extend the boundary around the fence, he walked next door to the cottage and knocked on the door before entering. Ericka, wearing pink pajamas with her hair piled on top of her head and sleepy-looking eyes, looked up from feeding Leo a bottle and smiled.

Treat felt his heart turn over at the sight of her. He'd seen her all glammed up, but something about the way she looked at this moment got to him. "Noisy night?" he asked.

"He had a rough time starting around four a.m. I think I'm going to throw a party when this tooth makes it through his gums," she said. "How about you?"

"I got my four hours, so I'm good. I got a call from the palace this morning," he said.

"I think I may have heard my phone vibrate, but I had to change a diaper and get his bottle, so I decided I'd check after he's feeling more human," she said. "Who was it?"

"Glendall Winningham," he said.

"Oh, my. Mr. Stuffy PR. Bet that was a fun call. Why in the world did he call you?" she asked.

Treat glanced down the hallway. "Before I finish, where is Nanny?"

"Asleep. She'll get up in an hour and leave this afternoon for her night off," she said. "What is this about?"

"Apparently an online paparazzi newspaper has published a photo of you. And me," he said.

Her eyes widened. "Where?"

"At the bar last night. The title of the article is Who Is Princess Fredericka's New Mystery Man?"

Ericka stared at him for a moment then burst out laughing, accidentally pulling the bottle from Leo's mouth. The baby glanced up at her, his little mouth forming a pout, clearly gearing up for a good wail.

"Oh, no, no. You're fine," she said to her baby, rubbing the nipple of the bottle against his lips. He let out a half cry then happily found the nipple and began feeding again.

"Why are you laughing about this?" Treat asked.

"Because it's Stefan's fault," she said, and giggled again, this time with more restraint so she wouldn't upset Leo. "I told him to get a low-profile security man or even a woman, but no, he chose you. No one will possibly believe that you're a nanny for Leo or my assistant. You're just too—" She sighed. "Male."

"So you're not at all worried about this?" he asked. "Because the PR guy warned you could receive additional unwanted attention because of this."

She made a face. "That's true, but I can't tell you how many times they've made up stories about me or my sisters or brothers. Hopefully it will pass soon enough." She paused. "There was only one photograph? If they'd taken one of me kissing you in the car…"

"Only one," he said. "But this means we have to be more careful."

"I think you mean I have to be more careful. I'll try to control myself in public," she said.

"I'm not sure it's a good idea for you and I to—"

"You're bailing on me after a dark photo. The palace will make a statement that there's no mystery man and that you are merely security." She closed her eyes. "I don't want to feel as if I'm begging you."

"You're not begging," he said, feeling torn between doing what he thought was best for her and what he wanted. "I just—"

"I don't want to talk anymore. I've had more than my share of wishy-washy men," she said, rising to her feet.

He blinked at her. "Wishy-washy?"

"Thank you very much for the information. I have other things to do. Good day," she said as she walked away from him.

Treat nearly got frostbite from her abrupt, icy and very royal dismissal. Whoa. He wondered if she'd learned that in princess school. Lord help him if he had to deal with that on a regular basis.

Treat returned to the man cave and focused on his work. He noticed Nanny's car departing the driveway and Simon arriving with food and fresh laundry delivery. The more the thought about Ericka, the more he realized that the woman had a point. Her husband had bailed on her and Treat had given her a ton of mixed messages.

He walked to the cottage and knocked on the door then stepped inside. Ericka was trying to lure Leo into turning over by moving one of his toys next to his side. "Come on," she said. "You can do it."

Sam scampered next to the toy, his head moving every time Ericka moved the toy.

Leo let out a loud guttural yell.

Accurately reading her baby's sound of frustration, she gave the toy to Leo and he clutched it as he continued his push-ups. Sam looked disappointed and wandered to Treat to wind around his ankles and stamp out his human smell.

"Close. Very close," she said, but didn't meet Treat's gaze. "If you're checking on us, as you can see we're fine."

"I came to apologize," he said.

Her head jerked upward and she gaped at him. "Excuse me?"

"I've been thinking about it and I have been sending you mixed signals. One minute, I'm pushing you away because I'm trying to be professional. The next I'm all over you and can't get enough of you."

She stood and crossed her arms over her chest. "Which is the real Treat Walker?"

"You already know the answer to that. Both. I could quit and we could see how things go," he said.

"I don't want you to quit. I want you to stay." She shook her head in frustration. "Can't we just take this one day at a time right now? Can you just let it be okay that you like me?"

His feelings for her ran much deeper than like, but he didn't want to muddy the waters any more than he already had. "Yeah. I'll give it a try."

"Good," she said. "Simon brought Chinese food tonight. Would you like to take it back to the man cave with you? Or would you like to join me?"

"I'd like to join you," he said. And it occurred to

him that she deserved a man who would court her. He suspected there had been plenty of men who had tried to win her over, but somehow he'd had the dumb luck of getting her attention. He wouldn't take the gift of her interest and passion lightly, but he still didn't know how this could turn out without a world of hurt for one or both of them.

Treat and Ericka shared the delicious meal and Ericka charmed him with more stories from her childhood years in the palace. It turned out her sister Bridget had instigated quite a bit of mischief, and the sisters had often plotted how to loosen up their stuffy older brother.

"Bridget was always a fashionista. She was very adept at getting out of palace duties until Valentina and I married our husbands. Then she fell for an American doctor who had become a father to his brother's baby's twins. At first, no one believed it. She's the kind to wear heels on the beach," she said, rolling her eyes.

"It sounds like you managed to enjoy at least part of your childhood," he said.

"I did. We all did. I think Stefan and Valentina took the brunt of the work. It was drilled into Stefan from the time he was born that he was the heir, so he needed to always excel. My mother died when my sister Valentina was in college," she said. "That was hard on all of us."

"You miss her," he said.

"I miss what I wished I'd had with her. I'm determined to make sure Leo has a totally different experience with his mother," she said.

Treat nodded. "Good for you."

"And what about you? What about your parents?" she asked.

He wanted to turn away, but her eyes were warm with compassionate interest. "My dad died young and my mother was overworked. She tried, but I can hardly remember time when she wasn't tired. Between taking care of my brother and trying to make a living, she could hardly catch a break."

"Your brother," she said. "You have a brother. Is he like you?"

He shook his head. "He had some health problems."

"Oh. I'm sorry," she said.

He shrugged. His inability to make life better for his mother and brother was his life's greatest failings. Now that they were gone, he would never have that opportunity again. They were gone forever.

Leo interrupted his sad memories with a plaintive sound.

Ericka immediately turned to him in his baby seat. "Are you feeling a bit ignored?" she asked her baby and rubbed his chin. He kicked and stared up into her face intently.

"How does it feel to have a little person adore you so completely?" he asked

She smiled softly. "It's the most wonderful thing I've experienced. Of course, he doesn't adore me every minute. If he's hungry or uncomfortable or teething, that whole adoration thing goes right out the window. Diaper change, bath and bottle now," she said, and then shot him a sly look. "Wanna help?"

"I think I'll leave that to the expert," he said, and rose. "I'll check the perimeter and confirm that the alarm system is in place." He paused. "I could come back if you like."

She nodded. "I'll see you in about an hour."

Anticipation thrummed through Treat as he conducted his evening duties. As much as he fought it, he wanted to hold Ericka against him and taste her lips again. He'd tried his best to stop thinking about the night they'd shared together, but her memory was blazed on his mind and body. And the more he learned about her, the more he wanted her.

Returning to the cottage, he gave a soft knock then entered and found her sitting on the sofa reading from her computer tablet. She looked up and rose from the sofa. "I just put the kettle on. Would you like a cup of tea?" she asked.

He wrinkled his nose. "The only kind of tea I drink is sweet iced tea. I'll fix myself a glass of water."

"As you know, I spent most of my pregnancy in Texas with my sister Valentina. Her husband is a big fan of your iced tea." She made a face. "I much prefer mine hot with a little milk." She poured her own cup and led the way back to the den. "I was just reading about the surgery Leo will be receiving as early as January or February. I'm terrified that they will have to perform general anesthesia. When I think about it, I'm not sure I can go through with it. But I must if I want to give him the best possible future. It will not magically heal him, but he will be able to hear when he's wearing the external device."

"Will it affect his speech?" he asked.

"It should. Even with the surgery, there are many adjustments that will need to be made and lots of training. We're fortunate because Stefan has connections in Italy where there are several highly trained surgeons who've performed the surgery many times. It's likely that Leo and I will travel there for the actual surgery. Every time I think about it, my hands shake from nervousness," she said, and set her tea on the small table next to the sofa.

Treat felt an odd twisting sensation in his chest. He hated seeing her so distressed. Put down his glass of water, he covered her trembling hands. "You don't need to let this upset you. My mom always said we've got plenty to worry about today. We don't need to borrow trouble from tomorrow."

"She sounds like a wise woman," she said.

"She was," he said.

"I'll bet she was very proud of you," she said.

"Hope so," he said. He hoped he'd been some comfort to her during her hard, hard life.

"Distract me," she whispered, leaning closer to him. "Distract me from worrying about the future."

She was so sweet and genuine he couldn't possible refuse her. He lowered his head and gently took her mouth. Her lips were sweet and plump, her response both giving and wanting. The combination made him hungry, but he was determined to take his time. As much as he wanted to run his hands all over her and sink inside her, he wanted to savor the taste of her, rub his fingers over the bones of her cheeks and stroke her silky hair.

He kissed her for what could have been seconds or hours, but he knew when she wanted more. She squeezed his shoulders and rubbed her breasts against his chest. Arousal thrummed through his body like a drum. Knowing the tempo and his need would only increase, he continued to make love to her mouth.

Her arms stretched around his neck, pushing her into him. He lowered his hand to cup her breasts and she gave a soft moan. The sound tripped his trigger and he was filled with a ferocious need to show her with his body how beautiful she was.

He unbuttoned her blouse and bra then touched her breasts, lingering over her swollen nipples. Her felt her breath hitch in her throat when he lowered his head to taste her.

"Oh, Treat,' she whispered.

Urgency pounded through him. He pulled off his shirt and felt her naked breasts against him. "So good," he told. "You feel so good."

He felt her lower her hand to where he was hard and aching for her. She stroked him through his jeans, and the fabric of her jeans and his became the worst tease. He reached for the top of hers.

Leo's cry broke through the smoke of his arousal. He heard the cry again as Ericka pulled back. They stared into each other's eyes for several seconds. Sam entered the room and mewed in complaint.

Ericka took a deep, deep breath and reached for her bra. "I have to get him," she said as she fumbled with the fastening of her bra. She tried to put her blouse on backward, but Treat helped her with it. His own hands were unsteady from the force of his arousal.

"Sorry," she managed and went to the nursery.

"I'll be here when you get back," he said, and paced the den to bring his body back to earth.

Ericka checked Leo's diaper, but he was as dry as a bone. She knew he couldn't be hungry. Picking him up, she saw him gnaw on his pacifier and she immediately identified the problem. "Your gums are sore. Let me get a cold rag for you."

She went to the kitchen and wet the rag, then lifted

it to Leo's mouth for his to gum it. Treat walked into the kitchen and gave a questioning look.

"Teething," she said. "You don't have to hang around. I'm going to rock him for a while."

"I can catch up on one of my football games if I get my laptop," he said.

"That's nice of you, but he can get pretty noisy," she said.

Treat shrugged. "I can handle it," he said.

"Okay," she said. "I'll be back when he falls asleep."

Unfortunately Leo awakened every time she put him in his crib. Not even the solar system helped. Hearing the faint sound of a ballgame coming from the den, she was surprised that Treat had stayed so long. Any other man would have given up hours ago.

She paced the bedroom until she grew tired then rocked, rapidly. If she didn't move quickly enough, he cried again. She guessed the movement distracted him from his discomfort.

She didn't know how long had passed when Treat appeared in the doorway, his broad shoulders blocking the soft light from the hallway. A twist of irony tightened inside her. The evening had held such promise. Being held by Treat had made her feel so wonderful she couldn't even describe it to herself let alone anyone else. Now, though, she had to focus on Leo. She had no regrets, but couldn't help feeling a little wistful. She couldn't blame Treat for wanting to return to his suite.

"You wanna let me take a turn?" he asked.

Ericka stared at him in disbelief. She couldn't have heard him correctly. "Pardon me?"

"I said, do you want to let me take a turn with him? If you're not afraid I'll do something wrong," he added.

Her heart swelled in her chest and she felt her eyes burn with unshed tears. Blinking furiously, she shook her head then nodded. "Are you sure you want to do this? He's very cranky. You'll either have to pace or rock."

"I can do that," he said, and extended his arms.

Ericka carefully placed her baby into his arms. "Cradle him a little," she instructed, moving his hands into position.

Leo pouted and wiggled. Treat began to walk and the baby calmed.

"Are you sure—"

"I'm sure," he said. "Remember, I can get by on four hours of sleep. Less if necessary. Go take a nap," he told her.

Ericka took in the sight of her big strong body-guard pacing the room with her helpless baby and took a mental picture she resolved to store forever. No matter what happened in the future, she wanted to always remember this moment.

Giving into her weariness, she went to her bedroom, changed into her pajamas and fell into bed. She slept so hard she didn't even dream. Some part of her must have sensed a ray of sunshine sliding past through her curtains, but she had a hard time rousing herself. Finally, she forced her eyes open and automatically listened for Leo, but she didn't hear anything.

Frowning, she rose, looked at the baby monitor and listened again. Uneasiness grabbed at her. Rushing from bed, she raced to the nursery. His crib was empty. Alarm swept through her and she ran to the den.

"Looking for us?" Treat asked as he sat on the sofa feeding a bottle to Leo. "I can't promise I did a great job with the diaper. He can be a squirmy little thing when you try to change him, can't he?"

"I—" She stared a him in surprise. "Did you stay the rest of the night?"

"Yep," he said. "He settled down for an hour twice, so I just dozed in the rocking chair."

Guilt nicked at her. "Why didn't you wake me?" she demanded. "I didn't expect you to stay the whole night."

"Why not?" he asked.

"Well, because," she said. "He's not your responsibility."

Treat glanced down the baby. "He is in a way," he said. "He's part of you."

She hadn't thought he could take her breath away

again, but he did. She sank onto the sofa. "I'm sorry the evening didn't turn out. I loved the idea of you staying the night, but I had really wanted to be conscious for it."

Treat met her gaze. "Next time," he said, his dark eyes holding the promise of pleasure.

Watching him feed Leo, she couldn't help taking another mental photograph. Some part of her sensed Treat wouldn't be around forever. Their relationship was a fleeting moment in time, but with each new day, being with him made her feel a little stronger. He reminded her that she was human and there was nothing wrong with that. He reminded her that she was a desirable woman. She couldn't imagine him wanting to deal with a single mother princess forever, but she would cherish these moments because it restored her faith in possibilities.

Chapter Eleven

Nanny never arrived at the cottage. By late afternoon, Ericka grew worried and called Nanny's house. An hour later, she received a call from Nanny herself. Nanny had been in an automobile accident and had been taken to the clinic for examination.

Horrified, Ericka gasped. "How horrible. Are you okay?"

"I'm so sorry, ma'am," Nanny said. "I'm sure it's just a scrape from the windshield splattering, but they want to make sure I'm not carrying around any extra glass. I'm so sorry."

"Please stop apologizing," Ericka said, worried for Nanny's safety. "I just want you to be okay. Take whatever time you need and get back to me with your progress."

Ericka hung up the phone and struggled with how to modify her arrangements for Leo for the evening. As she fretted over her options, she heard a knock on the door just before it opened.

Treat poked his head inside. "Checking in," he said.

"Thanks. I just received sad news," she told him. "Nanny has been in an automobile accident. She sounded shaken up, but she says she's okay."

"That's rough. Is she being checked out by a doctor?" he asked.

"Yes, of course, but I don't expect her in tonight or tomorrow, and I'm required to attend the palace outdoor Christmas tree festival tonight. Tomorrow the Sergenian royals are scheduled to arrive and I'm to represent my family."

He shrugged. "Do you want me to take care of him?"

"I hate to ask you, but I don't want him anywhere near cameras tonight. With his teething, I can just see him pulling off a hat to reveal his hearing aids. I just don't want to have to answer any questions right now. If my entire family wasn't supposed to be attending, I could ask one of my sisters, but they need to be there, too."

"What about your security?" he asked.

"The palace will send a car with your relief detail,

which you haven't used since you started. Even God rested on the seventh day," she said.

Treat grinned. "God doesn't sleep," he said. "I do."

"You could have fooled me," she said. "Are you sure you don't mind? This is a highly unusual situation."

"I'm okay with it," he insisted. "We'll watch football. He's gonna love it."

So grateful that she could count on him, she reached toward him and hugged him. "You really have no idea how much I appreciate this," she said, her voice breaking.

"Hey, hey," he said, stroking her hair. "What's this? You're not crying are you?"

"No, of course not," she said, blinking back tears.

"You don't have to worry. I'll take care of him. Your boy is safe with me," he assured, hugging her.

She took a deep breath and put a check on her emotions. "I know he is safe with you. Now, I'd better get ready for tonight. Simon has delivered another delicious meal. Coq au Vin. Eat as much as you like," she said, and went to her bedroom to get ready for her appearance.

Within an hour, a guard and driver appeared to take her to event. Darkness was beginning to fall over the island and holiday lights twinkled here and there. The palace would be lit from one end to the other. Stefan's wife, Eve, had insisted on creating more holiday traditions. Bit by bit, Eve was remodeling the palace both externally and in personality. The advisors still insisted on a certain level of decorum, but with toddlers roaming the palace halls, it was hard to require so much formality.

Arriving at the palace, she was escorted to one of the more comfortable meeting rooms. Bridget sat in a chair while her husband fussed over her and chased after their young twin boys. Stefan's daughter sat on the floor calmly coloring in her coloring book while his two-year old tried to keep up with the twins. Eve caught him just before he fell and scooped him up in her arms. Pippa carried her toddler daughter on her hip.

Eve spotted Ericka and moved toward her. "It's good to see you," she said, giving Ericka an affectionate squeeze. "I'm so sorry about Leo's nanny. Do you think she'll be okay?"

"I'll hear more tomorrow, but she was complaining about having to see the doctor, so I suppose that's a good sign."

"I'm glad. Who is watching Leo?"

"My security man," she said.

Eve widened her eyes. "Really?"

"Yes. He's been surprisingly good with Leo. He's not an expert with diapers, but—"

"I don't know many men who are," Eve said. "Hopefully we won't need to keep you too long tonight."

The press representative called them to attention

and reviewed the evening schedule. The children would appear briefly while Stefan ordered the lighting of the Christmas tree. Nannies would then take the children either to bed or to a playroom. Due to her advanced pregnancy, Bridget would be excused early. The rest of her siblings and their spouses would be required to stay until the end.

As she and her family walked toward the large imported pine tree, the crowd cheered with delight. Ericka smiled and waved as did her brothers and sisters and a few of the children.

"Good evening, people of Chantaine," Stefan said to the crowd. "Thank you for joining us for the lighting of the palace Christmas tree. This season celebrates hope, love and peace for the entire world. We are especially grateful for the peace our country continued to experience and I want to thank you, the citizens of Chantaine, for your commitment to your country and to your fellow citizens. You serve as an example to the rest of the world."

The crowd applauded.

"As you can see, the royal family is expanding by leaps and bounds with more expansion on the way," he said, glancing at Bridget.

He crowd chuckled.

"We, the royal family of Chantaine, wish you the happiest Christmas, full of love, hope and peace everlasting."

Stefan gave a nod of his head and the huge tree

was lit. More applause followed, the children waved farewell along with Bridget, and the festivities continued with a performance by a children's choir and a reading from a village priest and instrumental holiday music.

The entire time, Ericka wondered how Leo would have responded. The lights would have fascinated him. He wouldn't have been able to hear the children sing, the music or the applause of the crowd. Her heart twisted. She wanted so much for him. Maybe next year? she wondered and said a silent prayer.

Ericka arrived back at the cottage at ten o'clock, feeling worn out. She entered the cottage to find Treat holding Leo on his lap while he watched his laptop screen. He glanced up at her. "How'd it go?"

"It went very well. I feel as if I should be asking you the same question."

"I let him take the car for a spin, then we went for a swim in the ocean and we had a couple of beers before we got back to watch the game," he said.

Ericka rolled her eyes. "You want to tell me the real story now?"

"Gave him a bottle. Did you know that kid can burp like a trucker?" he asked.

Ericka chuckled. "Yes, and it's better for him to burp. He gets very fussy when he isn't well burped."

"I ate some of the coq au vin. It's a lot better than the peanut butter sandwiches I make, but not as good as your peanut butter and bacon sandwich. We both did some more push-ups. I gave him a bath—"

Ericka looked at him in surprise. "By yourself?"

He shot her an insulted glance. "It's not that hard. You just have to make sure the water's warm enough. I probably didn't do a perfect job, but I figure you can get whatever I missed on the next go-round. Since then I've been explaining different formations and plays. He dozed a couple of times, but I think he waited up to see you."

She sat down next to Treat and extended her hands to her baby. Leo fell toward her and she scooped him up against her chest.

"See? I told you he was waiting up for you," Treat said.

She cuddled Leo and kissed his chubby cheeks. "No signs of teething?"

"Not yet, but it's not the witching hour," Treat said.

"Thank you for taking care of my baby," she said.

"It was cake," he said. "Sam supervised me most of the time except when I bathed him. Then Sam suddenly disappeared."

"I'm sure you could tell that Sam doesn't like the water," she said, then sighed. "I have to get up early in the morning to meet the Tarisse sisters and their brother. Stefan has charged me with emphasizing the rules of our agreement. It's only fair since I twisted his arm. I can take Leo with me and one of the nannies for Eve and Stefan's children will watch him."

"Why would you do that when you can leave him here with me?" he asked.

"Because I feel that I've already imposed."

"I told you I don't mind," he said, rising from the sofa. "What time do you need me here?"

"Seven," she said. "I'll call the palace to give me a ride, but I'm told I'll be meeting them at an inn. I could drive myself."

"Not without security," he said. "I'm going to bed. Hate to admit it, but I'm starting to understand why moms of young ones feel tired."

She stood and pressed her mouth against his cheek. "I thought you're the tough guy who thrives on four hours of sleep."

"That's exactly what I'm going to get. My four hours. Your boy should be ready to hit the sack after one more bottle. If he gets fussy, give me a call. Night, princess," he said. Treat knew she didn't like being called "princess," but the way he said it made it sound sexy.

Seemed like lately the way he said anything was sexy to her.

Leo slept through the night. She almost awakened him the next morning, but restrained herself. Quickly dressing, she grabbed a quick bite to eat and sipped a cup of tea as Treat walked through the door. He looked her up and down then studied her face. "You look like you got a decent night's sleep."

"That's because Leo slept," she told Treat, still surprised.

"And that's because I had a little man-to-man talk with him about letting his mama get some sleep."

She chuckled. "And look how well it worked. I should have asked you to talk with him earlier."

He shrugged. "It's a guy thing."

"If you say so," she said, glimpsing the palace car in the driveway. "I should be back by lunchtime. Don't take him skydiving," she told him, and kissed his cheek.

"Hey, how did you know that was on my list?" he joked.

"Ciao," she said. "And thank you again."

Ericka reviewed Stefan's notes on the way to the inn where she would meet the Tarisse siblings. Stefan had initially requested the Sergenian royals to sign a contract, but Ericka had refused. The siblings shouldn't have to sign their lives away for a temporary stay in Chantaine.

Her security escorted her inside a small inn to a suite on the second floor. When she entered, she noticed one of her brother's top security advisors, Paul Hamburg, along with an assistant and the Tarisse sisters. Both princesses were beautiful, but at the moment both looked tired and irritated.

"Your Highness, Princess Fredericka Devereaux,

please allow me to introduce you to Princesses Sasha and Tabitha," Paul said, performing the formal introductions.

"Please call me Ericka," she said, moving toward the two women. "You must be tired. Would you like some tea?" she asked.

"Yes, please," Sasha said.

Ericka nodded toward the assistant. "Please get some tea and pastries."

Sasha, the elder sister, wore her dark hair in a loose chignon at the base of her neck while Tabitha wore her wavy hair loose over her shoulders. "We're grateful you've welcomed us to your family," Sasha said. "You'll forgive us if we're not at our most congenial."

"Because we've been tricked," Tabitha continued. "We made an agreement with our brother, Alex. He told us he would meet us in Chantaine, but he has disappeared."

"Oh, I'm so sorry. Do you have any idea where he could be?" Ericka asked.

Tabitha crossed her arms over her chest, her eyes nearly spitting sparks. "Who knows? He may be roaming the mountains on the border of our country. Or he may be partying in Italy."

"Tabitha," Sasha said in an admonishing voice. "I apologize."

"I can understand some of your frustrations. I've dealt with my share of sibling skirmishes."

The assistant returned with tea and snacks. Ericka made sure everyone had their own cup and a bite to eat before she began. "It's my pleasure to welcome you to Chantaine, but as you know, we have several conditions during your visit here. These are for both your safety and the safety of our citizens. I'm sure you've been told you'll need to assume different identities. You're not to reveal your true identity to anyone. Sasha, I know you're a talented concert pianist, but while you are here, we ask that you not play in public."

Sasha nodded with a sad expression.

"You can, however, play in private. We'll try to make sure you have access to a piano during your stay."

"Thank you," Sasha said. "It would be difficult for me if I couldn't play at all."

"Tabitha, we're working on finding a position for you within the next few days. In the meantime, the two of you can stay here. However, this is hard for me to say. You must not appear in public together."

Tabitha's face fell. "Never?"

"This is not forever," Ericka reminded her. "This is just during your stay while your country resolves its current turmoil. It's for your safety. Think about it. If the two of you are seen together, it's more likely that someone will figure out your true identities. Think of it as divide and conquer."

Sasha slipped her hand through her sister's. "We

will do what we must, but what do we do about our brother, Alex?"

Ericka looked at Paul Hamburg expectantly.

"We'll make inquiries, but we must tread carefully with the princesses visiting Chantaine. We don't want to arouse suspicion," he said.

"But we have contacts who have contacts," Ericka said.

Paul sighed. "Yes, we do."

"I know you don't take orders from me, but I hope you will give this your best discreet effort."

"I will," he said.

"Thank you," she said then turned back to the sisters. "Now let me tell you about Chantaine."

An hour and a half later, Ericka got into the car and returned to the cottage. She hoped she'd soothed some of their nerves, but she suspected that would take time. It broke her heart to see the fear in their eyes. She wasn't sure how she would arrange it, but she was determined to stay in touch with them. She was also going to make sure they had a Christmas celebration of some kind. After all they were going through, it was unacceptable for them to skip Christmas.

She exited the car and thanked her security man then opened the door to the cottage.

"It's not as bad as it looks," Treat called from the hall bathroom.

Alarmed, she raced down the hall to find Treat and Leo covered in red and blue. "What on earth?"

"I told you it's not that bad. We just need to get cleaned up," he said.

"How do you plan to do that?" she asked, wondering if her baby would be stained with red and blue paint for the rest of his life. "What are you doing?"

"You like art." Treat lifted a sheet of paper with Leo's footprints in red and his handprints in blue.

She reached for the precious image of Leo's sweet baby feet and hands and burst into tears.

"That bad?" Treat asked in a gently joking tone.

"Oh, be quiet. You know better." She swiped at her tears. "How can I help clean up?"

"Just go into the den and let us take care of it. This is a job for the men," he said. Leo giggled and planted a blue finger on Treat's cheek.

At that moment, Ericka felt herself fall hopelessly in love with Treat.

She forced herself to remain on the sofa despite the strong maternal urge to help. Pouring herself a cup of tea, she looked at the "painting" and cried again. She'd taken plenty of photos of Leo, but this was an image she knew she would always treasure. She visualized different frames for the art.

Finally after a few wails that caught at her throat, Treat returned with Leo scrubbed shiny clean, wearing only his diaper. Treat was still multi-colored.

"The bathroom is as clean as a whistle," he said. "I'm headed for a shower."

"Are you coming back?"

He met her gaze for a long moment then nodded. "Yeah."

Ericka dressed Leo and gave him a bottle. He nearly fell asleep, which led her to believe he'd had quite the active morning. She set him down in his crib and he nodded off right away.

She felt a rush of nerves as she waited for Treat to return. The events of the past few days had left her feeling more vulnerable than usual. She piddled in the kitchen and called to tell Simon she didn't want a delivery that afternoon.

She heard a knock on the door then it opened and Treat walked in, his hair damp from his shower, his gaze immediately searching hers. "How was this morning?" he asked.

"Challenging. They're afraid. I can't say I blame them," she said. "I'm hoping the peacefulness of Chantaine will be healing for them."

"It's not a bad place if you need to hide out for a while," he said, then took her hands in his. "You made it happen for them."

"I hope it will all work out," she said.

"What's on your mind?" he asked, dipping his head to study her face. "Looks like it's going a hundred miles an hour."

Her heart hammering in her chest, she wondered

why she was suddenly so shy. "I'm trying to think of a clever way of telling you that Leo is asleep and we have the house to ourselves."

Treat pulled her against him and kissed her. "That's the cleverest thing I've heard all day," he said, and scooped her off her feet and down the hall to her bedroom. "I'll try to take my time, but I swear I feel like it's been a decade."

"It hasn't?" she asked, unfastening his shirt while her fingers still worked.

He kissed her slow and deep, lighting the fire inside her. He ran his lips down her cheek and throat. "You skin is so soft," he murmured and unbuttoned her blouse.

He dipped his tongue in the hollow of her throat, taking her off guard. Another moment of caresses and her bra was gone. She loved the sensation of his naked chest against her breasts.

She rubbed her open mouth against his and he sucked in a quick breath, taking her mouth in another deep, hungrier kiss. His hunger made her hyper-aware of all the achy, needy places in her body.

He slid her skirt and panties down over her hips then followed her down on the bed. "I'm naked and you're not."

"I will be soon enough," he said, then kissed his way down her body.

Ericka fell into a delicious cocoon where only she and Treat existed. He pleasured and seduced her until she couldn't bear being separate from him for one more second. Then he finally slid inside her and they were as close as could be. Afterward, he held her tightly against him, as if he never wanted to let her go.

The rest of the day passed in a sweet haze of togetherness. They both played with Leo and ate leftovers. Treat turned on his laptop and attempted to teach her the finer points of football, but she was too busy soaking up every second. She knew this time together would soon pass. Nanny had already called, insisting she was ready to return to work the following afternoon.

The next day, Ericka found herself sighing in contentment. She couldn't remember feeling this happy in her life. Midmorning, she received a call from Treat. Unusual, she thought. He usually just walked over if he wanted to talk to her.

"Hello to you," she said, still feeling a buzz of happiness.

"There's a man at the gate," Treat said. "His name is Jean Claude and he says he wants to see his son."

Shock coursed through Ericka. She was so stunned she nearly dropped her cup of tea. "Is it really Jean Claude?"

"His identification checks out. But I can send him away."

Ericka closed her eyes and shook her head in disbelief. She'd been so sure her ex would never show any interest in Leo. Why now? Why now?

Remembering what Stefan had said, she felt a surge of raw bitterness and narrowed her eyes. "Let him in."

Chapter Twelve

"I'm here to demand shared custody of my son," Jean Claude announced as soon as he entered the cottage.

Ericka couldn't believe his audacity. At this moment, she couldn't believe she'd ever been in love with this man. "Hello, Jean Claude, I hope you're doing well," she said politely, because someone needed to provide some leadership in civility in this situation. Just beyond Jean Claude, Ericka could see Treat glowering with anger.

"I think you may be confused about the divorce agreement you signed concerning Leo. You waived all rights and responsibilities to your son," she said.

"That showed a lack of forethought," he said. "I

was impulsive because I feared you were trying to trap me in our marriage when I needed to be free."

The way he used the word *trap* made her stomach twist. Ericka had made every effort to save her marriage. "And you are now free."

Jean Claude shifted from one foot to the other. "I want to renegotiate."

"I see no reason to renegotiate. You haven't exhibited one drop of interest in your son since he was conceived let alone since he was born."

Jean Claude stretched his chin. "Must we discuss this in front of the staff?"

Ericka blinked. "Yes, we must. He's my security detail."

"Ericka, I know the Devereaux family has some hidden cash. Look how the royal yachts and the grand palace are always being redecorated. You have yourself a nice place here. You don't appear to be hurting for cash," he said.

"And your point is?" she asked.

"I want shared custody and support for when the baby visits me."

"Support," she echoed, her fury growing. "You don't know what the word means."

"We can make this easy, or I can make it very dirty in the press for you and your family," he said.

Ericka watched Treat move toward her ex and she held up a hand. "You do realize that if you have joint custody, you will also need to contribute to Leo's medical bills. Are you prepared to do that?"

"Why wouldn't I be?" he asked, a hint uncertainty flickering in his. "Is something wrong with him?"

"No, he's perfect. He's also profoundly deaf," she said.

Jean Claude stared at her in shock. "Oh, my—" He shook his head. "Now, I understand why you've kept him hidden from the press. How to explain a defective child. I can't say I blame you. I hope you'll keep him hidden. It wouldn't do anything for your image or mine."

Treat lifted Jean Claude from his feet and tossed him out the door. "Get away from her. You don't deserve either of them."

Jean Claude protested. "Don't you insult me. Don't—"

Treat punched him in the face, sending her ex reeling. Seeing Jean Claude for the opportunistic monster he'd become, she tugged at Treat's arm. "Stop. Please stop," she said, fighting back tears. She turned to Jean Claude. "Just leave."

"My attorney will be in touch," Jean Claude said, rubbing his jaw. "You can't hit just anyone with no repercussions," he said as he walked to the gate.

"I have to let him out of the gate," Treat said, his nostrils still flaring in anger. He did the deed then returned. "Are you okay?" he asked.

"I will be," she said, crossing her arms over her

chest protectively. "I still can't believe he just showed up with no notice."

"The palace keeps a watch over him and it appears he and his new companion have been spending more than he makes," he said as he escorted her back to the cottage.

Treat pulled her into his arms and she savored the protective sensation. "I don't think he'll be back," he murmured, rubbing his mouth over her forehead.

She sighed then pulled back slightly. "You were so angry. I could see it in your eyes."

He looked away. "I lost control. I'm going to have to deal with that," he said.

"What do you mean?" she asked.

"I'll figure it out," he said. "I need to file a report. Don't worry about it. You have enough on your mind," he said, then gave her a quick kiss. "We'll talk later. Put this in your rear view mirror. Your day is gonna get better, okay?"

She nodded, but something about his manner made her feel uncertain.

Treat rehashed the incident with Ericka's ex both verbally and in writing. Nobody was happy that he'd used physical force with Jean Claude, but nobody really blamed him, either. Still, the palace preferred to deal with all matters in a low-profile manner if at all possible. Treat supposed he could have restrained himself if he didn't have such strong feelings of protectiveness for Ericka and Leo.

Pacing the suite, he berated himself for his actions. He had acted out of his emotions instead of with the professionalism Ericka deserved. His partner deserved better. The palace deserved better. Ericka deserved better.

Treat knew what he had to do and it made him feel as if his heart were being ripped from his chest. He sent an official email to the palace, his partner and Stefan. Now for the hard part. He had to tell Ericka.

Treat tried to time his visit with Ericka for when Leo would be napping. He knocked on the cottage door and opened it, realizing this would be the last time he performed this little routine. He found her in the den. She glanced up from her computer tablet and smiled. "Hey, there. I've missed you," she said, rising from the sofa.

She put her arms around him and he inhaled the sweet fragrance of her hair. He wanted to remember that. He wanted to remember everything. Treat held her an extra few seconds then pulled back and took a deep breath.

"I need to talk to you," he said.

"Oh, sounds serious," she said.

"You could say that," he said, then looked away for a moment, searching for the right words. "What I did this morning was wrong. It was unprofessional and I broke my code of ethics by punching your ex.

I reacted emotionally. To tell the truth, I wanted to throw him out the door every time he opened his mouth. I was over the edge when he insulted you. It took everything I had to rein myself in when you held up your hand. When he said those things about Leo—" Treat broke off.

"I understand your feelings," she said. "The whole thing was so bizarre. I was just trying to stay sane."

"Well, you did a better job than I did." He nodded, feeling grim. "I've resigned from my position."

Ericka gasped, staring at him in shock. "What?" She shook her head. "No. No. You can't. Anyone could have responded to Jean Claude that way. He was so degrading."

"I can't be anyone. I've been given the responsibility of protecting you. My emotions were out of control. I lost control. I can't be your security anymore. I thought I could separate my feelings about you from the job I have to do. You don't need to be worrying about what your security guy is going to do. You've got enough going on with the rest of your life. I'm not good for you right now," he said. "I'm going back to the States."

"No," Ericka said. "Please don't do this."

He shook his head. "Ericka, you're not ready to have me in your life and I refuse to add to your troubles right now. I—" He broke off again. "You and Leo mean too much to me."

"But I don't want you to go," she said, her eyes filling with tears. "I want you to stay. Reconsider."

"I can't," he said. "It's done. Your temporary security guy is on his way now. I'm packed."

Ericka stared after Treat in disbelief. She felt as if she'd been spent her entire day in shock. *No, no, no.* She started to run after him, but Leo's cry broke the silence. Feeling as if her world had just been turned upside after everything had felt so right, she automatically went to the nursery.

"Hi, big boy," she said to Leo through her tears. "Need a diaper change?" She chatted with him until her throat closed tight from a wrenching feeling of loss. Then she picked him up and held his sweet warmth again her. Nothing could stop the love she felt for Leo. Nothing. But she'd finally let down her guard and she felt broken to pieces. Even though she'd instinctively known her relationship with Treat might not end with them together, she'd been unprepared for it to end so swiftly.

She'd just grown accustomed to his sense of humor, to feeling his arms around her and just basking in his presence. Her chest felt as if a heavy weight had descended on it. She could hardly breathe. She closed her eyes and his image stomped through her brain.

It was all she could do to keep from sobbing outright, but she had to hold herself together. Leo was counting on her. Within moments, Nanny appeared at the door with a small adhesive bandage on her forehead and a bruise on her cheek.

"Hello, hello," she called cheerily. "Now don't worry over the bruise," she said. "I may be a little scraped up, but not enough to stop me."

Ericka felt a trickle of relief at the sight of the woman although she wondered if Nanny had rushed returning to work. "Are you sure you're okay?"

"I'm fine, truly fine. Thank you, ma'am," Nanny said, then studied Ericka's face. "But you're looking a bit out of sorts. Are you feeling ill?"

Devastated was more accurate. "I'm not feeling all that well," she admitted, biting the inside of her lip to keep from bursting into tears.

"Well, let me take our sweet boy and you go take a little rest. It'll do you good," she said, opening her arms to hold him. "And don't you worry about a thing. I can take the night shift, too. You don't want to get worn down," she said, then made a clucking sound. "Off to bed with you, ma'am."

Following Nanny's encouragement, she went to her room and closed the door. She looked at the bed and all she could think about was the night she'd just shared with Treat. She wanted to run and hide, but he was everywhere. Ericka sank onto the bed and sobbed into her pillow.

Feeling like the emotionally walking dead, she went through the motions of her life. Leo still made her smile, but otherwise she felt joyless during this most joyful of all seasons. She avoided Nanny's worried glances. She shopped online for gifts for her family and visited a local store for toys for Leo and her nieces and nephews.

Just because she felt hollow didn't mean she was going to wallow in it. She bought a few gifts for the Tarisse sisters. Unfortunately, there'd been no sightings of their brother, Alex.

As Leo did his tummy time, Ericka wrapped packages, tossing the cat a shiny ribbon. Sam had been more affectionate lately, as if he knew she was grieving. She scratched the kitty behind the ears then glanced at Leo. He'd turned over and looked a bit disoriented from the experience.

"Look at you," she said, touching his chest and raving over him. "You rolled over. You're so strong," she told him, smiling down into his precious face.

Leo smiled and giggled in return. Ericka felt tears well in her eyes. She wished Treat could have been her for this. He would have been over the moon.

Ericka shook herself for thinking that way. Treat was gone and he wasn't coming back. She needed to face that fact. Her phone rang and she noticed the call was from her sister Pippa.

"Hello, Pippa. How are you?"

"I'm at the hospital," Pippa said breathlessly. "Bridget is in labor. When can you get here?"

"Oh, my goodness," Ericka said, feeling a rush

of excitement for her sister. "Nanny's taking a break watching a television show. How far along is she?"

"Well, you never know with Bridget. She's such a drama queen, but I will say she came in huffing and puffing and she wasn't wearing a drop of make-up," Pippa said.

"That's serious," Ericka said. Bridget refused to be seen in public without her cosmetics perfectly applied. "I'll be there as soon as possible."

Ericka took Leo to stay with Nanny while she watched her television show then rushed to the hospital with her new dour security detail sitting in the passenger seat. He hated when she drove, but he moved too slowly for her. Especially in this case.

Arriving at the hospital, she joined Pippa and Eve in a private waiting room. "I wonder how long it will take," Eve said. "I always get a little nervous when the Devereaux women go into labor."

Ericka nodded. "Valentina gave us a scare, but thank God everything turned out."

Eve continued to chatter, filling the time with conversation about Christmas. The door to the waiting room opened and Bridget's husband appeared, beaming.

"What a healthy mother and healthy baby girl! The boys have taken their turn to meet the baby. Would you like to visit?"

"Of course," Eve said. The three women were led to the birthing room where Bridget was sitting up in bed, her face make-up free, but her hair brushed into place.

She looked up and smiled. "Look what I have."

Pippa took her turn first and cooed over the baby. She kissed Bridget on the cheek. "You look entirely too composed for a woman who just gave birth," she said.

"I agree," Eve said, moving closer to get a better look at the baby. "Oh, she has a lovely pink complexion and that little spray of hair. A beauty," she said. "You did well."

Ericka peeked at the baby and agreed with Eve's assessment. "She truly is a beautiful newborn," Ericka said. "No lopsided head or scrunchy face." She kissed Bridget on the cheek. "I'm so happy for you."

"Thank you, all of you," Bridget said, growing suddenly teary. "I didn't want to let on how frightened I was when the doctor limited my activities. I'm so relieved she's here, safe and sound."

"That's our brave Bridget," her husband said, tenderly stroking Bridget's cheek.

The love between Bridget and her husband was so big it seemed to fill the room. Ericka was happy for her sister, but at that moment, she couldn't help thinking of Treat. She swallowed her bitter twist of loss and lifted her lips in a determined smile.

"We've gotten our peek. Let's give Mom and baby time to rest up," Eve said, and the three of them left the birthing room. "Beautiful," she said. "And

Bridget didn't look a bit ragged. I could complain, but her pregnancy wasn't the easiest. I'll see you and yours on Christmas Eve," she said, giving a quick hug to Pippa and Ericka. "We have so much to celebrate."

"We do," Pippa said as Eve walked away. She turned to Ericka and took her hand. "We need to talk. You look miserable."

Ericka demurred. "I'm fine. Just busy due to the holiday season."

"That's not what I heard. Let's go back to the private waiting room. There was a teapot. We weren't in there long enough to take any," she said, tugging Ericka to the waiting room where she poured tea for both of them.

"I should get back home," Ericka said. "I left a mess of wrapping paper on the floor. Who knows what the cat will do with it?"

"The mess can wait. I'm told your American security man abruptly resigned," she said. "There are rumors that you were romantically involved with him."

Ericka took a sip of tea, but it stuck in her throat. She coughed and set down the cup and the truth just spilled out. "It was a disaster from the start, but he surprised me. He was so kind to me and to Leo. It caught me off guard. I knew I shouldn't get involved, but I just couldn't resist. He was able to resist in the beginning, but the pull between us was so intense."

"He left because something happened with your ex," she said.

"Treat punched Jean Claude," she said. "Jean Claude visited and demanded I share custody and money. He was so insulting. Honestly, he wasn't like that when we first got married. I don't know when he turned into such a horrid person. Treat was horrified that he had behaved unprofessionally and he left," she said. "End of story."

"Is it?" Pippa asked.

"What do you mean?" Ericka asked.

"I must tell you that I see myself in your eyes right now. The misery and loss," she said.

"But you're not miserable," Ericka said. "You're glowing. You're happily married."

"I am now, but only because I went after the man I loved with all my heart. Did you ever tell Treat that you loved him?"

Ericka bit her lip and shook her head. "It happened so fast. I was afraid I would scare him away."

Pippa took Ericka's hands in hers. "How can you truly know what Treat wants if you don't tell him your feelings? You're not a teenager anymore. You're a woman with a child. You've been banged around a bit in the relationship department, but I think you know what you want. Do you think you'll ever meet another man like him?"

Ericka shook her head, feeling her chest tighten with grief again. "No. But I've lost him."

"You could tell him your feelings," Pippa suggested.

"But he's all the way in Texas," she said. "This isn't the kind of thing one sends in an email."

"We have jets leaving for the United States every day from Chantaine," Pippa said.

Overwhelmed by the prospect, Ericka stood and paced the small area. "I couldn't dare. It's almost Christmas. What would I do with Leo?"

"I would gladly take care of him for you," Pippa said.

Ericka's heart hammered in her throat. "I don't know if I can do this. I don't know if I have the courage. What if he turns me away?"

"There's only one way to find out. Let me know when you want to drop off Leo," she said, rising and giving Ericka a tight hug.

Ericka returned home, trying to digest Pippa's challenge to her. She couldn't believe her shy sister had become such a tiger. Ericka took care of Leo after she arrived home, but thoughts of Treat consumed her. She barely slept all night. The next morning, she awakened and decided to accept Pippa's challenge. She was going to Texas to see Treat and she was taking Leo with her.

Packing took little time and before she knew it, she and Leo were flying across the Atlantic. Her baby did surprising well on the flight, taking lots of naps and doing sign language lessons with her on her tablet. Nearby passengers looked at her curiously.

"You're teaching your baby sign language?" the woman from across the aisle asked. "Isn't he a bit young?"

"He is, but he's profoundly deaf, so there's no such thing as starting too soon," she said.

"I'm so sorry," the woman said.

"Oh, don't be. He's the joy of my life," Ericka said, and felt another weight lifted from her chest. One less secret to keep.

Treat sat behind the desk in his cluttered office space and stared at his laptop. Now that he'd messed up the job for the Devereaux family, he was chasing new leads for his business. It was a wonder his partner hadn't ditched him, but Andrew had seemed to sense his misery and chosen not to add to it.

Determined to make up for his failing, he was spending twelve hours a day at the office then falling into bed at night, but rarely sleeping. Visions of Ericka and Leo danced in his head. He didn't know which was worse—thinking about her when he was awake or dreaming about her during his rare moments of sleep.

He slurped down a cup of coffee that resembled tar and added another lead to his list. Unfortunately, with the exception of retail stores, most people didn't have security on the brain. He really should straighten up this office, he thought, looking around at the boxes of files.

A knock sounded at the door and then it flew open. Ericka and Leo swept inside the room. Treat stared at her in shock and shook his head. *Oh, no, he had gone over the edge.* He was seeing things. That was it. Time to check himself into the loony bin.

"Sorry. This isn't how I wanted to start our conversation, but we have a bad diaper situation," she said, and dug a blanket out of the gigantic bag slung across her shoulder. Struggling to hold squirmy Leo in place, she cleaned him, changed his diaper and put him on the blanket.

Leo immediately rolled over.

"He's rolling," he said.

"Yes," she said, smiling and sighing at the same time. "Now that he knows how to do it, he doesn't want to stop."

"Are you really here? Or am I just imagining this?" Treat asked, his heart starting to stretch and fill up at the sight of her.

"I'm really here," she said as she put her arms around him. "Don't I feel real?"

Treat squeezed her tight. "I don't know how or why, but—"

She backed away slightly. "Well, I'm going to tell you," she said, meeting his gaze. "I love you and I want you in my life. No secrets. I know I'll never meet another man like you."

"But I'm not royalty. I came up dirt poor," he said. "I'll never be as polished as most of the guys who've tried to win you."

"Do you have a prejudice against royalty?" she asked.

"No."

"Because you bring it up a lot. Haven't you figured out that part of the reason I fell in love with you was because I could be myself with you? You even seemed to like it when I was myself. You helped me become stronger and more confident. You took my heart by surprise and I'm just now catching up. Say you'll give us a chance."

Treat closed his eyes, feeling his heart nearly burst with joy. He couldn't turn down her offer. He had fallen for her like a brick and he knew there was no recovering from his feelings for her. "I love you," he told her. "Tell me what you want and I'll do my best to give it to you."

"Come home with me for Christmas," she said.

Five days later, the Deveraux family gathered for Christmas Eve. During Ericka's growing up years, she remembered the gathering as stiff and dignified. With all the babies, toddlers and love abounding, it was rollicking good craziness. Bridget's new baby girl was passed around from one adult to the other. Bridget's twin boys couldn't stop kissing the poor baby's pink cheeks. The rest of the children scampered around the room with parents preventing spills and upsets when possible.

Pippa held Leo on her lap and practiced some sign language she'd learned. The sight of her sister adapting to communicate to her son almost brought Ericka to tears. She couldn't remember feeling such love and support.

"Hey, princess, will you skip out to the garden with me?" Treat asked her.

She shot him a chiding look. "Princess?"

"Your Highness?" he said, teasing her.

Ericka asked Pippa to watch Leo for a few moments and walked into the garden with Treat.

He took her hand and loosened his tie at the same time. "Madness and mayhem in there. You Devereauxs sure know how to party," he said.

She chuckled. "Complete with diapers and sippy cups." She looked into his gaze. "Thank you for coming back to Chantaine with me."

"I wouldn't have it any other way," he said, and led her to a bench among the carefully tended blooms and shrubs. "In fact, I have a question for you…" He knelt down on one knee.

Ericka looked at him in surprise. She was even more surprised when he pulled a jeweler's box from his pocket.

"Fredericka Devereaux, I love you and Leo more than life itself. I never dreamed a woman like you could exist. Your strength, your humor, your passion. Will you marry me?"

Ericka was so overwhelmed she could hardly speak. "Oh, Treat. I—I—"

"Don't leave me hanging here too long," he said

"Yes," she managed breathlessly and urged him up from his knees. "I love you so very much. I don't ever want to live without you. Wherever we may go, I want to be with you. Forever," she said

"Will you wear this ring?" he asked and opened the box to reveal a brilliant ruby surrounded by diamonds.

"It's beautiful," she said. "Of course I will." Her hands trembled as he placed the ring on her finger. "The ring is beautiful," she said. "But the man who gave it to me is my true treasure."

Epilogue

Four months later, so many changes had taken place. The conference had been a smashing success. Ericka and Treat had married. Most harrowing of all, Leo had received his surgery.

Today, Ericka sat with Treat, Leo and the specialty audiologist in a small office in Italy. Both nervous and excited, she bounced Leo on her knee. Today the audiologist would activate the external device. This visit wasn't the pot of gold at the end of the rainbow. It was just the beginning. Leo would need to be trained how to best use the device.

"Okay?" Treat asked, covering her hand with his.

She took a deep breath. "A little nervous."

"It's gonna work out," he said, and offered Leo a ring of plastic donuts.

Leo grabbed the first one then tossed it several feet.

"He throws everything these days. It's all that football you let him watch," she whispered.

"Hey, the kid's got a good arm," he said as he gave Leo another donut.

Leo tossed that one on the floor, too.

The audiologist smiled. "I'm going to activate the volume levels on Leo's device now. I'll do it gradually, but as I told you, he may cry when he first hears noise because it can be confusing for the little ones. Here we go."

Ericka held her breath, carefully watching Leo's face. During the first few tests, he showed no response. Suddenly, though he stopped and his eyes widened.

"We may have something here," the audiologist said. "Say hello to your son," she told Ericka.

"Hi, Leo," she said. "Hello, beautiful boy. I love you so much."

Leo looked up at her and put his fingers against her mouth.

She gasped then laughed. "Can you hear me? You can hear, Leo. You can hear, can't you?"

Leo laughed in return and wiggled his head as if he would need to get used to the new sensation.

"That's what we call a late Christmas gift," the woman said.

Ericka looked into Treat's gaze and her eyes filled with tears. He'd been with her through all the upheaval and challenges of the past few months, and she knew in her heart that he would be there for her and Leo forever.

* * * * *

"So…" He took her cue and changed the subject, all business. "A real tree fetches a pretty good price in the city?"

Hanna nodded. "A king's ransom. Mistletoe is even more dear."

Oh, gee, did she *have* to bring up mistletoe? Around him, of all people?

"Oh, I know mistletoe is pricey," he said. "I bought some once."

"You have never bought a tree but you bought mistletoe?" Crazy to be curious, but she was. "Why?"

He looked off into the distance. "I think I had this cheesy idea that if I carried it around in my pocket I could haul it out and hold it over my head and collect lots of free Christmas kisses."

She felt a shiver along her spine at the thought of meeting Sam Chisholm under the mistletoe.

MEET ME UNDER THE MISTLETOE

BY
CARA COLTER

MILLS & BOON

Published in Great Britain 2014
by Mills & Boon, an imprint of Harlequin (UK) Limited,
Eton House, 18-24 Paradise Road, Richmond, Surrey, TW9 1SR

© 2014 Cara Colter

ISBN: 978-0-263-91338-5

23-1214

Harlequin (UK) Limited's policy is to use papers that are natural, renewable and recyclable products and made from wood grown in sustainable forests. The logging and manufacturing processes conform to the legal environmental regulations of the country of origin.

Printed and bound in Spain
by CPI, Barcelona

Cara Colter lives in British Columbia with her partner, Rob, and eleven horses. She has three grown children and a grandson. She is the recent recipient of an RT Book Reviews Career Achievement Award in the 'Love and Laughter' category. Cara loves to hear from readers, and you can contact her or learn more about her through her website: www.cara-colter.com.

To all my incredible new friends in New Zealand:
the Browns, the Burtons, the Emmersons,
the Pilkingtons and the Kalinowskis. Thank you.
Your genuine kindness and generosity
humbles and amazes.

CHAPTER ONE

"I QUIT!"

Hanna Merrifield held the phone away from her ear, and then tucked it in close again so her coworkers at the upscale accounting firm of Banks and Banks would not be disturbed by the loud, belligerent voice of her caller.

"Now, now, Mr. Dewey," she said, her tone conciliatory, "you can't just quit."

"Can't?" Mr. Dewey shouted, outraged. "Can't?"

"It's just that," Hanna said soothingly, resisting the temptation to hold the phone away again, "you would be leaving me in quite a pinch." Her eyes slid to her desktop calendar. "It's November thirtieth. Christmas is only weeks away."

"Hang Christmas."

That sentiment expressed how she had felt herself a million times or so. Hanna closed her eyes against the work, piled in neat stacks on her desk, each screaming its urgent deadline. *Not now,* she wanted to shout at Mr. Dewey, the manager of Christmas Valley Farm.

The farm had been in her family since the late 1800s. But Hanna had become the sole, and reluctant, owner of it upon the death of her mother six months ago.

Christmas Valley Farm. The place that she never wanted to go back to.

And it really, until this phone call, had looked like she might never have to.

"Isn't someone coming to look at it tomorrow?" she reminded Mr. Dewey. "A potential buyer?" She didn't add *finally*. "If you could just hang on until the showing, give me a chance to find someone else to manage it, I would be most appreciative—"

"Have a listen to this." A terrible noise came over the phone line: the screeching of tires and blaring of horns.

"What on earth?"

"It's that damn pony. Evil, she is. She's out on the road again. I'm done. I'm done with the midget horse, I'm done with people knocking on my cottage door day and night demanding trees and wreaths and sleigh rides. I'm done with all the ho-ho-ho and merriment. I hate it all, and the dwarf horse, Molly, the most."

Really, he was summing up the way Hanna herself had often felt growing up on the Christmas tree farm. But that feeling of being exhausted and fed up and one hundred percent done with all things Christmas didn't come at the beginning.

Her resentments—about all the work, and all the demands, and the elf costume, and her father's new and inventive gimmicks to sell trees and wreaths—piled up by the end of the frantic weeks leading to Christmas.

"Mr. Dewey," Hanna said tentatively, "Have you been drinking?"

"I have, but not nearly as much as I plan to be."

And with that, the phone went dead in Hanna's hands. She called back instantly—surely he didn't intend to leave Molly in the middle of the highway—but Mr. Dewey did not pick up.

She sat at her desk for a moment, completely paralyzed. A horse loose on the highway. And no manager on the farm's best—well, only—twenty-four income-earning days?

The farm's profits had dwindled over the past decade, but still rose in Hanna's throat when she thought of trying to meet those expenses herself.

The place *had* to sell. It was more imperative now than ever. She would have to meet the buyer tomorrow herself. Maybe that would be a good thing. She couldn't imagine Mr. Dewey, in his current frame of mind, doing the best job of presenting the farm for sale.

Then what? Hanna asked herself. She could not take the weeks until Christmas off work. She forced herself to breathe.

One thing at a time.

It was a two-hour drive to the farm in upstate New York. The cantankerous Molly could well be dead by the time Hanna reached there.

Hanna had the uncharitable thought—one she was sure she shared with Mr. Dewey—that Molly's demise could be nothing but a blessing. Maybe, if the pony was gone, he could even be convinced to come back to work.

It was a mark of her desperation that she would want him back.

But, right now, she had other worries. One thing working in a huge accounting firm had taught her?

Liability, liability, liability.

"I'm so sorry," Hanna stammered to Mr. Banks, a few minutes later, "I have to leave. Family emergency." This was, technically, not quite true, as she no longer had a family.

Or, she reminded herself sadly, any hope of one. Her fiancé, Darren, had broken off their engagement not a month after the death of her mom.

Not that she wanted to be thinking of that right now.

She had the immediate problem of a pony in the middle of the road just waiting to rain lawsuits into her life.

Mr. Banks did not look the least sympathetic. He pulled his glasses down on his nose and looked disapprovingly over the tops of them at her.

Since the end of her relationship, Hanna had been putting in twelve-and fourteen-hour days. Her work had been filling all the spaces in her life, and quite satisfactorily, too.

She had become Mr. Banks's darling, and she knew she was, at the moment, his first choice for the promotion coming up.

"How long will you be gone?" he asked sharply.

"Twenty-four hours," Hanna said rashly.

He considered this, and then sighed as if she was a big disappointment to him. "Not a minute more," he said sternly.

Her promotion now seemed to be in at least as much danger as Molly on the highway!

Her life, just a few months ago, had felt so comfortably solid, as though her future was chiseled in stone. Advancing nicely in her job, planning her wedding…but now everything seemed to be the way she hated it the most: totally up in the air.

Sam Chisholm turned his wipers on a higher speed as the fat snowflakes plopped on his windshield and melted. The early winter storm was thickening. Snow was gathering heavily in the boughs of evergreen trees, and drifting in white mounds along the road.

This part of rural upstate New York was Christmas-card–pretty, and the storm, despite presenting some driving challenges, was only adding to the charm of the picture.

Rolling hills were frosted in thick white. Golden light spilled out of farmhouse windows, casting shadows on towering barns. Cows and horses were dark silhouettes against the snowy backdrop. Sam's car passed over quaint bridges that crossed creeks as silver as Christmas-tree tinsel.

He knew this area of the country, but time had a way of changing things and he was beginning to wonder if he had missed the driveway.

There it was.

Christmas Valley Farm.

He'd almost passed right by it, and his shrewd businessman's mind made note that the sign had faded, and it was not lit. He was no kind of expert on Christmas trees—or Christmas for that matter—but presumably people might want to choose their tree in the evening. He glanced at his watch. The darkness of the night suggested midnight, but it was only eight o'clock.

Sam turned in sharply enough to feel his car skid a touch. There was a For Sale sign, even less visible and more faded than the farm sign. There were also fresh tire tracks through the snow, and he could see where the other vehicle had fishtailed on the slippery ground.

He felt his own tires hesitate, trying to find purchase on the slick track. He had an appointment. He would have thought, in the interest of making a good impression—not to mention the convenience of customers doing early Christmas shopping—the drive would be plowed.

Suddenly, an apparition materialized on the drive to the right of him. A creature, gnomelike and hooded, hunched against the storm, led a fat pony toward the golden glow of a distant barn.

It was another Christmas-card–worthy picture, except

that when it was caught in the sweep of his headlights, the pony started, and leapt onto the track in front of Sam's vehicle. The gnome didn't have the good sense to let go, and went to its knees, and was dragged along the ground.

Sam had been creeping along, but when he punched his brakes, he felt the car slide, then heard the sickening thump.

Sam slammed to full halt, and leaped from his vehicle and raced around the front. The gnome was on its knees, untouched by the vehicle, spitting out snow. A tubby, dun-colored pony with a scruffy black mane, snow caught in a shaggy coat, was nearly beneath his bumper.

It wagged its fur-and-snow-matted legs in the air, then grunted, and leapt to its feet. It gave him a look that appeared to be loaded with malice before it staggered to one side of the road and glared balefully back at them. Sam moved toward it, but the pony shuffled away, backing up one step for his every step forward.

"Don't try and catch her—she'll bolt," the kneeling gnome said, in a surprisingly feminine voice.

The gnome was right. When he stopped, the pony stopped. He had more immediate things that needed his attention, anyway.

"Are you all right?" Sam dropped to his knees in the snowbank beside her. "Why on earth didn't you let go when the damn thing bolted? It nearly dragged you right in front of the car!"

"If it hadn't taken me an hour and half to catch her, I might have!"

Something about the tone, annoyed and clipped, and yet husky and smooth, sent a little shiver along Sam's spine. He reached for the hood and brushed it back, aware he was holding his breath.

The hood fell away, and Sam found himself staring

into the most beautiful eyes he'd ever seen. They were an astonishing hazel, part brown, part green, part gold.

He should have started breathing again, but he didn't. Her hair, light brown, turned to honey as it caught the distant light from the barn. It tumbled out from under the hood. It looked to Sam as if her hair might have started the day piled up on top of her head, not a strand daring to be out of place. Now, part of it had escaped its band and part of it had not, and it hissed with static from the hood being pulled away.

Recognition stole his breath away.

Hanna Merrifield was all grown up, and she was not in the least gnome-like.

CHAPTER TWO

SAM REGARDED HANNA with astounded awareness. Under a ridiculously large and cumbersome plaid jacket—she had obviously thrown it on over the top of what looked to be a beautifully tailored black slack suit—she was lovely, and slender, and surprisingly curvy in all the right places given that slenderness.

She glared at the pony in frustration, running her fingers through the lush tangle of her burnished hair, scraping a mat of snow from it, but failing to restore her locks to any kind of order.

Despite the wildness of her hair, her makeup was subtle and expert: a hint of green shadow bringing out the spectacular hazel of eyes that were enormous with a combination of both fright and annoyance at the moment.

She had a touch of gloss on her mouth that made her lips look plump and kissable. Sam remembered, suddenly and in almost excruciating detail, the flavor and texture and warmth and invitation of those lips.

He realized his hand was still resting at the edge of her hood, and he snapped it down by his side. He noticed she had a brush of color on high cheekbones—from the crisp air or chasing the pony or an expert hand with a makeup brush—he couldn't be sure.

But in a face that was otherwise winter-pale, her skin

as delicate as porcelain, the color on her cheekbones made them look sculpted and accentuated the breathtaking perfection of her face. It occurred to him that once she had been cute. That cuteness had transformed into beauty.

"Hanna. Hanna Merrifield," he said, and then ran a hand through his own hair, sending melted snow flying. "Mr. Dewey told me you didn't live here anymore. He said you haven't lived here for years."

"I haven't, I don't," she said, a slight tremor in her voice, more shaken than she was letting on.

"Then what are you doing here?"

"Mr. Dewey quit two hours ago, though I'm hoping by morning he will have reconsidered. He let me know the pony was loose on the highway."

Hanna would, he knew, be super annoyed to know that despite the polished perfection of her makeup and hair, and the clear indication of education in her voice, he still saw the girl who had been pressed into service as a Christmas elf to help with selling trees, visits with Santa, and pony-pulled sleigh rides on her family's Christmas tree farm.

Maybe it was because the too-large parka over her suit reminded him of her as an elf all those years ago. The boots, comical in their largeness, obviously did not belong to her either, but added to the impression of a child playing the grown-up.

He remembered, suddenly, as clearly as if were yesterday, the day he had seen her in her green elf costume in her father's Christmas tree lot. She had probably been all of fifteen.

It was the first time he'd ever noticed the girl who went to the same high school as he did, but was in the grade behind him, and therefore invisible.

But in that elf suit? Anything but invisible. Cute and comical, but with the length of her legs being shown off by the shortness of the green tunic, there had been just a whisper of something else...

She'd been mortified that he and his friends had seen her, and if he had been then the man he was now, he would have possibly had the grace to pretend the encounter had never happened.

But he had just been a boy himself, and after that day, he had not been able to resist teasing her when their paths crossed. He had liked seeing her looking flustered and adorable, spitting at him like a cornered barn kitten.

But then, he reminded himself, she had shown him she had some claw, and that was a lesson about Hanna Merrifield that he would do well to remember.

Her focus moved off the pony, and she was regarding him intently now, curious how he had known her, and then recognition dawned in her features.

"Sam?" she asked, and it was evident she was as stunned by this unexpected reunion as he was. "Sam Chisholm?"

"One and the same."

Hanna Merrifield's fingers combed through the lushness of her thick hair once more, and she sent a flustered look and a frown at the clumsy boots on her feet, and muttered, "Oh, sheesh."

Sam raised an eyebrow at her and she flushed.

"A person just wants to make a good impression when they meet someone from their past," she said, tossing her head a bit defensively. Then she bit her lip, regretting having said it, even though it was true. "I'm an accountant. Banks and Banks."

Sam realized she was trying to divorce herself from the very image that had first leapt into his mind: of Hanna as an adorable Christmas elf. Still, he tried not to look too shocked. Hanna, an accountant?

"Why on earth didn't you let go of the pony?"

"Easy for you to say," she said, tearing her gaze away from her boots, and glaring sideways at the pony. "I'd just caught her."

Was Hanna cradling one of her hands in the other? "Did you do something to your hand?"

"It's nothing," she said.

"I seem to remember pony frustrations in your past," he said, and earned himself a sharp look that clearly said *I'm an accountant now. I just told you.*

"It's the same pony," she said, reluctantly and not at all fondly. "And now she's on the loose again."

His fault entirely, from Hanna's tone of voice.

"Well, she doesn't appear to be going anywhere. Can I have a look at your hand?"

"No. And she never appears to be going anywhere. She's not fond of wasted motion. She's saving all her energy for when I make another attempt to catch her."

Against his better judgment, Sam held out his hands to her. He noticed she reached out with only one. Still, he could feel the warmth of that hand rising past the Merino wool of a very good glove. He set his legs against the slippery footing, and then pulled Hanna to her feet.

They stood regarding one another. He looked for signs that she had changed, and despite the cut of her *I'm-an-accountant-now* suit and the passage of nine years, he found very few. If he was to wipe away that faint dusting of makeup, Hanna Merrifield would look much the same as she had looked at fifteen. The bone structure that had promised great beauty had delivered.

Except there was something faintly bruised about her eyes, like she carried sorrow around with her, which Sam

knew she did. It made him want to squeeze her unin-
jured hand, which he realized, uncomfortably, he was
still holding.

"I'm sorry about your mom," he said, and gave in to
the impulse to offer comfort. He gave her hand a quick,
hard squeeze before dropping it. "Wasn't it six months
ago now?"

Hanna nodded. She was looking down at her hand as
if even through her glove she had felt the same nearly
electrical jolt as him.

Sam shoved his own hands in the deep pockets of his
long, leather jacket.

"I'm also sorry about nearly running you down. You
and the pony just seemed to materialize out of the night.
Do you think the pony is all right?"

"I'm afraid so," she said gloomily, and he couldn't help
but smile at her tone. "She's the reason I'm out here. The
farm manager has just quit because of her dreadful antics.
Though I'm hoping I can talk him out of it."

Though he wondered about the wisdom of trying to
talk the manager out of quitting when he had obviously
left her in a complete pickle, Sam kept that to himself.

"Bad timing, isn't it?" he said. "Right before Christmas? His defection explains why the driveway isn't
plowed for customers."

"I don't think the tree stand or gift shop has been
open at night."

The businessman in him couldn't stop from comment-
ing, "But that's when it's convenient for people who work
during the day to shop."

"It's early in the season," Hanna said, a bit defensively, and then sighed. "You don't know the half of it."
Her gloom seemed to deepen.

"Why don't you tell me?" Sam told himself it was

purely his interest in the farm, and not any kind of interest in her, that made him want to know the details.

She hesitated, then shrugged. "Things have been different the last few years and the farm has been run by managers. It has been on a downward slide ever since."

Then she seemed to realize she did not want to confide in him after all, and bit down on that plump bottom lip.

Hanna pulled herself to her full height, which was not very high, maybe five foot four or five, and said with graceful polish, "And you, Sam? What are you doing in the driveway of Christmas Valley Farm on a night when it would seem wiser to stay inside and drink cocoa? Are you shopping for your Christmas tree?"

"I'm not exactly the stay-inside-and-drink-cocoa kind of guy," he said with a snort. "And I'm even less of a shopping-for-a-Christmas-tree kind of guy."

And he saw something flash through her eyes. Crazy to think it might be a memory of that one kiss they had shared so many years ago.

"I understand you've put the farm up for sale," he said. "I'm here as a prospective buyer."

"You?" Hanna could hear the disbelief in her voice, and she saw the hardness settle around his features at her tone.

Still, it *was* shocking. Sam Chisholm buying Christmas Valley Farm? The shock of it took her mind off the throb of dull pain in her hand that had been caused by hanging on to the pony's rope when she should have let go.

Though, now, too late, after the disbelieving words had come from her mouth, Hanna saw there were differences between this man and the one she remembered from years ago.

Sam Chisholm's shoulders, gathering snow on them

already, were immense under a tailored long coat that was not buttoned. It was the kind of coat people around here did not wear: a beautiful dark leather, turned up at the collar. He had a plaid scarf casually threaded under the collar of the coat.

Would she have recognized this man if she had passed him on the street? Of course, she had the fleeting thought that if they were going to meet unexpectedly, she would have much rather passed him on the street.

In her rush to get home to deal with the Molly emergency, Hanna had not packed proper farm wear.

So she stood before this gloriously attractive man in a too-large mackinaw of her father's, and boots that may have been her father's too, which she had found still standing at the back door of the farmhouse though he had been gone for years.

Her fault that her father, too young for such things, had collapsed in his tracks, hands over the heart that had exploded in his chest? The heart that she had broken.

The thought blasted through Hanna. Her life in the city was so full, so busy. Planning for the wedding, her pace had become even more frantic. She hadn't had time for thoughts like that. And she had loved the fact that her life was too full for thoughts of the past. Maybe that was why, even now, she filled every spare second with work…

The guilt she had been running from seemed to have settled over her like a cloud as soon as she had opened the back door of the farm, stuffy from being shut up for so long.

Easier to focus on the distraction of Sam Chisholm than the guilt she knew had been waiting for this moment: her return to her childhood home after a six-year absence.

Sam looked deeply sophisticated, and gave off the unconscious air of wealth and control. He also radiated a certain power that went beyond the perfection of his physique, that perfection obvious even beneath the line of that expensive jacket.

His hair was devil's food-dark, cut short and neat. His face was clean-shaven and exquisitely handsome: wide-set eyes, straight nose, honed jawline, strong chin with just the faintest and sexiest hint of a cleft in it. His lips were full and sensual, and there was something faintly intimidating about the set of them.

But right underneath those surface impressions of strength and confidence lurked a certain roguish charm— of a pirate or a highwayman. In fact, that remembered rogue seemed to dance in the darkness of those eyes, so brown they appeared black in the shadowed light of the snowy night.

"You don't think I'm a suitable buyer for your farm?" he asked, those dark eyes piercing her. His voice was faintly amused, but challenging at the same time.

His voice reminded her of a large cat: a growl that could be pure sensuality, or could be danger, or some lethal combination of both. It had an almost physical quality to it, as if sandpaper had whispered across the nape of her neck.

Hanna registered, as a sad afterthought to her sizzling awareness of how damned attractive Sam was, that she had managed to insult the only prospective buyer the farm had seen since it was listed six months ago. And she'd unwittingly revealed its slow decline to him, as well.

"I'm sorry," Hanna said hastily. "No insult was intended."

"None was taken," he said, but his voice remained the pure raw silk of a gunslinger just as prepared to draw as to smile.

"I can see you've changed," she said, but the brightness in her voice felt forced. In truth she felt a certain unfathomable loss at the change in him. "You are certainly not the renegade boy I remember, though I must say you don't strike me as any kind of a farmer."

The sense of him having changed in some fundamental way was underscored by the deep confidence in his voice. And by the way he was dressed, which backed up what she had just said about him not being a farmer.

She had a sense of being very aware of him, as if she was tingling all over, maybe because of the jolt she had felt when he had taken her hand.

Likely just static, she told herself firmly. *Or the chill of the night penetrating her clothing.*

Or maybe not. The lights from the headlamps of his car had illuminated them in an orb of pure gold. His breath was making puffs in the crisp air.

Hanna had the oddest and most delicious sense of breathing him in.

CHAPTER THREE

SAM DID CUT a breathtaking picture, standing here in the crisp chill of a winter evening, his hands deep in his coat pockets. His coat was undone, and his look underneath it was casual, but not casual in the way that was interpreted around here, certainly not *farmer*-casual.

No, around here, in the rural community that surrounded the upstate New York village of Smith, casual was plaid shirts and faded jeans, work boots and ball caps.

Sam's casual was more in keeping with Hanna's life in the city, a look that could have taken him for drinks at an upscale club after work or to the theatre or to dinner at any of New York's finest restaurants.

He was wearing a long-sleeved, creamy shirt, which looked to her like fine linen. With its thin blue pinstripe, the perfectly pressed shirt looked casually expensive. It was open at the strong column of his throat, and tucked into knife-creased, belted, dark slacks that definitely did not look as if they had come off the rack at a chain store.

"Renegade?" he asked, lifting a dark slash of an eyebrow at her.

Was there a nice way to say he looked very respectable now? Back then, respectability was what she—or anyone else—would have least predicted for him.

They had done a silly thing in the Smith High School

Annual every year: under each photo of a graduating student, it had said *Most likely to*...sometimes flattering, but mostly not.

Most likely to become president, most likely to make a million, most likely to rob a bank.

She recalled Sam's had said *Most likely to sail the seven seas.*

Just a silly thing, and yet, those few words had captured something of him: a restlessness, a need for adventure, a call to the unknown.

Of course her own, in her senior year, before she had left Smith forever, had said *Most likely to become a nun* and how ridiculously inaccurate had that proven?

Sam had been older than her by a year, the heartthrob of every single girl in Smith Senior High School, so he had graduated and gone before her own senior picture had appeared in the annual.

"You aren't going to deny that, are you? That you were, uh, something of a renegade?" It occurred to her it might have been better to pretend she could barely remember him at all, but she simply wasn't that good at pretending.

Sam had been a force unto himself then, and she suspected he still was. Even though he had just hit a pony with his car, he looked entirely unflustered, radiating a kind of self-certainty that was immensely attractive rather than off-putting.

"Something of a renegade" was an understatement. Sam Chisholm had been an absolute renegade, which of course, had only added to his lethal charm.

It looked to Hanna as if he was still dangerously and lethally charming, even if he claimed to have left a part of himself behind.

The thing was, she was not sure you could leave something like the person he used to be behind. The essence of it was still clinging to him, and it was like a nectar of wild enchantment that called to her and that could not be resisted.

She of all people should resist its pull, and frantically. But she could not. Hanna reluctantly gave herself over to remembering Sam.

Even back then, a senior in high school, Sam Chisholm hadn't been in sync with the town of Smith's sense of style.

He had favored faded jeans so worn that nothing was left but white threads over the large muscles in his thighs, and below the back pocket of his butt.

He had sported the world's sexiest leather jacket, the leather distressed by real age and wear. He had worn that jacket through all seasons, even when it was far too cold for it. He had arrived at school in a rumble of noise, and often blue smoke, on an old motorbike.

He'd never ever worn a helmet, his too-long deep brown, silky hair always raked by the fingers of the wind, his features always made even more attractive by the fact they were kissed by sun and the elements.

"A renegade?" he asked again now. Sam raised a dark brow at her. She could not really tell if he was amused or annoyed.

"A renegade," she said with prim firmness, a voice very well suited to *Most Likely to Become a Nun,* a voice that would never give away the fact she had found the wild version of him to be unreasonably sexy and that she had given in to the pull of remembering him with a nary a protest.

From the brief touch of his hand on hers just moments ago, he still had that mystical *something* that just made some men sexy and almost unbearably so.

He was dangerous to her, part of Hanna shouted. Danger, danger, danger. He was the kind of man who made a woman who had given up on love—after all, she had been jilted by her fiancé while she was still raw from the death of her mother—long for the very things she had sworn to harden herself against.

It made an eminently reasonable woman such as herself, who had vowed to dodge the wounding arrows of love by burying herself in her work, think unwanted thoughts of looks so heated they could scorch through to the soul, and breath coming in ragged, wanton gasps, and the silken caress of forbidden kisses...

It was because she had once tasted the nectar of his kiss, she warned herself, that she was being drawn back into the wild and dangerous enchantment of him.

Embarrassed by her weakness, Hanna remembered all too clearly how she had been caught in this particular spell once before.

"What made you arrive at that conclusion?" he asked.

"Which one?" she stammered, thinking remembered kisses must be showing in her face.

"That I was a renegade?" he reminded her.

"Oh, really!" she said annoyed. "Of course you were one. Anybody with a motorcycle in a place where tractors—and ponies for that matter—are more common, would be seen as a renegade headed straight for a life of debauchery."

He actually laughed at that, and Hanna had to inwardly kick herself for *liking* his laughter.

And liking, too, the look of unguarded fondness that now crept across his handsome features. "Ah, my motorcycle, that old Harley-Davidson Panhead. Did you know I rescued it from a dump? And restored it myself? As much as I could, anyway. I seem to remember being stranded by the side of the road a lot. And none of those guys driving those tractors that you mentioned would stop and give me a hand, either."

"The leather jacket sent out danger signals—clearly you were seen as a threat to the wholesome, country image of the town of Smith, poster child for an all-American town."

Again that look of tenderness softened the features of Sam's face. "I remember when I saw that jacket in a store window, saving up money to buy it that could have been better used for..."

His voice drifted away, and the look of fondness faded abruptly. In fact, he looked suddenly annoyed with himself. "I'm sure I was not the rebel you recall."

"But you were. Sam Chisholm, you were the town of Smith's answer to James Dean."

"I suppose," he said, his tone dry, "it must have appeared like that to you, the town of Smith's answer to wholesome all-American girl."

He would not have seen the high school annual that proclaimed her *Most Likely to Become a Nun*, but seeing her as the proverbial, sheltered, wholesome girl next door was just about the same thing.

But of course, he did not know the truth about her. Everyone had thought that she was so good and pure and could do no wrong. And she had let everyone down.

Of course, most just believed she had gone away after graduation, called, as so many rural young people were, by the bright lights and lure of the big city. The truth remained one of her most closely guarded secrets.

The truth that had left her father clutching at his heart on the pathway to his beloved Christmas Workshop.

"There was plenty of evidence you were wild," Hanna told Sam, suddenly most anxious to stay focused on his past rather than her own, "It wasn't just my perception, a girl looking at you through the eyes of complete innocence."

Innocence that would soon enough be lost in the incident that had destroyed her family and had kept her from ever coming back here.

"Evidence?" he said, his tone mocking. "You need a little more than a motorcycle and a leather jacket to be a rebel."

"You were always being kicked out of school. For smoking—"

"I'd forgotten that," he said with a half smile. "I still sneak the occasional smoke, but rarely. Only when I'm stressed."

Why did she care? Unbidden came a memory of that one time, when she, the good girl, had done the most unexpected thing of all. She had boldly tasted his lips. She did not remember anything about smoke, just something delicious and forbidden unfurling within her.

"And fighting," she continued, hearing that prudish note deepen in her voice, a defense against the power of that memory of their lips joining, that sense of the universe shifting and aligning, of all being right in her world, when it had been such a *wrong* thing to do.

And if she recalled, and she did, he had been very quick to point that out to her, too. What had he said?

Don't start fires you can't put out.

Hanna could actually feel her cheeks burning at the memory, but Sam's mind, thankfully, was apparently not on stolen kisses. Far from it, evidently.

"Ah," he said reminiscently. "I did enjoy a good fight. But only if I won."

"I recall you always winning."

He lifted a lazy eyebrow at her, and she knew she had

probably revealed more than she wanted to about her girl-
ish days of dreaming about him.

"And drinking," she said swiftly, inserting the stern
note back into her voice.

"You're mistaken there. I did not drink then, nor do I
drink now." His voice had gone taut.

"So," Hanna said, her own tone deliberately light,
"just now, you nearly killed the pony and me stone-cold
sober?"

He laughed, reluctantly. "Guilty."

"And for skipping school," she finished, triumphantly.
"You were always being suspended because you skipped
classes."

The laughter left him instantly. "I did do a lot of that,"
he admitted.

"Why?" Her curiosity felt like a form of weakness,
but it really did seem, around him, that she had always
suffered one form of weakness or another.

He considered her carefully for a moment, and she
was aware his gaze was suddenly shuttered. "It's really
not important anymore," he said.

And he was so right. It was *not* important anymore.
Hanna was not the same person she had been back then—
far from it—and neither was he.

He would probably be shocked by the direction her
life had taken after he had left Smith, how the girl he
had called "Goody Two-shoes" had managed to be such
a tragic disappointment.

"Are you sure you're all right?" he said, and stepped
toward her. He looked down into her face and concern
furrowed his brow. "Your hand still hurts, doesn't it?"

Though it had been nearly nine years since she had
laid eyes on Sam, looking into the quiet strength of his
face, she felt a sense of familiarity, of knowing him.

"Yes," she said, "it does."

He took her arm, having seen all along which one she was favoring. He slid her glove off her hand, and turned it over in his own.

"That looks nasty," he said, and Hanna glanced down to see her hand was already swollen and discolored. The pony rope must have caught in between her fingers and her thumb and scraped the skin away.

But the pain seemed numbed by the warmth of his thumb making a circle in the cold palm of her hand.

It felt as if her whole world dissolved into a forbidden sense of longing, the present melting into the past as Hanna experienced the same feverish awareness that Sam had always created in her.

The first time she had ever seen him, she had been in her first year of high school, and he'd been in his last. Naturally, he hadn't known she was alive. And she would have been quite happy to keep it that way.

Worshipping him—his beautiful confidence, his way of moving, the unconsciously sexy light in his eyes, and in the upward twist of his mouth—from afar.

But, to her eternal regret, it had *not* stayed that way. He had noticed her, under the very worst of circumstances, and it had all just gone downhill from there.

When other boys struggled with acne and awkwardness, Sam had always walked like a king.

It was the Christmas he and some friends had shown up at the farm. That year, as always, her father had, in his never-ending quest to attract more people to buy real Christmas trees, shoveled off the old pond and advertised free skating and free hot chocolate.

Hanna remembered, sourly, that when they had added it all up in the end, it had, as always, barely balanced out.

Still, wasn't it that final tally of the season where her love of the order of numbers had been born?

But Sam and some of his friends, skates slung over their shoulders, had shown up at Christmas Valley.

Also that year, gritting her teeth and doing her bit for the family business, just as she had every year since she'd been twelve, Hanna had put on the green elf costume. When she was twelve she had *liked* contributing, being a part of the excitement of Christmas. She had loved the fact that her father had given her the cutest pony, Molly, and they were going to be a Christmas team: an elf offering rides in a minisleigh to children.

But by that year, at fifteen, Hanna had not been a compliant elf, but an awkward teenager. While her need for her father's approval had kept her from being overtly rebellious, she had been humiliated by the elf costume, and seriously jaundiced about the whole Christmas thing.

That year it felt as if the blinders had come off her eyes. Christmas had seemed less about wonder and magic than endless work and chaos, and ultimately, when they counted up the receipts, disappointment.

Even Molly, whom she had managed to love unconditionally up until that point, just seemed like a mean-spirited little beast whom Hanna had to be constantly vigilant with as the pony had a terrible tendency to nip small children.

Still, her father overrode her protests and no amount of sulking, begging and outright crying could convince him she had outgrown her job as the Christmas elf.

And just like a Christmas elf, she was needed everywhere on the farm. When she wasn't shoveling snow off that rink, she was in the workshop flogging wreaths and mistletoe. Or she was in the gift shop selling nauseatingly cute Christmas bric-a-brac. Or she was in the lots, shaking snow off racks and racks of trees. Or guiding people down the aisles of live trees. Or giving sleigh rides, the sleigh pulled by the always evil-natured Molly.

The elf costume had been the worst part of all of it, and all of it had been bad: endless work, smelling of pine, the stubborn Molly trying to bite children, her father's latest crazy idea of an attraction to get people in.

Oh, yes, by the time Hanna Merrifield was fifteen, Christmas had totally lost its magic for her.

And then Sam had seen her in the elf getup. She had instantly abandoned the pony that she had just been putting on the harness to offer a horribly misbehaved child a ride.

Hanna had made a run for it as soon as she had seen Sam and his friends pile out of Tom Brenton's pickup truck, but it was too late. They had seen her. Their hooted calls had followed her mad dash for the safety of the house.

She had heard Sam's voice, above the others. Not hooting.

"Shut up, you guys." Strong, firm, mature. "You're embarrassing her."

Which was even worse, of course, than the hooting. As Hanna had closed the farmhouse door behind her, and leaned against it, she had been aware of the horrifying fact that her secret heartthrob now saw her as an object of pity.

CHAPTER FOUR

IF IT HAD ended there, with a silly moment in time quickly forgotten by everyone involved, that would have been excellent.

But no, having been caught in her elf costume had unfortunate consequences. It made Hanna no longer invisible to Sam. When he saw her at school the next time, he grinned that slow, sexy grin of his, and said, "Hey, Elfie, how's it going?"

Apparently, after coming to her defense with his friends, it was okay for him to embarrass her.

So, her first words to her secret heartthrob were, "Don't call me that."

But he'd just grinned, and the next time he'd seen her, he'd said the very same thing. "Hey, Elfie, how's it going?"

She thought he was making fun of her. And her family's farm. By the time school was letting out for Christmas, she was on edge: she was tired of the elf costume, tired of making wreaths, tired of sales figures that were, as always, mediocre in the face of her father's beginning-of-the-season optimism.

Added to all that, "Hey, Elfie, how's it going?" had grown into yet more teasing. In those days before school ended for Christmas break, Sam called her his favorite

Goody Two-shoes. He asked after her homework. He teased her about doing his.

Her girlfriends were totally titillated by his attention to her. Hanna had *hated* it. She was desperate for Sam to see her not as an amusing child but as a woman.

She could still remember the feeling of his dark eyes on her, the shiver along her spine, the desire to be seen as anything but Elfie or Goody Two-shoes.

And so, in a moment of total desperation, she had decided she must show him that she was not a child. She, the least impulsive of people, had acted on pure impulse.

He had been outside the door of the school, his backside leaning against his motorcycle, his hair ruffled. Who rode a motorcycle in December? And with panache, besides? That day, school had been over, and she had been late coming out.

"Detention, my little Elfie?" he'd asked incredulously, his dark eyebrows lifting over those soft-as-suede eyes. Strangely, he had not seemed amused. In fact, his eyes had narrowed to slits, as if he would personally go take on anyone who had treated her unjustly, even if it was a teacher.

There had been no other students around, the parking lot empty of vehicles, the buses gone for the day. Maybe that was why Hanna hadn't ignored him or ducked her head, and grasped her books tighter to her chest and scurried away. Or maybe it was the protective look in his eyes that had made it feel safe to stop.

She had said, with all the dignity she could muster, and over the hard beating of her heart, "I am not *your* little Elfie." And then, in the interest of seeming very adult and perhaps even sophisticated, she had added in her haughtiest tone of voice. "I was, in fact, discussing iambic pentameter with Miss James."

The dangerous glitter of amusement had left his face. For a moment, Hanna thought she had succeeded. Sam had been totally silent, expressionless.

But then he had bitten his bottom lip. His shoulders had started to shake.

And then he seemed unable to contain himself. He had thrown back his head and roared with laughter.

Other than the fact Sam's laughter was about the most beautiful thing she had ever experienced—and it was an experience on so many levels—the fact that he was laughing *at* her had felt unbearable.

She had thrown down her school books and stalked over to him. So close. So close she could smell the leather of his jacket and the heady scent of his soap, and the faint engine and exhaust smells of the motorcycle.

He stopped laughing, but the amusement was back in his eyes, dancing, as they both waited to see what she would do.

Obviously, she should have smacked him.

But she didn't. Obviously, she had failed, utterly, to convince him of her maturity by opening a discussion on iambic pentameter.

This close to him, she felt intoxicated. Iambic pentameter was the furthest thing from her mind, even if this was the kind of moment that had probably driven poets to create since the beginning of time.

Hanna felt a *need* to let him know she was not a dull little scholar who had temporarily enlivened his world, provided amusement for him by putting on an elf costume and trying to engage him with discussions of poetry.

She felt a need to let him know her days of being an amusement to him were over.

She had needed to let him know she was not the child the elf outfit had implied that she was.

And so, seeing the astonishment in his eyes, she had leaned closer. And then she had taken the lapels of that leather jacket and pulled him into her.

There had been the slightest resistance to her tug.

But she had ignored it.

And she had, in one moment of misguided boldness, done what she had done a million times in her dreams.

She had kissed Sam Chisholm.

She, who had never kissed anyone, had taken his lips with her own, and covered them. For a moment he had been stunned into stillness, but only for a moment.

Then his hand had rested, lightly, as lightly as though he were stroking a bird, on the back of her neck, and he had brought her gently and more fully into him. Any illusions that she'd had that a kiss was merely a chaste meeting of the lips were swept away.

The initial frosty chill on his lips melted into warmth, and then warmth became heat, and then heat became fire.

Sam explored her, discovered her with a leisurely thoroughness. What he didn't know, and she didn't know either, was until that moment she had not been fully alive. Sam had breathed his life into her.

And then, way too soon, he reeled back from her, and stared at her, and the chill crept back across her lips and into his eyes, that were narrow again, darkly angry.

"Look, mistletoe girl—"

Mistletoe girl? Hanna thought furiously. It was another dig at her family's Christmas tree farm, and it made her feel as if she was standing in front of him in the elf costume once again.

"—don't play with a fire you can't put out," he warned her, his voice stern and flat, and his brown eyes turned black. "You are heading for all kinds of trouble that you don't have the first clue how to deal with."

The anger at what she perceived as his rejection—as him acting like her father, instead of a potential boy-friend—chased the chill away again, for a far less satis-factory reason. Anger flared, white hot and consuming, inside her.

It was made worse by the fact he pushed off from his bike, and gathered her fallen books, held them out to her casually, as if nothing at all of importance had happened between them.

As if he, the town bad boy, was a gentleman who had spurned her kiss for her own good.

"As if I would ever start a fire with the likes of you," she had snapped, grabbing her books from his out-stretched arms and holding them like armor against her heaving chest.

She could have and should have left it there, but he had cocked his head at her, unperturbed by her anger, forcing her to go on.

"I know where you live, Sam Chisholm, and I know what your father does."

It had been so childish, proof really that he was en-tirely correct, that she was not in the least ready for what his lips had just told her existed in the world.

Looking at the man now, she could still remember the look on his face back then.

It was about the furthest thing from the look he had now: of confidence and composure, a man in control of his world.

No, that afternoon, her words had hit him hard, dashed that self-assured look from his face. He had momentarily looked completely stunned. And then his face had gone cold as he had leaned once again, his rear against his motorbike, regarding her with those turned-earth eyes narrowed to dangerous slits.

Because here was what she knew about his father, since her own father hired him sometimes to work on their farm.

Sam Chisholm's father was a drunk, who took work as a farm laborer if anyone was desperate enough to hire him.

The school's sexiest boy lived in the most dilapidated trailer on the worst road in Smith, the one right by the railway tracks and the shut-down flour mill.

His face had gone cold as ice, and he'd looked at her hard enough and long enough for her to feel ashamed, but not to take back words that could not be taken back.

And now he was back in Smith, and she was back in Smith, and he wanted her family's farm and presumably had the means to buy it.

Was it a moment of vindication for him?

"So, what do you want my farm for?" Hanna asked.

My farm? Where had that come from? Hanna had not thought of the farm as hers, or even as home, since she had left here—in disgrace that it seemed Sam might have been predicting that afternoon all those years ago when he had admonished her so sternly not to play with fire.

"I own Old Apple Crate. Maybe you've heard of it?"

It was a moment that should have brought Sam great pleasure, because Hanna struggled to hide her awe. Old Apple Crate was a model of success that was drooled over in business circles.

Relatively new on the business front, Sam's company specialized in locally grown produce, much of it organic. The company was taking advantage of people's desire to shop closer to home and know about what exactly they were getting, how it was grown and who grew it.

"I've heard of it, of course."

She noted he looked pleased, but not smug.

Really, he had no reason to be so pleased that she had heard of his company. She was in business. Success stories like his were what businesses like hers paid attention to.

"And Christmas Valley Farm would be a good fit for you because?"

"I like this property for two reasons—one, it's got a great location, with highway frontage. And two, to certify produce as organic, I need soil that hasn't been altered by chemicals for a specified number of years."

"So, you wouldn't keep it as a Christmas tree farm?" She evaluated the tone of her voice with a bit of dismay.

"Are you disappointed by that?" he asked.

Hanna wanted to say no, and found she couldn't. He had read her with alarming accuracy.

"Christmas tree sales," he said mullingly, as if to appease her. "Personally, I'm not a Christmas kind of person, but maybe professionally it could make sense."

Don't pursue it, Hanna begged herself. It was way too personal. But he was the one who had mentioned it.

"What does that mean, *not a Christmas kind of person?*" She had remembered he had also said something tonight about not even shopping for a tree. And not being a sipping cocoa kind of guy, either. So, despite his denial, he still was a bit of a renegade, out of step with the very kind of wholesome family image this business catered to.

Sam hesitated. When he spoke his voice was gruff, stripped of emotion.

"I always just felt, in that season of good cheer and merriment, I was on the outside looking in. We never even had a tree when I was a kid."

He looked as if he regretted having said that, instantly. She regretted his saying it, too, because it was hard enough keeping up your defenses around such a good-looking, confident man.

But then to picture him as a small child, feeling left out on Christmas, wrenched at Hanna's soft heart. "Oh, Sam, we always had some we gave away. Fully decorated. We had a contest every year. You could have had a tree."

He gave her an annoyed look that rejected her sympathy at the same time as letting her know the impossibility of what she was suggesting.

She felt driven to show him he might not be alone in his sentiments about Christmas.

And so Hanna offered something, too. "I'm not sure it was much better being on the inside looking out. I haven't bothered with a tree since I left here, either."

"Really?"

"I grew up believing *artificial* trees were the devil's own work, and somehow I couldn't bring myself to pay what they wanted for a real one in the city. Never mind working out the logistics of getting it home and thinking what to do with it in my tiny apartment once I got there."

It was, of course, way more complicated than that.

"Oh, well, I'm sure they always had a giant one up when you arrived home."

Easier to let him think they had remained the family he thought they were, and not to share the truth about that with him, and yet the words came out of her.

"My dad died the year after I finished high school. My mom remarried and moved away, which is why it was left to managers to run. This farm hasn't been home for me for quite some time. And Christmas...well, Christmas." Her voice drifted away.

He was looking at her way too closely. "I'm sorry," he said softly.

"Nothing to be sorry for," she said tartly.

"So," he took her cue and changed the subject, sud-denly all business, "a real tree fetches a pretty good price in the city?"

Hanna nodded. "A king's ransom. Mistletoe is even more dear."

Oh, gee, did she have to bring up mistletoe around him, of all people? she berated herself, silently cringing. *Mistletoe girl* seemed to suddenly be there between them.

"Oh, I know mistletoe is pricey," he said. "I bought some once."

Not remembering *mistletoe girl* at all then, but some-thing else, from the faraway look on his face.

"You have never bought a tree but you bought mistle-toe?" Crazy to be curious, but she was. "Why?"

He still looked off into the distance. "I think I had this cheesy idea that if I carried it around in my pocket, I could haul it out and hold it over my head, and collect lots of free Christmas kisses."

"Did it work?" She felt a shiver along her spine at the thought of meeting Sam under the mistletoe.

"Lost my nerve," he said, but she had a feeling she was not hearing all of this story, and she wasn't sure why.

"You know, mistletoe was popular around the turn of the last century because the only time people could kiss in public was underneath it. That would hardly seem to be the case today." *Least of all for a guy like him.*

But he was not going to have his personal kissing his-tory probed. His interest in mistletoe, now at least, was all about business.

"Do you grow that here?" he finally asked. "I remem-ber you selling it, all those years ago."

"No, we imported it," she said stiffly, "from a grower in Texas."

"Hmm. Mistletoe. Trees."

"Wreaths," she filled in helpfully, trying to stay focused on what was between them now, which was strictly business.

"I already have the stores, and keeping local product at the forefront can be a problem during the winter months. I wonder. I'll check on the viability of a line of Christmas products. It could be a good fit for our company."

Hanna was taken completely by surprise by what she felt when he said that, because it seemed to her any research on his part would only serve to seal the fate of the farm.

She already knew what he would find out. Christmas products of the natural, home-grown variety were not particularly viable. Or at least they hadn't been on her family's farm, certainly not in comparison to a success story like Old Apple Crate.

For as long as she could remember, her family's business had limped along from year to year, barely making ends meet.

And so why, at the thought of it not being a Christmas tree farm anymore, would she feel these emotions? Loss. Sadness. It seemed impossible. She should feel nothing but relief. And yet…that's not what she felt.

Not at all.

CHAPTER FIVE

HANNA WAS TRYING not to let all the feelings that were washing through her show on her face.

"That would be ironic," Sam said. "Me, getting into the Christmas tree business."

"And me getting out of it," she added softly. Out of the business, her last remaining link to her family. Good grief! She had the awful feeling she might start crying.

He was looking at her too closely and she turned away from him, acting as if she had just noticed she had a horse on the loose.

"You're here a day early," she said, her tone neutral. "You should come back tomorrow. I'll be ready for you, then."

She'd been in the house only briefly, to grab a jacket and boots, and she had barely glanced at the barn when she had run in to get a halter and lead rope. But even peripherally, it had been hard to miss that things looked a touch shabby. If she had until tomorrow at noon, when he was supposed to arrive, she could do a few cosmetic spruce-ups.

And talk to Mr. Dewey, and then be on her way.

"My appointment was for tonight," he said.

She certainly wasn't going to argue with his word against Mr. Dewey's.

"I have to catch the horse," Hanna said, fumbling through her pockets for the limp carrots she had found in the barn. "You know tonight just isn't going to be a good night to discuss business, Sam. If you could come back tomorrow, around noon?"

She left it hanging, realizing she wasn't sure when she wanted him to come back, which, given how eager she had felt to sell the farm, was just plain dumb.

But there was something about being back here, even with Molly misbehaving, that seemed to be pulling on a place in her that she hadn't thought she had anymore.

A place that *wanted*.

That wanted all the things she had lost a long time ago. Tradition. Family. The warmth of the kitchen at night. Cookies fresh out of the oven. A gathering around a board game. Laughter.

Maybe she even wanted the kind of Christmas her family had once had: yes, they had worked hard.

But they had worked together.

And Christmas had been the day the madness stopped, and they enjoyed the same things they had tried to give everyone else: a beautiful tree, a fire in the living room hearth, laughing around a turkey dinner, a sense of closeness and family that she had never recaptured since she had left the farm.

But hadn't she thought she and Darren would recapture all that was best about being a family? That they would have that sense of family and all that came with it, safety and security?

From what he had said, Sam hadn't even had that.

Every single year, Hanna remembered, *she had always gotten what she asked for. Even if sales had not gone well, there it was under the tree. The impossible: new skates, the down-filled parka, or a silk blouse. And*

*her dad smiling one of his rare smiles, with such shy,
proud pleasure.*

Oh, Dad, I am so sorry.

Those things, she reminded herself, when push had
come to shove, were the very things that had hurt her the
most. Love had hurt the worst of all.

And Sam had just reminded her of that, anew. That
love, that holding out hope and then having it utterly
dashed, was what hurt worst of all.

She suddenly *needed* Sam—with his double threat,
her awareness of him and the fact he could take the farm
and her remaining sense of family from her for good—
to be gone.

"Come back tomorrow," she said again to Sam, her
tone now clipped and much sharper than she wanted it
to be, "if that's convenient."

She turned toward Molly, proffering the carrots.

Sam did not take the hint. He came and took one of the
carrots from the bunch in her hand, uninvited.

"I can manage," she said too snappishly, and took a
step toward Molly, who snorted and leapt away.

"Maybe I better just stay until you have her under
control. I don't want you to hurt that hand any worse
than it already is."

And again, that forbidden place of *wanting* breathed itself awake within her. Wanting someone to lean on, someone to share with, someone to laugh with, someone to
love…

But when she looked at the fiasco of her now-ended
relationship with Darren, it seemed to Hanna all that
wanting had led her to a poor relationship choice; all
that wanting had left her vulnerable, weak instead of
strong, way too ready to read things into situations that
were not really there.

So she said uninvitingly, firmly, "I can manage on my own."

And she felt both exceedingly irritated and exceedingly vulnerable when Sam said, his voice a seductive croon, "Come on, sweetie. Give it up."

For a moment her heart stood still.

Then she threw back her shoulders and tossed her head. Sweetie, indeed! It was as bad as being called Elfie! She was not starting her *new* relationship with Sam Chisholm in the very same way as her old one.

No, wait. *Relationship* was way too strong. They *might* reach a business agreement. In the distant future.

But not if he was going to be like that. What did he mean, *give it up*? Give up what? Her precious hold on control?

Hanna sucked in a deep breath, and turned to face him. She meant to tell him in no uncertain terms not to call her sweetie, and to tell him she didn't intend to give up anything.

Maybe not even her family farm.

She was contemplating with alarm the troubling thought that she might be reluctant to part with the farm, when she realized Sam was totally ignoring her, and sidling toward Molly.

"Sweetie," he said again, his voice that same croon, though now there was absolutely no mistaking he was talking to the horse, "Give it up."

Sam held his breath as the pony took one tentative step toward him, and then another.

He glanced over his shoulder at Hanna. "Ah," he said, wagging an eyebrow at her, "that old irresistible charm."

That desire to tease her had come back to him as naturally as if nearly a decade had not passed.

And her reaction was about the same as it always had been. Hanna folded her arms over her chest. She was unaware she was favoring her hurt hand, and letting him know in no uncertain terms that his irresistible charm was wasted on her.

It suddenly occurred to Sam she might have thought he was calling her *sweetie*.

She wouldn't like that any more than she had liked being called Elfie. The very thought filled him with an almost irresistible urge to continue teasing her.

But then sanity regained its foothold and Sam knew the last thing he needed in his life was the complication of teasing a girl like Hanna Merrifield. She was the kind of girl who would see teasing as interest and interest as the potential for things to go deeper and further.

And he knew what deeper and further with her would mean.

She was the kind of woman who would deny she needed traditional things. But she would need them nonetheless. Hanna Merrifield would need an old-fashioned courtship, followed by a wedding with her floating down the aisle in a white gown. And then there would be babies and a house with a picket fence.

She would need a man who knew how to give her those things, as if by second nature. A man who had grown up with those concepts of family as ingrained into him as his own name.

Hanna's man, when she settled on one, would probably come from a farm not unlike this one, one that had been in the same family for generations, and had produced stable, trustworthy, hard-working men of the earth who liked sipping cocoa and bringing home the family tree for Christmas.

Even while the thought of those things created a physical sensation in him—a throbbing ache at the back of his throat— Sam was not like that man. In fact, he already knew he was the man least likely to give her the cozy traditional life—cocoa and the Christmas trees she had so obviously missed even while she denied herself the pleasure of having one—and he knew that because he had already failed, spectacularly, in the traditional department.

"I'm divorced," he told Hanna bluntly. There was no sense her thinking the teasing—or worse, the electricity that had jumped between them when their hands had touched—could ever mean anything.

He did not miss Hanna's slight flinch at the word *divorce*, confirming what he already knew.

"That would interest me, why?" she said coolly.

"I just know my charm to be completely superficial and unworthy of a girl like you. Don't worry about me trying to exercise it on you, though I don't mind trying it out on the pony."

Despite how she wanted to hold the fact that she was a career accountant out in front of her like a shield, he knew she was solidly traditional. Her dreams were written all over her.

"What do you mean, a girl like me?" she asked, her voice stiff, as if he'd insulted her instead of giving her a gift.

"You want things a guy like me could never give you, Hanna."

"I don't want you to give me anything! You don't know me well enough to make presumptions about what I want," she said huffily. "You never did, and you don't now."

He went on as if she had not protested. "You're a forever kind of girl. When you get married, you will never ever get divorced, will you?"

"I'm never getting married, so it's a stupid question."

"You? Never getting married?" It was too easy to picture her amongst the Christmas trees, with a doting husband, two or three chubby babies in a sled and a golden retriever gamboling through the snow. "That's ludicrous."

"It isn't," she said, tilting her chin up, her eyes flashing dangerously. "Just because I never made it to the altar doesn't mean that you are the only one with a failed relationship under your belt. I was engaged for two years."

Despite her attempt to say it lightly, as if it didn't matter one little bit to her, a world of pain swam in her eyes.

"That louse," he growled.

"Wh-wh-what do you mean?" she stammered.

"He dumped you."

Her mouth fell open, and then snapped shut. "How do you know?"

"Because if you said yes to a proposal, that would be as good as taking a vow to you. You would hang in there long after you'd figured out it was a mistake."

"I never thought it was a mistake," her tone was tight and did not invite any more comments.

"Louse," he said again.

"No," she said firmly. "He did me a favor. I love being single."

He said nothing, and she apparently felt driven to continue.

"Not that I would want you to interpret that as an invitation to exercise your charms on me."

"I won't," he said.

"I have been able to absolutely devote myself to my career."

"Terrific," he muttered. Sam knew he should let it go right there, but he couldn't. Hanna Merrifield in love with her job? As an accountant? Ludicrous! He had to let her know he did know things about her…and they were things she would do well to know about herself.

"It is," Hanna said stubbornly. "Terrific."

"Uh-huh."

"You're acting as if you know me!"

"You're a certain type. You're the type of girl who stays inside and drinks cocoa on a snowy night," he said softly. "You long for the very things you have denied yourself, like a Christmas tree."

She was glaring at him with naked annoyance, which was a good thing, an antidote for the way he knew they both had felt when their hands touched.

There had always been something between them. Always.

Once, she had been too young.

Though, even then, had he not recognized that she needed something a person like him could never give her?

His failed marriage was ample evidence that he had been right then, and he was right now.

He was not a man accustomed to failure, and that one still had the power to sting. Though he would take it, instead, as a reminder not to tangle too deeply with the lovely Miss Merrifield.

He knew it would be a good note to leave on—with animosity shimmering off her like a heat wave off the desert.

The problem was that he felt honor bound to help her catch the horse. What was he going to do? Leave her here to deal with it when her hand was probably more injured than she was admitting?

Sam looked away from her impaling gaze to see the pony watching him. Who knew a horse could manage an expression of such deep suspicion and dislike?

It was almost identical to her owner's.

And then, with startling swiftness, Molly leapt forward, snapped off the carrot with her slanted yellow teeth—nearly taking his fingers with it—and leapt away again. She stood just out of reach munching on the carrot, leaving him holding the green top part, all the while watching him out of the corner of her eye.

"She outwitted me," Sam said, stunned. He slid Hanna a look when he thought he heard a muffled giggle.

She had looked lovely with the snow catching in her hair and her cheeks pink from a combination of irritation with him and the winter air.

But now, with that faint, reluctant smile tickling her lips? It seemed as if she could outwit his every defense without half trying. Probably while denying, to herself and to him, that she was doing it.

He glanced around at the serene, snow-covered fields, the barn in the distance, the old house that had stood in the same place for a hundred years and raised generations of contented Merrifield babies.

No one would ever see this tranquil, Christmas-card-worthy scene as dangerous.

Except for him. Sam knew somehow he found himself in the most dangerous place of all. That ache was back in his throat. He would help her catch the damned pony, because doing the right thing was important to him, his way of rising above the manner he had been raised.

And then he was out of here. He was not looking back. He had people who could handle the purchase of a small farm. He could have someone else here to meet her at noon tomorrow. He didn't need to do it personally.

Why had he even come here in the first place? Sam suspected he had come because, from the moment that paper advertising this farm had crossed his desk, he had remembered the town of Smith and this farm and Hanna

Merrifield, and all the things that had been out of his reach when he was a young man.

He had come *hoping*.

And he had found out what he already knew. That hope was the most dangerous thing of all.

But if he wasn't coming back, not tomorrow and not ever, what would the harm be in giving himself over to the tiny bit of magic in the wintry air tonight?

And if he was not coming back, not tomorrow and not ever, what would the harm be in giving himself over to the natural curiosity about this girl who had intrigued him from the first moment he had noticed her, in a little green elf costume?

Even though he had not expected to see her, even though the farm manager had told him she was no longer here, underneath every other motive, wasn't that really why he had come? To satisfy his curiosity, to ferret out a few facts, so that he knew all about whatever had happened to Hanna Merrifield?

CHAPTER SIX

HANNA WOULD HAVE liked to kick herself around the Christmas tree lot. Instead of Sam seeing her for what she was, a deeply ambitious, successful and fulfilled businesswoman, he had seen her with frightening clarity.

She *would* have stuck it out with Darren. She *had* said yes to his proposal. She had accepted his ring. The church had been booked. The invitations were on order.

Hanna could have ignored that little voice whispering no. When Darren had broken it off, she had been hurt. Of course she had been. His timing was terrible. Her mother had just died. She needed the stability she had planned for herself. No, for *them*.

But when he'd called it off, sheepish that he was having feelings for someone else, what had she felt right underneath the hurt and anger and sense of betrayal?

Relief.

"You're lucky she didn't bite you," Hanna told Sam, anxious to keep him from knowing just how clearly he had seen her.

He looked at the clump of carrot tops in his hand. Something changed in him, some tension eased, as if he had made a hard decision. Sam smiled at her.

Despite kicking herself again, she smiled back. Better, though, to focus on her very naughty pony than the loveliness of Sam's smile, the straight whiteness of his teeth, the glint of devilment that sparked in the deep brown of his eyes.

"There is good reason she is the world's most unpopular pony," Hanna said drily. "A full-grown man has just quit his job and been driven to drink because of her. She comes with the farm, by the way."

"That's what negotiation is for. If I buy the farm, you take the pony."

"I live in an apartment."

"You said that when you mentioned no room for the tree. That's funny. I never imagined you living in the city."

Hanna felt something go still inside of her. She had to discourage these way-too-insightful observations. "I can't think why you would have imagined me at all."

"The advertisement for the farm came across my desk. When I inquired, I heard your mother had died and that was why the farm was up for sale. It did make me wonder," he admitted. "I wondered what had happened to you."

"To satisfy your curiosity, not a whole lot," she said. She hoped it would sound lightly self-deprecating. Instead, she thought she sounded pathetic.

Sam frowned. "Somehow, I imagined you and an all-American husband and a brood of apple-cheeked children being fitted for elf costumes."

She looked at him closely. "I would never make my children wear elf costumes," she said, and then saw from the faint satisfaction that played briefly across the hard line of his mouth that he had found out something he'd already suspected.

That she *wanted* those things, especially children,

after all, even though she tried hard not to, even though she denied it.

"As you can see," Hanna told him, stiffly, "the reality of ponies is quite different from the dream of ponies. The same goes for life. And probably children."

She was not able to completely strip the strain from her voice, and his frown deepened, as if he was aware he had stumbled on her broken dreams.

She rushed to set him straight. In a breezy tone, Hanna said, "Dull as some people might find it, I actually love my job."

"What's to love about being an accountant?" he asked with insulting skepticism.

"There is great order in numbers," she said. She didn't add that after growing up with the chronic Christmas chaos, and the world she had thought was so secure blowing apart, she had gravitated to her career like a shipwreck survivor to a rescue boat.

"Ah," he said, still sounding doubtful.

"I'm single and I live in New York City. They make television shows about women like me."

"Those women aren't anything like you," he said softly.

"That's probably true," she rejoined sweetly, "because almost all of them would fall for your superficial charm."

For a moment, he just looked at her. And then his gaze went to her lips, and she found herself, foolishly, licking them.

She suspected they both knew he could make her fall for his superficial charm in an instant if he applied himself. And if he used his secret weapon. She remembered the taste of him all those years ago, his lazy expertise, and she turned swiftly away from him and focused on

Molly before she flung herself at him and refreshed her memories. She tried to creep up on the horse.

"It's pretty hard to be sneaky in boots that are that big on you," he commented.

She was aware she was clomping despite the snow. Hardly the picture of the sophisticated big city girl she was desperate to create.

"Maybe if you go that way and I go this way," he suggested, "we will have more luck."

The term *get lucky* blasted, completely uninvited, through Hanna's brain. That was the problem with being around a man like him...her brain was getting ideas of its own.

Or maybe it wasn't her brain. Her brain was that reliable part of her that enjoyed the order in numbers.

It was some other part of her entirely, that wanted to relive the attractions of one very foolish kiss she had shared with this man before she was old enough to know better.

Obviously, she needed to get rid of him. He was a threat to the life she was determined to build for herself: unadorned with the responsibilities of husband and children, she could devote herself to the order of those numbers she loved, rise through the ranks of Banks and Banks, be their first female CEO, possibly by the time she reached forty.

Sam Chisholm, unexpectedly and annoyingly chivalrous, had made it clear he wasn't going until they caught the pony. Okay, they'd catch the pony. And if that meant working as a team to make it happen more swiftly, then that was what she would do.

But she was not—*was not*—going to have fun doing it. Her brain agreed. Another, entirely different, part of her snuck a look at the swell of Sam's bottom lip, and without permission from her brain at all, her tummy did the funniest downward dip as if she was going full speed on a roller coaster down the world's steepest incline.

Trying to catch his breath, Sam contemplated the pony. A full hour had passed and Molly was proving shockingly difficult to catch. Lazy but cagey, she was managing to avoid capture without exerting herself too terribly. With a seemingly effortless, ambling gait, she was crashing through snowbanks and over hill and dale.

"This is called the insider's tour of the farm," Hanna called, breathless as well, trying to fight her way through a particularly deep snowbank. "This is the seven acres of Douglas fir. You've seen nearly the full sixty acres now."

Something had relaxed between them. As aggravating as the situation was, the pony was hilarious: kicking up her heels at them as she darted away, farting as she went. Molly was also a master of the sly look of malice, and the triumphant head toss.

Sam reached back and gave Hanna his hand, and she took it. He was aware she was still being very careful with the one hand.

"The phrase dashing through the snow keeps running through my mind," Sam said, panting, "and I don't even like that song."

He was rewarded with a smile from Hanna. "I think we nearly have her now."

"Sure we do," he said cynically, and then found himself laughing with her.

"And at least we have ample evidence she's not injured after you hit her with your car," she said.

"You really care about her," he said, watching Hanna.

"How could I? She's awful."

He looked at her shrewdly. He suspected Hanna had lying to herself down to an art form.

"And there she goes," Hanna said. "Right into the corner."

Sure enough, they finally had the pony trapped against a fence at the very back of the Douglas firs, where a fence separated Christmas Valley from their nearest neighbor's property.

"At least she came this way, and not toward the highway."

"You like her," he insisted.

"I don't. I mean only in the generic way, where I would not want any living thing to come to harm."

He sidled up to the horse, who finally realized it was trapped, grabbed the proffered carrots and gulped them down greedily while he took up the lead rope Molly had been dragging the whole way.

Molly swallowed her carrots, and just to prove she was not a willing captive, lowered her head, took a sliver of his pants—and his thigh—between long, yellow slanted teeth, and nipped.

He yelped and dropped the rope, which luckily Hanna scooped up before Molly made yet another escape.

"I'll add an extra five thousand to my asking price," Sam said, "if she's not included in the sale of the farm."

He was joking, hoping to coax that smile out of Hanna again, but he did not miss the fact that she looked troubled instead. "But where would she go?"

"A petting zoo?" he said, hopefully.

"You just saw how unsuitable she'd be. She nips."

"How about one of those carousels at the fair, where the little ponies go round and round all day long? I don't even think they can get their heads around to nip."

Hanna was probably not even aware of how aghast she

looked at the suggestion. "She's way too old for that. I wouldn't even let her pull the miniature red Christmas sleigh here anymore."

The pony capitulated to capture, but with ill grace. As they walked her back over the quiet, snowy fields, she would stop and balk and set herself mulishly.

It took both him and Hanna pushing and pulling and begging and yelling to get her moving again.

Some wall tumbled down further between them as he pushed on the pony's substantial rump and Hanna pulled at her halter. The snow had stopped, and just behind wisps of remaining cloud, bright stars were crusting a black sky. The night rang with their laughter.

Finally, the pony was put in her stall, munching with seeming contentment on sweet-smelling hay that Hanna forked expertly into a manger.

There was a piece of that hay in Hanna's hair, and Sam had to shove his hand deep in his pocket to keep from picking it out.

"She doesn't have salt," Hanna noted, unhappily. "That's likely the appeal of the highway. They'd be putting road salt on it to make it less slippery. Her straw isn't fresh, either."

Sam saw her eyes dart around the barn, and a furrow develop in her forehead.

"I should have stayed more involved," she said, her tone laced with guilt. "This place is a disgrace to my father's memory."

He would have liked to reassure her in some way, but it was true. There were signs of benign neglect everywhere. This was not the same farm he remembered from his youth: manicured and perfect, a setting worthy of a Christmas card.

As they moved outside Hanna paused and drew the

clear air into her lungs as if she was breathing in nectar. Their evening should have been over, but instead they stood outside the barn shoulder to shoulder, gazing up at the star-studded night.

"Did she break your skin?" Hanna finally asked, "when she nipped you?"

"I think so."

"I should have a look at it. That could lead to a nasty infection."

He thought of where the bite was, and he thought of Hanna having a look at it. Apparently she thought of those things, too, because a blush stained cheeks already high with color from the exertion of chasing the pony and the cold, Christmasy air.

"I'll be fine."

She was gazing at the house, and he sensed she was reluctant to leave the beauty of the night to tackle whatever was inside. No doubt, more neglect.

"Has the house been closed up since your mother died?"

"Yes." She sighed heavily, but when she turned and looked at him, her face was a mask.

"Good night, Sam," she said. "Thank you for your help. I'll see you tomorrow."

Would she? Hadn't he told himself he would honor his obligation to help her catch the pony, and then designate someone else to make her an offer on her farm? Hadn't he recognized there was something about Hanna that put him in a dangerous place that he had to back away from, rather than walk toward?

For a moment, he saw that same awareness of danger flit through the glowing depths of her eyes.

He saw her look around: at the darkened house where she had grown up, at the barn, and then she looked down the road further.

That's right, there was a large shed back there. After people drove by the quaint house and the barn, they came to the shed where all the Christmas magic happened.

He remembered it had been painted bright red, with crisp white trim. A jaunty sign over the door proclaimed it the Christmas Workshop. Full-bodied wreaths and luxurious swags were displayed against the red exterior walls. Racks and racks of cut Christmas trees were to one side, and a well-worn trail led to the live trees, where families could choose their own and even help cut it down.

After he and his friends had chased poor mortified Hanna in her elf costume into the house, the pony had stood where she had been abandoned, hitched to a sleigh that matched the building.

Sam had been ready to leave right then, after their short-lived encounter with Hanna. But his friends had insisted on availing themselves of the free skating and then had wanted to go to the Christmas Workshop for free hot chocolate.

The shed was huge inside and unfinished, bare studded walls adding to the sense of largeness. At the front by the door was a cash register, manned by a woman who could have easily been Mrs. Santa, but who he'd heard greeted as Mrs. Merrifield, Hanna's mother. That area had gift displays of Christmas decorations and handmade chocolates, pouches of specialty cocoas and ciders and teas.

If his recall was correct, and Sam was fairly certain it was, the next section housed long tables where you could watch wreaths being made. And beyond that was a huge open space, with a bandstand at the far end, and brightly painted red benches around it. There was a play area and old-fashioned toys to entertain kids: wooden rocking horses, handmade spinning tops, an old train set under one of several beautifully decorated trees.

Despite how large it was, that day the workshop had had a festive air and had been crowded with people.

It had a pot-bellied stove burping out warmth at its center and a vat of help-yourself hot cocoa on top of that. A church choir had been on the bandstand, singing Christmas carols, the notes feeling plump and rich inside the large, crowded space.

There had been barrels filled with mistletoe, and wreaths hanging from every available surface. There had been handmade centerpieces constructed of boughs and candles, and bough swags for front doors. The scent—cedar and pine and spruce—of all those freshly cut boughs, had been heady, the smell of the Christmas Sam had never experienced.

There had also been half a dozen trees on display, decorated for a contest. Sam recalled one had been done entirely in shades of violet, and another had had an outdoor theme, hung with miniature rifles, fishing rods and shiny brass bullets.

The trees, once decorated and judged—one done all in white angels had won the grand prize of an eight-foot Colorado blue spruce—were then donated to people who couldn't afford a tree.

Sam would have never, in a million years, said his family was one of those who needed a tree.

In fact, when Hanna had mentioned tonight that Christmas Valley Farm had always kept trees for those who could not afford to buy them, Sam had felt the burn of remembered shame. And not just about the tree, either.

CHAPTER SEVEN

THE CHURCH CHOIR was taking a break, but Sam's friends remained, swilling gallons of hot chocolate and being too loud. One of them had started to say something about the elf, but Sam had silenced him with a look.

None of his friends seemed to notice he had gone very quiet.

Sam had felt as if he was soaking it in: the scents, and the happy people going in and out the door, arms full of purchases. The recent notes of music felt as if they were still inside him. Two boys were stretched out on the floor, playing with the train set that was under one of the contest trees, and a little girl was rocking on one of the wooden horses. The jingle bells over the door rang merrily and constantly.

There was a quality of happiness in the air.

Sam had the thought, *So, this is Christmas,* and he'd felt a strange lack of desire to leave this place.

A grumpy older guy, whom Sam knew to be Hanna's father, had come in and glared meaningfully at him and his friends. Obviously the "free" hot chocolate was really intended for people who were shopping at Christmas Valley Farm.

He and his friends had taken the hint and left, but Sam, ashamed of taking advantage of these people—using their skating rink, drinking their cocoa—had made an excuse and ducked back inside. He had purchased the only thing he could, a single sprig of mistletoe with the five-dollar bill in his blue jean pocket, the only money he'd had.

He wondered now if that was the day he had become the kind of guy who didn't drink cocoa, as if it always had the faint taste of shame to him after that.

"Going to get the girls to give you a Christmas kiss, eh?" Hanna's mother had said, giving him a wink as if it was a great plan, and wrapping his mistletoe carefully, as if it was her most important sale of the day.

He'd ducked his head and mumbled yes, and even thought it was a good idea, but somehow he'd never followed through with it.

Crazily, he still had that dried-out sprig of mistletoe, and through a dozen moves and a divorce, he knew exactly where it was. It was as if it held something of that day: the music and the scents and those beautifully decorated trees, the jingle of bells and the kids playing with the train set and rocking horse.

And him, making a decision that would begin to separate him from his father. He had not been able to afford that mistletoe. There hadn't been a sip of milk or a slice of bread in his house that day.

Yet still, he had done what he had felt was the honorable thing. But what did that say of his life that, even now, that was his best Christmas memory?

"You don't have to sell this farm if you don't want to," he told Hanna softly.

He saw memories in her own eyes, stronger than his own, because that had been her daily life, not a single moment in time.

Sam thought—and even wished—that Hanna would tell him she did not want to sell anymore.

But she got a mulishly determined look on her face. "Of course I want to. And, seriously, I need to know what you would do with the pony."

"At the moment, I'm thinking the glue factory."

She tried to look stern, but she giggled instead. But the giggle was dangerously close to something else. She blinked hard, and pressed her lips together.

"What?" he asked.

"Nothing," she said.

They were both silent for a moment, the quiet of a sleeping, snowbound farm surrounding them, making it feel as if they were alone in all the world. He suspected *this* was her nothing, this place that seemed like sanctuary in a too-busy world. How could she not miss it?

"How many places," he said softly, "are left in the world that feel like this? Places where you can feel this kind of silence and see the stars so clearly, and be surrounded by such quiet beauty?"

She gulped, and then said, her tone breezy but a little forced, "Careful, Sam. The price is going up with every word you say."

"Uh-huh."

The beauty of the moment was suddenly destroyed by the deep rumble of a badly tuned diesel engine starting. Startled, they both turned and squinted down the road that led to the Christmas Workshop shed. Headlights came on and they were caught in the glare.

"Who is that?" Sam asked.

"It must be Mr. Dewey. His living quarters are back there. He must have noticed us up here and is coming to investigate. That's good. Hopefully, I can talk some sense into him. I know he won't really leave me in the lurch this close to Christmas."

The vehicle trundled toward them, the headlights glaring.

Sam realized the truck did not seem to be slowing down as it got closer. If anything it was gaining speed.

He yanked Hanna to the side of the road, and the truck swept by them. It was loaded with furniture, poorly tied. A rocking chair, covered in stained fabric, wobbled precariously on the top of the load.

"But he can't leave!" Hanna said, horror-struck.

"For someone who can't," Sam noted uneasily, watching the truck swerve out to squeeze by where he'd left his car in the driveway, "he is."

The truck barely stopped where the driveway met the highway: a pause, a slither, and lights becoming red pinpricks in the distance until they disappeared altogether.

"I have to be back at work," Hanna said, her voice desperate. "I told Mr. Banks I would be back in twenty-four hours. That would mean I have to leave here by two tomorrow afternoon."

She would arrive back to work when everyone else was leaving for the day? Hanna poring over numbers deep into the night in an empty office was so far from the life Sam had pictured for her that he wanted to shake her.

When she turned her gaze to him, that something that Hanna was so dangerously close to minutes before sparked anew in her eyes, and then spilled, like a single liquid diamond, out of the corner of her eye and down her cheek.

Sam stared at her. Intellectually, he knew he'd done the right thing by already deciding he was done here, by deciding he would send a representative of Old Apple Crate to talk to her about the farm tomorrow.

A better man than him, a good man, would see her distress and know what to do.

A good man would take her in his arms, and hold her, and feel her tears wet his shirt, and tell her it would be okay.

He wasn't that man.

On the other hand, he was never going to see her again, so just for now, just for this second, he would pretend that he was.

A good man who knew what to do with a woman's tears.

What was honorable, after all?

He stepped up to her and put his arms around her, and tugged her in close to him. He felt Hanna's tears slither past his overcoat and down through the opening in his shirt, warm on his chest. He tucked her head into his chest and resisted, barely, the desire to kiss her forehead.

But he did hear himself whisper, like the man he had always hoped he could be, "Shhh, everything is going to be okay."

For a moment she relaxed into him. And for a moment, just like long ago, sitting in the shed sipping hot chocolate, everything felt amazingly right and good in his world.

But then, as if ashamed she had allowed herself a weak moment and let herself lean on him, Hanna pushed back from him and scrubbed at her eye with a furious knuckle.

"I'm fine," she said, her voice a squeak that indicated she was not. But, thankfully, before he could repeat his efforts at being a good man, she turned and headed for the house. "Tomorrow, noon."

He accepted her dismissal and walked back to where his vehicle was still parked way up the drive. Sam left the farm and drove ten minutes to the town of Smith. It was night-quiet, the way it had always been, a quaint farming community, so sleepy that the phrase "the streets were already rolled up for the night" could have been coined for it.

He had booked a room at the only hotel, a beautiful old building proudly displaying a plaque that declared it a historic treasure. He drove to it and stopped in front of it, but at the last minute, he did not go in.

Instead he pulled back out onto the deserted main street. Even the Christmas decorations, adorning every light standard, usually lit, had been turned off. Sam felt like a man on a mission as he drove to the part of Smith that was not quaint, the neighborhood of dilapidated trailers and falling-down houses that stood in the shadow of a bleak flour mill that had been closed for fifty years.

He stopped in front of the Mill Road trailer he and his father had shared during his high school years. It did not look any worse than it had back then, because it seemed places like these reached a point where they could not get any worse.

There was a handwritten For Sale sign planted in the mounded snow that, no doubt, hid trash in the front yard. The sign had hung there so long that the S had faded completely, and the sign now read For ale, which was way too appropriate, a fitting remembrance of his father.

Sam stared at it for a long time. He didn't wonder why he had come. He knew why he had come.

Because, for a moment, holding Hanna, playing at being the better man, it had felt so right.

But this was where he came from, and it seemed to him, looking at it now, he was able to recognize that he'd been trying to rise above this place all his adult life. He had traveled the world. He had enjoyed every perk that being a very wealthy man could offer. He had tried to achieve that most elusive of states—"normal"—when he had married. Despite giving Sandra what he thought mattered most beyond the trinkets and the trappings of success—honor—their marriage had not survived.

He had come here to remind himself that the exquisite longing that had unfurled in him when Hanna's tears had washed down his shirt and her hair had pillowed his chin was not something he could give in to.

This was where he came from. He had risen above it professionally—maybe even been driven by it. But personally? It still influenced him in a million subtle and not so subtle ways, from stocking his pantry as though he were preparing for the Apocalypse, to having a collection of leather jackets so extensive they needed their own temperature-controlled closet, to needing to feel in control.

He could not outrun the sense of not having enough, the sense that while he had achieved every success, true happiness eluded him. This was the only legacy he had to give.

Sam fished his cell phone out of his pocket, determined to send someone else out to discuss the sale of Christmas Valley Farm with Hanna tomorrow.

But when his assistant, a middle-aged wonder named Beatrice, who seemed to have no other purpose in life but to make him happy, answered, he found himself not immediately talking to her about Christmas Valley Farm at all.

"Bea, I want you to have the real estate team buy a trailer for me." He gave her the address of the trailer on Mill Road and the details off the sign.

If Beatrice was surprised by the request, her utter professionalism did not allow her to comment. It was only after Sam had hung up that he realized he had not got around to mentioning the farm.

He told himself he would do it in the morning.

But in the morning, when he looked out his hotel window at Smith, the sun was dazzling on the snow, and he felt annoyed with himself for thinking there was anything about the sale of Christmas Valley Farm that he could not handle.

Besides, he couldn't really ask his real estate team to bring horse salt out to the farm and check Hanna's hand.

And an assistant would have never seen the farm before, so how could he possibly evaluate what needed to be done?

Sam had just put things in motion to buy his childhood home. That should serve as a constant reminder to keep things from getting personal with Hanna, or anyone else for that matter.

It should keep him right on track about his goals for the farm. What needed to be done, Sam told himself firmly, was all those Christmas trees needed to be felled so Old Apple Crate could use that virgin soil to certify its produce as organic.

But that no longer felt as cut-and-dried as it had only twenty-four hours ago. It was a warning to him, because if anybody lived by cut-and-dried rules in a cut-and-dried world, it was Sam Chisholm.

But this morning, reading Beatrice's text—they already had an offer in on his old childhood home—Sam trusted his strength. He trusted that his boundaries were firmly back in place.

And so, an hour later, fueled with coffee and a huge hometown-style breakfast, Sam knocked on the kitchen door at the back of the farmhouse. There was no answer, and Sam put his head in the door.

"Hanna?"

A fire burned in the wood heater at the center of the kitchen. The Christmas Valley Farm sign that he had noticed was faded had been taken from the gate and was on the kitchen table with open paint pots beside it.

The kitchen was old. It was not the granite-and-stainless-steel masterpiece of space and light that his own kitchen in his very upscale Park Avenue condo was.

It was dark and cramped and way too hot with the wood heater going. The sink had chipped enamel, the cupboard doors were thick with layers of paint and there were gaps opening up between the wooden slats, rich with an aged patina on the floor.

Despite the lack of sophistication, or maybe because of it, Sam felt a sense of *home* here that he had never managed in his own house.

He snorted at himself. "Home." The thing he knew the least about, as he had been reminded last night.

This neat farm, this old house with its cozy kitchen, was about the farthest thing from what he had grown up with.

He had a sudden unwanted vision of his father lying in the middle of the sagging kitchen floor of that trailer, an empty bottle beside him, the doors long since smashed off the cabinets, and the one broken window boarded over.

This, this room that he stood in, where a family had gathered around a table and shared a meal, and played a game or two, this place where Mrs. Merrifield had once stood and pulled fresh-baked cookies and Christmas turkey from the oven, this was Sam's deepest longing.

To be normal.

To be part of that union called a family.

To have a safe place to put down one's head, and a soft place to fall.

He recognized the longing as a weakness he had thought long since banished. It had led him down the wrong road once, to a marriage where he had allowed the most dangerous thing of all—*hope*—to come alive in his world.

He had done the one thing he was most contemptuous of. Sam Chisholm had failed. At marriage he had not just failed, he had failed spectacularly.

And he had, after that, resigned himself to that fact that he was never going to have what other men would have, and he had steeled himself against those unexpected moments of longing.

He was pleased he was taking the first steps toward buying the trailer, which would be a constant reminder to him of that.

Because a space like this kitchen filled him with yearning in a way he had not felt in years. He felt sideswiped by it, as if he could nearly taste the cookies out of that oven, see the look of welcome when people walked through that door.

He had a sudden, urgent need to escape.

It had not been necessary for him to come back to the town of Smith, in the first place, and he was not sure why he had.

He should not have come back here today, not after last night. He should not have been arrogant enough to trust his own strength. A lawyer could easily handle this transaction. Sam backed hastily toward the door, not turning his back on the kitchen, as if its promise of warmth would sneak up behind him and swamp him.

His hand had nearly reached the dull bronze of the old knob that would release him back to his world—his world of success and accomplishment, and admiration and respect, where no one really *knew* him, when he saw the sign at the door.

At the Christmas Workshop shed.

The house had been bad enough to go into, but Sam drew a deep, steadying breath at the challenge of returning to the shed.

Had he really been contemplating running away? He had never run away from anything in his life. Not even when he should have.

Where'd you get that jacket? Christmastime. He'd finally saved up enough money to buy the leather jacket, brand-new.

A Christmas gift to himself and probably the only one he would get… Sam felt a tremble along his spine at the memory, but squared his shoulders, just as he had then. He faced things dead on. He was not going to run from these things inside of himself. It was time to banish these longings, to get rid of them for good.

What better place for him to do it than in the place it seemed they had begun?

Sam could not help but notice the farm did not look as magical in the brilliant brightness of the day, as it had last night. The house needed painting, and badly. The barn boards were so gray and rotted, Sam was not sure how the structure was holding up the sagging roof. Fences were down.

Sighing, he opened the trunk of his car, retrieved the salt block, went into the barn and hefted it into the pen with Molly.

As he approached the Christmas Workshop shed, he could see it had not fared much better than the rest of the farm. The paint was peeled off to gray board in places, and where paint remained, the red had long since turned to a washed-out rust color.

There were a few desultory trees against racks to the side of the building, and one wreath on the door that looked as if it might be a remnant from the previous year. The snow on the path to the cut-it-yourself trees was undisturbed. There was not a single car in the customer parking lot.

Sam felt relieved by all of it.

His longings, just like this farm, could not stand up to the bright light of reality.

CHAPTER EIGHT

IT WASN'T UNTIL the bell over the door jingled and Hanna looked up to see Sam coming in that she realized that despite the sheer and overwhelming amount of work she had to do, part of her had been waiting for this moment.

To see him again.

She had even dressed this morning in anticipation of it. She had not been prepared for a long stay, and so she had had to go through her old closet.

She'd found a casual pair of khaki work pants that still fit, and a beautiful red angora sweater—one of those gifts from her father in one of those years that she thought she could not even hope for what she wanted.

She knew why she had left the sweater here. Like so much of her past, the pleasure the sweater had once given her was overshadowed by the disappointment she had caused him.

The memory came unbidden, as the voice of her younger self whispered inside of her.

I'm pregnant.

Two words that could blow a family to smithereens. She had lost the baby early in the pregnancy, but Humpty had already fallen off the wall, and there was no putting anything back together again.

Looking at herself in the mirror, she'd realized the

red was beautiful on her, the softness of the sweater delightful. This time, she had not been swamped with guilt; although she still felt sad, there was also a sense of it being time to leave something behind her that she no longer needed.

The pause as Sam entered the workshop now was a moment of stillness in a morning that had been hectic. The list beside her did not have as many check marks on it as she wanted, particularly those items that appeared under the heading of "Urgent."

First on her list was to find out what had happened to the Christmas tree decorating contest that the farm held annually, when the fully decorated trees were donated to families who might not otherwise have one.

Rationally, Hanna knew this was probably not the most urgent thing on the list, and yet, her heart said it was. So far, though, she had been able to find out nothing. No one even seemed to remember the contest.

Then she had been calling agencies and placing ads in search of a new manager. After that, she had started trying to track down what kind of promotional campaign was in place for the farm this season. She was coming up empty there, too. Ditto for a staff list. And where the heck were the beautiful New Brunswick trees that should be filling the racks in front of this building? Where were the little Christmas trinkets and stocking stuffers that usually sat up by the cash register?

She was working on item number seven on her list now, trying to make sense of the wreath orders, but giving herself over, just for one second, to this moment of looking at Sam without his being aware of it.

That wasn't particularly sane, because Sam seemed to add to her sense that her life was falling into confusion and chaos, rather than what she wanted it to be, which was calm and controlled.

But if this was chaos? Something inside her sighed as she watched Sam stand inside the door, his eyes adjusting to the darker interior. Hanna took advantage of his temporary blindness to study him.

She had hoped that somehow her mind, tired and vulnerable last night from her drive up from New York, chasing the pony and the unexpected shock of seeing Sam again, had somehow managed to exaggerate his attractions.

Now she could see that was the farthest thing from what her mind had done. Backlit by the bright sun, the man was nothing short of glorious.

His mink-dark hair shone in the sun that spilled in the door behind him and silhouetted the male perfection of his frame. He wasn't wearing the elegant leather overcoat today. A plain white shirt—expensive-looking and very tailored—emphasized the broadness of his shoulders, the expanse of his chest, the narrowness of his waist.

She remembered the way his arms had felt around her last night: that splendid feeling she had had of being completely safe in an unsafe and unpredictable world.

As Hanna looked at Sam, she felt momentarily cowardly, as if she should duck and run, pretend she wasn't here. It was the same way she had felt when she ran away from him last night. Instead, Hanna ordered herself to suck it up.

She was not fifteen anymore, given to idiocy and helplessness because of the presence of a good-looking man. Okay, a spectacularly good-looking man. She had learned her lessons from life—the love of men was extremely capricious, look at her father and then Darren—and she wouldn't give her happiness into anyone else's keeping.

"I'm back here," she called, and busied herself sorting through the stacks of wreaths she was trying to match to orders as she took inventory of the contents of the Christmas Workshop.

Despite her stern reminder to herself that she was not fifteen anymore, Hanna felt as gauche and shy as a young girl when his shadow fell over her.

She forced herself to look up and smile casually, a woman in complete control, one who did not fall apart because of the possible loss of her childhood pony.

And childhood home.

And a man's arms around her, the whisper of his voice on the nape of her neck, not just telling her, but making her *feel* as though everything could be all right.

But last night, after he had left and she had gone into the house, Hanna had decided she wasn't relying on Sam Chisholm to make her feel safe and secure. She had sought solace where she so often found it—in numbers. She had done what she did best. She had looked through the farm's books.

Her mother, who had remarried with shocking swiftness after the death of Hanna's father, had moved to Florida and the farm had been left in the hands of a series of managers. Hanna really hadn't had the heart to look into it before now. Her feelings about her mother were nebulous, which made her death harder to bear rather than easier. Right on top of trying to deal with that, Hanna had been jilted by Darren. Then Molly had forced her hand.

Deep into the books and the inventory, Hanna had seen, late last night, that her avoidance—of everything—had not been a good plan. The state of Christmas Valley Farm was gut wrenching.

"I would have called you this morning," she said, "if

I had thought to get your number last night. To cancel our appointment for today."

"Why's that?"

"I'm just in a total mess, here. How can I possibly show you the place in a good light when I barely have a grasp on what's going on myself? If you give me a few days, I'll have a better picture for you."

"A few days? I thought you had to be back at work this afternoon?"

Hanna thought of Mr. Banks's voice when she had called him this morning to let him know she needed a bit more time to set things straight at home. It had occurred to her, stunned her, really, that she didn't like her boss very much.

"No choice," she told Sam. "Mr. Dewey's defection means the twenty-four hours I allotted myself to fix all things farm are now completely unrealistic. Plus, there is this." She held up the hand she had clumsily bandaged herself this morning. "Alas, this is my adding hand."

A smile tickled his lips.

"It's not really funny."

"I've just never heard anyone use *alas* in a sentence before."

She wagged her fingers in an approximation of a hand on an adding machine, to let him know this was serious business. She told herself to be quiet, but her voice just kept on going. "I've been in line for a promotion at work. From the tone of my boss's voice this morning, I seriously doubt I will get it now."

"Not moved by your pony plight?"

She shook her head.

"All those days of staying late and working weekends haven't earned you a little bit of leeway to deal with some urgent personal business?"

"Apparently not."

"Sounds like a jerk."

Why did she resent that comment, when she'd really reached a similar conclusion herself this morning? And wasn't she forfeiting her right to resentment by confiding in Sam as if he was a long-lost friend? Or worse. A long-lost love.

"Would you mind if I had a look at your hand?" Having declared, with utter and aggravating confidence, that her boss was a jerk, now Sam was leaving that topic behind.

"It's fine." Hanna bet Sam was a really good boss. "The bandage is making it look much worse than it is. I just wrapped it to keep it clean and as a reminder not to use it too much today. You don't need to look at it. Really."

He frowned at that, and then took her bundled hand in his own, just as if she had said he *needed* to look at it, instead of the exact opposite. He'd be a good boss because he cared about people.

"I have to protest your high-handedness," she said. She tried to sound haughty. Instead, she sounded faintly breathless.

"Protest away. We are on the topic of hands after all."

It felt like a weakness to smile, and to enjoy the fact that he looked up from her hand and smiled back.

Oh, what was the point of being surly? Despite the impossible number of items on her "to-do" list, she had come out the door of the house this morning and taken a breath of air so clean it had tasted like champagne on her tongue.

Right now, sunshine was bursting through the skylight above her head, anointing them both in a sparkling glow.

"It's quite the messy attempt at a bandage," Sam said. "It looks like something from the movie *Mummies of Munson County*."

"You have not seen *Mummies of Munson County*," she said.

"How do you know?" he asked mildly. She realized he was distracting her, deliberately, because he was already unwinding the bandage from her hand.

"You're not the type who would enjoy that kind of mindless, poorly plotted carnage."

"Really? What type am I?"

"*Green Hills*?" she guessed, naming a current suspense thriller. "Or *Halls of Valhalla*?" It was a film that was a historically accurate look at Vikings, that still provided plenty of action.

He smiled at her. "I don't have time for movies. How about you?"

He didn't have time for movies, and yet here he was, making time for her. Mr. Banks had made it clear he only had time for her if she was providing something of value to him.

Maybe, she told herself, as a defense against the unraveling within her at Sam's touch, his investment of time was not really for her, either. It was about the farm. He was just making small talk and showing concern, until they got to the part where he tried to buy it off her. Why not just follow his lead? "You have to guess."

"If you have time to watch movies?"

"What kind of movie I like."

He considered. "*The Sound of Music*?"

"That's old!"

"But classic. I see you as being a classic kind of woman, somehow."

Silly to be flattered by so casual an observation. The

truth? If she had to list her ten favorite movies of all time, that one would probably be in there.

Giving herself over to his ministrations was a surrender, and she knew it. Still, given the stress of her morning, with her job in jeopardy and the farm a mess, why not just enjoy this simple and unexpected pleasure? His scent was scrumptious: clean and crisp and masculine.

His expression was neutral, nothing but focused, but his touch was exquisite and tender. He unwound her sloppily applied bandage slowly, and the cuff of his shirt kept brushing her naked forearm. The shirt was silk and the whole exercise seemed impossibly sensual.

He set Hanna's clumsy dressing aside, and inspected her hand carefully. He ran his thumb over the swollen webbing between her own thumb and fingers and when she gasped, he frowned at her.

"That hurt?"

Actually, pain had been about the farthest thing from her mind, but she squeaked out a yes.

"That's looking a little nasty," he said, studying her hand. "Did you put antiseptic on the scrape?"

"The first-aid kit was down here. I was at the house when I did it."

"Would you mind if I put a little antiseptic cream on before I rewrap this?"

Say no. But just like last night, there was something about leaning on him—about being taken care of—that was proving irresistible.

So, that was not necessarily *him*, Hanna told herself primly. She had been holding her whole world together on her own for months now, absorbing shock after shock, until she was in a weakened state. The phone call with Mr. Banks this morning, finding the farm like this, had been final straws. She told herself Sam Chisholm could have been Attila the Hun, and she would have gladly let him bandage her hand.

She was exhausted and stressed. Giving in whilst in this state was perfectly acceptable.

She directed him to the location of the first-aid kit behind the counter at the front, and pulled herself together before he came back.

He swabbed the scraped skin, and this time her gasp was real.

"That stung," she said.

"Sorry." And then, Sam lifted her hand to his lips and placed a gentle kiss on it.

Her mouth fell open. He looked appalled at himself. He quickly and efficiently wrapped the tension bandage back on, avoiding her eyes.

"Thanks," Hanna said, shakily. "I'm sure that will help." She should clarify she meant the antiseptic and bandage so he didn't think she was referring to the *kiss-it-all-better*.

On the other hand, maybe the less she said about that the better. Or maybe she needed to distract him from the shakiness his lips on her hand had caused.

"Don't you have an injury, too?" she asked, sweetly. "Where the pony nipped you? Do you want me to have a look at that since we're doing first-aid this morning?"

"Ah," he said, unruffled. "A long time ago I warned you about starting fires you didn't know how to put out."

And so he had.

"Well," she said brightly, "we've established you are in no need of first-aid. Can I call you in a couple of days? By then I should be a better spokesperson for the farm."

Take it, Sam ordered himself. She was offering him a way out, and he needed to take it. She was way too pretty in that soft, red sweater. Her hair was loose today, and fell in a shining wave to her shoulders. She had on the faintest dusting of makeup, but he had a feeling the rosiness of her cheeks was completely natural. A hint of gloss drew his eyes to the lovely line of her mouth.

Now he had, very foolishly, kissed her hand, and she was teasing him, and it could all get out of control way too quickly. Sam Chisholm did like to be in control.

All good reasons to take the out she was giving him.

But looking at Hanna, he could see smudges of exhaustion under her eyes, and he wasn't at all sure she could be trusted not to use that hand. It looked to him like the kind of injury that could easily get infected if it was not properly tended.

He remembered the soft vulnerability of her accepting his embrace last night.

"Do you need some help with something around here today?" he asked her. To himself he asked, *Sam, what the hell are you doing?*

"Oh, no," she said quickly, but even as she said it, he saw her eyes slide to the stacks of wreaths on the table in front of her.

"What are you doing with these?"

"Sorting them into two piles. Keep and Toss. I was trying to match orders to inventory, but I actually think I'm just denying the awful truth. Most of these wreaths need to be replaced. How can I sell these?"

She lifted a particularly bad one for his inspection. "They're pathetic," she said, as if he couldn't see that with his own eyes. "Sad and saggy. I hope I'm not describing my future self."

She rushed on, as if to erase that picture from her mind, but in fact, he did not think she would grow old pathetically. He thought she would be one of those rare women who grew more and more beautiful with age.

"This one?" she said. "Half the bundles have no white pine. And this one, the grand fir has been skimped on. Look at this one, straight balsam, and missing two or three bundles to boot.

"You can't sell a wreath like this and say it's from Christmas Valley Farm. Already brown in places," Hanna said with disgust. "How could Mr. Dewey sell such rubbish? He'll destroy our reputation."

Our reputation, Sam noticed.

"You can't trust a man to make a wreath," she muttered.

"What? On behalf of myself and my brothers, I'm offended."

"No, it's true. Men cannot make wreaths. They just don't have a good sense of the aesthetically pleasing."

"That's stereotyping, Hanna. Please do not put my sense of the aesthetically pleasing in the same category as Mr. Dewey's."

"You don't even know Mr. Dewey."

"I spoke to him on the phone. I caught a glimpse of him last night. The fact that he is the kind of man who would abandon a pony on the highway and leave someone in the lurch at a precarious time of year for their business tells me a great deal about him. It tells me I could certainly make a better wreath than he could."

He saw, suddenly, how he could help her without her really even knowing until it was too late.

Get out of here, a voice inside him shouted.

But if he left right now, how was he any better than Mr. Dewey? Or his father, for that matter? He'd been trying all his life to live with honor, and this opportunity had been given to him to do it.

Hanna was in way over her head. Christmas was barreling down on her, and there was no way she could tackle it all herself.

He took a deep breath. He tossed down the glove.

"I challenge you to a wreath-making contest," he said.

CHAPTER NINE

HANNA GAVE A shout of disbelieving laughter. It should have been insulting, but Sam was reluctantly enchanted by how her mouth curved and her eyes sparkled.

"You can't be serious," she said. "You are challenging me to a wreath-making contest?"

"I am."

"You don't know any more about wreaths than you know about mummies, Sam Chisholm."

"But I'm a very quick learner. And you would question what I know about mummies after the expert wrapping of your hand? You seem determined to offend me."

She hesitated, and then smiled again. The smile tickled the edges of a mouth that was nothing short of splendid, and it was a smile that could make a man put his whole life on hold to do the honorable thing, to play Galahad to her maiden in distress.

"I can't be offending a potential buyer of my farm, can I?"

"Absolutely not."

She studied him for a moment, and then lifted a slender shoulder "Okay. You're on. What's the prize for the winner?"

He forced himself not to look at her mouth. "How about if the loser provides lunch?"

She considered that, and why shouldn't she? It meant he was planning on still being here at lunchtime.

"Let's make a wreath," she decided, the moment she gave up the struggle more than evident in her face. "Grab that box there, and those pruners beside it."

He took the empty apple crate she had pointed at and the pruners and followed her out the back door of the shed. He wondered if she knew how pretty she looked this morning in that red sweater.

A mountain of boughs was stacked behind the workshop.

"This is balsam," she said. "Take one branch out of the pile, like this, and snip it into pieces in your box, like this."

He watched her and did as she said. "Not rocket science, so far," he said.

When they had nearly filled their boxes, she moved on to another stack of tree limbs. "This is grand fir. See these beautiful fans at the end of the branches? Cut those."

He cut until there was a collection of those on top of the balsam.

"Now these. It's white pine. You don't need much, just a single sprig in every bundle."

"That's what the horrible Mr. Dewey missed in half of them?"

"And it's essential," she said seriously. "You'll see."

With boxes full of fragrant clusters of tree branches, she brought him back in the shop and cleared a place on the table.

"This is my childhood," she said quietly. "The sale of the trees paid the bills, but mistletoe and centerpieces and swags, and especially the wreaths, were the profit. Every day, from mid-November, after school and on weekends, my Mom and I made wreaths. We tried to have enough for when the real Christmas rush started, but we never did. I remember working until midnight, sometimes. I still dream I'm making wreaths. It feels so real I wake up and smell my hands."

Sam was aware of a desire to lift her un-bandaged hand, and see if the sweet scents of the branches they had cut were already clinging to it.

Hanna shook herself out of her reverie. "So, for the contest, what would you like to make? A small wreath, a medium one, or a large one?"

"A large one, of course."

"Ah, bigger is better."

He raised an eyebrow at her, but failed to make her blush.

Instead, she shook her head at him. "Precisely why men are not good with wreaths. So, for the large wreath, we'll need this frame."

She reached up above her. Even standing on tippy-toes she was straining to reach where metal wreath rings were hanging from a nail on the rafter.

He came over, reached above her and snagged it handily. For a moment, his body was pressed against the length of hers, and the scent of a delectable shampoo rose above the scents all around them.

He snapped back from her quickly, but once that awareness was there, it was like a racehorse out of the gate. Putting it back in the starting box was nigh near impossible.

Still, he tried.

"This," he said, backing up a careful step from Hanna, and wagging the ring at her, "is precisely why men are good at making wreaths. We can reach the equipment."

He inspected the frame, rather than the blush that had

risen in her cheeks. It was an ugly circle of wire with lethal-looking prongs sticking out from it.

"Humph." She took the ring from him. Was she extra careful not to make contact? He was fairly certain she was.

Hanna, he noted gratefully, was determined to be all business. "I'll just set it here by the press. So, we need sixteen bundles for the large wreath form. I'll show you how to make a bundle. First you take a really nice fan of this grand fir, and put it in the back."

She laid the frond of fir across her bandaged palm. "Then, on top of that, balsam, bigger pieces at the back graduating to smaller at the front. And then you finish with one precious sprig of white pine." She winced as she tried to close her hand around the bundle, and he went and took it from her.

They were close again. The fragrance of the cut clusters of branches was thick in the air around them, but mingling with it was Hanna's scent, sweet and unperfumed. Clearly a soap-and-water kind of girl.

She looked as if she was going to protest his commandeering of her bundle, but then looked at her hand and accepted what was.

What was. The two of them together. Was she savoring, as he was, the contrasts? The danger of awareness, mixed with the almost hypnotic wholesomeness of building a wreath?

No, she seemed intent with wrapping an elastic around the stubby bottom of the collection he held. Her tongue was caught between her teeth with concentration.

But when her eyes rose to his, he knew she felt something sizzling in this room that could not be explained by the fragrance surrounding them, or the warmth chugging out of the heater at the center of the room.

"That," she said, trying to stay focused, trying not to appear flustered, "is a bundle."

Sam looked at the neat cluster of different kinds of pine and fir. His awareness of Hanna was dampened, somewhat, by the enormity of what he had gotten himself into. "And you need sixteen of these to make a large wreath?"

"Uh-huh. It's fourteen for a medium, and twelve for a small."

"How many orders for wreaths do you have?"

"About a hundred that I could find. There may be more. I'll have to call the people we have always had standing orders with."

"And how much do they sell for?"

She told him.

"Pretty labor-intensive," he said. "How can you make any money at this?"

"You'd be surprised. It actually moves along fairly quickly once you get the hang of it."

"Okay," he said, drawing in a breath, "I'd better get started, or I'll still be here tomorrow morning."

Now, *there* was a distracting thought. Still being here tomorrow morning. He frowned down, and chose a fan of grand fir to lay across his palm. And then carefully, he added the other ingredients until he was ready for an elastic. He finished and held it up for her inspection.

"Well?"

"It's not bad for a first effort."

"You mean it's not perfect?" He was surprised that he felt a little crestfallen by that. He ran a multi-million-dollar business. How could such a small thing bother him? But the truth was he was tremendously competitive. And he liked perfection.

"It's a little fat at the bottom. It'll make it a little

harder to press it into the form. Don't worry about it this time, just remember that your hands are bigger than mine."

The comment, off the cuff as it was, intensified the awareness of her that was a constant in the background. It made Sam aware of Hanna's femininity and his masculinity, her tininess compared to his height, of her softness in comparison to his strength.

A woman like her made a man feel as if he had been born to be bigger and stronger and to use his size and his strength to protect.

"Make a bundle that would fit in my hand."

"Okay."

"And could you do my elastics?"

He noticed now that she had done six bundles to his one, but laid them out carefully, awaiting elastics, because of her injured hand.

Ridiculous to feel manly about doing it for her. But nonetheless, Sam did. He wrapped the bottoms of all of the completed bundles.

"Should I keep my bundles separate?" he asked her. "In the interest of a totally fair competition?"

"I'll help you with this part."

"You're pretty cocky about winning."

She snickered at that and kept working. Finally, they had completed the thirty-two bundles necessary for two large wreaths. Though he was pretty sure she had made twenty-two bundles, and he had done ten.

She was gracious enough not to point that out—not the fierce competitor that he was nor being prematurely smug about her win.

"Okay," she said, "now you take the form and set it in the press, and place a bundle in it. And then you step on this to activate the press."

He watched as the press folded the metal prongs on the ring form down over the completed bundles of needles. She did it sixteen times, and then handed him the first completed wreath.

"Wow," he said. "I'm no expert on wreaths, but this is spectacular."

The wire frame was invisible and the wreath was full and heavy, abundantly beautiful.

"Here, you try it." She stepped back from the press, and he put the second wreath together and then studied them both as they lay side by side on the table.

"They look the same," he decided. "How do we decide who won?"

"Oh, we are not nearly done yet. Why, are you bored already?"

His doubts about how you could make any money at this had increased, but he was surprised to find, given the repetition of the task, he was not bored at all.

He liked being with her in this room, intensely focused on this task. He liked how they were deeply immersed in a world of fragrance and creation, underlaid, always and subtly, with an awareness of each other.

"No," he said, realizing he was a bit surprised. "I feel remarkably Christmasy."

"What does that mean?"

"I'm not exactly sure." He contemplated the fact that this was the same place—inside the Christmas Workshop at Christmas Valley Farm—where he had felt like this once before. It had something to do with creating this beautiful object that would hang on a door in welcome, holding within its boughs the warmth and cheer and the spirit of the season.

"I guess," Sam said slowly, feeling his way through his confused emotions, "the wreath feels like a gift I'm extending to a stranger, and the spirit of Christmas seems to be in that."

There was that smile again, the warmth of it touching him as certainly as the warmth of the sun pouring in the skylight, and the warmth coming from the wood heater at the center of the room.

"That's nice," she said. "For a guy who claims not to be *Christmasy* you seem to have a handle on it."

Sam knew that was not possible. There had been no *spirit of the season* in his house. Lots of spirits, but all the wrong kind. *Where'd you get that jacket?* He could feel sweat breaking out on his upper lip at the memory.

Hanna said, "We are not exactly giving the wreaths away, but they are extraordinarily beautiful. I've compared every wreath I've come across in my years away to these ones, and nothing holds a candle to them."

Her voice soothed the hard beating of his heart and brought him back to this moment.

And the realization of the fact that him helping her was part of what was going on for him. That Christmasy feeling unfolding in him might be because he was helping someone else, putting their needs ahead of his own.

Maybe, given the electrical awareness he had of Hanna and the fact that being here in Smith was triggering memories he thought he had left far behind him, it was even placing himself in the danger zone in order to help her out.

"Okay," Hanna said, while he was contemplating all of this, "moving right along, next station."

She moved to another table and he followed her, carrying the wreaths. "So, choose three pinecones, and wrap the bases in this fine wire, like this."

She did it expertly, a task she had performed a million times. "And then choose three of these Christmas decorations and attach the wire to them."

Expertly she was attaching her pinecones and three sparkling silver Christmas balls, hiding the wires deep in the clusters, twisting the wire behind the wreath so it was completely invisible. Even with the use of only one hand, Hanna was finished before he had attached his first pinecone.

He was studying it sadly—you could see the wires, and it obviously had to be redone—when she materialized beside him. "Which one?"

She was balancing four spools of two-inch-wide ribbon: pure white, pure red, one with reindeers and one with silver snowmen.

"If none of these appeal, there's a ribbon room. My mom literally collected a lifetime supply. There's still probably four or five hundred spools of Christmas ribbon in there."

"The thought of picking a Christmas ribbon from four or five hundred choices gives me hives," he said, shuddering. "That one."

He pointed at the reindeers.

Seconds later, while he was attaching his second pinecone, she came back with a luxurious bow, huge and full, already wired for him to attach to his wreath.

"How are you doing this with one hand? My fingers feel too big for this," he said as he finally attached the ribbon. "Don't take that as evidence guys can't do this."

She came and looked at his wreath. "It looks great," she said generously, though when he slid a look over to hers, he could see his was not quite as polished-looking as hers was. The silver snowmen on her ribbon were a perfect complement to the silver balls. The pinecones looked as if they had grown from the wreath.

"We just have one thing left to do before these are done. They have to have a word."

"A word?" Sam asked.

Hanna looked around, then went out of the workshop. The door swung open in the breeze. The smart thing to do would be to see that as an invitation, to make an excuse and leave. But he was in this thing now, committed to a course of being a better man, of doing the honorable thing.

Hanna came back triumphant, swinging a big galvanized metal bucket, shutting the door behind her. "Here they are."

She set the bucket down and fished through it. It was filled to the lip with words, and she pulled samples out and laid a line of thin, painted tin words on the table.

"*Merry Christmas* was the most popular one, but there were other good sellers."

One by one, she took them out and laid them on the table.

Believe.

Faith.

Hope.

Love.

Miracles.

Each of those words felt like a nail going through him. All the things he had wanted with such desperation when he was growing up, and then, when he was married... he'd had just one normal Christmas. Just one.

"I'll take *Merry Christmas*," he said gruffly.

CHAPTER TEN

"GO AHEAD," HANNA SAID. "Choose *Merry Christmas*. Be boring. Couldn't possibly be a winner."

It made her feel slightly giddy that she had just called Sam Chisholm boring. She could feel Sam's eyes on her as he waited to see which one she took. Her tongue was caught between her teeth, with fierce concentration, and she felt like a child picking a favorite flavor of ice cream from the parlor.

"This one," she finally decided. She held it out for his inspection.

Miracles.

"Why that one?"

"Right now, I feel as if I need one."

Hanna contemplated her choice as she attached the word to her wreath. She did feel she needed a miracle.

And it felt hopelessly naïve to think that a miracle was standing beside her.

When Sam thought she wasn't looking, he put *Merry Christmas* back in the bucket. She saw him take out *Hope* and look at it for a long time, before passing it over for *Season's Greetings,* which really was just as boring as *Merry Christmas*, but she had given him quite enough help.

Just as they finished attaching the words the bell over the door jingled, and a customer walked in.

Miracles, Hanna mouthed silently, and then called out, "Excuse me? Could you come back here for a moment?"

A middle-aged woman walked toward them. Hanna hoped she would recognize her, as a returning customer might be able to fill in some of the blanks about the farm, but the woman was a stranger to her.

"We've just had a wreath-making contest," Hanna told her seriously. "We were wondering, could you be the judge?"

Sam didn't miss a beat. He held up his wreath and turned up the wattage of his smile.

Oh, boy, Hanna thought, a first-row seat to his lethal charm at work. The woman preened under his attention and took her task very seriously.

She looked over both wreaths and asked to see them more closely. She looked at the workmanship and stood back from them, pursing her lips.

And then she pointed at Sam's.

"He snuck you five dollars, didn't he?" Hanna protested.

"No, I just like the reindeers on the bow. In fact, I'd like to buy both these wreaths. And I saw a tree outside I'd like too." She batted her eyelashes at Sam. "It needs to be cut down."

Hanna was going to protest. The man the customer wanted to cut down her tree was the CEO of a very important company. And the possible buyer for her farm! She couldn't—

But Sam looked over their customer's head, mouthed the world *miracles* again, and winked at Hanna.

And she surrendered. There was no missing it when you were in the presence of a miracle. None at all. It had a feeling to it—as if the very air was shimmering with light—and a mere mortal would be toying with things they did not understand to refuse a moment like this one.

Half an hour later, Hanna was ringing in the sale. The woman went back outside, all smiles, as she chatted with Sam while he strapped a ridiculously large Scotch pine to the roof of her very small vehicle.

Sam was right.

Despite the fact she had taken money, Hanna had a sense of having given a gift to a stranger.

She was blindsided by the wave of emotion she felt.

She had a sense of loving this place and what they did here. How was it that she had forgotten the moments like these ones? The kind of quiet joy of making a really lovely wreath, each one so different than the one before it? The moments of intense satisfaction? Of giving joy, yes, but also receiving it.

It erased all the other things Christmas had been for her family, the invisible things that you did not sew into wreaths. Pressure. Stress. Financial concerns.

Sam came back in. His white silk shirt was covered in dirt and needles. His hair was faintly messed.

"What?" he said, gazing at her.

A long time ago Hanna had felt an overwhelming compulsion to kiss this man. She was stunned that she felt it again, just as strongly as if not a day had passed since the last fateful time their lips had met.

Thankfully, the bell over the door jingled again, and she leapt back from him. This time it was not a stranger who walked in.

"Mrs. Stacey!"

Mrs. S. was Christmas Valley Farm's oldest employee—both in age and years of service. Hanna had lost touch with her over the years. Her mother had certainly never mentioned that Mrs. S. still worked at the farm.

"You're home," Mrs. Stacey said, her voice firm and welcoming. And, indeed, that was how Hanna felt.

As if she had been a wanderer who had finally found her way home.

"Mr. Dewey quit," she told Mrs. S.

"Well, thank the Lord for miracles both large and small," Mrs. Stacey said with a sniff.

Hanna was reminded again of the word sewn into the frothy greenery of her wreath.

"I have so many questions," Hanna said. "I am so glad to see you."

"We'll catch up in a minute," Mrs. S. said. "I saw some folks wandering in amongst the trees. I'll just go give them a hand."

Hanna blushed. She had been so caught up in her desire to taste Sam's lips she hadn't even heard cars arriving with more customers.

Hanna made her way back to Sam. "That's Mrs. Stacey. She's been here as long as the farm."

"Could she do Mr. Dewey's job?"

"I was just wondering why she hadn't been," Hanna said pensively. "My mother never mentioned her, and they were good friends, so I thought Mrs. S. must have moved on when my mother did."

"You could probably be back at the beck and call of Mr. Banks by this afternoon if Mrs. S. can do the job," Sam said. He was watching her way too closely.

She realized it was true. She could leave everything in Mrs. S.'s more than capable hands. She could make her twenty-four-hour deadline after all. But she thought of the dull mounds of paper that awaited her, and the snippy tone in Mr. Banks's voice this morning, and felt suddenly and deliciously rebellious.

She waved her damaged hand at Sam, her excuse not to return.

He smiled with approval.

"I need to stay for a few days, just to get things back the way they should be," Hanna said, but she was aware of a wobble of emotion out of her voice. "The selling of this farm has been a bullet dodged for a long, long time. But if I'm going out, I'm going out like this. Giving joy. Giving people more than they expected, not less. Giving people the highest quality product they can find anywhere."

"Don't cry," he said, softly. "Please, don't cry."

"I didn't realize I was," she said. Good grief, she had to stop having these breakdowns in his presence. He would think she was just trying to weasel back into the warmth and safety she had felt last night in his arms.

He reached out to her and his hand rested on her shoulder. Hanna scrubbed furiously at her wet cheeks with her fist.

"I'm being ridiculous," she said. She scanned his face for agreement, but really he just looked terrified of the tears. "I'm sorry. I'm just a bit overwhelmed. There are things I have to satisfy myself about before I can go back to New York. So many things. That's why I'm crying."

"Of course it is."

"It's about the farm's legacy. The state things are in right now? This is *not* how I will have my family's farm remembered. I'm fixing it."

"Fixing it how?" Sam asked tentatively.

"I'll do it the way my dad would have wanted it done— beautiful wreaths, a well-organized Christmas tree lot."

What? Hanna screamed inwardly. What she was suggesting was impossible! Never mind her promotion, she wouldn't even have her job at Banks and Banks to return to if she followed through on this foolhardy and emotion-driven decision to save her family's farm.

She was only staying a few days, just to make sure

Mrs. S. could handle everything. She was not as young as she had been once. And there had to be a reason she was not managing the farm already. What was it?

"Are you going to wear an elf costume?" he asked silkily.

"I might," she said, with a toss of her head. "I am not a self-conscious fifteen-year-old anymore. If it sells trees, I'll do it."

She realized she sounded like her father.

"That's the spirit," he said.

"We can resume the discussion about you buying Christmas Valley Farm later."

Sam was silent.

"And that will give you time to think of a solution for Molly."

"A solution for Molly?"

"I'll need to know your intentions for her."

"You haven't asked me anything about the price I plan to pay, but you want to know what's going to happen to the pony?"

Her boss would be appalled at her. Where were all her years of accumulated business acumen?

But there would be time enough for that later. Right now, Hanna had Christmas to whip into shape. And so very little time to do it in. How long could she stay here before there would be no job to go back to? Probably a week at the outside.

Sam rocked back on his heels and regarded her thoughtfully.

"Is there anything else I can do for you, Sam?"

"There is the small matter of lunch," he said, "since I did win the wreath contest. Though, I'm willing, sportsman that I am, to give you another chance."

She went very still.

"I think we should try it again. Double or nothing."

She knew what he was really doing. He could see she was overwhelmed by the decision she had just made.

"What you're really doing is offering to help me, isn't it?" she said.

He lifted a shoulder.

"Because you pity me? Because I cried?"

She needed to be strong enough to say no to his offer to rescue her.

"It's not really about you, Hanna." His voice was cool. "I'm thinking of buying the farm. I had already clearly stated my intention to see if Christmas trees and all the rest of this would be viable for me. What better way than this?"

She wanted to make sure his offer to help was motivated by a desire to learn the business and not because he pitied her, but the expression on his face, cool and detached, answered her question. Mrs. S. stuck her head in the door.

"The truck with the trees from New Brunswick is coming down the driveway. Nearly a week late, but at least they're here."

Mrs. S. seemed to notice Sam for the first time.

"Young man, what are you doing standing there with your hands in your pockets? Get out there and help those people load that tree they just bought. And then you can unload that truck."

Hanna started to correct her. She slid Sam a look. The powerful CEO of Old Apple Crate looked stunned, like a fighter who had just been blindsided by a punch.

Instead of correcting Mrs. S., Hanna giggled.

Sam gave her a look.

She giggled again. And then, as quickly as she had found herself crying, she found herself laughing.

When she stopped, Sam was still watching her, the detachment gone from his face, something there that she could live to see again, though when her eyes met his he looked away.

"Young man!" Mrs. S. bellowed.

"Yes, ma'am," Sam said and with a wink at Hanna, sauntered out the door.

Hanna took a deep breath and went up to the front. Mrs. Stacey was ringing in the sale, frowning at the contents of the cash register.

"I think that devil, Dewey, cleaned you out," she said.

Hanna barely heard her. She peeked out the open door and watched as Sam easily muscled a tree into the back of a family van. Then he walked over to the truck that had just come in, stood on the running board and said something to the driver.

Sam threw back his head and laughed at the driver's reply, and then the driver got out and opened the back door of the semi.

Really, Hanna had already let things go far enough. She needed to stop this right now.

Then she considered another possibility. She had sewn the word *Miracles* into the fragrant boughs of her wreath. After you did something like that, wouldn't there be some kind of cosmic penalty to pay if you refused the ensuing gifts?

Surrender, she told herself. Just surrender.

Surrender?

Was she mad? She squared her shoulders. She *had* surrendered to love. After she had left this farm, she had *craved* love. And along had come Darren: handsome, funny, smart.

Hanna had thrown herself into loving him, putting her whole life on the back burner to be in love. She had manufactured homemade cards and cookies, sewn into each offering a barely acknowledged dream for *them* of a solidly traditional life like the one she had left behind. He had asked her to marry him. Okay, it hadn't been the romantic proposal she had envisioned—a casual, *let's get married someday*—that had nevertheless thrown her into paroxysms of preparation that had ultimately frightened him away.

Hanna, I'm just not the man for you.

And within weeks of that—when she thought he should be changing his mind and coming back to her—he was really finding out he was the man for someone else.

Like her mother, Darren had moved on with shocking swiftness!

Still, even with that fresh in her mind, and even with all the important things on her list, Hanna could not believe it when she turned to Mrs. S. and said, "I'm going to go to town and pick up some things for lunch. I thought we could roast some hot dogs over the wood burner."

As they had always done.

Rather than looking as if she thought that was a terrible idea, Mrs. S. looked rather pleased.

"Good idea. You won't be much use with your hand like that, anyway. Get lots. We can offer them to the customers. And the workers. Morale has been terrible around here, because of that fool, Dewey. Morale terrible on a Christmas tree farm," Mrs. S. said with a disapproving *tut* and a shake of tight, iron-gray curls.

It begged the question what Hanna's mother had been doing hiring managers when she'd had Mrs. S. to do it for her, but that question could wait for now. It seemed to Hanna that close observation would give her a better answer than asking Mrs. S. herself.

"There's a girl from the high school coming at four to make wreaths. Her name is Jasmine. And the young man, Michael, who works in the tree lots, will be here in a few minutes. I'm glad you've hired that extra man."

The time to correct her was now, but Hanna was silent.

"He's a looker," Mrs. S. said.

"Ha! And is there anything worse than a good-looking man?" Hanna shot back.

"Well, I guess I can think of worse things," Mrs. S. said mildly and then winked, and turned away with a smile when Hanna blushed right to the roots of her hair.

"Oh, gosh! Before I go to town, I better check on Molly," she said, as if she had the most urgent business in the world to tend to. She scurried away from the knowing look of Mrs. S.

But, once in the quiet barn, looking at Molly, Hanna realized if she had thought she was somehow going to escape the knowledge that had bloomed in Mrs. S.'s eyes of her own attraction for Sam, she was wrong.

Because there was a block of fresh salt in the pen, and Molly, far from looking as if she was eyeing up a new escape route, looked unusually content, her tongue sliding lovingly along the block. She had already worn an indent into the square blue surface of the salt.

Hanna tossed in some fresh hay, but Molly ignored it and came over to the stall divider that Hanna stood behind, and nuzzled it. It was an invitation and Hanna opened the gate and went in.

The world's meanest pony came and shoved her head right against Hanna's tummy and nudged. Everybody else had to be wary of those teeth, but the truth was Molly had never nipped Hanna, not even once.

The scruffy pony wanted her ears scratched. With her good hand, Hanna complied. Molly closed her eyes and sighed with contentment, rocking her head back and forth so that each ear got equal treatment.

Anybody watching might have thought the little horse loved Hanna. Or that she loved the little horse.

Love.

Hanna felt just about as vulnerable as she had ever felt. And foolishly, crazily, stupidly, as if she was doing the very thing she wanted least to do.

She could fall for that guy out there who had brought salt for this pony this morning and not said a word about it, who was helping her when she needed it most but without wounding her pride doing it. That guy out there who was, as she stood here having a moment with Molly, hefting trees off the delivery truck.

Or maybe, there were things left between her and Sam from all those years ago, that had never been undone.

Maybe, she already had started falling for him!

"Stop it," Hanna told herself sternly. This was her whole problem. She fell too hard and too quickly and it frightened people away. It should frighten her as well, this loss of herself to the forces of love.

Besides, she had vowed to herself that her days of falling at all were over. Even before Darren's defection, love had hurt her so terribly.

Her mother and her father had given her such a solid, traditional life. And yet when she had disappointed them—never mind that she had also disappointed herself—everything had changed and drastically, too. It seemed when she had needed it most, love was withheld. So, she had gone to Darren already wounded, already needy. Catastrophe had been predictable.

No, Hanna was determined to be a career woman now, through and through.

She was going to test her resolve with Sam. She was

going to eat hot dogs with him and work with him, and then she was going to turn away as easily as Darren—and if it came to that, her own parents—had walked away from her.

Sam could be a lesson in getting her own power back, and she was taking it. In a few days she would be back at her job at Banks and Banks, more dedicated to being their most prized employee than ever!

CHAPTER ELEVEN

"Battle of the Balls," Sam said.

Hanna leveled a disapproving look at him—she was taking her power back after all—but then she spoiled it all by dissolving into giggles.

The official workday was over at Christmas Valley Farm; the workshop and tree stands had closed for the day. It was just after 9:00 p.m., and Hanna was aware she should have sent Sam home.

He had been invaluable today. The farm was seriously understaffed, and without being asked, he had made wreaths, cut trees, unloaded tree deliveries, wrapped and loaded tree purchases and manned the cash register.

But he wanted to know the ins and outs of running the farm, and the truth was, at this time of year, the day never ended. Besides, she wanted to prove to herself she was over her romantic notions.

So, here was a good test. They were alone in her house, shoulder to shoulder, her laptop open between them on a print program.

After a full day on the farm, she could clearly see Mrs. S. had a handle on the business end of Christmas Valley. But they were understaffed, and they never seemed to get caught up on the wreath orders. And Mrs. S. was not as young as she had been.

Hanna couldn't just dump all that on her and head back to New York. It was obvious, after one day, Mrs. S. would never have time to put together the Christmas tree decorating contest and somehow that event seemed pivotal to restoring the farm's place in the community. Hanna would just get that organized before she left.

Besides, when Sam was giving so unstintingly of himself—he had never once complained today—how could she, the owner of the farm, not match his effort and energy and enthusiasm?

"That," she said, managing to look stern again, after she had stopped giggling, "is a terrible name for a Christmas tree decorating contest."

Hanna realized, warily, that underneath all her other excuses for staying here on the farm when she really should be leaving, the truth was that she had not giggled as she had today for a very long time. The truth was she was having fun.

Without her really making note of it, her life, including the job she would have said just yesterday that she was devoted to, had become a somber affair. It was as if some kind of dullness had crept up on her.

If she was honest, she could trace that dullness back to even before her mother had died and Darren had jumped ship.

"Why is it such a terrible name?" Sam asked, feigning innocence.

"You know darn well."

"No, I don't."

"It sounds faintly naughty."

He wagged his eyebrows at her. "Good. Sex sells."

It was more than evident to her that Sam, even though his life was no doubt way more exciting than hers, was having fun, too. "It doesn't go with a Christmas tree decorating contest," Hanna admonished him.

"But you could make it go with a Christmas tree decorating contest with a simple stroke of the pen." He took
the pen she was holding and the paper she was writing
their brainstormed ideas on, and leaned in close to her.

He smelled so good. Of the trees he had handled all
day, and faintly, of soap and aftershave, and that indefin-
able something which was pure man.

Be a professional, she told herself. *Quit sniffing the
man. He is a prospective buyer for the farm, nothing
more.*

He wrote, his handwriting firm and slashing, "Battle
of the Balls," and then he squeezed an arrow in between
the and *Balls* and scrawled in *Christmas*.

She found herself giggling again, and then surrender-
ing just the tiniest bit.

"You want something for dinner?" she asked.

"Nah, you don't have to feed me."

It wasn't the same as making Darren cookies, or going
through her cookbooks looking for the perfect romantic
meal to cook. So far, she'd fed him hot dogs for lunch.
Hardly high romance! Now she'd whip up a quesadilla
for dinner. It didn't mean anything, and she was quick
to tell him that.

"You are working for free. The very least I can do is
feed you."

"I told you, it's win-win for me. I'm getting the insider's look at the farm."

So, they'd both established it wasn't personal. A few
minutes later she passed him a quesadilla, and was horrified when she felt a certain womanly satisfaction when
he bit into it with a groan of appreciation.

"I can't believe I have the CEO of Old Apple Crate
working as a laborer for food. How is it that you don't
have blisters on your hands?"

* * *

Sam contemplated that question…and the fact that he was still on Christmas Valley Farm. But technology really turned the entire world into an office, and he had been able to handle urgent matters with his phone.

He also had a great team at Old Apple Crate, and they were used to him taking off to source out ethically grown coffee beans in Brazil, or to check out the work practices of the cocoa plantation in West Africa, where the beans for chocolate that his company sold were sourced from.

No one at Old Apple Crate was surprised that their CEO was taking such a hands-on approach to checking out the Christmas tree farm he was thinking of acquiring. He was always thorough and meticulous about details that others might overlook.

The truth was, Sam was finding he had enjoyed his day on the farm, and particularly working physically. He liked the labor involved in the tree farm—cutting down trees, wrapping them in netting, lifting them to his shoulder and bringing them out to people's vehicles. He liked the pleasant ache in his muscles…and okay, stupidly and dangerously, he liked the look on Hanna's face when she thought she was watching him and he didn't know it.

But, so what? Some things never changed, and a man liked a woman to know he was strong, liked to see *that* look on her face.

But working so hard physically had also made Sam aware that he had missed it. It had been a long time since he had done anything physical for his business, though when he had started he had put in exactly the kind of long and relentless hours they were putting in now.

"Blisters?" he said to Hanna. "Blisters are for wimps. You weren't suggesting I was a wimp, were you?"

He loved it that her blush was a confession of how often she watched him.

"I've got really tough hands," he told her, and then, despite his order to himself to shut up, he found himself still talking. "This isn't my first stint as a laborer, you know."

"It's not?"

"No, that's how I got my start."

"I didn't know that."

There was a lot about him that she didn't know. And it felt as if it would be a darn good idea to keep it that way! They were a man and a woman alone in her house.

It was all business. He needed to keep it that way.

"My dad was a farm laborer," he said, and then was annoyed with himself. He changed the subject. "How about Showdown at Christmas Valley?"

She wrote it down on her list of possible names for the tree decorating contest, then set down her pen and took a bite of her own quesadilla. But she wasn't distracted. "I knew what your dad did," she said quietly. "He worked here from time to time. I remember that day that I—"

Her eyes went to his lips and then skittered away. "I remember that day I was so mean to you. Have I ever told you how sorry I was that I said those things?"

He could pretend he didn't know what she was talking about, but he wasn't that good at pretending. Instead he said, a bit desperately, "Christmas Chaos?"

But instead of distracting her—and himself—that just reminded him even more of where he had come from.

She wrote it down. "It was terrible to say those things to you about your father and your house, and I'm sorry."

Instead of coming up with another really stupid suggestion for a name, he felt something go quiet in him. She didn't try to fill the silence, and after a long time, he said, "My dad used to work out at the Hansens' quite a bit. South of town? Mixed farm?"

"I know who they are."

Of course she would know who they were. When he had gone into Smith to run errands with her earlier in the day, people had shouted, across streets and down aisles, "Welcome home, Hanna!"

They came out from behind store counters to hug her. When locals came to the farm to get their trees, they squealed their pleasure when they saw her.

Everywhere they went, people welcomed her. That's what happened in a town like this when you were fourth or fifth generation. Like the Merrifields and the Hansens.

No one welcomed him home. His family, if it could be called that, had been transient farm laborers.

"Herb Hansen gave my dad more work than anyone else. But sometimes my dad was too hungover or too drunk to go."

Why was he saying this to her? Not to reveal anything of himself, he decided. No, it was to warn her off.

"So I'd go. That's why I missed so much school."

Hanna was staring at him, her eyes wide and beautiful, and filled with a light that was more unnerving than sympathy. It was pure compassion. And it made him keep talking when he wanted to shut up.

"I got suspended for it all the time. For missing too much school."

"If you had just told—"

He stopped her with a look. "You don't just tell those things. I was ashamed of it. Everyone, including the teachers, thought I was skipping because I thought I was way too cool for school. They thought I was out riding my motorcycle and doing whatever else it is a cool guy of eighteen does. I wanted them to think that."

This was warning her off? It felt a lot more like he was unburdening himself at her expense.

"Oh, Sam." Her hand crept across the table and took his. Hanna did not seem warned off at all! He should have pulled away from her, but he didn't.

"It turned out okay," he said, a faint hoarseness to his voice. "Herb saw some potential in me, probably the first person who ever had. He took me under his wing, and I found out I actually liked farming.

"He helped me buy an old wreck of a farm when I left high school, which is part of why I left here. It was in a different part of the state. It turned out I was ahead of the curve in seeing the demand for locally produced and organic produce. He was really the first investor in Old Apple Crate."

He dared look at Hanna. She didn't look at all perturbed by what he had just told her.

"I think," she said softly, "that you are amazing."

He gulped. He did what he should have done as soon as she took his hand. He stole his own hand back out of hers.

"I'm not, really," he said gruffly. "Those things, Hanna, growing up without enough of anything—" he stopped himself from saying *including love* "—that changes a person."

"In what way?" she said softly.

"I can't ever have what you've had," he said. "I can't ever have a warm and loving family. I don't know how. I tried it once and I failed, and I'm not trying it again. It has its plus side. I'm driven in business, and I don't let anything get in my way."

She looked at him long and hard. He had the awful feeling he had not succeeded in warning her off. He had the awful feeling that she saw right through what he had just said to the longing that lay underneath it, to have those very things he had said he could not have.

That was why he was really hanging out here, wasn't it? He was soaking up the atmosphere of family at the farm, the joyous expectation for Christmas that came through the doors of the workshop every time someone arrived to buy a tree or walked out with a beautiful wreath, or that very special Christmas decoration.

He tilted his chin at her, daring her to call him on it.

But she didn't. She looked at her list and said, "How about Season's Shenanigans?"

"That's terrible. It doesn't begin to say what a serious and cutthroat competition this is going to be."

"So far," she reminded him, sadly, "it's a competition with no one in it. Mrs. S. says there hasn't been one for the past half dozen years. People have forgotten about it. I don't know if they'll come back. And," she glanced at a calendar, "I'm not sure about the timeline. Can we put it together this quickly?"

Sam felt relieved by this conversation. This was what he did. This was what he excelled at. He put things together. He fixed things. It was way more comfortable ground for him. He took his cell phone out of his pocket.

"Hi, Bea. Look, this farm I'm on is having a contest to decorate a Christmas tree. It's a great cause. They give the fully decorated trees to families who need them. Book some rooms at the Smith hotel for the weekend of December fourteenth and bring a team out from the office."

He read the silence on the other end of the phone as stunned.

"Well, doesn't that sound fun," she finally said, as if they had never had fun at the office before. Which they probably hadn't. He had never been an office-Christmas-party kind of boss.

"Fun?" he said gruffly. "Bea, I fully expect to win."

He smiled when Bea said that of course they were going to win. He hired people who were as competitive as he himself was.

"I'll fax you a poster with the rules and what you'll need to bring." He hung up the phone and looked at Hanna, who was smiling. "There. There's your first team entered."

"Humph. Well, Christmas Valley Farm will have its own team, too." She seemed to realize she was committing to something, and frowned. "I mean I may not be here, personally, but no one can decorate a tree like Mrs. S."

"You're going back to work?"

"I have to, though my hand isn't quite there yet. I'll give it a few more days, until I'm convinced things are running well here."

But he heard the lack of enthusiasm in her voice. She might not know it yet, but Sam seriously doubted the firm of Banks and Banks was going to be seeing Hanna anytime soon. But he went along with her for now.

"So, let's get these posters done while you're still here, then," he said. His voice was, thankfully, all business. That was what he was here to do, learn a business. "Name?"

"How about Christmas Miracles at Christmas Valley?"

"Sheesh. That doesn't make it sound like a cutthroat competition at all."

"It's making a miracle happen for whoever receives that tree," she said stubbornly. "My dad and I used to deliver them after the contest every year to the families who needed them. I remember lots of tears when we arrived with those incredible, fully decorated trees. We had a man come in to the workshop the other day who had been a kid in a family who got one of those trees. He said it was a miracle."

"It's too smarmy," Sam protested.

"It won't just be about decorating the trees," she said, a bit dreamily. "It'll be a family day. We'll shovel off the pond and have hot dogs and hot chocolate, just like in the old days."

Her phone dinged that she had a message, and she looked down at it and smiled, and despite his every effort to harden his heart, her smile lit up the room. "Guess what?"

"Please don't tell me a miracle," he said drily.

"You judge. Mrs. S. says her granddaughter is a cheerleader at the school and the squad wants to enter a team to decorate a tree."

"It is a miracle. Mrs. S. *can* text. And she's older than Methuselah."

Hanna hit him on the arm. He frowned at her, but the truth? There was a dangerous camaraderie building between them. The truth? He *liked* Hanna smacking him on the arm.

Business, he reminded himself sharply. "All I can say is you better buy lots of hot dogs. Because where those cheerleaders go, lots of teenage boys will follow."

"It's going to be a great day," she said with wonder.

"Yeah," he said. And dyed-in-the-wool cynic that he was, Sam had to admit he was beginning to feel just a little bit of wonder himself. He crushed it. "You should do an analysis. I'd like to see how the contest translates to farm sales."

Her eyes met his, and something zinged between them.

"I have to go," he said abruptly.

She looked at the clock. "Yes, you do. Morning comes early on a Christmas tree farm."

When he got back to his hotel, his phone pinged that he had a text. He glanced down at it. It was from Bea.

Forgot to tell you when we spoke, pushed through Smith trailer sale. Offer has been finalized. Will close within two weeks.

Good. Buying that trailer was like finalizing his reminder to himself that there was no place for wonder in his world, and definitely no place in it for a woman like Hanna Merrifield.

If he was smart, he wouldn't even go back to the farm the next day. But somehow, he found himself there, bright and early, and much as he tried to tell himself otherwise, he hadn't been drawn here only to learn the business.

The thing was, she didn't have to know that. And so, over the next few days, he was determinedly and grimly strictly professional. He worked like a dog and so did she. As her hand got better, she did more and more.

It was as if they were soldiers on a mission together. Let's get 'er done. They made wreaths and hauled trees. Despite his attempts to keep the barriers up, a quiet and somewhat reluctant camaraderie continued to develop between them.

Now, it was once again after-hours. She had insisted on giving him dinner again. He ate and checked his emails while she worked on her computer. Sam glanced up at Hanna.

She was glowing. He had been at Christmas Valley Farm for a week, and it seemed each day, as she immersed herself in the multitude of details of getting that farm up and running in time for Christmas, Hanna grew more beautiful.

Sam felt something stir in him. "Don't you have to get back to work?" he said gruffly.

She frowned and stared at her computer screen. "According to my boss I should have been back yesterday."

"But?"

She sighed. "I don't really see how I can leave before the contest. It's too much to put on Mrs. S."

Hanna was coming home, though Sam suspected she may not have admitted that to herself yet. And he was helping her do it.

Even if it was bittersweet that he was helping her back to the place he could never go, and even though he knew with each passing day that he was probably moving further from his goal of attaining this farm, rather than closer to it, the look on her face right now made it all worth it.

She was studying the computer intently, her hair forming a curtain, her tongue caught between her teeth.

She always did that: caught her tongue between her teeth when she was working hard or thinking about something.

"How's that?" she said, leaning back from her computer.

He stood up and went behind her, bending over to look at it. She had created a draft of a poster.

It was simple: a tree with snow-laden boughs in the background, with printing over top.

You're invited to a day of Christmas Miracles. Skating, free hot chocolate, hot dogs.

And in bigger letters: *Christmas Tree Decorating Contest, Christmas Valley Farm,* with the date, and a contact number to enter a team for the decorating contest.

"What do you think?" she asked him.

What did he think? The wonderful smell of her hair was tickling his nose, shampoo mingled with the scent of pine and fir, and it made it hard to think at all.

"The poster looks great," he said gruffly. He made a great show of looking at his watch. "I've got to go."

"Just wait a sec, you can bring some posters with you and distribute them around town before you come back out here tomorrow."

He contemplated that. He contemplated that it was a given he was returning to the farm tomorrow. He contemplated how she was not going back to work, even though it seemed her choices might be putting her career in jeopardy. It seemed to him that despite both their best efforts to control their worlds, they were failing, as if it was impossible to fight something else that was going on.

Something that was greater than both of them.

It wasn't until he left, a few minutes later, a stack of posters under his arm to distribute around town before he came back out to the farm in the morning, that Sam was able to think clearly again at all.

And his thoughts?

Sam, you are getting in way over your head.

It was easier, once her scent was not tickling his nostrils, to see this as a business opportunity.

And, to see, ever so clearly, it was up to him to keep it that way. Even if they never ended up doing a deal after all.

CHAPTER TWELVE

HANNA CAME AROUND the corner of the workshop and crashed headlong into Sam. He righted her and then quickly put her away from him.

She was aware that today he was trying to keep the distance between them, and she was also aware that while she should be nothing but grateful to him, she was finding his chilliness frustrating.

"What are you doing?" she asked.

"Nothing," he said, too quickly. He ground something into the snow under his foot.

"Oh, my God, Sam Chisholm, were you smoking?"

He glared at her. She leaned into him, and sniffed. How wrong was it to find that faintly smoky aroma dangerous and sexy?

"You said you only smoked when you were stressed. What on earth are you stressed about? It's a Christmas tree farm!"

His eyes flitted to her lips. So, he wasn't quite as indifferent to her as he had been letting on! she thought, trying to squash the curl of satisfaction she felt.

"I'm not stressed," he said. "I'm freezing. It snowed last night. I've spent the whole morning shaking snow out of trees."

"You'd think you would figure out that there is not

a leather coat for every occasion," she said, eyeing his beautifully distressed bomber style jacket meaningfully. She could smell the aroma of that, too.

"That's sacrilege," he warned her.

"No, sacrilege is smoking at Christmas Valley Farm. This is a wholesome family operation."

Or had been. Until—

"Like Disneyland," he said sardonically.

"Exactly."

He took a slow look around.

"Okay. Maybe not exactly like Disneyland. Still, there's no room for crankiness here. If you don't have the right attitude, I might not be able to sell you the farm."

It felt as if she had told him a secret. And herself, too.

"Are you reconsidering selling me the farm?" he asked her.

She didn't say anything.

"Because of my crankiness?" he demanded softly, "or because of something inside you?"

"Because of your crankiness," she said, firmly. She was not ready to look at the longing being home on the farm was creating in her.

"Huh," he said with utter disbelief. "If you are not going to sell me the farm, there is absolutely no reason for me to be freezing my backside off shaking snow from trees."

"I didn't say I wasn't going to sell it to you. I said you need the right attitude."

"Oh," he said, "wholesome."

He took a step toward her. The look in his eyes was about as far from wholesome as you could get!

She felt her eyes go wide. Was he going to kiss her? Just to show her he was not the least bit interested in being wholesome? And never had been? She gulped. She ordered herself to step away from him, but she didn't. She held her ground and tilted her chin.

He moved slowly toward her, a wicked light gleaming in his eyes, and an unreadable smile on his lips.

And then he ducked down, picked up a handful of snow and began to form it into a ball in his hand.

She read his intent immediately. With a small shriek, she turned and ran. The snowball whistled by her ear.

"How's that for wholesome?" he called.

She ducked behind a stand of trees, picked up her own handful of snow. If there was one thing he could not beat her at, it was a snowball fight! She stepped out from behind the trees, and threw.

The snowball hit a glancing blow off his shoulder, and exploded. He looked astonished, and then with a war cry, the fight was on!

Hanna shrieked with laughter, ducking in and out of the noble firs as his snow missiles landed all around her. Finally, he caught her, tugged her to the ground, and straddled her.

He shoved snow down her coat until she begged for mercy, and then he rolled off her, and they lay side by side in the snow gasping for air, looking at the sky.

"How did you leave all this?" he asked her. "Why didn't you ever come back? You must have missed it."

She contemplated that. "I think I'd convinced myself I didn't miss it. I remembered all the hard work and not any of the good parts. My relationship with my parents wasn't good by the time I left here. Returning seemed painful."

"It wasn't good? That surprises me. You just seemed like one of those families who could weather any storm."

"I know," she said pensively. "It surprised me, too,

when we couldn't weather the storm, when we just all fell apart."

"It must have been a hell of a storm."

Suddenly, she did not want to ruin this perfect moment revisiting that storm.

"Are you warm now?" she asked, changing the subject.

"Yeah, fine," he said gruffly. "Trust you to have a wholesome way to warm up."

She hesitated and then she said, softly, "I'm not as wholesome as you think I am." In fact, that was at the heart of the rift between her and her parents. She had the awful feeling if he showed even a hint of interest, she would unload the whole seedy story on him.

He lifted himself up on his elbow and stared down at her. "Miss Merrifield," he said, his voice hoarse, "that is somewhere I do not want to go."

And then he got up, shook snow off himself and sauntered away, leaving her feeling breathless, and not just from the mad dash through the snow, either.

And so the days unfolded in counterpoints. Playfulness seemed to be followed by tension, closeness by distance, moments of sizzling awareness followed by hours of deliberately ignoring one another.

The day of the Christmas tree decorating contest arrived.

"Look what you've done to this place," Sam said quietly. "You've brought it back to life."

She looked at him. The feeling she had was that somehow, being around him, with all the tension and all the playfulness mixed in, it was not the farm coming back to life.

It was her.

Hanna looked deliberately away from him and at the area that had been cleared in front of the Christmas Workshop. Ten trees were set up, Christmas Valley's homegrown and very best noble fir. They were ready for the decorating contest. Each tree even had its own power source, a detail Sam had worked on late into last night.

Tears pricked her eyes. At first, as the 3:00 p.m. start for the contest had approached, there had only been a trickle of people. Hanna's anxiety was compounded by the fact she'd just had a text from Mr. Banks, the latest in a series she'd been receiving all week, which told her in no uncertain terms to get her priorities straight.

What if she'd invested all this time and effort—when really she should have been at work—and Christmas Miracles was a colossal failure? What if she'd invested all this time and effort into Christmas Valley Farm, and it was already too late, the farm, and all it had once stood for, already lost?

But then, when Mr. Banks texted her again, Hanna didn't read it. Firmly, she had turned off her phone. And all of a sudden, the trickle of people had thickened to a flood. Now, the parking area had long since filled, and there were cars parked out to the highway.

There was a throng of people waiting for the contest to begin. It was a beautiful day, the sun sparkling on snow, and they were going to decorate the trees outside.

Hanna looked up at Sam, and the tears pricked harder behind her eyes. Now look what she had done.

Look what *they* had done.

"Is it just like you remember it?" he asked.

"No, it's better. And quit glaring at those boys, for heaven's sake."

"They're swilling back the hot chocolate like pigs at a trough."

"That's what it's there for."

"Next year, we're charging for it," Sam said. "We can

give the proceeds to charity, but it will stop the bottomless pits from taking advantage."

One part of her registered what a good businessman he was. But another part of her registered something else, altogether.

Next year? He didn't necessarily mean next year, together, she told herself firmly. He meant next year when he owned the farm, of course.

Mrs. S. took a microphone, part of the electronics that Sam had worked tirelessly on setting up. She had declined Hanna's invitation to join the Christmas Valley decorating team and said she wanted to "run the show" instead. She was dressed in her most horrible Christmas sweater and obviously thrilled at the crowds and her position as MC. After welcoming everyone, she introduced the ten teams who would be competing for the grand prize of a ten-foot Fraser fir to take home. The "prize" tree had been carefully chosen, and was the farm's best.

When Mrs. S. announced the Old Apple Crate team, Sam gave Hanna a wink, and removed his leather jacket.

Underneath it, he had layered a bright red T-shirt over a sweatshirt. The T-shirt had the Old Apple Crate logo on the front. But when he turned his back to her, the T-shirt proclaimed he was the leader of the Battle of the Christmas Balls team.

His team of four, all in identical shirts, surrounded him.

Hanna had met his people earlier, and had seen instantly how devoted they were to him. Now they gathered around him, and she wondered if he knew himself how much he was the center of them, the hub of the wheel that all the spokes turned around.

Sam was not the warm and fuzzy type—or *smarmy*—as he would call it. In fact, he could be downright cranky!

But she had noticed in his days spent here at the farm that people, customers and staff gravitated to him naturally for leadership.

He was straightforward, and a take-charge kind of guy. He was strong and funny. He radiated a kind of unconscious confidence that inspired trust. And loyalty.

Looking at him with his staff, Hanna was not sure that love would be too strong a word to describe what she saw in the air around them.

She contemplated that for a moment. *Love.* It seemed as if the world had gone silent around her.

She reflected on the time that they had been working together, and the warm feeling she had in her heart every single time she thought of him. She thought about the laughter and his quick wit and teasing. And she thought of the deep comfort she felt with him as they shared hurried lunches and hot dogs, as she consulted him about orders, or one of the myriad problems and challenges that came up every single day.

She thought of how she had come to trust him and rely on him. Sam Chisholm was one of those rare people who followed through on every single thing he promised. If he said something would be done, then it was done.

And it was done perfectly, no shortcuts, no weaseling out of extra work, no excuses.

His word was pure gold.

Hanna wondered suddenly, with a sick downward swoop of her stomach, whether she had been fooling herself about her reasons for staying on the farm when she needed to be back at work.

No, what she was fooling herself about was the nature of love! It was a fickle beast, and if anyone should know that, it was her.

She would see the contest through. She would enjoy

this little interlude with Sam. And then, without so much as a backward glance, she would go back to her other life. Her real life.

"And last, but of course, not least," Mrs. S. said, "representing our very own Christmas Valley Farm, Hanna and the Elves."

Hanna, and her two helpers, Jasmine and Michael, smiled and waved. An enthusiastic cheer went up from the crowd, and Hanna marveled at how she had been accepted back into this community as if she had never left at all.

Of course, it was the fact she was leaving again that made her so brave. Taking a deep breath, Hanna peeled off her own overcoat. She had a surprise for Sam, too.

Underneath it, she had on the short green tunic and wide black belt of her elf days. She had on dark green tights and green buckled shoes that turned up at the tips. The outfit still fit her after all these years, though from the look on Sam's face, it might have been a little tighter than it had been before.

She looked over at Sam and grinned as she tugged the green elf hat out of her pocket and pulled it over her hair. She had added a jaunty little sprig of mistletoe to the brim.

But Sam was not smiling. His mouth had fallen open, and his eyes had darkened.

He made his way back to her, and stared down at her. "No fair," he said, his voice a growl that sent a shiver down her spine. "You are quite the distraction in that outfit. I think you are doing it deliberately to break my focus."

"For heaven's sake," she said, "there are six teenage girls over there in cheerleading outfits shaking their pompoms. And Jasmine looks pretty stunning in her elf outfit, too. *I'm* breaking your focus?"

He barely spared Jasmine a glance, and didn't even look at the cheerleaders. "The mistletoe is a particularly diabolical touch, because you know darn well what a man's thoughts go to when he sees mistletoe."

"All is fair in love and, er, battle," she said with a gulp.

There was that word again, love.

Yes, she told herself, that stupid word that represented impossible dreams and lost hopes and unfathomable betrayals.

But despite telling herself all that, as they stood there for a moment, looking at each other, it was as if the crowds had faded to nothing.

They were in a place they had been in once before, at her family's Christmas tree farm with her in an elf costume.

Only this time everything was different. This time she wasn't running away. This time she was holding her ground.

"Really?" The growl in his voice became even more menacing. "All is fair?"

Hanna nodded, her throat dry.

"Well, Miss Merrifield, you are standing under the mistletoe. It's clearly an invitation."

What had made her put that sprig in the brim of her hat this morning? Had she wished, in some secret part of herself, for this exact moment? For the awareness to be like a fire in his eyes, and for the air around them to sizzle with possibility?

At some level, had she hoped to erupt the tension that had been right below the surface ever since that snowy night when he had knocked her pony to the ground, and come to her rescue?

Even though they were in a very public place, he stepped in to her, put his arms around her, and drew her against the length of himself. And then his head dropped over hers and he kissed her.

Thoroughly.

It was strange, because even as her heart sped up, Hanna could feel her whole world slowing down, melting into this moment, until that was all there was. She and Sam, motionless, in the center of a kaleidoscope of action and color and noise.

Hanna was aware, in the deepest part of herself, where awareness has no words, that her sense of homecoming was complete.

And that she was complete.

This was the moment all that tension and playfulness and awareness had been building toward. When she felt as if she was as limp as a wrung-out rag, as if her knees were going to buckle beneath her, Sam stepped back from her and raised that dark slash of an eyebrow wickedly at her.

"I think," he said gruffly, "Miss Merrifield, that we may be even in the distraction department."

Then he frowned, plucked the mistletoe from her hat and shoved it in his pocket. "Just in case anybody else is getting ideas," he said, sending a warning look at Michael, who Hanna was one hundred percent certain had not been getting any ideas!

And then Sam wheeled away from her and went back to his team.

She stared after him. The woman he had introduced earlier as his assistant, Beatrice, gave Hanna a subtle thumbs-up.

Her cheeks burning with equal parts of embarrassment—she was not one given to displays of public passion, even if the mistletoe *did* allow it—and the heat of his kiss, she forced herself to lead her team over to the Christmas tree they had been assigned.

"Complete, indeed," she muttered to herself, annoyed.

He had done it to distract her, nothing more, and he had been totally successful. She was thoroughly distracted, but she forced herself to look at the tree. It was six feet tall, a Scotch pine.

"All right," Mrs. S. called. "Teams, get ready. You have exactly one hour to decorate your tree. Ho-ho-ho and go!"

To the best of her ability, Hanna shook off the distraction of that kiss. She and her team had decided they would do a heritage tree, which meant they didn't have to start with the strings of lights like every other team.

Hanna had found boxes and boxes of vintage decorations in the workshop. At one time, her mother had run a sideline specialty business selling them, but that had been before the days of internet shopping, and it had not taken off. They sold a few in the gift shop every year, but that was all.

Hanna's team began by attaching the candle holders and putting a candle stub in each one. And then they placed the popcorn that she and Jasmine had been secretly stringing for a week. After that they filled every space in that tree with handmade ornaments and small wooden toys and little tin flutes.

"Half an hour left," Mrs. S. called.

The time was flying by way too quickly! Hanna and the Elves was the smallest team, and it placed them at a disadvantage.

"Look at Old Apple Crate," Jasmine said with a moan.

The last thing Hanna needed was the distraction of looking at Old Apple Crate, but she did.

The team, under Sam, was like a well-oiled machine. And their tree was breathtaking. They had chosen totally white lights as a backdrop for what appeared to be hundreds of tiny red apples and bright green pears, crusted in diamond glitter.

"The cheerleaders look pretty good, too," Michael said.

The cheerleaders did look pretty good, hopping around in their short skirts and leading cheers from the crowd, but to Hanna's experienced eye, their tree was something of a disaster. The electrical cords for the lights showed, and the angel at the top was leaning precariously. As far as she could see they had no theme, just a mish-mash of decorations. There were gaping bare spots in the tree, and spots so full the decorations were crunched against each other.

Hanna glanced around at the others. The Smith Mercantile team was doing a wonderful job and so was the Feed Store, though she was pretty sure Sam's tree and hers were the frontrunners.

The rest of the hour passed in the blink of an eye.

Hanna's team had barely got their candles lit when Mrs. S. called time. Hanna stood back and looked at their tree. Because they were outside and darkness had not yet fallen, the magnificence of the candles was not showing properly.

Naturally, Sam's tree was perfection from the top, a lit star, to the bottom, where an abundance of wrapped parcels had appeared under his tree.

"So, sadly," Mrs. S. announced, "we have a disqualification. Hanna and Her Elves, representing Christmas Valley Farms have been disqualified."

Hanna's mouth fell open. "He paid you!" she cried.

"Who paid me?" Mrs. S. asked, clearly both insulted and confused.

"Tut-tut," Sam called. "You are always accusing me of paying someone when you lose competitions against me. Don't be a poor sport, Hanna."

She stuck out her tongue at him.

"My dear," Mrs. S. said, "these trees are given to families with young children. As beautiful as your tree is—the clear aesthetic winner—we can't have lit candles on it. It's a hazard. In fact, I think one of your branches is catching fire right now."

It was true, a gust of a breeze had fanned one of the candles, and the closest needles were catching fire. Michael quickly reached up and doused the lit branch, and then he and Jasmine went and blew out the rest of the candles.

"Now, we will judge the winner by audience vote, and it will be decided by whoever gets the loudest applause."

That was another twist Hanna had not been expecting. Usually the mayor and a committee of dignitaries decided which tree was the winner.

"So competitive," said a voice in her ear. "It's written all over your face."

"Now you're going to win," Hanna said sulkily.

"What do you need to win for? You're already surrounded by trees. The last thing you need is to win your own tree back," he teased.

"It was for the glory," she pouted. "What are you going to do with the tree?"

"Put it up in one of the stores, probably. With a sign saying where it came from. Good advertising for you."

"Oh, quit being a good winner," she said.

But Sam's team did not win. Not even close.

The high school cheerleaders won handily: the roar of approval from their fan club of high school boys practically shook the workshop on its foundation. The girls jumped up and down and did a cheer, and then they huddled.

One of the girls stepped forward to accept the beautiful prize tree, which Hanna had to admit would look fantastic in the lobby of the high school. She was clearly thrilled by what Hanna thought was an undeserved victory.

But Hanna was humbled by what happened next.

"We would like to donate this tree we won to a girl in our school, Laura Lindy. Her little brother has been diagnosed with cancer, and it is going to be a very hard Christmas for the Lindys." She waited for the applause to die. "And we would like all of you to help us decorate it."

In that moment, it went from being a contest to a community pulling together. The true spirit of Christmas was suddenly in the air as grandmothers stood beside their grandchildren to put decorations on the new tree, as the doctor stood beside the farm laborer, as the strongest of men stood beside the frailest of women.

Leftover decorations were taken from the boxes of all the teams who had competed, and when that wasn't quite enough to satisfy the ring of people around the tree, each team pulled a few from their trees to make the "new" tree happen. People went into the gift shop and bought more decorations to load onto the tree.

The air was filled with chatter and shouts and laughter and giggles.

And when they stood back from it, that tree was clearly the winner. It was beautiful. The chatter disappeared, and the laughter quieted.

One of the cheerleaders began to sing, her voice tremulous at first, and then gaining strength.

"Silent night, holy night…"

And then other voices joined that sole, brave cheerleader's. "All is calm, all is bright…"

Hanna heard Sam's voice, rising above them all, deep and confident. His breath whispered along the nape of her neck. She tilted her head back, and as she looked up at him, she felt a shiver as she remembered his lips on hers.

She let the spontaneous celebration of Christmas tingle along her spine, and she was aware she had never experienced a more beautiful moment than this one.

For the first time in a long time, it seemed her life was ripe with possibilities.

All of them dangerous. But for this moment, she found herself not caring, not caring one little bit if being here for this day and this moment had cost her the job that only two weeks ago she had lived for.

CHAPTER THIRTEEN

SAM STOOD IN the driveway, watching the last set of red headlights disappear into the night.

The day of Christmas Miracles was over. The nine o'clock closing of Christmas Valley Farm had come and gone with no one showing any sign of leaving. As night had fallen a bonfire had been started by the pond and skating had begun.

Now, it was just after midnight. He contemplated what he was feeling: a deep sense of satisfaction. Contentment.

It seemed to him the thing that had eluded him all the days of his life—happiness—was unfurling like a flag before a tender wind inside of him.

"We made five hundred dollars on hot dogs," Hanna said, coming out of the workshop, and pulling the door closed behind her. Almost as an afterthought, she locked it. There was a lot of money in there.

They stood side by side drinking in the silence, and the loveliness of the trees that had been decorated, still lit up, twinkling against the darkness of the night.

She was part of it. Maybe even the biggest part of the happiness he was feeling right now.

"How much did you make on the trees?" Sam asked, trying to get back to his safety zone. Money. Business. He was pretty sure the sales would set a record for the farm. After the tree decorating contest, the cash register had started ringing, and it had not stopped until close to midnight.

He and Hanna, Jasmine and Michael and Mrs. S. had been run off their feet.

"I'm not sure. I'll count it in the morning."

Sam smiled at that. There was one of the huge differences between them. Trust her to know exactly how much the hot dogs had made, when that money was going to charity. He had hastily constructed a sign charging for the hot dogs before the high school boys had descended and eaten up all the profits for the day.

"We're completely sold out of wreaths," she said with a sigh. "I think I see wreaths in my future, as well as my past."

He went and began unplugging the trees. She joined him. One by one, the lights on the contest trees winked out.

"They're still gorgeous," she decided.

"They are," he agreed. It was as if those trees, imbued with the nobler purpose of bringing joy, were saturated in light even now, when their lights had been turned out.

"Are they hard to deliver, all decorated like this?"

"Oh, yeah. And worth every second of it."

"Are you exhausted?" he asked. He hoped she would say yes, and wish him good night. He hoped she would say no and that he could hold onto this feeling just a bit longer.

If there was one thing life had taught him, it was that moments like this did not last.

"Kind of," Hanna said, "but kind of wired, too, like the excitement from such a good day is jumping around inside of me."

That's how he felt, too. Reluctant, if he admitted it to

himself, to let go of the wonder of the day. He pointed to the benches around the dying embers of the fire. "You want to have a hot dog before we call it quits? I noticed you didn't stop for supper."

"We have hot dogs left?"

"I hid a few."

"My hero," she said, and Sam felt something ripple along his spine. A man could live to be her hero.

She went and plunked herself down on the bench. There were nothing but embers left, perfect for cooking. He threaded a hot dog onto a stick for her, and sat beside her.

"Wasn't it an incredible day?" she said softly a while later, after having tucked away three hot dogs. She was looking at the fire, as if she had no plan to move. And no desire to either.

Then again, neither did he.

"It was," he said. "I've never, ever felt the spirit of Christmas the way I did today when everyone came together to decorate that last tree."

"I saw quite a few tears when we were singing 'Silent Night,'" she said softly. "I was blinking them back myself. That was, totally, the spirit of Christmas."

"Have you felt it before?" he asked softly.

"Working here? Growing up here? Yes. Lots and lots of moments of pure magic. I don't know how I became so blinded to them. It was a good note for me to finish on," Hanna said. "Mr. Banks has made it clear to me if I'm not back at work on Monday, I won't have a job to go back to."

"I don't know how you can leave a place like this," Sam said. He could feel the hesitation inside of him. "It's magical here. I felt just a hint of that once before. And it was here, too, the day I first saw you in your elf costume.

Today and that day, those are the only two times I've felt as if I had any idea what Christmas was all about."

"But why?" she asked, troubled.

It was time to tell her, Sam thought. All of it. He had never told anyone all of it before. Never. It was all well and good to entertain thoughts of being her hero. All this tension, interspersed with playfulness, their awareness of each other, it was going a dangerous place. It had been dangerous before he kissed her, and now that he had tasted her, how could he go backward?

But he had to. It was time to lay the bald truth on the table. She would know after she heard it that he would be the worst possible guy to take any kind of chance on, not with what she wanted. He was no one's hero, and probably never could be.

This evening, after having enjoyed the full day of festivities, his assistant, Bea, had given him a set of keys.

"I almost forgot. These are for that trailer you bought. It's all yours." Typically, Bea, if she was curious about this odd acquisition in Smith, never said a word.

Now, those keys seemed to be burning a hole in his pocket, reminding him of who he really was, and what he had to offer.

Or more accurately, what he didn't have to offer. What he would never have to offer, what he was a prisoner to. He'd seen what was unfolding between him and Hanna. It bothered him that his attempts to keep it in check had been useless.

Today, he had kissed her. He had said it was to distract her, but it wasn't. He had been driven by that adorable little elf costume and by that sprig of mistletoe, to taste her. It had overwhelmed his customary caution, his need for absolute control. And now that he had, how did you put that particular tiger back in its cage?

She didn't know everything there was to know about him. And when she did? Kisses between them would be unthinkable. He had to scare her off, plain and simple. For his own self-preservation and for hers.

"Hanna," Sam said slowly, feeling his way carefully through the minefield of his past, "I shouldn't have kissed you. I shouldn't even be here with you right now."

She looked stunned. "What? Why?"

"It all implies it's going somewhere, and it's not."

Now she looked hurt. And that, he told himself, was nothing but a good thing. He should leave it there. He should just get up and walk away.

But somehow he could not be that cold. Not to her, not with her sitting there in her little elf costume, looking so lovely and innocent and adorable.

"Look," he said, "I've never had what you had. Look around you. This was your reality. And maybe it will be again.

"A beautiful farm, a family that had worked the same place for a hundred years. You grew up with traditional values, and those magic moments you just spoke of, strung together, one after another like pearls on a thread."

"It wasn't quite like that," Hanna protested. "There's a price to pay if anything happens to rattle those values."

She wasn't getting what he was saying. He had to be blunt. "I'm trying to tell you, you and I are worlds apart. My dad was a transient laborer, we moved from town to town, following work, outrunning his reputation. Smith is the only place we ever stayed more than a year, and it was only because I was old enough to start filling in for my dad at the Hansens' and Herb took a liking to me."

Sam took a deep breath. He could feel something shudder inside him. Hanna moved closer to him, pressing her shoulder and hip into his side. It was the hardest thing he'd ever done, but he moved away from her, committed to saying what he needed to say.

"Christmas was a horrible time for me, Hanna. My dad drank more, we had even less money. We never once had a tree. Sometimes he'd get me some presents, never wrapped. Usually, he didn't wait until Christmas morning. He'd just roll in drunk, all pleased with himself, and say *here*.

"When I was little, it was a cheap toy. A plastic tractor, a little car. I cherished those things, but we moved so much and in such a hurry that things often got left behind.

"One year he came home with a puppy."

Sam's voice cracked. For a moment he thought he couldn't go on. He needed to say this, so she would know not to take a chance on him, know why this could not go anywhere.

But then Hanna's hand crept into his, warm and small and surprisingly strong. It was the opposite of what he wanted, so why did he let it stay there?

"I thought it was the best thing that had ever happened to me. It *loved* me. It followed me everywhere. It slept with me. But then it got sick. I had to take it to an animal shelter because we couldn't afford a vet. I didn't even know it should have had shots. When the lady at the animal shelter told me it should have had shots, she was so disapproving of me. I felt so ashamed.

"You can be written up in every business magazine in the world, win every award, have the best profits you've ever seen. And right below all that? That shame is still there."

Her hand tightened on his. He glanced at her out of the corner of his eye. A tear was sliding down her cheek.

He wanted to stop. He was causing her pain. But in

the end, that was a good thing. That she knew, completely, who he was, and that it would cause her pain if she got involved with him any further. That they had to stop this runaway train of feeling they were both riding. So he forced himself to go on.

"Another year, he gave me a bicycle. It disappeared a few days later."

"What do you mean, disappeared?"

"He told me it was stolen, but I knew he'd sold it. He bought booze instead."

Hanna gasped, and Sam absorbed her shock.

"I'm not telling you this to make you feel sorry for me," he said. He wanted her to see him, and he wanted her to run the other way when she did, so he kept on talking, even though it was painful.

"I used to save my money to buy him something for Christmas. I was always looking for the gift that would solve it all. I'd save my money and buy him something I was sure would make him happy. A little TV one year, expensive shaving lotion, a good shirt. The year after the bike thing, I gave up. And then, at some point, I thought I'd just start buying my own Christmas present, instead. I decided I was not going to rely on anyone else to make me happy. Sometimes I'd save a whole year to get myself what I wanted. I didn't wrap it up or anything. I just got it and felt the satisfaction of getting it.

"One year," he said softly, "It was that leather jacket. The one you remembered from high school. My dad noticed that it was new. He was drunk. Mean drunk. *Where'd you get that jacket?*

"I was so sick of it all. I told him it was none of his business, that I was earning most of the money in the house, and that I'd spend it on what I damn well pleased and that wouldn't be booze for him. It was the first time I'd ever raised my voice to him. He came at me, and he pummeled me within an inch of my life. I didn't go to school for a week after Christmas holidays, I was so banged up.

"But when he was done clobbering me, I stood up, and I took him by his collar, and I lifted him right off his feet, and I told him, 'Old man, if you ever touch me again, I'll kill you.'

"And we both knew I meant it."

He could feel her body shaking where it was touching his. Tears were coursing down her face.

"That's who I really am, Hanna, a man with crippling baggage, a man who could have killed his own father. I wanted to be something different. I wanted to rise above it, but my marriage showed me I couldn't. Our only Christmas together was the same fiasco I had grown up with.

"It's in me. It will always be in me—bitterness and anger just waiting to boil up at the slightest disappointment."

"I don't see you as bitter and angry."

"And let's just keep it that way," he said firmly. "I'm better just to fill every moment with work, that wondrous place where I can, for the most part, immerse myself in something else, and forget all that baggage in my past."

"What happened to your marriage?" Hanna asked, wiping away the tears with the sleeve of her elf costume. "I simply can't imagine you failing at anything."

He didn't want to confide in her about his disastrous marriage. But if it helped her to see how impossible things would be with him, why not?

"I disappointed her at every turn. That disastrous Christmas? She wanted to go to the Bahamas. I wanted to stay home. She wanted a very expensive necklace, I gave her an antique dresser. She wanted to go out for dinner, I thought we should try and cook a turkey at home.

I wanted a real tree, she didn't want to clean up needles. She ended up getting drunk, knocking over the artificial tree and throwing the turkey at me.

"It was all like that. Endless squabbling over nothing, her drinking more and more. I could see I would eventually turn her into my father. It seemed like the kindest thing for both of us to let her go."

"I think you're being unfair to yourself," Hanna said. "Maybe you weren't turning her into your father. Maybe, at some level you married someone just like him, hoping you could resolve it."

"No, it was me. I made my father like that, too."

"That is the most ridiculous thing I have ever heard."

"Is it? At my dad's funeral, I found out he wasn't always like that. He had a brother and a sister and old college roommates who talked about how fun he was and how smart."

"But what happened to him? And don't say you!"

"It appears his downward spiral began when my mother died. I gather theirs was quite a love story. He couldn't handle her loss. He didn't know where to go with all that grief."

"But when did she die?"

There was a long pause. "She died having me. So, you see, it was me, after all."

CHAPTER FOURTEEN

THERE. SAM FELT absolutely done. Spent.

Hanna had heard all of it. He had killed his mother and destroyed his father, and managed to release his wife before he destroyed her, too. He could bring nothing to Hanna but damage and bitterness and a deep shame he could never quite outrun, no matter what he did. If Hanna had any sense, she would get up, thank him for all his help on Christmas Valley Farm, and then run for her life.

But that was not what Hanna did. She took the hand that she still held, and she lifted it to her lips and kissed it. She laid her head on his shoulder.

He had thought he was telling her for her benefit, but now he realized it had been for his own.

He had laid every ugly truth about himself on her. And she was not running.

It seemed she was accepting him for exactly who he was, and what he was. That had never happened to him before.

And he felt the most incredible sense of lightness unfold inside of him, as if he had been holding onto something heavy for so long, and now he was finally able to let it go.

"Sam?" she said.

"Uh-huh?"

"I'm glad you told me."

That stopped him short. He was supposed to be chasing her away, not feeling this close to her.

He reviewed the last few weeks, the way he couldn't wait to get to the farm in the morning, the way the smile came to his lips the moment he saw her. The way they worked together, a perfect team, laughing and teasing. The way his nose, like a hound dog's, sought her scent. The way he looked for excuses to touch her. The way he loved to make her laugh.

This day, in particular, seemed threaded through with the light.

This was what happened, when day after day you got pressed into service making wreaths that they could not keep up with the orders for.

You chose a word to put in a wreath. Day after day, his hand had hesitated over the word *Hope*. He'd never chosen it, though sometimes he had picked it up, and felt it in the palm of his hand, before laying it back down. Sam had passed over other words, too.

Words like *Believe*.

Miracles.

While Hanna chose those words with a certain lightness, enthusiasm, even joy, he instead continued to pick the more generic wishes: *Merry Christmas, Season's Greetings*.

But even though he hadn't picked *Hope, Believe,* or *Miracles,* was it possible the essence of them had eased up through his palm, through the fingertips that hovered over them? What if each of those words held a power that, once planted in a mind, would not be denied? A power that crept by his guards and filled his heart with something so strange it felt forbidden?

Hope.

That was what Sam Chisholm felt right now, sitting with Hanna under a star-studded sky with the fire dying in front of them. He felt hope.

And he was like a man whose strength had been tried to the breaking point, and he could be strong no more.

His strength had begun to ebb away when he had kissed her today, using the mistletoe in her elf's hat as a pretext.

The kiss, he had told himself at the time, had been light and teasing, a distraction, nothing more.

Now, he saw he had only been kidding himself. The seeds for the confession he had just made had been planted in that moment, as surely as working with those wreath words had planted something in a heart he thought was too hard to be a fertile ground to grow new things.

Sam had felt as if he was protected by all the things she did not know about him. He had held those things to use as a secret weapon when the moment came when he most needed to put his shield back up.

But his secret weapon had not worked. At all. It had not driven her away, but instead brought her closer.

He had to taste her again. Fully this time. As his complete self.

He dropped his head over hers, and experienced the exquisite and delicate welcome of lips that told him, without words, that she knew all of him.

And delighted in his every truth.

Sam reeled back from her. She was still dressed in the cute little elf costume. No wonder she had trouble comprehending the cold, hard truth about him. She lived with one foot in a fantasy. She had always lived like this. Surrounded by a different reality than his.

One thing about working on the farm? He had discovered people really liked Christmas. It was not an act. It was not contrived. It was not manufactured by companies selling things.

The spirit of Christmas was real. It was a genuine joy in the air.

And Hanna had grown up breathing in that magic. That was what made them so different. And that was why what was in him could destroy her.

He carried darkness. It could snuff out her light.

He had to make her understand that. But that elf costume, and the glowing embers of the fire, and the scent of fresh cut trees in the air, and the light in her eyes were all proving a terrible distraction.

On the other hand, those keys for the trailer that he had been given earlier were still burning in his pocket. A trip back in time should remind him of the danger of hoping for too much. And if he took her with him, it would be more than words. It would be the stark reality of that brutal world.

The words hadn't been enough.

"I need to show you something," he said grimly. "It's too late tonight. I'll pick you up in the morning."

She looked as if she was going to argue, but then she just nodded, slid her hand over the roughness of his cheek, and left the fire. He watched her go, a little elf finding her way home after a hard day of Christmas merrymaking.

In the morning, thankfully, the elf costume was gone. Still, Sam had to steel himself against the temptations of her: her scent, the light in her hair, the solemn largeness of her eyes as she slid into the seat of his car beside him.

Hanna tried to make conversation, but gave up in the

face of his surly silence. Hardly a word passed between them as they drove through the quiet streets of Smith. The streets were decorated for Christmas now, but naturally none of that spirit extended to Mill Road.

"What are we doing here?" she asked, as they passed the hulk of the abandoned flour mill and pulled to a stop on the unplowed road in front of the trailer.

It looked particularly nasty in the bright morning light.

"This is where I grew up. I just bought it."

"Why?" Hanna asked, taken aback.

"To remind me of who I really am," he said grimly. "Now I need to show you that too. I don't think you got it last night. How mean it is, and how ugly, and how that still lives inside of me and probably always will."

He got out of his car, went and opened her door, and then plowed a path with his feet through the drifted snow to the door of the trailer. Hanna came behind him, but he sensed her reluctance.

He unlocked the door, held it open for her, then stepped inside after her.

The heat had been turned way down for a long time, and it was cold inside. She shivered. He was sure that the grimness of that interior would slap them both back to reality. He stood there, waiting for memories to swamp him, to drag them into the real world, to prove to him the folly of what he was allowing to happen between him and Hanna.

But to his shock, bad memories did not swamp Sam.

It had never occurred to him the trailer would not be the same, but it wasn't.

"I wasn't expecting this from what it looked like on the outside," Hanna said thoughtfully. "Someone has worked very hard to make it cozy. Look. The curtains are homemade."

She wandered over and touched them, while he stared. The furniture was worn but clean. In fact, when he walked through the trailer, feeling like an intruder in someone else's home, everything sparkled with cleanliness.

In the smaller of the two bedrooms, the one that used to be his, there was a child's bed, the comforter with colorful pictures of spaceships and planets. There was a toy box—still filled with toys—in the corner of the living room, and a worn teddy bear sat next to a huge cushion on the floor, surrounded by tidy stacks of children's books.

Hanna came behind him, and peered around him.

"What had happened here to make someone leave all their belongings?" she asked, worried, "Their child's toys?"

What indeed?

Sam called Beatrice and asked her to find the answers to some questions. When she called him back a few minutes later, his mission wavered.

It occurred to Sam maybe he wasn't here to renew his bonds with the past at all. All those years, acquiring more and more success, he'd been driven like a man running a marathon.

Now, it occurred to him, he had been running the wrong way.

He had been running away, when he should have been running straight toward this.

He was standing in his opportunity to banish his past's hold on him forever. By doing the same thing the cheerleaders had done when they had donated their prize back. By entering the spirit of Christmas in a deeper way, in a way that could heal instead of hurt.

He had, here, the opportunity to change one other life,

the life of another little boy, a boy who, despite his mother's best efforts, had known only poverty, and all the uncertainty that came with that.

Sam Chisholm took a deep breath.

Maybe all those words that they wove into the wreaths were more than words, after all.

CHAPTER FIFTEEN

HANNA STOOD BESIDE Sam in the abandoned trailer, shivering, despite the fact she still had her winter jacket on. Sam put his phone back in his pocket. He looked deeply troubled.

"Do you know who Udo Burfermer is?" he asked.

Hanna felt her nose wrinkle in distaste. "Not one of Smith's finest citizens. What does he have to do with this place?"

"He was involved with some kind of rent-to-own scheme. He owned this place—I wouldn't be surprised if he owned it when I lived here. She was a single mom working as a nurse's aide, and jumped at the chance to 'own' her own place, even though it stretched her thin financially.

"Her little boy got sick and she lost a few days' wages, and couldn't pay one month. She came home one day and the locks had been changed."

"Is that legal?"

"She obviously didn't have the resources—or possibly the will—to find out."

"That's awful."

"I might be able to make it right."

"But how?"

"What would you think of this? I'll have a team come

in. They'll check the place out for electrics and heating and insulation. Then I'll have Beatrice track her down and we'll give it back to her.

"Well, not me exactly,' he added. "She'll never know who did it."

"Like a secret Santa," Hanna breathed.

"I think it's too big a project to hope to finish it before Christmas," he said. "Cosmetically, you can see it needs everything. So, what about the stuff you can't see?"

"It has to be done for Christmas," Hanna said firmly. "We absolutely have to have it finished for Christmas."

We. In that moment, Hanna admitted the truth she had been hiding from herself for two weeks.

"We?" Sam said, raising his eyebrow at her. "You're going back to work."

But he said it in a way that made her think he already knew the truth she had been hiding from herself for two weeks. She was never going back to Banks and Banks.

"Even if you chose not to go back to work at the accounting firm, you have enough to do on the farm. Your busiest ten days are coming up."

"I could give seven of those days to this," she decided. "Mrs. S. has been running that farm since before I could walk and she's told me she's happy to carry on working there. Do you think new floors are a possibility? I hate this carpet."

"I guess they're a possibility," he said, and she heard the surrender in it. "Seven days to fix this place?"

"If she could be in on the twenty-first that would still give her a bit of breathing room before Christmas."

He snorted. "Now you're asking for a miracle."

"We need to paint it all, and that bathroom is a disaster," she said quickly, taking advantage of the fact he was giving in before he changed his mind.

For the first time in a long, long time, Hanna believed in miracles. It seemed as if one after another had unfolded since she arrived back at her farm. Banks and Banks was shimmering in the distance, like a mirage on the desert, that she could never reach.

And why would she need to, now? The thirst within her finally felt quenched.

"We could decorate it for Christmas, and put up a tree." She heard the wistfulness in her voice, and when he didn't say it was impossible, she rushed on, "And get some presents. It looks like it's a little boy."

She realized she was spending Sam's money rather freely. Embarrassed she said, "I bet if I approached the merchants, we could—"

"No."

"No? But why? You saw what happened when everyone decorated the tree."

"This is different. No approaching the merchants or the community. The hardest thing, when you're poor, is to accept charity. It's everyone in town knowing your business."

And a hurt teenage girl throwing it in your face.

She realized she would always feel bad about what she'd said to Sam all those years ago, even though she'd apologized to him for it recently and he'd forgiven her.

"I want to do this quietly," Sam said. "I'll have a lawyer contact her and set it up so she can still pay a small, affordable mortgage. Eventually, she'll have the dignity of knowing she earned her home back herself."

Hanna was well aware he had come here initially, to his old childhood home, to prove something to her. But the moment had passed, and she had been able to tell from his face the exact moment his agenda had changed.

Yes, he had come here this morning to discourage her from loving him. And instead she only loved him more.

She suspected, whether he knew it or not, he was about to prove something to himself instead. Something that she had known all along.

He was just a good, good man. Strong, successful, compassionate, giving.

"I can't wait to get started," she breathed. "We have to start right now. I'll break down the seven days until the twenty-first, and we'll make a list of what has to be done on each day."

In her mind, she wrote down number one on her list: resign from Banks and Banks.

He regarded her solemnly for a moment, and then, reluctantly, he laughed. She loved it when he laughed.

From that moment on, the time passed in a blur of excitement and exhaustion and activity.

For Hanna, every moment they spent together seemed suffused with light. She had not told him that she loved him, and yet she knew she could not stop that emotion from shining out of her.

Every fiber of her tingled with electricity from being near him. Every little detail of life became amazing when she shared it with him: the way coffee smelled when they ground it in the morning, the taste of pizza as they sat on the newly finished floors, sharing it after a long, long day.

The sound of his voice seemed to vibrate within her, his laughter was like a wave of energy that she rode. She could not get enough of him—the way his hands looked as he wielded a paintbrush, the way his brow creased when he looked at a cabinet that had not been installed properly, the way he effortlessly pitted his strength against the stubborn old bathtub that resisted being removed.

If Hanna and Sam had worked well as a team on the farm, she was aware they had moved to a different level now. The differences between them, and there were many of them, became assets. They both came at problems from entirely different directions. Sam was analytical and Hanna, despite her accounting background, was largely creative in her approach to problem solving.

Their acceptance and respect for each other's differences brought them to solutions that amazed them both.

And right below the surface of all the activity and problem solving and labor was a sharp, physical ache that was made worse and not better by his hand touching hers. By his lips brushing her forehead or her cheek. By the hugs they shared as one project would reach completion and another would begin.

Sometimes, after the day's projects were completed, they would sit side by side on the floor, backs against the wall, holding hands, and breathing it in.

Breathing in the scents of new paint and freshly laid floors and cozy heat pumping out from the new furnace.

But breathing in more than that. Breathing in deeply what was happening between them, an intense and abiding awareness of each other. Sometimes, they would kiss until they were both breathless, until they both knew the state they were in was suspended from reality and time.

They had to move forward. They were being driven to move forward. To the next level of knowing each other, to the next level of intimacy.

And yet they both seemed to understand that a greater level of closeness would require all the energy they were now giving to this project. It would require them to focus on each other, and pour that energy they were putting into the house, into each other.

This project was the means to the end. And it was unspoken, and yet understood, that after Christmas would be their time.

Hanna knew, with an opening of her heart, what that end was going to be. She was going to spend the rest of her life with this incredible man, the man she had given her heart to years ago, when he had been the first boy she had ever kissed.

In her heart, for the first time, she was so grateful things had not worked out with Darren.

Had she ended up married to him, she would have settled for so much less than what love was meant to be. She would have missed this. The glory and the bliss of falling so totally in love it consumed her.

Those tiny moments of each day—a look, a touch, a brush of the lips—became so infused with meaning. Getting this Christmas gift ready for someone else, for a complete stranger, was the best way to fall in love that Hanna could imagine.

Completely exhausted in the loveliest of ways, Sam and Hanna were sprawled out on the floor together. There was no furniture yet—that would be coming tomorrow. There was an empty pizza box on the floor and their hands were intertwined.

Hanna felt as happy as she had ever felt.

"Have you ever wondered if everything happens for a reason?" she asked softly.

He cocked his head at her.

"Molly brings me out here just in time to see that the farm was heading toward financial ruin, I hurt my hand, so it isn't really even a choice whether to stay and look after things here, or go back to work.

"I feel as if fate had a better plan for me than anything I could have ever planned for myself.

"In fact," she admitted, "when I look at my original

plan for myself, to stay at Banks and Banks and work until I dropped, I feel faintly ashamed. Why was I settling for so little? When did I become so dull and safe?

"Now, I feel as if from the moment I answered that phone and Mr. Dewey yelled at me that he quit, I started on a journey. And it's been the best journey of my life."

"Because you've come home," he murmured.

"Yes, to the farm."

"Not just to the farm," he said, "but to who you really are."

That was true. When she thought of the last weeks, Hanna had a sense of coming back to herself after a long absence.

"You, too," she told him. "You've come home to who you really are, too, Sam."

A week ago, he would have denied that. Now he drank in her words, then rolled over on his elbow and looked down at her.

He kissed her.

He kissed her thoroughly, like a man who meant business. This was the final step in her journey toward homecoming and she could feel the rightness in it, the welcome in it.

She explored the mystery of his lips with exuberant abandon, her heart racing to meet him. The kiss deepened.

The house around them faded, everything faded. It was just her and him, alone in a world made amazing by their presence in it, by the intensity of their awareness of each other.

The very air seemed infused with that intensity, that shivering delight in being fully alive, that felt both pleasurable and painful, like the pricks of a million pins along her skin. They kissed with hunger and abandon, until they were both gasping for air, gasping with need.

"Let's go home," she whispered, her voice hoarse with wanting him, "back to my place."

But Sam pulled back from her and shook his head, and traced the line of her cheek with his fingertip. "That's not who you really are," he said.

"Yes, it is."

"No, it isn't." He rolled away from her, and then with great effort, got to his feet. He looked at his watch. "Do you know what day it is?"

"December twentieth?" She felt sulky. She rose up off the floor, touched his arm, pleadingly, wantonly. She wanted nothing more than to kiss him again, and to follow that kiss wherever it took them.

But with a regretful smile, Sam backed away from her, reminding her of his absolute strength.

Why was he resisting this?

"Tomorrow's going to be unbelievably busy," he said, as if that was the reason. "We have to get all the furniture in. Mallory—" that was the name of the woman who was getting the trailer "—has been promised keys for tomorrow."

"There's nothing left to do, except add the furniture."

"And a tree," he pointed out.

He was right, even though Hanna did not have to be happy about it. There would be time for them after all this was done.

Done.

She looked around at what they had created and was aware of feeling sad that it was over, and eager for what was promising to come when the busy Christmas season ended.

"You know what I just realized?" Sam said, his voice that deep and pleasant growl she loved so much, "I haven't done my Christmas shopping yet."

"You don't strike me as a big Christmas shopper," she

said, smiling past the disappointment that the incredible passion unfolding between them had to be postponed for such trite things as Christmas shopping!

"I'm not. But I have to let Bea know how much I appreciate her. And there's a few other people, too."

His eyes rested on her in such a way that her heart leapt to her throat, that confirmed their time was right around the corner.

"You're right." Hanna said. "I have to get something for Mrs. S. And Jasmine and Michael." *And you.* "I can't believe it. I haven't given one thought to Christmas shopping. Except for Marshall."

Marshall was Mallory's little boy. They had found out he was turning six right before Christmas.

"Do you think that you haven't thought of shopping because that's the most superficial part of Christmas?" Sam asked her solemnly. "I feel as if we've been *living* what Christmas really is."

He was right, of course, but still, not to have something from her to give him on Christmas Day? But what could she possibly get for him that could tell him completely about the fullness in her heart and her hopes for the future?

And then, with a sigh of deep satisfaction, Hanna knew exactly the right gift to get for Sam Chisholm for Christmas.

CHAPTER SIXTEEN

LOOKING AT HANNA, Sam was rigid with the effort it was taking not to give in to the temptation to get back to that kiss. And then it occurred to him that he knew exactly the right Christmas gift to get her. Given the way things were going between them, it was really the only Christmas gift to give her.

The thought filled him with a mixture of excitement and fear. He realized he needed to go back to his hotel and think it through. Was it too soon?

But the following morning, as he and Hanna put the finishing touches on the house, his resolve solidified.

Hanna radiated complete joy as they placed furniture and did final polishes. Then, they brought in the tree.

It was Hanna's heritage tree that had been disqualified from the contest. They had taken all the decorations and candles off, and strung it with more traditional lights. And then they had put all those handmade decorations back on.

The decorations were not the throwaway kind so popular today. They were made to last a lifetime.

Finally, they wrapped gifts together, small, useful things for Mallory, oven mitts and tea towels, larger things for Marshall, a two-wheel bike with training wheels, a collection of story books, a huge teddy bear.

"I think we should have just put bows on the bear and the bike," Hanna said, stepping back to survey their handiwork. "The wrapping looks terrible, as if there are misshapen trolls underneath all that paper."

"It's not about how it looks," Sam said. "It's about how it feels. I know the bike and the bear would look pretty sitting there with bows on, but imagine that little boy tearing the wrapping off to discover what was inside."

She smiled at the thought, but Sam could sense sadness as they put the final touches on the trailer, locked the door and left the keys in the mailbox.

He knew they were both aware that they would probably never again set foot in this place that had taught them so much about love.

He went down the walk, freshly shoveled in welcome, and retrieved the wreath from the back of the farm truck that they had brought in to make it easier to transport the rather large, fully decorated tree.

He and Hanna had made this wreath together, early, early this morning, shoulder to shoulder, in the now familiar Christmas Valley Workshop.

This wreath was the last one to be made this year. Sales had dwindled to nearly nothing with Christmas so close, now.

If it was possible, it was the most beautiful of all the wreaths that had come off Christmas Valley Farm this season. As he had helped Hanna put it together, Sam had marveled at how familiar this felt to him now, the bundles thick and fragrant across his palm. He had marveled at how much he enjoyed the contemplative quality of making a wreath, the comfortable silence between him and Hanna.

He was so aware, and he knew Hanna was too, that they were sewing something sacred into this wreath. All the decorations on it were white; even the pinecones were frosted in white. The ribbon was pure white, and crisp, flocked with snowflakes in a deeper white.

And so, two words were chosen to adorn this very special wreath, instead of one. Two words were sewn into the fragrant fronds of the pine and fir. He had, finally, allowed his hand to settle on the word *Hope*.

Hanna had chosen *Believe*.

Now, together, they attached the wreath to the door, and stood back to look at it. They had made the impossible, possible. Wasn't that a miracle, by any definition?

In an hour the new homeowner would arrive. This was not a reality TV show, where they would wait for Mallory and her little boy, Marshall, and with every tear and squeal, congratulate themselves on what they had done for them.

No, Sam and Hanna had decided together, that this was Mallory's moment. Hers and Marshall's. A miraculous moment of being restored to belief, to a hope for the future.

It was a private moment, and they would not intrude. He put his hand on Hanna's shoulder and guided her back to the farm truck. They drove home in the blissful silence of two people who understood the gift they had just given was flying back toward them at the speed of light.

Later, it was just her and Sam and Mrs. S. left in the Christmas Workshop, sipping hot chocolate.

Hanna noticed how naturally she and Sam chose to sit together on the bench, shoulder to shoulder, a bond between them that felt unbreakable.

"Slow day," Mrs. S. said.

"It's getting close now," Hanna said. "Not even three full days left until Christmas Eve. Most people have their trees and decorations up. Most people don't want to put out money now for things they'll be throwing away in two weeks."

Hanna remembered this from her youth: she couldn't wait for everything to be done. And yet, as things wound down for another year, there was a feeling of emptiness, as if the purpose for life was gone.

Today, this familiar feeling was compounded by finishing with the trailer.

And yet, this year, there was something to hope for as the Christmas season ended. As she gazed at the now-so-familiar cast of Sam's profile, Hanna told herself the miracles weren't ending, they were beginning.

The miracle of love was just beginning for Hanna and Sam.

After she and Sam had left the trailer, Mrs. S. had put Sam to work on dismantling the tree lot. There would be few sales now. The rest of the trees went to a chipper, and the mulch would be sold as break-even by-product.

So now, sitting beside Hanna, Sam had the scent of the trees clinging to him. It was more appealing than the best of colognes.

The slow day at the farm had allowed Hanna to catch up on some much-needed bookkeeping.

Now, pleased, she passed an envelope to Mrs. S.

"A bonus?" Mrs. S. said, peeking in the envelope. "It's been years since we had a bonus."

"We had a really good year," Hanna said with satisfaction.

"People wanted to see the farm the way it was before," Mrs. S. said. "I don't think they realized how much it was part of their traditions until it started to go so badly downhill under Dewey's direction."

"This is for you, from me," Sam said, a little awkwardly. He gave Mrs. S. a small box. She opened it and her eyes filmed over as she drew out a broach, a tiny Christmas tree, constructed entirely of gems.

"Oh," she said, "I don't know how to thank you."

It had been Jasmine and Michael's last day, and they had already gone home, thrilled with their Christmas bonuses and the gifts Sam had given them: gift cards to download music.

"No," Hanna said softly, "I don't know how to thank you. I'm going to ask you to do something that should have been done years ago. Will you manage the farm?"

"But you're staying, aren't you?"

"Yes," Hanna said, without one ounce of doubt. She had emailed her resignation to Banks and Banks when she had finished doing the books for the year.

She was home. It could be aggravating and the work was never-ending. Home came with a mean-spirited pony who loved only her, and a house that was old and crumbling, and a future full of chaotic Christmases.

Or did it? Would Sam want to make this his home? She slid him a look. She had never seen him look so deeply relaxed, content.

Yes, she was pretty sure Christmas Valley Farm was about to become home to both of them. Besides, she knew he had a condo in New York. That was no place for the kind of gift she had gotten him for Christmas.

"I am staying here," Hanna told Mrs. S. "But I need you too. I need you to guide me and teach me."

Mrs. S. cleared her throat, and dabbed at her eyes. "Ah, well, the first thing you need to learn is there is no rest for the wicked. I'll be back on January second. The trees we didn't sell will have to be dealt with. Sam made a start today, but that is a big job.

"And items from the gift shop should be wrapped and put away for next year. And after that, there's the pruning and shaping. And those ten acres in the northeast corner have to be replanted. I don't supposed Dumb Dewey ordered trees, though. Fraser, I think, continues to be our bestseller."

"Why on earth did my mother not make you manager in the first place?" Hanna asked. "You've been with us forever. You would have been the natural choice when she decided to move away."

"She would have never hired me as manager."

"But why?"

Mrs. S. hesitated before she spoke. "I'd had a falling out with her. Actually, it had been with your father. She carried the grudge even after he'd died."

"What? You were friends!"

"Not after I gave your father a piece of my mind, we weren't."

"About what?" Hanna asked, laughing.

"About the baby."

Hanna felt Sam go very still beside her. The laughter died in her.

"He should have never treated you that way, Hanna. As if your getting pregnant was an affront to him. He was so hard and unforgiving. When he sent you away from your home—and your mother went along with it—I gave them both a piece of my mind. The joy went off the farm that day. I didn't blame you when you never came back, even though you lost the baby."

Hanna was aware of the stiffness in Sam's posture. She sent him a pleading look, but he was avoiding her eyes.

"Those fools," Mrs. S. said sadly. "A baby is always a blessing. Anyway, I continued working here, but it was never the same, and your mother would have never, ever considered me as a manager. I think she harbored the thought that I helped kill your father."

Mrs. S. seemed to realize the sudden silence was strained. She looked from Sam to Hanna and then got up.

"I must go, the grandchildren are arriving shortly. Merry Christmas to both of you."

And then she left them.

Hanna turned to face Sam. It felt as if the temperature in the workshop had plummeted, even though the wood heater was still blasting away.

She scanned his face. This must be how people who survived a tornado felt: dazed by how suddenly everything could go from being okay to nothing left but wreckage and rubble.

Sam stared at Hanna. It felt as if an Arctic front was moving in, freezing everything in its path, including his heart. How could it be possible that she had not told him about this? How could it be possible he had trusted her with every single detail about himself, and she had told him nothing about her?

"A baby?" he said quietly. "You left the farm because you were pregnant."

She nodded, her eyes still pleading on his. She knew that she should have trusted him with this piece of her past, but for some reason, she had chosen not to.

"I was at a party," she said, her voice shaking. "Someone spiked the punch. One thing led to another...probably my own fault. You did warn me all those years ago about starting fires I didn't know how to put out."

He registered that, and hated—furiously, savagely hated—whoever had done this to her. He wanted to be the man who could overlook her lack of trust in him and just comfort her, but all he could feel was cold.

"How is it?" he asked, his voice rigidly controlled, "we have spent all this time together—you know my every secret—and somehow you never told me something as important as that?"

"I don't know," she whispered.

"Didn't you trust me with it?" he asked. His voice was soft, but there was already a distance in him. It already felt as though something precious was slipping away from them.

"That's not it," she said, and he could hear her desperation to bring him back. "I suppose I was ashamed. No one around here knows anything about it. I left after high school, and they all thought it was to follow my dreams. And then I lost the baby. My mom and dad just thought I'd come back once I'd miscarried, but somehow, I couldn't. Nothing here was as I had thought it was. I thought love, true love, wouldn't be as conditional as it turned out to be. Anyway, I didn't come back.

"My dad had a heart attack shortly afterwards and died, and my mom was remarried and off the place before I knew what had happened."

For a moment, he could feel himself soften. He wanted to relax, to take her in his arms, help her carry this burden of pain.

Instead, Sam Chisholm shoved his hands deep in his pockets. He fingered the sprig of mistletoe he had shoved in there this morning.

Really? It was all too soon. It had been so intense between them. But none of it had been about the real world.

Her pain, so apparent in her face, was the real world. Maybe that's why she hadn't told him, because she had known intuitively he would not have the skills to deal with it.

"I have to go," he said, his voice terse and strained.

"But, weren't we going to spend Christmas together?"

Weren't they going to spend Christmas together and

exchange gifts and share their hopes and dreams for the future? Hadn't this quiet moment of just the two of them been what they were waiting for?

"I'm just not sure about anything anymore," he said quietly. He got up off the bench and stood looking down at her for the longest time. "I need some time to think."

He should have been thinking all along! That was what he was good at. This emotional intensity that he was feeling right now? He was definitely *not* good at this.

When she reached out to touch him, he took a step back and her hand fell short. He hated himself for it. But this was a truth he should have made more apparent from the start. He was a jerk. He was absolutely terrible at relationships. He had let her—and himself—be filled with false hopes.

He turned on his heel and walked away. It wasn't, he knew, exactly because she did not trust him. There was a far more poignant truth: he did not trust himself.

Hanna stared after Sam as he walked out the door. It was everything she could do not to run after him, begging for another chance. Instead, she waited, proudly until the door had closed behind him, before she let the tears fall.

She turned away from the door and went to the ribbon room. She opened the door and the puppy with the bow around his neck—impossible to wrap a puppy, no matter how fun unwrapping gifts was—gamboled out and whined up at her.

She picked him up and buried her nose in his golden fur and wept all the tears that she had held inside since her whole world had blown apart all those years ago.

And then again today.

CHAPTER SEVENTEEN

SAM ENTERED HIS hotel room and packed quickly. He was amazed, in fact, how fast a man could pack up a few weeks' worth of his life.

He checked out of his room. It was starting to snow when he put his car on the highway, but he was aware he was making no allowances for the poor driving conditions. He just wanted to leave Smith and Christmas Valley Farm and especially Hanna Merrifield behind him.

He was back in New York in record time. He had a very upscale Park Avenue condo, and when he went in the door he was aware he wanted something.

He wanted to feel a sense of homecoming. He had always liked walking in the door. With its modern aesthetic and great view of Central Park, the condo whispered *arrival*. The condo was one of the testaments to his wealth and success.

It was the place a guy like him was least likely to arrive at.

But now Sam was aware a sense of arrival was not a sense of home, and that wealth and success were not the least likely place for a man like him to arrive at.

Home was.

Love was.

He didn't even take off his shoes. He tossed down his

suitcases in a heap inside the door, slammed across the Brazilian walnut floors and threw himself down in the deep brown leather of his custom sofa.

He was aware that he was vibrating with a furious kind of energy. At first he thought he was angry.

Sam had trusted Hanna with every single detail of himself. And she had given him nothing in return.

Nothing? a voice inside him chided. His mind insisted on remembering *everything:* a gnome collapsed in front of his car, the way her throat looked when she threw back her head and laughed, the smell of the wreaths all around them, the sense of companionship and comfort and trust he felt when he was with her.

His mind insisted on remembering the tree decorating contest and the mistletoe in her elf's hat and the intense days in that trailer together, and the way her lips had felt crushed under his.

The memories took the edge off his anger and Sam realized the truth about himself. He *wanted* the energy to be anger. Fury felt powerful. It was the force that had lifted his father up by his collar that day so long ago.

But this thing he was really feeling? It wasn't anger.

He recognized it as fear. There was nothing worse in the world than a man feeling afraid.

He had not felt it for so long, he had forgotten how its tentacles could reach into every part of a man and render him helpless.

He'd fallen for Hanna when he had vowed to himself he would never fall for anyone again. He loved Hanna even though he didn't want to.

It was an out-of-control feeling, falling in love. And with the way he had grown up? Out of control led to catastrophic failures. That's what he feared. Being out of control.

A grand love was what his father had experienced with his mother. Love might have built his father up once, but in the end it had destroyed him completely.

Love felt so good. The last few weeks of Sam's life had been the best he'd ever experienced. But this was what he had to remember: love hid a dagger just beneath that cloak of warmth and comfort. It made you feel alive, as it waited to steal the life's breath from your lips.

This was what Sam knew of himself as he sprawled amongst his wealth, feeling as poor as a man could feel: he had been looking for an excuse to run. And finding out Hanna had once been pregnant and never shared that with him had been a feeble one, at best.

But he had taken it.

His eyes flicked to his liquor cabinet. He kept it well stocked for entertaining. He never drank himself. He had seen, close-up, the devastation of that. He was afraid that weakness probably ran in his genes as surely as the color of his hair and the shape of his nose.

But eyeing the cabinet now, he felt, for the first time ever, an affinity with his father. Sam Chisholm understood the despair and desperation of feeling like a man with nothing left to lose.

A man who would do anything to outdistance his pain.

He got up off the couch, like a man broken. He went to the liquor cabinet and opened the door.

Christmas Eve. It was always a quiet day on a Christmas tree farm, and Hanna was alone. She considered the possibility it was not too late to send Mr. Banks an email begging his forgiveness, begging for her old life back.

But then two people came for last-minute trees in the afternoon. She sold the trees for a fraction of their cost. Then she had a call from a woman who had seen one of Christmas Valley Farm's centerpieces at her friend's house. She just *had* to have one for her own Christmas table. She said she would pay anything for it.

Thank goodness, Hanna thought, as she put the pieces of the lush Christmas centerpiece together, that it wasn't a wreath. But even though it wasn't, being out here in the workshop, at the same table where she and Sam had created so many wreaths together, was an exercise in agony.

Why hadn't she told him?

Because it was the truth she had hidden even from herself. She had closed the door on that chapter of her life completely, as it had been simply too painful to bear. The loss of her family, and then the loss of the baby, and then the guilt over her father dying, as if she had killed him herself.

She had been burying herself in *busyness* ever since. And avoiding coming back here.

But now she allowed herself to feel the pain of that old loss, and this fresh one, too. Her tears crusted the fronds of grand fir like diamonds.

The new puppy whined at her feet. She could not help but smile as he gazed at her, utterly trusting her to do what was right by him. And so, when the centerpiece was completed, she set it outside the workshop door with a bill attached to it, and a hastily scrawled somewhat insincere Merry Christmas.

Oh, those words felt hollow. It wasn't going to be a merry Christmas, obviously. It was going to be the worst Christmas of her entire life.

She went to Molly's stall. Though, thanks to Michael, her stall was meticulously clean, the poor little horse had barely seen the light of day since the day she had been hit by Sam's car.

Not that she seemed unhappy about it with her pile of

sweet hay and her salt lick and her fresh bedding. She gave Hanna a suspicious look when she entered the stall with the halter.

"Don't worry," Hanna told her. "You're way too old to pull sleighs. How about just coming for a walk?"

She slipped the halter on, and the pony plodded along beside her, her hooves making muffled clip-clops along the snowy path that led through the farm.

As she walked the puppy and Molly, Hanna found herself smiling at the puppy's antics with the brand-new experience of meeting a real, live pony.

There was a small knoll, the height of land for the farm, and Hanna made her way there and stopped on the top.

She looked around. The trees were thick around her, their boughs drooping under the weight of snow. She could smell the sweet scent of the pony and the sweet scent of the trees mingling. The pup gamboled down the hill, and then, seeing she had not followed, wheeled back and then skipped ahead again.

When Hanna looked around, she could see the workshop and the house and the barn. She could see acres and acres of trees, balsam and grand fir and Colorado blue spruce.

She thought of Sam and waited for the beauty of the moment to dissolve into the agony of loss.

But instead, Hanna realized she was able to appreciate this moment of extraordinary beauty, because of him.

Because of love.

If it was really love, it didn't tear you down. It didn't do what it had done to his father. It made you better and stronger. It made you more able to see, more willing to throw yourself at life, and trust its caprice would bring you, eventually, to this.

This, she realized, was the place she had never been.

Where she was absolutely alone. And still it was enough.

Somehow, Sam's love for her, even if it was gone, had not destroyed her. It had given her the best gift of all.

It had allowed her to forgive herself.

And to love herself.

She was never sending an email to Mr. Banks begging for her old life back. She had her life. She had the life she had been born to.

Hanna Merrifield had found her way home.

She heard a car in the distance. The woman had come to pick up her centerpiece. She wished, suddenly, she had not put a bill with it, but had given it away.

She shrugged and continued her walk, coming down off the knoll to a familiar loop through the trees and back toward the house. It was snowing gently, a perfect Christmas Eve, and she could feel the crispness on her nose and cheeks.

The puppy, galloping forward and barking, alerted her that someone was coming.

Her heart began to beat harder, as if it already knew what her mind was terrified to believe.

But her heart was right.

Sam was striding through the trees, looking for her. Did he not know a leather jacket like that one was not warm enough for today?

The puppy greeted him with wild enthusiasm, as if it knew that was who he was intended for.

Sam bent for a moment, stroked the pup, but he was barely distracted, coming toward her with the long, confident strides of a warrior.

She stopped. And Sam came to her and halted.

"That can't be the jacket from high school," she whispered with recognition, "It can't be."

"It is. I collect jackets. I'm sorry. It's a fault. I have so many faults, Hanna."

She stared at him, uncertain what to say, uncertain she could even make herself heard over the hard beating of her heart.

"You know what my worst fault is, Hanna?" he asked softly.

She shook her head.

"It's a guy thing, not that that is an excuse."

She still could not think of a single thing to say.

"It's not all about me," he said. "Isn't that what I've been learning practically since the moment I arrived at Christmas Valley Farm? That if I ever wanted to know joy, it was about making it about someone else. It's about decorating a tree for someone who needs one, it's about allowing a single mom to be home for the holidays.

"When I left here, I thought I was angry at you, Hanna, and I let you believe that. But I wasn't angry, I was scared.

"I was terrified of what I was feeling.

"Stupid scared.

"And then, in my fear and loneliness and anguish about what I was throwing away, I opened the liquor cabinet at my apartment, with every intention of drinking it dry.

"But something stopped me. I think your love stopped me. It asked me not to take the easy way, the familiar way, learned from my father. It asked me not to be cowardly but to be brave. It asked me if I had been self-centered and self-focused this whole time.

"I'm a guy. The answer is probably yes to that. But isn't the whole point of loving someone wanting to be better, letting love make you a better person?"

He registered the shock in Hanna's face, and smiled tenderly.

"Yes," he acknowledged. "I used the word love. That 'something' I've been speaking of is love.

"And love asked me to acknowledge I was afraid, and then to move toward that fear and not away from it.

"Love asked me to earn your trust, as you had earned mine, to become the great listener that you have been, to encourage you to entrust me with your secrets, as you had encouraged me to come to you, not in pieces, but whole.

"Love asked me to ask myself, Good God, how did it feel for Hanna to be that young girl, just getting ready to graduate from high school, who found herself pregnant? It was probably nearly more than you could bear that you had been taken advantage of. You took responsibility for it, when you were not responsible.

"And then the people who should have loved you through it didn't.

"Instead of thinking about me, Hanna, I've been thinking about you. I've been thinking of how you must have felt when your father died, and if you took responsibility for that, too, when it is so obvious you were not responsible."

"I was responsible!"

"No," he said, "you weren't. I want you to tell me every single thing that happened. I don't want you to carry it by yourself anymore. Not for one more minute."

Hanna stared at him. She took a deep breath. Sam's love, so evident in his face and his eyes, made her stronger than she had ever been.

And ready. It poured out of her, all that pain and anguish and betrayal, it poured out of her as if it had been waiting, water behind a dam. And at first it came out like dammed water: murky and full of debris, ugly.

But behind that, right behind that, as Sam put his arms

around her, and she wept, the water flowed clear and pure. And that part forgave. Her father and her mother. And Darren.

And finally, finally, herself.

Sam loved *all* of her. It was so evident from the strength and acceptance in his embrace. He loved all of her, and she needed to love all of her, too.

"I've been thinking about you," Sam said, his voice low and sure, "How, despite all that, you found the bravery in you to go on with life. And now, to come back here, to find your way home.

"To know—to insist—this is your birthright, and you are claiming it. Not a farm, but to feel worthy.

"That is my birthright, too, and we are going to spend the rest of our days, if you will have me, teaching that to each other," he finished.

She was shaking. The tears were coursing down her face. He put his finger under her chin and tilted her face up toward him. He gazed down at her.

The truth of his love for her shone out of him.

And then, from that long-ago jacket, he pulled something.

It was dry and colorless, and looked as if, at a single touch, it would turn to dust, and yet there was no mistaking it for what it was.

It was a single sprig of mistletoe. He smiled down at it, and then looked her square in the eyes, and held it over both their heads.

The sensation was of homecoming, of the world sparkling with love. It was so strong it made her feel as if she could not breathe, as if her knees had turned to pudding.

When his lips greeted her, she was glad for the strength of his arms around her, for Hanna felt herself melting into him.

As if from a long way away, Hanna was aware that Molly whinnied and the dog barked. She was aware that all of creation, even the animals of the manger, realize when they are in the presence and glory of love.

All of creation stands still, and understands what Christmas really is, a celebration of hope, a rebirth of life.

CHAPTER EIGHTEEN

HAND IN HAND, Hanna and Sam walked home. They put Molly away and went to the house. As soon as she let him in, he threw back his head and laughed.

"What's so funny?"

"No tree. No Christmas cookies. No wreath. No parcels. You were so busy making Christmas for everyone else that you forgot about yourself. And that just won't do."

Together, they went back outside and picked a tree. Together they cut it down and dragged it through the snow to her house. Together, they set it up and decorated it. Together, they baked cookies and ate them for supper. Together, they listened to Christmas carols and played board games. Together, they fell asleep on the sofa, the dog, now wearing his Christmas bow, snuggled up with them.

Together, they woke on Christmas morning and greeted the new day and the new life.

Sam Chisholm began courting Hanna Merrifield with all the old-fashioned earnestness he had known she would need from the first day that he had seen her again.

He respected her decision to stay on the farm, but he needed to be back at the helm of the Old Apple Crate. And so they began their courtship with weekends. Sam wooed Hanna in the most tender and traditional of ways.

He took her to movies. He took her to dinner at some of New York's finest restaurants. They went to live theater. He cooked dinner for her at his apartment.

When they spent weekends at the farm, Hanna showed him how to toboggan and build snowmen and bake cookies and prune the shape of the Christmas trees. They watched all their favorite movies, and went to dog training, and popped corn over the wood heater.

There was a tendency in a man to rush things, but Sam had recognized he needed to fight all his tendencies.

He felt that to be worthy of Hanna's love he had to dig deep every day, and find new ways to be a better man.

They graduated, slowly, from weekend dinners and movies and tramps on the farm and dog training. In the spring, he took her to Paris for a few days. In the summer, he talked her into skydiving, and on a mule trip down into the Grand Canyon. In the first chilly days of fall, he took her to Brazil on a coffee-buying trip, and to West Africa to see how cocoa was grown.

But it was Hanna who moved them in a different direction, from filling their space together, to just being in their space together. On Christmas Valley Farm, they went from "doing" to "being".

A quiet night sitting in front of the fireplace talking was the best. Or walking, hand in hand, through the newly shaped Christmas trees, the fragrant boughs on the ground all around them. Or sprawled out, on separate couches, reading books, the puppy, now a gangly adolescent, snoring contentedly on the floor between them.

It was the most natural thing in the world that all that love would begin to radiate outward. Love was not stagnant. It did not stay in one place. It grew and it evolved, it was the force that could change the whole world.

At the end of November, close to the anniversary of

Sam knocking Molly over with his car, Hanna heard of a young woman in Smith who, just as she had once been, was pregnant and lacking support. Sam bought a small house, and he and Hanna returned to their greatest joy.

Expressing their love by helping someone else. In those hectic days before Christmas, Sam and Hanna remodeled the house and set up an education fund for both the mom and the baby. Supported by Old Apple Crate, Home for the Holidays was born.

Sam felt as if he was the richest man on earth.

"He's up to something," Hanna said to Jasmine, eyeing Sam's Christmas tree-decorating team. "He lost last year. He's very competitive."

"And you aren't?" Jasmine said. "Honestly, we have been making the decorations for this tree for months. No, correction, I've been making decorations for months. You've been buying houses and remodeling and falling in love."

Hanna knew that even after all these months she blushed.

It was all true. She had been relying heavily on her staff to run Christmas Valley Farm because her life was so full and so busy.

Her dull days at Banks and Banks seemed like a distant and not very happy memory.

Mrs. S. ran the farm like a lovable tyrant. This year she had decided the annual tree decorating contest could be made more interesting if each tree had a theme. Hanna had decided on "A Homemade Christmas," but that was before she and Sam had acquired the house, when she still had time.

The decoration responsibility had fallen largely on Jasmine, who had risen to the challenge as if born to it.

The Hanna and Her Elves team's tree was completely decorated with handmade bows and other simple home-made, but time-consuming, decorations. It was turning out even better than she had expected.

And so was the crowd turnout for the second annual Christmas Miracles day. They had nearly double the number of people they'd had last year.

"Our tree is clearly the winner," Hanna said, but looked over at Sam's Old Apple Crate team and frowned. "But he's definitely up to something."

His tree was a confection in white: his helpers had even flocked the edges of all the branches right after they had put the lights on.

Now the green boughs of the tree were barely visible for the abundance of tiny, white, beautifully wrapped gift boxes adorning every branch of the tree. They looked like jewelry boxes. There appeared to be hundreds of pure white bells in that tree. How had his team accomplished so much in so little time?

The tree was spectacular and possibly better than her own, Hanna admitted with resignation. But it didn't matter, anyway.

Because the cheerleaders were here again. They had declared their theme was "Toy Story". Their tree, a nice Concolor fir, though heavily laden with toys, was every bit as much a jumble of styles and decorations as it had been last year. But, just as last year, the cheerleading squad had brought a contingent of teenage boys with them.

So, if the judging was by the loudness of the cheers again…at least Sam had got a sign up on the hot choc-olate, charging for it but saying all the proceeds would go to charity.

His charity. Home for the Holidays. Just thinking about it made her heart swell with love and pride in Sam.

She realized it really didn't matter to her if Hanna and the Elves won the competition or not.

When you had this feeling in your heart—of being home, of being complete, of being loved—being competitive felt rather silly.

"That's an hour," Mrs. S. called. "Teams, put down your decorations! Hanna, would you go look at Sam's tree? I'm considering disqualifying it. We did have to have a theme this year, and I'm unclear about the theme of Mr. Chisholm's tree."

Hanna felt the laughter ripple up within her. Laughter, so much an ingredient of each of her days. She loved the spirit of this day: fun and playful. And wouldn't that just be tit for tat if Sam's team was disqualified? He was forever ribbing her about being disqualified last year.

Hanna went over to the Old Apple Crate's tree and folded her arms over her chest, setting her brow in what she hoped was a critical expression. The truth was she could barely keep from laughing, with the joy bubbling up within her. She tried to discern a theme.

The tree took her breath away with its white lights and little wrapped boxes, beautiful white, sheer ribbons all over it. Sam's team stood by smiling secretive smiles. Sam's assistant, Beatrice, whom Hanna had come to love as part of her new Old Apple Crate family, suddenly stepped forward.

"Oh, my," Bea said theatrically, "I've forgotten the topper."

Her other team members brought her a ladder, and she climbed to the top of the tree.

She removed the tree topper from a small sack she had carried up the ladder. With grave care, she placed a bride and groom on the very top branch.

Hanna's mouth fell open. She was suddenly aware that

it was way too quiet. There were even more people here than last year. How could such a large crowd be so silent?

She recognized the theme of the tree. It was a Wedding Tree.

With her heart pounding in her throat, Hanna turned away from the tree. Sam was in front of her, on one knee. Her fist flew to her mouth.

"Hanna Merrifield," he said solemnly, "I have never known joy such as I have known with you. I have never known gifts as I have known them with you. I am asking you for one more gift. I am asking you to do me the grave honor of agreeing to be my wife. Of walking through the years with me, allowing me to give you the best gift of all, a gift I would not have, save for your presence in my life.

"That gift is your love. Your love has restored me to laughter, your love has saved and rescued me, your love has given me a reason to live.

"Now I ask if you will allow me to give you my love in return, for the rest of our lives."

The cheer was deafening. The very branches of each of the contest trees trembled with it, but the branches of the Wedding Tree trembled most of all. The hundreds of tiny bells, which Hanna suddenly realized were not Christmas bells but wedding bells, tinkled merrily.

When she nodded through her tears, and he came and picked her up, his shout of exuberance reverberated even more loudly than the applause that rolled on and on and on.

"Well," Mrs. S. managed to say, sniffing through her tears, "we have a clear winner here."

"Just a sec," Sam called.

And from the pocket of the old, old leather jacket he wore over his Old Apple Crate T-shirt, Sam pulled a sprig of mistletoe from his pocket.

Hanna knew that mistletoe. And she knew the story behind it. How a young man had felt the spirit of Christmas for the first time on the day he had bought that sprig.

The sprig looked even worse than it had last year. It was so dry with age it looked as if it would crumble to dust if a breath whispered across it.

But Sam cupped it in his hands, like a match in a wind, and then, carefully, he held it up over their heads.

The gathered crowd went wild. This most private of men, who had made his declaration of love so public, kissed her and kissed her and kissed her.

"Will you?" he whispered, in between kisses. "Will you marry me?"

Hanna gazed up into the familiar depths of Sam's beautiful eyes. She saw her future in them: she saw babies yet to be born, and challenges yet to be faced. She saw that ribbon of road called love stretched out before her.

It beckoned with its promise of adventure and discovery, with its promise of warmth and comfort, with its promise of strength to sustain through the storms ahead.

It beckoned like a road that led, eventually, to that one place everyone wanted all roads to go to.

And that place was home.

"Oh, yes," she whispered back. "Yes, yes, yes."

* * * * *

MILLS & BOON®

Why not subscribe?
Never miss a title and save money too!

Here's what's available to you if you join the exclusive **Mills & Boon Book Club** today:

◆ *Titles up to a month ahead of the shops*
◆ *Amazing discounts*
◆ *Free P&P*
◆ *Earn Bonus Book points that can be redeemed against other titles and gifts*
◆ *Choose from monthly or pre-paid plans*

Still want more?
Well, if you join today we'll even give you
50% OFF your first parcel!

So visit **www.millsandboon.co.uk/subs**
or call **Customer Relations on 020 8288 2888**
to be a part of this exclusive Book Club!

14_ST_7

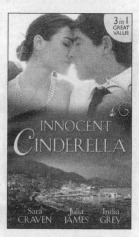

MILLS & BOON®

Exciting new titles coming next month

With over 100 new titles available every month,
find out what exciting romances
lie ahead next month.

Visit
www.millsandboon.co.uk/comingsoon
to find out more!